MW01256726

BROKEN
WINGS

WSJ & USA TODAY BESTSELLING AUTHOR

JAYMIN EVE

USA TODAY & INTERNATIONAL BESTSELLING AUTHOR

TATE JAMES

Cover design by Tamara Kokic
Book design by Inkstain Design Studio

To Rebekah,

Delta is watching!

BROKEN WINGS

Chapter 1

Death. So fucking final. I'd never realized just how final until that fateful night.

"Riley, hold on, honey!" my dad yelled as our car screeched and he swerved across the icy road, but there was no way for him to stop the inevitable.

Black ice.

Ancient car.

No chance.

We hit the embankment and the car rolled over and over. Since I was the only one with a seatbelt on—my parents' had both jammed the day before, due to either cold or age probably—it held me locked in place as we tumbled.

They screamed my name, but I was beyond words. I was just plain screaming in terror. My mom's side of the car slammed into something, halting us abruptly, and then there was silence. My head and ears rang as

I fought against the darkness. I'd definitely hit my head at some point, and sharp pains in my chest and hand threatened to pull me under further, but I had to help my family.

Through the haze, I could have sworn a shadow moved outside my window, but my focus was shot to shit and couldn't hold onto anything solid. My mom made a noise then, a whimper which almost broke through the ringing in my head, but that pained, terrified sob was cut off swiftly, and I heard a thump.

I wanted to call out for her, but consciousness slipped my grasp, and an infinite amount of time passed while I hung heavily against my belt.

When hands touched me, they grabbed onto my arm first. The shot of intense pain to my system dragged me completely into the blissful darkness of unconsciousness.

I WOKE TO THE STRONG smell of antiseptic. Blinking through the heavy haze, I tried to focus, but an incessant rhythmic beeping kept trying to drag me under again. "Riley Jameson?"

My eyes caught a flash of dark blue. Cops.

"Riley, we need to tell you something," he tried again, but I was already shutting down. The darkness once again taking hold.

The second time I emerged from the pressing veil in my mind, I found my best friend, Dante, sitting by my side. His head was down, cradled in his tattooed hands, as his elbows rested on the side of my hospital bed. There was less fuzziness in my mind now, and before I could stop it, a whimper crept up from my chest and escaped.

His head snapped up, and I met his light, seafoam green-eyed gaze. I'd seen this look on his face only one other time and that had been a really bad night for all involved.

"Riles!" He reached out and touched my right hand, scooping it up and squeezing tightly. I barely felt it over the pounding in my chest and the panic trying to gain traction in my cloudy mind. I lifted my left hand to rub at my face, but it felt heavy and lifeless. I was too out of it to pay attention to why, so I just dropped it to the bed again.

"Are you okay?" he asked, leaning further into me. "Should I call the doctor?"

I shook my head. "No," I rasped, my throat dry.

A cough shook me then, and Dante turned away to grab a cup of water. He was dressed in his usual black, ink visible on any uncovered skin. His head was shaved short again, that thick dark hair barely a quarter of an inch long.

It seemed like years since I had seen him last, when it was…

"How long have I been here?" My words were clearer this time, and I sighed in relief when he placed the straw against my lips and I sucked in the cool water.

He set it back down before taking my hand again. "Three days. You've been in and out of consciousness."

"What happened?" I whispered, not wanting the answers, but understanding I needed them anyway. A screech of tires played through my mind and then screaming, but the finer details were fuzzy.

His strong jaw tightened. Dante was a big guy, almost six and a half feet, tough, and relentless when he wanted something, yet in that moment, he almost looked scared. Which made me search for the oblivion of unconsciousness again. It was too late, though; apparently my brain thought

3

I had slept enough.

"Your car slid on black ice," he said, his voice rumbling. "You hit an embankment, and it started to roll. You were the only one with a seatbelt on, Riles."

Panic built in my chest, a pressure so intense I wondered if I might have been having a heart attack. "Where are my parents?" I asked, my voice breaking as that pressure increased.

I wasn't religious at all, but in that moment I started to pray.

Please, please let them be okay.

"Riles ... they ... they didn't make it."

He said it as quickly as possible, like he was trying to get the words out before he couldn't.

A keening cry left my lips, and I sucked air in, trying not to scream. He leaned farther into me, like he could protect me from this truth, but there was no protecting me from it. The only people I had in the world. The only people who gave a fuck about me ... were no longer here.

I lost my battle with the pressure then, and I screamed, a high pitched cry I'd never heard from myself before, and the ache in my chest increased to where I dry heaved over the side of my bed. Dante must have called someone, because I heard people rushing into the room, and then there was cloudiness in my head as darkness took me again.

THE DAYS AFTER THIS WERE disjointed. The police returned and asked me thousands of questions. About the accident, where we had been going that night, why my parents had chosen to ignore their faulty seat belts despite the icy conditions. Any moron would have known that was asking for trouble, but we'd gone out anyway. Why? I couldn't remember. Only that it had been urgent.

After they'd gone, a CPS worker came in with an older woman who looked exhausted, and they were the ones to tell me all about the accident. The stuff I didn't know. The fact my mom's neck was broken on impact, and how my dad had suffered a severe head injury and blood loss. He'd died at the scene. My injuries were serious, but not life threatening. Mild head injury, fractured wrist, and some cuts and bruises. Dante visited me every day, but I didn't remember most of it as I sank into a pit of despair and grieved for my family. They were laid to rest four days after my accident, and I couldn't even be there. Not that I wanted them kept on ice for fuck knew how long it'd take for me to be discharged, but still.

Dante had footed the bill for their funeral, and it was yet another thing I added to the mental tab I'd been running since he'd become my friend years ago. He'd made it a respectful service, or so he told me, but the whole concept made my chest feel like it was being torn in two.

Buried. In the ground. The thought of my parents like that was breaking me, and when Dante told me, I cried more than I thought was possible.

Two days later, as I stared listlessly at the white ceiling, one of my nurses walked into the room.

"Sweetheart," she said softly.

My heart lurched, because my mom had always called me sweetheart. God, the pain was so bad that I wasn't sure I could survive it.

I didn't turn to her, but she continued anyway. "You're being discharged tomorrow, and someone from child services will be by to pick you up."

I didn't acknowledge her words, and wasn't surprised by them. Mom and

Dad were only children, both of their parents had died young, and I had no other family.

I was alone.

And it was now time to find out exactly what that meant for me.

"IT'S TWO MONTHS UNTIL YOUR eighteenth birthday," the social worker said, leaning forward so I got a decent view of the cleavage straining against her white button down. "We planned on putting you into a group home here, so you could finish up your senior year, but … something else has come up."

That got my attention, because I had a feeling things didn't usually "come up" for almost-eighteen-year-old orphans.

"Did you know you were adopted?" She was blunt, those icy blue eyes seemed to have seen too much already. Probably jaded from her job, and I didn't blame her.

I adjusted my broken arm then, trying to ease the mild discomfort it still caused me. "Yes, my parents told me when I was younger, but it made no difference to me. Blood or not. They were my family."

The ache in my chest started to strangle the breath in my lungs, and I gritted my teeth, making a conscious mental effort to shove my emotions aside.

The stages of grief could kiss my ass, because there was no way I was ever getting past this pain and anger. I couldn't deal with their deaths, I just couldn't. However, I'd become an expert at compartmentalizing when needed, so I breathed in and out for a moment, then I was able to function again.

She watched me closely, and it wasn't like she enjoyed my pain exactly, but she did seem fascinated by the way I'd pulled myself together.

"So this thing that came up," I distracted her from whatever bullshit brewed in her mind. I was not up to being shrinked today, even if this chick did hold my fate in her hands.

"Your birth parents have come forward," she announced happily, and then she paused like she was waiting for me to cheer.

I leaned into her, narrowing my eyes as I did, fingernails digging into the arm of my chair so I didn't punch her in the nose. "You talking about the people who threw me away as a child? The ones who gave so little fucks about me, that I've never even heard from them once in seventeen years?"

Her smile faltered. "I don't think you understand how wonderful an opportunity this is. They're wealthy, very wealthy. You'll have a proper home. Go to a top school. This is the chance for you to finish out your year with a bang and go to college. Your future will be set."

If I could have stormed out, I would have, but I still wasn't completely recovered from my injuries, and it would have taken me far too long to get to my feet. Crossing my arms as best I could with the cast, I met her gaze with my own. "No."

She blinked, and unlike me, she easily rose to her feet. "What do you mean, no?"

Fuck it. I dragged myself up. "I mean that I will not be going with those assholes. Send me to the group home."

It was starting to hit me now just how odd this all was. My adoption had been closed, which meant no birth parents involved at all. My mom told me they had no idea who they were, and they'd even tried to find out at one point because of some medical issues. So how the hell were the DNA donors strolling back into my life now? How did they even know my mom and dad were de … gone?

"How rich did you say they are?"

My random question didn't take her by surprise. I guess she thought everyone was only interested in money, but that wasn't the reason I'd asked. The way her eyes lit up told me all I needed to know about who was *really* paying her salary. Fucking everyone could be bought these days.

"Rich enough that you've probably seen their names on the Forbes list."

Right. Well, that explained how they'd found me. They had enough money to keep tabs on anyone. My beaten up body ached again, so I lowered myself back down, and tried to think this through clearly. "Do I get a choice here at all?" I asked. "And … why would people … rich *people* throw me away in the first place and then want me back?"

Something wasn't adding up here. This CPS chick was clearly taking bribes but to what fucking end? Why would my bio-parents suddenly want me back?

She nervously shuffled some papers before finally meeting my eyes. "Unfortunately, you have no choice. You've already been signed over to them, and they'll be here in…" Checking her watch, her eyes lifted to the door behind me. "Five minutes." It didn't escape my notice she'd only answered my first question. She probably had no idea why I hadn't been wanted, but it had all worked out for the best anyway. *I have amazing parents who love me and that is worth more than all the money in the world.*

Had. Past tense. I *had* amazing parents. Now … now I was alone.

Her estimation of an arrival time proved a little off, because the door swung open. I turned my head to find a woman framed in the doorway. If I'd had any doubt she was my birth mother, it was all swept away in that moment. She looked like my older sister: the same bright blue eyes most people thought were contacts, and wavy dark hair. She'd clearly learned how to tame hers, or maybe it was the rich person hairdresser she no doubt went to—mine was always a mess of unruly curls. She stood about my height, five foot nine, but would have been shorter if hers wasn't jacked up by four inch heels. Very shiny. Very expensive looking black heels with red soles.

"Is she ready?"

Not even a word to me, the cold question was directed right over my head.

The lady, whose name I couldn't remember, started to fidget nervously. "Oh, yes, Catherine, she's ready on our end. Her belongings were packed up and are being held downstairs."

"It's Mrs. Deboise," Catherine said in that same icy tone. I made a mental note to always call her Catherine, because she was a stuck up bitch. Mrs. Deboise ... seriously...

Deboise...

As in Deboise banking? *No freakin' way!* The Forbes thing made even more sense because Deboise was a huge, worldwide bank, originating in Europe. Or at least that's what their ads said on television.

I'd been staring at the impressive shoes again, and when I lifted my head, I was disconcerted to find impassive blue eyes on me.

"Let's go," she said shortly.

I remained seated, continuing to stare at her. She let out a little huff. "I don't have all day, if you're going to be difficult about it, let's get that out of the way so we can make our flight."

My heart stuttered, and I swung back to the child services chick. "Where am I going exactly?"

I had no idea why I'd assumed this bitch lived in New Jersey too, but I should have guessed that wasn't the case.

Papers shuffled again, and I was five seconds from reaching across and swiping all of her shit right off the desk, when the corrupt CPS worker spoke. "I believe Mrs. Deboise lives in upstate New York."

Of course she did, probably had a huge estate out there.

"That's only a few hours away, why are we flying there?" My brow creased in a confused frown. Shit wasn't adding up.

"I'm a busy woman," the older version of myself snapped back, not even raising her face from her phone for a second. God forbid she want to spend a couple of hours getting to know the daughter she threw out like trash.

Whatever, at least I wasn't moving too far away if I ever needed to escape back to Dante. And speaking of…

"I need to let my friend know what's happening to me, I don't want him to worry." I had no idea why I directed that statement to child services. They were not my guardians, but I just couldn't bring myself to speak to the ice queen directly. She was actually scarily intimidating, and I felt zero comfort around her.

Nevertheless, it was *Catherine* who responded to me.

"Your friend?" She spat the word with distaste. "Yes, we were told you've been getting visits from some tattoo covered gangbanger. All that will change now. No child of mine will be seen associating with such individuals."

The way she sneered it made Dante sound like some kind of criminal. Like he was the scum of the earth and the type of person this woman wouldn't piss on if he were on fire. My stomach churned and bile rose in my throat as I processed her words.

"I'm not going to abandon my best friend just because he doesn't suit your lifestyle, *Catherine*," I snapped back at her, leveling a glare at her that I could only hope carried as much ice as hers did. "For your information, not every person in Jersey with tattoos is in a gang."

The elegant, stuck up bitch of a woman who had donated her DNA to my creation just looked at me like I was a simpleton.

"Come on, we're late." She totally ignored my response, checking her expensive wrist watch and turning on one of those sharp heels to exit the room. The arrogant woman didn't even glance behind her to check I was following, just assumed I would be.

Anger bubbled up in me, choking out the fear of never seeing my best friend again. If this was how she wanted to play it, I was going to do everything in my power to piss her right the fuck off. I only had two months until I was eighteen, and then there was nothing she could do to keep me in her custody. It was going to be a very long two months for her.

It was too painful to think about the fact that my parents just died, so I'd embrace that fury. Mrs. Deboise had no idea who she was messing with.

Chapter 2

The Deboise house was exactly what I'd thought it would be. As Catherine's chauffeur-driven Bentley paused outside the wrought iron gates, I allowed myself a quick moment of awe.

It wasn't a house. Not even close. It was a sprawling mansion like something out of one of those fantastic Christmas rom-coms. The ones with a girl who meets a prince in a foreign, made up country and they fall madly in love… what a shame happy endings weren't real, and pretty mansions were just bricks and mortar.

"This is where you live?" I muttered, unable to bite my tongue any longer. We'd been silent the entire helicopter flight and car ride, and I was starting to get twitchy.

Catherine turned her condescending glare on me. "This is where *we* live. You're a Deboise now, Riley. Start getting used to it." She grimaced, her mouth twisting like she'd licked a lemon. "That name is atrocious and not at all suitable for my daughter. We'll have to change it before the school term starts."

I spluttered in shock and choked on a stray droplet of saliva.

Smooth, Riles. Real smooth.

"Excuse me?" I demanded when my coughing subsided. "I could have sworn you just said you wanted to *change my name.*"

My birth mother turned her attention back to her phone that she'd been tapping away at for the whole journey. "That's exactly what I said, child. Perhaps you suffered a worse head injury than the doctors realized."

I clenched my teeth together. Hard. My temper had always been a bit short, but no amount of deep breathing and counting to ten was going to save me now.

"You can't just change my name because it doesn't suit you," I declared, a growl of fury underscoring my words. "That's not how it works. It's *my fucking name*, you egomaniac."

This finally seemed to capture her attention entirely, and her icy glare snapped back to me. "I'm going to let that slide, just this once, because you don't know what you're saying. But hear this, child. I'm Catherine Deboise. I can do anything I please, and if I want to change your name, that's exactly what I'll do." Her response left me gobsmacked, at a total loss for words. I had no idea people like this even *existed.* "As for that appalling, vulgar language, I can only imagine it's a result of your poor upbringing. Deboise ladies don't swear, so don't *ever* do it again."

Her swipe at my parents—my *dead* parents—had me seeing red.

Before I could even process what I was doing, I spat in her face. "Fuck you, Catherine."

She sat there a moment, just staring at me in shock as my saliva ran down her cheek. For a millisecond, I regretted my actions. Spitting was revolting, and not something I'd ever done before, but Catherine Deboise brought out the worst in me.

My moment of regret was gone as quick as it came thanks to the crack of Catherine's hand across my face. She'd used the back of it, her huge diamond rings cutting my cheek in the process.

"The next time you treat me with disrespect, I'll have you beaten." She delivered the threat in such a cold, uncaring way that I really questioned if maybe I'd died in the crash after all. Surely this was Hell.

I touched my fingers to my cheek, dabbing at the blood trickling from the fresh wound and looking at them in stunned disbelief. She'd just *hit* me!

Catherine pushed open her door and stepped out, disappearing into the mansion without another word and leaving me to find my own way. After a few minutes of struggling I finally managed to clamber out of the car, only to find the fucking driver just *standing* there.

"Thanks for the help, asshole," I growled at him in anger. Not because I expected servants to wait on me hand and foot, but because I was in a goddamn cast and blood still dripped down my face. It was only common courtesy, wasn't it?

The driver raised his brows, giving me an aloof look. "Word of advice, miss. Keep your head down and your mouth shut. You do not want to get on the Mistress's bad side."

I glared at him, then decided it wasn't worth the effort to argue. All he'd done was confirm what I already suspected... Catherine Deboise was a fucking psychopath.

#

"This is your room," she said, acting like the confrontation in the car hadn't even happened. "I'm heading out right after this for a business meeting. You will stay in here until I get back, and then we will go over the rules."

I didn't even bother to acknowledge her. I'd already decided that whatever she told me to do, I was going to do the opposite. I might not have much power against someone with Deboise banking money, but I'd take what I could. She'd made a big mistake thinking she could just pick me up and drop me back in her life again, and now that I had met her it was making even less sense that she had.

She turned away from the door, and I had to ask: "Why?"

She didn't pretend not to understand. "Because I have need of you now. I didn't when you were born."

Then she strode off, the heels clicking on the shiny wood floor.

I blinked after her, trying to figure out what the hell she was talking about. *Had need of me? Need for what?*

Panic and pain swirled inside of me again, and I had to steady myself against the door frame. From the outside it no doubt looked like I'd hit the jackpot: mega-rich birth parents bringing me back into their lives. Their sort of money was beyond anything I'd ever known. From my first step onto the marble floors of the Deboise mansion, I knew I was so far out of my element it wasn't funny. I grew up in a loving, but very poor, home. We had never had a single extra, but we got by. That was how I'd met Dante. He'd been my neighbor growing up, until he graduated to his own pretty impressive condo. I'd never asked him how he afforded it, and he never dragged me into whatever he was low-key running for the local gangs.

Yeah, I'd lied to *Catherine* earlier. I knew my friend wasn't completely innocent, but from our neighborhood, very few were. I didn't care. Loyalty meant a lot to me, and I would have Dante's back for the rest of my life.

My room held no interest to me. Despite the fact it was huge, more like a mini-suite than a bedroom, I mostly hated everything about it. The bed was white, the walls were white, the rug was black, and there was a fireplace. I also had a black leather couch and what looked like an impressive black and white bathroom through an open door across the room.

Everything was clean, sterile, and ultra-modern. It all just screamed of that cold bitch. I fought against the urge to go across and mess the perfectly fitted blankets on the bed. Because this place was giving me the creeps.

I'd moved further inside when a knock sounded from behind, and I turned to find yet another man standing there. It was not the driver, though, this man was in his late-fifties, with a thick head of gray hair.

"Good evening, Miss Deboise," he said politely. "I'm Stewart, and I'm head of staff here at Deboise Estate. If you require anything, simply ring that little buzzer." He pointed toward a black and gold button near the side of the bed. "And someone will be straight by."

I nodded, and he turned to leave when I called out, "Where is all of my stuff? The lady at child services said they packed up the things from my *home*." I near choked on that word, because the pain at knowing I'd never go back to that crappy little house was too much for me to handle. I'd take it over this cold mansion any day.

Stewart slowly turned, his face expressionless, although it did seem there was a slight softening of the lines around his eyes when he replied, "Mistress informed me that you had everything you needed in your room. We don't have any other belongings for you."

I stumbled back, and he reached out as if to grab me, but I waved him away before he could. "She didn't bring any of my things?" I seethed. *That fucking bitch.*

As if it was poor Stewart's fault, I glared at him and he just gave me a polite nod before backing up and closing my door as he left. Yeah, I'd bet that I wasn't scary when he was used to working for the bitch of Upstate New York.

Fury burned and swirled in my gut, and since I generally wasn't someone that held onto anger, I knew I needed to do something to blow off steam. My life had been ripped apart in the last ten days, I'd lost everything, and now ... this was a bad situation. I knew it. I could feel it deep down. It was all too much for me to process—I needed a car. I needed to race and forget everything in my current shitty life. I'd been given no car privileges though.

In fact, I didn't have a phone or any way of actually reaching the outside world. I was a veritable prisoner right now...

Except...

I didn't have to be. What was stopping me from sneaking out of this house and taking my chances in the big wide world? I mean, Dante would help me, I was sure of it. He was probably going out of his mind with worry right now knowing that I'd just disappeared from the hospital never to be seen again.

A plan was already forming, but I knew it would be safest at dark. The expensive looking gold clock on the wall told me it was almost 4:00 p.m., which meant I had at least another hour before it was dark enough.

With nothing else to do, I explored my very temporary room. The bathroom was exactly as I thought, sleek and expensive, with the most tempting looking deep tub. Not quite tempting enough to put up with Mrs. Debitch though. A large room joined the main bedroom, and it was filled with clothes and shoes and makeup and … it was basically a mini-mall with every conceivable item a rich young chick would need. My mouth watered when I realized that there was a wall of shoes, and more than one pair of black heels with the red soles. I reached out and lifted one up, finding some swirly signature on it starting with an L. I had no idea what this brand was, but I was starting to see I had at least one thing in common with my birth mother. We were hooked on shiny black heels.

With reluctance, I placed it back on the shelf. I wouldn't be taking anything from here with me.

The time ticked away at an agonizingly slow pace, but I had one shot at this. If she caught me, I would be under twenty-four hour security, I had no doubt. She wouldn't have gone to all of this trouble to get me back, unless she really did "have need of me."

When it finally got dark enough, I eased open the bedroom door and snuck a quick look to make sure no one was around. Normally I would have gone out the window, but with a broken arm, I couldn't climb. My heart beat rapidly as I crept along the hall and down the stairs. There was a huge double staircase, which led to the impressive entrance to this house. Crystal chandeliers twinkled above, cascading lights across the marble.

I didn't see anyone around, and was relieved when I managed to get outside and into the darkness without incident. From what I remembered, the front drive was long, which meant I was not safe until I was off Deboise land. Pausing,

I realized that anyone this rich would have security. They were probably patrolling the perimeter right now, and I wondered if they shot trespassers.

I almost hesitated then, but I'd come this far, so I stopped thinking and started running.

Holding my broken arm against me, my legs pounded the pavement, and I veered off so I was away from the lights lining the main drive. The grass was thick and soft, and my pace picked up. My body still hurt. My head ached on and off, as it had done since I woke up, and no doubt this sort of sprinting was not recommended by my doctor when recovering from a car accident, but I didn't care.

I needed out.

The Deboise estate was fucking huge, of course, but I still managed to make it to the imposing fences in under ten minutes. Speed had always been my thing; running and cars anyway … not so much the drug. The fence was my next obstacle, because it was three times my height, and had thick bars lining it. There was a symbol etched in the middle of each bar, on a round plaque. Something that looked like an M and a D, possibly, but it was hard to tell in this low light. I was guessing the D was for Deboise, and the M … mansion. Who knew what pretentious bullshit she was representing here?

Moving along the fence line, I stayed behind the hedges which lined it. I was close to the gates we'd entered through, and I wondered if they were on a sensor. There would have to be a code, I was sure of it. While I was trying to figure out what to do, a set of headlights turned into the fence, and I dropped to the ground, holding my breath. *Fuck fuck fuck.* The bitch was back.

Chapter 3

The car paused for a brief moment at the gates while they silently slid open. Once my panic faded, I realized that this was my best chance of getting out of here. I pulled myself up while still staying out of sight. I'd have to time it perfectly, but I knew I could do it. I had to do it.

The thrum of an expensive car echoed past me as she accelerated, and I waited until the gates were just starting to close again before I pushed off hard from the ground and pumped my legs. My cast hit the side of the gate when I dived through, and I bit back the cry, trying my best to shake off the pain. It was worth it though, because I was on the outside, exactly where I wanted to be. Well, sort of. I remembered another set of gates at the start of this section of exclusive estates, but I was sure I'd manage to get past them too.

The second set had guards on them, but they were definitely more interested in who was coming in, rather than who was going out. I snuck through at the same time a black Bugatti Veyron rumbled out. *Holy fuck.*

My legs didn't want to move, I just wanted to stare at the perfection of that fine ass piece of machinery. But there was no time for me to drool over my unicorn car. I had to get the hell out of Dodge.

As soon as I was a short distance from the guards, I started to relax. Right up until another set of headlights flared to life right before me. My muscles tensed, prepared to run, when a figure stepped out from the driver's side and headed toward me. With the lights blinding me, it took me a few minutes to figure out who it was, and then I was running. Right into his arms.

"Dante!" I whisper-yelled. When his arms wrapped around me, I sank into the warmth and comfort. "How the hell did you find me?" I asked, pulling back from him.

His lips tilted up slightly, as he ran his gaze across me. That smile disappeared the moment he saw the cut on my cheek.

The hold he had on me tightened. "What the fuck happened to you?" he seethed, almost shaking me.

I jerked myself out of his hold. "My birth mom is a fucking psycho, that's what happened."

He didn't seem surprised to hear me say "birth mom," and I wondered how much persuasion it took for CPS to divulge my location. Dante could be very convincing when he wanted something.

"Is she dangerous to you, Riles? Do you think she'll actually hurt you?"

I thought about it for a moment. "No way to know what that crazy chick would do, but I get the vibe that if I obey her rules, she'll leave me alone."

His anger deepened; ignoring this, I pushed past him and hurried across to the car, my hand already reaching out to touch her sleek lines. It was my baby, a dark blue Aston Martin V12 Vantage S. Okay, technically it was Dante's baby, but he let me race her whenever I wanted.

"Why were you sneaking out, Riles?" he asked, watching me closely as I loved up on the car.

Pulling my hand back, I let out a low breath, facing him. "I don't know what's going on, but apparently my birth parents want me back. Catherine Deboise is completely insane, though. I'm not even kidding. She threw away all of my stuff. She wants me to change my name. She's going to try and mold me into a Stepford child."

He let out a low chuckle, and I wanted to punch him. "It's not fucking funny, dude. This is serious. I can't stay there."

His eyes flicked to the cut on my cheek again, and then his jaw was tense, all signs of his laughter gone. "I agree, but you can't just run from people like this, Riley. She has more power than you can fathom, and it'll be nothing for her to hunt you down. Especially when you're only seventeen."

Two fucking months.

"What exactly are you saying, Dante?"

I was going to make the bastard spell it out for me. He reached forward and wrapped an arm around my shoulders. "I'm saying, that you need to be smarter than this. I have connections, but not even I can go up against the Deboise family."

"I have to go back," I said resigned.

"Just for now," he promised. "But ... follow her rules, Riles. Don't let her hurt you again."

Part of me was pissed he didn't fight harder for me to run, but I could tell that he knew more about this than me and that he believed running wouldn't work. Or he was too scared to risk it. Dante was tough, don't get me wrong, but I'd seen him act like a bitch on more than one occasion when he got in over his head. Granted, that was something which hadn't happened in the last few years, so maybe the Deboise threat was legit.

"Can I drive her before I go back?" I all but begged, knowing this might have been my only chance to blow off steam.

He laughed, and nudged me toward the door. "There's actually a race here tonight, in Jefferson."

"You drove four hours just so I could race?" I joked, already sliding into the driver's seat.

Dante dropped into the passenger seat. "I drove four hours to make sure you were okay."

His words were casual, but I knew my friend well enough to know when he'd been pissed off and scared. He changed the subject. "You wanna race?" His gaze flickered uncertainly to my plastered arm, then he nodded to himself. "Left arm, you should be good to drive at least half as good as usual."

I laughed, a note of hysteria creeping out. "Only half? Don't insult me, Dante." I dragged in a deep breath and released it on a heavy sigh. "I'll take the risk. Mommy dearest is already going to beat the living shit out of me, might as well make the most of my night of freedom."

Dante froze. "Don't let her fucking hurt you, Riles. Do whatever the hell it takes to make sure she doesn't. I'll figure out a way to get you out quicker, I just need some time."

I shrugged. I could take a few beatings if it meant I'd eventually be free of this family. I did not want to have to run and look over my shoulder for the rest of my life.

He dropped a phone into my lap then. "Call her. Tell her what's happening. Maybe she won't be so angry."

I doubted that, but since he apparently had her number … somehow, like that wasn't fishy as fuck. I stored that in my brain to hit him up over later, and hit dial. Two rings. "Where are you?"

She knew it was me. Everyone here had far too much in the way of information.

"I want to spend this one night with my friend," I said, getting to the point. "Give me tonight and I won't fight you on anything else. I will dress in your clothes," *especially those heels*, "and follow your rules."

I held my breath, hoping she couldn't sense how badly I needed this.

"You have one night," she finally said, and I could practically feel the ice in her voice. "Tomorrow you belong to me."

The line went dead, and I let out all the air from my lungs. "Holy fuck she's scary," I choked out before handing the phone back to Dante.

He shook his head. "Keep it, I want to be able to stay in touch with you."

I shrugged before slipping it into the back pocket of my jeans. The engine roared to life a moment later, and I could have cried at the familiar feel of this car under my hands. Well, hand, for now, because one of them was broken.

"You're going to have to be careful tonight," Dante warned me as I swung her around and took off. I had no idea where we were going, but there was only one path from this estate. "You won't have the same level of control with a broken arm."

My speed picked up, and I didn't even bother to reply. The flash of the butterfly symbol across the back of the car caught my eye in the mirror. It was my calling card, the butterfly. I wouldn't let a broken arm stop me from flying, especially not tonight.

Dante muttered something about a death wish before settling back and letting me do my thing.

After we reached the edge of town, he started to direct me along a dark and deserted part of the county.

At least it seemed deserted until I drove around a sharp bend and through a small pocket of trees. When I emerged on the other side, all the tension in my body eased.

This was my happy place. Illegal street racing. Except this one was somewhat different from the ones Dante usually took me to back home.

"Damn," Dante breathed as I rolled past some of the most expensive cars on this planet. "Was that a Bugatti Veyron?"

I glanced in the direction he was gaping and spotted that same gorgeous car that had come out of the gated compound Mrs. Deboise lived in. These kids really did have too much damn money if those were the cars they were choosing to race in.

"Over there," Dante directed me, pointing to a guy in a ball cap who was receiving a fat wad of cash from a pimple faced kid in an obnoxious striped blazer, white pants and loafers. Fucking *loafers*.

Hat-dude was clearly the one in charge. They were usually easy to spot—the ones with their pockets bursting with money. I pulled my—er, Dante's—car to a stop and popped my seatbelt before pausing with my hands on the steering wheel.

"I don't know if we can really afford this one, Dante," I murmured, eyeing the crowd assembled. They were all clearly "locals" in the sense that their shoes probably cost more than my mom earned in a year.

The thought of my mom stabbed grief through me, and I smothered it with anger. It was the only way I knew how to handle it. Anger at life for taking my parents away from me. Anger at myself for not putting up more of a fight at CPS. Anger at Catherine fucking Deboise for thinking it was okay to throw me away as a baby then just pick me up again now that she needed me.

"Whatever their asking price, I've got us covered," Dante assured me with a mysterious smile. He had new ink on his neck, just below his ear, and I reached out to trace the raised lines with my fingertip. It was a little butterfly. Totally out of place amongst his skulls, guns, bleeding roses and gang symbols, and I got the feeling he'd gotten it for me.

Neither of us spoke for a moment, then someone rapped on my window, making me jump with fright. Blushing, and dodging Dante's way too intense stare, I pressed the electric window down and gave the sandy blond guy who'd knocked a tight smile.

"You here to race?" he asked, wrinkling his nose in confusion then looking straight past me to Dante. "That's brave of you to let your girlfriend drive your car, bro. I wouldn't trust any chick behind the wheel of a nice car." He gave an annoying little guffaw, like he was sharing some sort of private man-joke with Dante. I pitied this dude's girlfriend—if he had one.

"She's not my girlfriend, this is her car and I'm not your *bro*," Dante replied in a voice cold enough to give Catherine a run for her money. He clicked his seatbelt off and stepped out of the car, coming around to my side.

The guy who'd knocked on my window looked at a loss for words, but Dante just pushed him out of the way and opened my door for me to get out and join him.

"That's uh," the blonde dude stuttered, casting a glance over his shoulder to where a group of guys leaned against cars near the ball-cap guy. "I don't think we allow chicks to race," he finally spat out, then paled when Dante folded his tattooed arms over his muscular chest and glared. "But hey, I'm not the one in charge. You're welcome to check with Jimmy."

Blond guy scurried away as quickly as he'd appeared, and I exchanged a look with Dante.

"You want to kick their rich-kid asses even more now, huh?" He asked me with a small smile, and I grinned my response. The only thing better than winning a race like this: rubbing it in their faces that they got beat by a girl.

Holding my plastered arm against my body, I wandered across the gravel to where Jimmy was counting out a sickeningly thick wad of cash. "Jimmy?" I called out when I got within a few paces of him.

The guy looked up, then tilted his cap up a bit when he spotted me standing there. "You're new," he commented with an odd tone. Excitement? Curiosity? "Come to place a bet on your newest crush, darling?" he asked me with severe condescension.

Dante snickered a laugh beside me but didn't try and speak for me. This wasn't the first time we'd come up against this attitude, but it had definitely been a while. I'd been driving since I was twelve, and racing Dante's cars since I was fourteen. Back home, I'd earned a name for myself. People *knew* how good I was. How good my baby, the Butterfly, was.

It was almost thrilling that I would get to prove that all over again to this bunch of posers.

"I'm actually here to race," I informed him, stuffing my good hand into the back pocket of my jeans. For the first time in a long ass while, I felt totally out of place. My jeans were worn and ripped—and not in a designer sort of way—and my sneakers had definitely seen better days. In fact, I think my mom had gotten them from goodwill. My purple sweater was too small, and the top of my electric blue bra was showing.

Jimmy tilted his hat up even further, peering at me with mossy green eyes as he stepped closer. His gaze ran up and down me, judging, before a small smile touched his lips. "You're definitely new around here, sweetheart. We don't allow girls to race."

My eyes narrowed at him. A light smattering of freckles decorated his nose, and the hair poking out of his hat was mouse brown. If it wasn't for that arrogant air of money he carried, he would be totally unassuming. "Why?" I challenged. "Because your egos can't handle it?"

Jimmy smiled back, but it wasn't a kind one. "No. Because girls can't drive for shit." He dismissed me with a shrug, turning away and starting to head back to his friends before someone else spoke up.

"Let her race, Jimmy," a deep, husky voice said, and my attention jerked to the left where a tall figure leaned against—ugh, against that sexy as fuck Bugatti. When had he arrived? We'd driven past him some hundred or so yards back. "She can take Jasper's place."

"Whoa, what? No way, man!" A guy with platinum blond hair protested from where he sat on the hood of a canary yellow Lamborghini Aventador. As fast as he reacted, though, he backtracked. "I mean, sure, whatever. I didn't want to drive tonight anyway."

I squinted into the shadows at the guy who'd spoken up for me, but all I could make out was his broad frame and a flash of a wristwatch. If only he would step a foot to the right, I could see his face...

"Are you sure?" Jimmy asked the mystery guy—not Jasper, whose place had just been offered up.

"Absolutely," the dude replied, then as though he'd read my damn thoughts, he shifted into the light. My breath caught in my throat, and I could have sworn time slowed down. His dark hair was the perfect length, styled like he'd just stepped off a photoshoot. His dark gray top was tight across a broad, muscled chest and hugged his thick arms all the way to the wrists. Probably Dante's height, but where Dante was all lean, street strength, this guy was buff. Solid.

Put simply, he was possibly the most stunning guy I'd ever laid eyes on. Ever. Of course it made sense that such a perfect creature drove my unicorn car. "Maybe when she loses her pretty car she will think twice about turning up where she doesn't belong."

My jaw dropped at the cruel twist to his words. His dark eyes seemed to burn as he met my gaze across the shadowed space between us, and a shudder ran through my whole body.

"Excuse me?" I squeaked out. "My—"

A mean smile curved the dark haired guy's lush lips. "Your car. The Aston, right?" I nodded, glancing over my shoulder at my baby. "Buy-in for these races is two hundred, but I seriously doubt you *or* your boyfriend have even seen that much cash, let alone carry it on you. So we will accept your car as buy-in." A sneer curled his lip. "Not that a 2015 model is worth anything close to that, but it'll do."

Stunned, I turned to Dante. Two hundred *thousand* dollars buy-in? That was insanity! He met my eyes as I started to shake my head, and responded to the sexy, smoldering stranger himself.

"Done," he replied, giving me a small, confident nod. "It's just a car, and you never lose." Ignoring my gaping jaw, he turned to face Jimmy. "If that's acceptable to you? I take it you *are* still the one running this race?"

He'd hit a nerve, as Jimmy gave the dickhead with the Bugatti a small glance, then nodded to Dante. "Of course I am," he replied with an edge of annoyance. It was a tough position. He clearly took his orders for Bugatti-boy but didn't want anyone else questioning his authority. "If the other racers are fine with it, then I guess you're racing, sweetheart." He curled his lip at me in a small sneer. "Don't say I didn't try and stop you."

Shocked into silence, I started to follow Dante back to our car before someone's snickering, cruel laughter made me pause. It was a girl who'd crawled up on top of Jasper—the dude with the yellow Lambo. Her long, dead straight hair was a sheet of honey blonde silk, and her red dress was so short I could see her matching lace panties.

"I'd be tempted to say 'break a leg,' but it looks like you're already down a limb," she sneered with a laugh, and Jasper just grinned like a damn hyena. His hands roamed her body like he owned it, and my stomach churned in disgust.

A moment ago, I'd been terrified and ready to pull out. How could I risk Dante's car? The most expensive buy-in we'd ever done wasn't even a tenth of this one! Now, though? Now I wanted to beat these pretty rich boys and shit all over that misogynistic attitude.

"Come on, Riles," Dante murmured to me as we reached our car again. "Show these pretentious fucks who they're up against. If you win, it's a million dollar payday." His eyes sparkled with excitement, and I recognized the fact that he was getting off on the risk.

"Yeah, and if I lose, you lose your car," I muttered, the sour taste of fear rolling across my tongue.

Dante just grinned and winked. "But you never lose."

Chapter 4

I was the last to roll my car up to the line. There were already five others with their engines running, their noses flush with the spray painted line. We were at a wide stretch of road, but even so it was a tight squeeze to fit six sports cars across. I was on the outside, and I knew I would need to pull ahead quickly or I'd get pushed off the road when it narrowed out again.

A crowd had gathered, much bigger than I was used to, and nerves were fluttering in my belly. Dante was on the sidelines, his eyes locked on me, even though he wouldn't be able to see me through the dark tints of my windows.

To my surprise, Bugatti-boy wasn't racing at all. Maybe he was just all talk? Instead, he leaned on his sleek black car with a perfectly proportioned brunette girl in a mini-skirt and high heels hanging all over him. Not that he seemed to notice her... that smug, arrogant smile was all for me.

Rage boiling, I tightened my good hand on the gear shift. Once again,

I thanked fuck for small mercies that it had been my left wrist broken. Otherwise I really would have been screwed when it came to driving.

A girl with short, messy blonde hair tapped on my window, and I rolled it down to see what she wanted. So far, my reception had been somewhat less than warm, so call me suspicious.

"Hey." She smiled at me. "I'm Eddy."

"Riley," I responded with a tight smile. "What's up?"

She cast a glance over my car at someone calling her name, then flipped them off and turned back to me. "I figured no one would have run you through what to expect. This road seems wide, but pretty much right after that first corner it narrows to two lanes. After that it's about a mile of turns on the narrow road and then it opens into a motorway. You don't need to worry about cops, but you will need to keep your eyes open for traffic in the other direction." She rolled her heavily made up eyes. "The guys don't close the roads because they like the element of danger."

I raised my brows at her in surprise. The fact that they even *could* close the roads for their race spoke volumes about the amount of power and influence these kids had.

"Thanks," I murmured. "Why are you helping me?"

She shrugged, but her smile really seemed sincere. "Because I'm so sick of the guys around here acting like it's nineteen fifty three and all women are good for is cooking, cleaning and sucking cock. I have a feeling you'll be the one to prove them wrong." Someone yelled her name again, and she glanced over my car with a pissed off expression. "I better go, but good luck, new girl!"

As she ducked back off the "race track," I noticed she was the only girl I'd seen so far who was actually dressed for the cold weather. Sure she still had designer heels on, but at least she was in jeans and a warm coat.

In stark contrast, the girl who stepped out in front of us with a red scarf in her hand was in nothing but a crotch length bandage dress. She must have been freezing her fake tits off, which might have explained the prissy look on her face.

There was no more time to ponder on the locals. Her scarf dropped and my body moved on sheer instinct as I slammed my car into gear and pressed my foot down hard on the accelerator.

Eddy had said that the road narrowed out after the next turn, which meant I needed to pull ahead or behind in exactly... *now*.

My wrist protested as I jerked my steering wheel, cutting off the guy in an Audi R8. My tires grabbed the road just in time to make the turn alongside a cherry red Porsche 911. We were out in front, but it was a long race—much longer than I was used to—so I needed to hold the position. I couldn't lose Dante's car; it was simply non-negotiable.

For several turns, the Porsche and I stayed neck and neck while a Corvette and Mercedes hugged our back bumpers like barnacles. It wasn't long, though, before the Porsche started pulling ahead of me. Not because he was a better driver, simply because he knew the roads.

Every turn I hesitated, unsure of what the next stretch of road would be like, or if we'd encounter oncoming traffic. All those hesitations, where my foot eased on the gas, they all added up so that when we hit the motorway the Porsche was almost two car lengths ahead and the Corvette was starting to pass me.

"No, no, no," I hissed under my breath, slamming through my gears and pressing my foot down harder, "Not today, you entitled asshole. Not my baby."

From the corner of my eye, I noticed small piles of old snow beside the road, dirty and melting. I'd raced in winter often enough that I could handle myself on cold roads, but a chill of fear rippled through me and for a flash of a second, I saw the crash. I saw our car spinning out of control, heard my mother's screams, smelled the sickening, coppery tang of blood.

It was only a flash, but it was a flash too long. It broke my concentration, and I suddenly found myself sandwiched between the Corvette and Mercedes while a truck barreled toward us.

I screamed as the headlights blinded me and the driver leaned on his horn. Panic and fear locked up my muscles, and my plastered hand spasmed. The wheel jerked in my grip, sending me careening sideways into the Corvette.

Metal crunched and my head snapped to the side as our cars collided, then in the next second I bounced across into the Merc. My ears were ringing, my vision blurred, but survival instinct kicked in. I slammed my foot down on the brakes as my beautiful blue Aston entered a spin and skidded off the road into the grassy shoulder.

It seemed like forever that my car skidded before finally coming to a stop with a hard thump against a tree. My heart, though, continued thundering so hard I worried it was about to burst. Tears stung at my eyes and my breathing came in heavy, harsh gasps while I desperately tried to get a grip. But the fresh memories of my parents' death refused to be silenced, and a low, keening sound began to wail from me.

Get a grip, Riley! Hold it together. You're not dead, you're fine. You're fine. You're fine.

Dante's car, though...

"No," I sobbed, trying and failing to unbuckle my seatbelt several times before my trembling fingers made it work. My door was stuck, and I needed to kick it a couple of times before it popped open and spilled me out onto the chewed up grass.

In short... my beautiful Butterfly was destroyed.

I was no mechanic, but I could only imagine how much it would cost to repair the kind of damage done. The idea made me sob, and I hugged my knees as I sat in the dirt beside Dante's hundred and eighty thousand dollar write-off. Or, not even Dante's anymore. By now the other drivers would be long finished, which meant Dante had just lost his car.

As I sat there, rocking back and forth, fighting down the mounting despair, a sleek black car rolled up and stopped on the road where I'd spun out.

Sickness pooled in my belly, and I quickly swiped the tears from my cheeks as that dark haired, arrogant asshole stepped out of his Bugatti and crossed the grass toward me.

"Come to gloat?" I snapped at him, scrambling to my feet. He was still an easy half foot taller than me, but at least I wasn't cowering.

The smile he gave me was tight and humorless. "I hope you learned your lesson, Butterfly," he said in a cold, serial killer sort of voice, flicking his gaze over the decal on my poor, destroyed baby. Behind him, several more cars pulled up—probably to gawk at the poor little new girl who couldn't handle racing with the boys. "Go back to where you came from. You don't belong here."

He started to walk away again, and I spluttered a protest. "Hey, wait!" I yelled. "What about my car?"

Turning slightly back toward me, he arched a brow over one of those dark eyes. "You mean my car?" He gave a cold half-smile. "I'll probably get it towed to the wreckers. It was a piece of shit anyway."

I was left speechless, and he strolled back to his sexy-as-sin car and slid in. In the dim light while his door was open, I spotted that same brunette girl who'd been all over him before the race, and her smug grin was enough to make me see red.

Bugatti-boy took off, closely followed by three other insanely expensive cars—including Jasper in the yellow Aventador. The other kids who'd stopped to stare all left a bit slower, the last one leaving just as a vintage mustang pulled up and Dante leapt out of the passenger seat.

"Riley!" he yelled as he barreled toward me, sweeping me up in a huge hug. "Are you okay?" he demanded when he finally set me down. His hands cupped my face as he peered at me, like he was a human x-ray machine and could scan me for injuries.

"I'm fine," I replied, peeling myself out of his grip. "Just a bit shaken up. And Butterfly..." I choked up, looking over the wreckage of the beautiful car again.

"Fuck the car, Riles," Dante growled. "When we saw the wreck, I thought you'd—" he broke off with a cringe, and I swallowed past the lump in my throat.

"You thought I'd died. Like my parents did." I shivered hard, and not just because my sweater was too thin for the winter temperatures. In my attempt to avoid Dante's too intense stare, I spotted Eddy standing awkwardly on the edge of the road.

"Hey," I called out to her. "Your car?" I indicated the mustang, and she nodded.

"Yeah. Want a lift home?" Her smile was sympathetic, and it made me want to burst out crying again.

With one last look at my poor, broken Butterfly, I heaved a sigh and trudged back to the road where Eddy waited beside her car. "Thanks," I muttered, taking the front passenger seat as Dante hopped in the back.

Suddenly something occurred to me. "Fuck, you're going to think I'm a total spaz, but... I don't actually know how to get to, uh, the place I'm staying."

Eddy arched a brow at me in curiosity, and I felt my cheeks heat.

"She's going to the Deboise Estate," Dante offered, slouching across the backseat so he could look between Eddy and me.

My new friend spluttered and coughed a laugh. "Excuse me?" she exclaimed, gaping at me. "Why are you going to the Deboise Estate?"

I heaved a sigh and cradled my plastered arm to my middle as I peered out the window. "Long story," I mumbled. "Do you know how to get there?"

Eddy snorted. "Of course I do. I just live two houses down." I gave her a puzzled frown and she rolled her eyes. "Edith Langham," she explained, pointing to herself. "You sort of met my brother Jasper earlier."

Blame the head injury, but it took a moment for my brain to make the right connections. "Langham," I repeated slowly. "Langham Finance?"

Eddy nodded. "Yup, that's the one. So behind those ridiculous gates there are just the five estates. Ours—Langham—as well as Rothwell, Grant, Beckett, and obviously Deboise." She flicked a quick glance at me while she drove. "You met Sebastian Beckett tonight, of course, and my brother Jasper Langham. You didn't see them, but Evan Rothwell and Dylan Grant were tagging along in Beck's shadow like they *always* are." She rolled her eyes and drummed her fingers on the steering wheel.

"Sebastian Beckett?" I repeated, and that sexy, smoldering asshole popped into my head. Of *course* that was him. I groaned and dropped my head into my hands.

"You didn't know?" Eddy exclaimed, with a small laugh, then tossed an accusing look at Dante in the mirror. "That was rude of you not to introduce her."

I frowned, turning in my seat to glare at Dante. "You knew who they were? What the fuck, Dante?"

He just shrugged and looked unapologetic. "Like I give a shit about a bunch of entitled rich kids. I just wanted to see you shit all over their egos."

Grumbling, I turned back to my window. "Look how that worked out."

There was a long, awkward silence, then Eddy hummed under her breath. "School is going to be so much fun this semester."

Chapter 5

Eddy wasn't questioned at the first set of gates, driving through with barely a pause. I was still pretty shaken up, my pulse racing. Heavy emotions pressed on my chest as well. Not only was that the first car I'd driven since my parents, it was the first race I'd ever lost, and I'd had to do it in spectacular fashion in front of a bunch of rich fucking assholes. Poor, butterfly.

"So, are you going to tell me your story? Or should I guess?" Eddy picked up the conversation, as she maneuvered along the dark road.

I looked over my shoulder and exchanged a glance with Dante. He didn't give me his usual head shake, and I was surprised that my jaded best friend seemed to be okay with Eddy. Usually it took him ages to warm up to someone new, especially enough to trust them with life stories.

Deciding I could use one friend in this piece of shit place, I decided to give Eddy a chance. A real chance. "My parents were killed—" I choked on that word, swallowing hard and attempting to stuff all of my burning pain down again. "In a car accident. The Deboise are adopting me, or re-claiming me more accurately, because I'm apparently the biological daughter they threw away at birth."

Eddy blinked at me and slowed her car before pulling it to a stop. We were in front of the gates I'd escaped from only a few hours ago. "Fuck me. Seriously, the Deboises are your birth parents?" Something seemed to occur to her because her eyes widened and she sucked a deep breath.

I nodded, shrugging off her weird facial expression. "Oh yeah, and Catherine Deboise is an ultra bitch. She is trying to morph me into a rich asshole. The next time you see me, my name will be impossible to pronounce and I'll be wearing designer heels."

Dante snorted from the back. "You'd kill yourself in heels."

He wasn't kidding.

Eddy was quiet, her face drawn. "Is this about Oscar?" she asked quietly.

I blinked at her. "Oscar?"

The name was not familiar to me at all.

"Oscar Deboise…" she trailed off.

"Is that my father?" I wondered. I had no clue what his name was, or if he actually existed. If I had to guess, I'd say Catherine had long ago diced him into small pieces and cemented him in her basement wall. Psycho.

Eddy went really pale then, reaching out to grasp my hand. "Holy shit, you don't know. Okay, so Oscar is—was—your brother. He was killed a month ago."

I had a brother? "How old was he?" I asked in a breathless whisper. Why the fuck a dead brother's age was important, I'd never know, but for some reason I pictured him as a tiny child, and that made me feel even more ill.

"Twenty," she said, surprising me. "Almost twenty-one. His birthday would have been in April."

Something dark and painful slithered across my mind, adding to the layers of confusion about this new life I'd found myself in. "My birthday is in March," I said softly. We'd been born almost in the same month, just three years apart. *A brother.*

"Why the hell did I get the boot when they kept *him?*"

I had no idea if this was something Eddy would know, but it didn't hurt to ask.

She cleared her throat before swallowing hard. "Oscar was the planned successor for the Deboise fortune, and you—according to my parents anyway—were an accident. I seriously just remembered the story when you said it before. But here's the thing… she said you died during the birth."

It shouldn't have hurt to hear her say that, because I didn't give a single fuck about the Deboises, but for some reason, my chest was aching.

"Catherine isn't really a 'kid person,'" Eddy continued. "And maybe it was just easier to fake your death and then put you into foster care, rather than deal with another crying child? Even with nannies, my mom said she still struggled with Oscar."

Her lame reasoning was a clear grasp at straws, but there wasn't much she could say to justify Catherine pretending I was *dead.*

Dante made a rough, angry sound from the back, but didn't interrupt.

Eddy grinned, and it was a little evil. "It's not all bad news. You were a breeched birth, and you tore Catherine to pieces. She ended up having all of her shit ripped out to stop her from bleeding out," Eddy finished, and I blinked at that unexpected ending. "So, she couldn't have more kids, and that was the perfect karma. You got your own back."

"Maybe that's why she hates me so much?" I pondered.

Eddy shook her head. "Catherine hates everyone."

I was distracted then by the gates opening. Catherine knew we were out here, and that was my signal to get my ass inside.

"How did Oscar die?" I asked as I opened my door.

Dante opened his as well, even though there was no reason for him to get out. Catherine Deboise would not let him within five feet of her house, that was for sure.

Eddy leaned over so she could see me, the interior light in her car illuminating her doll-like features. "No one really knows. He took off one night, on his own, and then his body was found in the lake behind town the next day. He was banged up pretty badly, but there had been a storm that night so the local police believe it was just an accident."

"That's a lot," I whispered, not sure what else I could say. It didn't sound like Eddy believed the police, and I was sure she had a lot more information, but there was no more time for questions tonight. I probably wasn't in the right headspace for any more life changing revelations like that anyway. Switching subjects, I turned to Dante. "What are you going to do? Thanks to my fuck up, you don't have a car?"

He shrugged, looking relaxed. "I have friends in town; I'll crash there tonight. Don't worry about it." His eyes narrowed. "Still got your phone?"

I patted my pocket, having completely forgotten about the little device he'd given me. "Yep, still there," I said, pulling it out and checking it for cracks. Everything looked good.

"Keep it on you at all times," he warned me. "My number is speed dial one. If you get into any trouble, any at all, you call me immediately. Okay?"

I saluted him. "Whatever you say, Sir Dante, sir."

He relaxed before winking at me. "That's my girl. Okay, I'll let you go now, but I'll be around."

He took off into the dark, Eddy and I watching him until he disappeared completely into the night.

Eddy let out a low whistle. "Holy fuck. My panties are seriously wet right now." Her wide brown eyes met mine, and she looked a little flushed.

I grinned. "Dante has that effect on chicks. They're always hanging off him."

Eddy fanned her face. "Is he yours?" she asked. "Just say the word, and I will remove him from my vibrator spank bank."

I was already shaking my head, laughter bubbling from me. "Nope, Dante and I are just friends. Best friends. There's never been anything romantic between us."

Except the recent "lingering looks" had caught me off guard. And that damn new tattoo. It almost felt like he'd gotten my name on his ass or something. We probably needed to have a chat soon, establish those boundaries again, but right now I had too much other emotional shit to deal with.

"I better get inside," I said, gesturing over my shoulder to the open gates. "Debitch doesn't strike me as the patient type."

Eddy snorted. "She's been way worse since Oscar. He was her pride and joy."

I felt a sliver of sympathy for her then, having suffered my own loss recently. Had she gotten me back just to fill the void Oscar's death had left in her life, or was this about needing another successor? I mean, surely, she didn't need a child that badly to inherit the money. Give it away to a charity or something.

"Thanks for the ride," I said to Eddy.

"Wait!" she called. "What's your number?"

I actually had no idea, since this was a phone Dante got for me. "Just put your number in here," I said, handing the screen across to her.

She took about eight seconds, clearly familiar with the device. "Okay, awesome. Send me a text and we can catch up. School starts Monday, and I'm guessing you'll be going to the same school as me. Catherine doesn't strike me as the type to send her child to public school."

"As long as I have one friend there, I can deal," I said. School was school. And I was almost done, thankfully.

"I'll show you the ropes," she promised before she gave me a wave, and I closed the passenger door. Her engine revved, and she took off in a rush, tires slipping on the soft grass for a beat before finding traction. When the tail lights disappeared, I let out a low breath and faced my new home.

As I took the first step inside, it almost felt like I was walking to my death. I'd barely made it five feet from the gates, when they slid closed. I looked up into the trees and hedges nearby. It took me a minute, but I eventually found the cameras, hidden away and covered in greenery.

Baring my teeth, I raised my good hand and flipped her off.

Of course, it could have just been some overworked security guard watching, but I sensed it was Debitch herself. She had that psychotic air about her—particularly when she'd smacked me across the face.

Touching two fingers to my bruised cheek, I winced. It was a long trek back up to the main house, and I didn't see anyone hurrying down to collect me in one of the ridiculous golf buggies that I'd seen parked by the front door. Why were rich people so lazy?

I folded my arms across my body, hugging my plaster cast close and gritting my teeth at the twinge of pain I was feeling. Somehow in my failed race, I'd cracked the plaster between my thumb and forefinger so it was no longer limiting movement like it should.

Stewart was waiting at the door when I finally arrived, and he politely held it open for me to enter before shutting and locking it.

"Did you have an enjoyable evening, Miss?" he enquired with a totally straight face. Was he fucking with me or actually serious?

Unsure, I responded with a tight smile. "Delightful."

"Splendid," he murmured, following me as I made my way up to the room I'd been assigned. Just as I was about to enter, I paused, staring at the door opposite mine. The door with an intricate, twisted gold "O" on it.

"Stewart?" I started, chewing my lip as I stared at that letter. "What happened to Oscar?"

The gray-haired man grimaced, glancing at the door in question. "I suggest you don't say that name again, if you value your skin, Miss." His lips pursed, and it was clear he wasn't saying anything more on the subject.

I sighed and pushed open my door. I'd try getting more information out of Eddy at school on Monday.

"I do apologize, Miss," Stewart murmured as I sat on the edge of my bed to take my shoes off. "Madam Deboise gave me clear instructions. You're not to leave your room until she returns from her business trip."

Outraged, I gaped at him. "And how long is that?"

"Monday morning, I believe." He cringed a little as he said this and my jaw dropped further.

"That's two whole days from now! What am I supposed to do in here?" I stood up to gesture my anger but he just stepped back and place his hand on the door handle, preparing to close it.

"Your school books have all been delivered. Madam suggests you might start catching up on everything your subpar education might have missed." He indicated the pile on my desk, which hadn't been there earlier. "I'll ensure that meals are brought up as permitted."

Without waiting to hear my protests any longer, he pulled the door shut and locked it with a heavy turn of a key.

"Hey!" I screamed, rushing to the door and banging on it with my fist. "You can't do this! This is illegal or something!"

"Good night, Miss," Stewart called through the door, and the distinctive sound of his footsteps faded away down the hall.

I screamed pure fury into my empty bedroom, then threw myself down on the bouncy, king sized bed. All my dark emotions were crowding my brain, making me feel panicked and out of control. Suddenly the prospect of being locked in my room was giving me intense claustrophobia. What if there was a fire? Would anyone bother to let me out or would I burn to death in my gilded cage?

Breathing in harsh pants, I scrambled off the bed and made a beeline for the window. Fuck my broken arm, I needed an escape route so I didn't die of imagined smoke inhalation.

I threw the curtains open, then fumbled with the latch before unclicking it and yanking the sash window up only to find...

"You have *got* to be kidding me!" I screamed, slamming my hand on the fine but impenetrable mesh covering my window. It was the same sort of

46

stuff that people used on fly-screen doors so that burglars couldn't break in. Apparently it worked just as well on teenagers breaking *out*.

Despair threatened to choke me, and I sunk to the plush carpeted floor in a defeated ball of emotions.

#

I must have dozed off on the floor, because when I woke again the sun was just starting to peek over the horizon and my neck was stiffer than my horny ex-boyfriend Nathan. Sleeping on the floor was partly to blame, but I wouldn't have been surprised if I didn't have a bit of whiplash from last night's crash.

The images of Butterfly's mangled frame, and of myself spinning out of control in a car—just like how my mom and dad had died so recently—flashed across my mind, and I shuddered. I'd been an idiot, thinking I could race so soon. And now I owed Dante the better part of two hundred grand.

Good thing money seemed to run in my blood—even if I'd never known it.

Stretching out the kinks in my spine, I decided to explore my prison. If I was going to be stuck in my room for two full days, I needed to find something to do.

Thankfully, there was an attached bathroom so I wasn't going to need to be escorted for toilet break—or worse, use a bedpan like it was the dark ages. On the flipside, though, there was no TV.

When I finally realized this, after searching *everywhere*, I needed a moment for that to sink in. Surely, given all the Deboise money and opulence, that was a deliberate choice. Probably another of Catherine's archaic views. It went nicely with her insane "ladies don't swear" mentality.

"Well shit," I muttered, turning to the stack of school books. "Looks like I'm learning shit after all."

The first book I picked up was on calculus. Gag.

I tossed it aside and reached for the next one—A complete guide to Ducis Academy.

"Ducis Academy," I read out loud, rubbing my thumb over the gold embossed crest on the cover and rolling my eyes at the money that must have gone into a simple about-the-school guide. "Let's learn about where I'm finishing out senior year."

I flipped the cover open and started reading. The first chapter was all about the school's founder—some stuffy old rich dude—but the basic summary when read between the lines was it was a privately owned academy with enough money and influence not to be restricted by the board of education.

The first clear sign of this fact was outlined in the next chapter. According to the guide, Ducis Academy was not a high school at all. It was an *academy*, and as such it only took students from their junior year of high school, but provided classes all the way up to sophomore year of college. The guide suggested it was incomparable to any other school in the country, as Ducis Academy was "one of a kind."

"Ugh, uniforms?" I groaned, flicking to the next chapter. "You've got to be kidding me!"

The school I'd attended back home wouldn't have known a uniform if it vomited all over us. It was the sort of school with metal detectors on the entries and armed security guards patrolling the grounds. Without a doubt, Ducis Academy was going to be a culture shock.

Throwing the brochure down, I decided I'd had enough of scaring myself and instead explored the impressive closet. It still took me by surprise, the sheer size and amount of clothing rich people owned. I could wear a new outfit every single day for the next ten years and I probably wouldn't have worn everything in here.

Moving past my favorite part—the shoes—I stopped on something I hadn't noticed last time. An entire section of school uniforms. There were dozens of them, neatly pressed and covered in those plastic protective sleeves that I'd seen dry cleaners use. The school colors were a dark blue, with red and gray piping across the pleated skirt, white blouse, with a fancy embroidered D on the pocket, and a jacket that matched the skirt. No doubt there were knee high socks and shiny black shoes somewhere here to complete every dude's porn fantasy.

With a shudder, I turned away, pausing at a thump which came from outside the *clothes room*. I was going to call it that from now, because this shit was not a closet. It was a fucking room.

"Miss," Stewart called, and I hurried out to find him hovering in the doorway. "I have your food."

I eyed the open door behind him, but Dante's warnings were still strong in my mind. If I ran, there was no way they wouldn't find me. I had to be smarter, which meant playing her little game.

And maybe playing an extra little game with Stewart, because I could certainly use an ally in this house.

He walked slowly, but somehow still urgently, across to the small table near the black couch. He placed the tray down and fussed over it for a few seconds, fixing things up and lifting up the protective coverings. I followed close behind, and when he straightened, I pasted the broadest smile I could across my face.

"Stewart, you're seriously the best," I gushed. "Thank you so much, I was literally starving to death."

He stared at me, and it was like he was waiting for me to slap him or something. The look on his face almost had me feeling bad for trying to manipulate him, but desperate times and all that.

"You're very welcome, Miss. If there is anything else … anything at all."

Reaching out I patted him gently on the shoulder. "You're doing a fantastic job. I appreciate you."

He froze, and for a second I thought I'd laid it on too thick, and he knew I was up to something, but then he straightened his shoulders and smiled. It looked so weird on his wrinkled face that I was almost certain he didn't smile like that often. If ever.

"I'll bring you dessert as soon as you're done," he promised before he hurried out of the room.

He wasn't so happy he forgot to lock the door, but that was okay, step one of my plan was already initiated.

I just had to have patience.

Chapter 6

By the time I'd scraped up the last morsel of food and licked my plate, I decided to be okay with remaining locked in my room if I continued to eat like that. There had been bacon on my plate. Real bacon, like from an actual pig. The last time I'd eaten bacon was when my dad took me out for dinner on my sixteenth birthday. My mom had been on a hardcore vegan kick since I was eight, but both Dad and I still loved our meat in secret. Anyway, back to the bacon. It had been wrapped around chicken breast, which was stuffed with garlic and butter, smothered in red wine jus and it was still hands down one of my favorite meals ever.

All of the delicious food swirled in my stomach as memories relentlessly assaulted me. My parents had so little in their lives, always struggling to make ends meet, trying to provide me with the basics just to survive, and then, before life could get any easier for us, they were stolen from me in a freak stupid accident that didn't even make any sense.

My dad was an amazing driver; he'd never lost control. Not once in my entire life, and we'd driven in way worse conditions than that night.

I miss you.

The truth of that had me scrambling up, and I just barely made it to the toilet before I hurled everything up. Tears poured down my cheeks as I sobbed against the white seat, not even caring that I had my face pressed to the very place an ass had sat.

I just wanted my parents back, I wanted my old life back, I wanted answers to why the fuck I was now a prisoner inside some rich psycho's house. I wished she'd just continued to be the sort of parent she had been for the first almost eighteen years of my life. Absent.

Now that I'd started to cry, I couldn't seem to stop, and I hugged my legs tight to my body as I rocked back and forth, trying to relieve the deep ache in my chest. Eventually though, my tears dried up, and I was able to get myself under a semblance of control again.

Since I was already in the bathroom, I took a long, hot bath, which was another luxury I'd never had in my life, and by the time I was dry, dressed in some stupidly comfortable silk pajamas, fatigue was pressing in on me again.

Might as well sleep the rest of the day away.

Crawling into the bed, I snuggled under the covers, closing my eyes and breathing in deeply. The scent of the sheets were so clean and light and fresh that my head went dizzy at the sheer opulence of this bed.

Just as I was drifting off, a weird noise jerked me awake. Blinking, I sat up, looking around as I tried to figure out what it was. It sounded again a moment later, and I let out a little gasp before reaching down to where I'd left my jeans, dragging the phone out of the pocket.

The phone! I'd completely forgotten I had it.

Sliding the bar across, I saw there were three messages waiting for me.

Dante: Girl, is everything okay? Do I need to bust a fucking bullet in her ass?

Dante: Riles, I'm not fucking around. Answer my message or I'm coming for you.

Then the last one, which had come through two seconds ago. *Dante: I'm on my way.*

I frantically typed out a reply, my fingers stumbling over the keys, so that half of the words were messed up. *Me: I'm fiene. Just lcked in room. Stupid bitchh.*

I held my breath, hoping he hadn't smashed his phone when I didn't reply. It wouldn't have been the first time. Not that Dante and I fought much, but when we did...

Air rushed out of me when the phone vibrated again. *Dante: Are you okay? Don't lie to me.*

Me: Yes. I'm good. I promise.

Dante: Are you going to school on Monday?

Me: I assume I will be. Debitch hasn't been here since I got back, so I'm running low on information.

There was some time before his next text arrived.

Dante: I will check in again later. I'm going to see what I can find out for you.

I glared at the phone, wishing I was with him right now. Being locked in this room was messing with my head—I'd always had so much freedom. It was the one thing I'd had in spades.

Me: Don't get into trouble. Love you.

Dante: Trouble? Me? Love you too, Riles.

I threw the phone onto the bedside table, confident that I'd hear it if Dante messaged me again. As I dropped my head down again, I remembered that I had to send my number to Eddy too, but I'd do that when I woke up. For now, I was sleeping some of this nightmare away.

##

The rest of the weekend passed in slow motion. By the time Monday morning rocked around I'd tried on half my wardrobe, texted Dante twenty times, and set up a time for Eddy to pick me up for school. I hadn't seen Debitch, and I almost wished she'd come back so we could get this confrontation out of the way. I would not remain a prisoner like this long term. There was no way in hell. So we needed some sort of compromise.

Stewart, who, with a little encouragement, was turning out to be so helpful—he'd even found me a phone charger—knocked on my door. "Riley, the Mistress wants me to inform you that you'll be going to school this morning. Everything is set up for your enrollment, you just have to go via the office to get your things."

I flung the door open and grinned at him. "Stew, seriously, that's the best news I've heard all weekend."

I tried to peer around him to see if Catherine's coldly beautiful face was close by—she was supposed to be back today—but the hall was empty.

"Am I no longer a prisoner?" I asked, watching him closely.

He smiled. "She is granting you the freedom to go to and from school, for now, and when she returns you will discuss the rest of the rules."

I was both ready and dreading her return.

"I'll get dressed," I said, turning away.

He cleared his throat, and I looked back. "Please wear the uniform correctly," he said. "I will send one of the day maids up, she will lay it out on the bed."

I shrugged, having met a few of the day maids already. They never spoke, kept their eyes locked on the ground, and hurried around cleaning.

"I'll be in the shower then." Turning the other way, I crossed to my bathroom, as the main bedroom door closed behind me. There was no distinctive click of the lock this time, and I tried to contain the happiness bubbling in my chest.

Freedom had never tasted so sweet, even if I did have to attend a preppy rich school to experience it.

My shower was short because I was more than a little anxious to get out of this room. I slapped on some makeup, taking a little extra care with my eyeliner—I was not rocking up to some rich-kid-school looking like a raccoon. It took me a tad longer to blend makeup around the healing cut on my cheek as well, and nothing could hide it completely, but it was at least harder to see.

I exited the bathroom, clad in matching black underwear, and stopped short when I saw the outfit on the bed. Or more accurately, the shoes perfectly positioned on the floor below.

"No fucking way," I choked. Were they actually serious right now?

Striding across to the door, I swung it open and called out: "Heels? You want me to wear heels all day?"

I slammed the door then and grumbled the entire way back to my bed. I loved heels as much as the next girl, but I was usually drunk when I wore them, and as Dante said, I usually ended up on my ass at least once during that period of time. My feet already ached just looking at shiny black school shoes.

Knowing I had no choice, I quickly shimmied into the skirt and blouse, not at all surprised they were my exact size. Everything in my *clothes room* had been my exact size, because Debitch was a weirdo stalker.

The skirt was pretty short, falling to mid-thigh, and I tucked the blouse in. Sitting on the bed, I pulled on the knee-high socks and then gingerly slipped my feet into the shoes. They fit so well. Like, my toes weren't pinched and nothing rubbed even though they were new.

I wondered if they'd feel this good eight hours from now.

The last piece of the uniform was the jacket, and I slipped into the custom made number, surprised that it slid easily over my cast. Before I could stop myself, I turned to check myself out in a nearby mirror. The floor to ceiling piece, with a wide gilded frame around it, reflected back a stranger.

I'd left my unruly waves out, because it was easier than trying to manhandle it into a bun. My skin looked pale against all the dark colors in the uniform. The shoes made my legs look long, and considering I was just a bit above average height at 5'9, that was a nice change. But everything else about this made me uncomfortable.

Picking up my phone, I snapped a pic and sent it straight to Dante with the caption "I look ridiculous, shoot me now."

His reply was almost instant.

Dante: Riles…

I wasn't sure what to make of that, so I didn't reply, just threw my phone into the pocket of my blazer, and took a few wobbly steps across the room. Stewart had told me that the books on my desk were my home books, for study outside of school—yeah, okay—and that when I got my welcome pack at the school, it would have my school copies.

So I didn't have to break a nail carrying my books home with me.

My phone buzzed again, and I pulled it out of my pocket.

Dante: *You're going to get me killed. That skirt…*

Me: *I'm wearing fucking heels. Forget about the skirt, it's not going to get anyone killed. The heels though…*

Dante: *Riles, watch this school. I've been warned about those guys from the race. They're bad news. Really bad news. You need to keep me updated. I'll be around.*

Me: *If I can deal with Debitch, I can deal with some punk ass wannabe rich gangstas.*

It took him another minute to reply, and I knew he would be running his hands over his shaved head right now, face screwed up in annoyance.

Dante: *Have you actually dealt with her yet?*

Bastard. No need to poke holes in my brilliant plan so quickly.

Dante: *Don't argue with me. Keep your head down, don't go searching for trouble. I got your back.*

Since I trusted him with my life, I had no doubts of those words. Still, I was getting pretty sick of being dictated to so much. Ever since I was thrust into this world, I felt like everything about me was out of control.

I was losing myself.

None of my friends back home would even recognize me now, not that I had many outside of Dante. But I had plenty of acquaintances, if that counted, and not one of those would know who the hell I was if I rocked up like this.

I wobbled out of the room again, but thankfully got a handle on the heels pretty quickly. Lucky for me they weren't six inches … more like four. I briefly considered switching the shoes out for converse, but a dark part of me enjoyed the *Clueless* look I was rocking. No harm in looking good for my new school, right?

There was no sign of anyone as I stumbled down the stairs and crossed to the door. Eddy had texted me a minute ago and said she was on her way, which meant I'd have to figure out how to get to the gates.

"Miss Riley?"

I turned to find Stewart in the doorway that I was pretty sure led into a massive kitchen. I wouldn't know because I was not allowed such privileges as walking outside of my room. In his hand he had two things, one was an expensive looking leather satchel, and the other some keys.

"This is for you to take the golf cart to meet your friend," he said, jingling the set. "Mistress approves of your friendship with Eddy, so she has no issue with this arrangement."

I blinked at Stewart a couple of times. "How does *Mistress* know about Eddy?" I demanded, cringing at the fact that we sounded like house elves waiting to be gifted socks.

Stewart just gave me a *don't-be-so-dense* look.

Eddy was lucky she was so awesome, because knowing Debitch approved of her, almost had me regretting our new found friendship.

"And the bag?"

He held it out to me, and with a sigh I stepped forward and relieved him of both items. "The bag has your identification, some cash for essentials, and a few other things that…" he cleared his throat. "Young ladies require."

I snorted. "Catherine bought me tampons? Well, look at that, she's almost a mother now."

Stewart looked even more uncomfortable, if that was possible, and I couldn't help reaching out and patting him on the arm again. "Thanks for putting up with me. I'll see you this afternoon."

"Straight home from school," he warned as I rushed out the door.

I waved over my shoulder, too focused on my freedom to pay much heed to his words.

There was a cart already prepped and waiting for me, so I threw the bag to one side and slung myself into the driver's seat. I'd never driven one of these, of course, golf was a rich person sport, but I figured it out quickly enough.

My heart started to beat faster as I took off, leaving the house behind me. By the time I reached the main gate, I was actually smiling. Parking the cart near it, I got out and grabbed my satchel.

A horn beeped, and I swung to find Eddy smoothly pulling up to the gates. My jaw dropped at the view I caught of her through the window. She looked so ... proper. Her hair was slicked back in a demure bun. There was no cleavage or funky adornment to her uniform. I barely recognized her.

Until she opened her mouth...

"Come on, bitch, we're gonna be late!"

My smile grew, and I rushed through the opening gates.

When I dropped into the seat, she eyed my outfit. "We're legit gonna have to do something about that skirt. I can't even see your ass."

Her voice went falsely high, as she rolled her eyes at me. "I mean, how will you show the boys you're available to them, if they can't see your vag?"

I snorted. "I'm not available to them, so I'm giving the exact right impression."

JAYMIN EVE + TATE JAMES

She winked at me. "That's the way to approach it. Trust me. You're new, and they're going to be all over you. Fresh meat."

She took off in a squeal of tires, and I let out a breathy sigh. This was my shit. Speed. The thrum of a powerful engine. Of course, my thoughts went immediately to my car, my butterfly, and when Eddy pulled out of the second gates and onto the main road, I wondered if we would cross near the crash site.

"Uh, so … what did those assholes do with my baby?"

Eddy shot me a sympathetic look. "Your car? I'm not totally sure, but I think Beck had it towed to a junkyard."

"Beck…? As in Sebastian?"

She nodded. "Yeah, they call him Beck. Everyone does."

Of course they did. Beck suited the bastard. I was gonna try my best to call him Sebastian from now on. I had no idea why I was even planning out his name in my head, because I was not talking to him at all, so I could just skip the name thing.

"What's his middle name?"

What the fuck is wrong with me?

I couldn't seem to help myself. Eddy shot me the sort of knowing look friends had been giving each other since the dawn of BFFS. "Don't waste your time, girl. Sebastian Roman Beckett is off limits to all of us mere mortals. You don't want to mess with any of that crew. They're the elite of our world."

Elite. That explained so much. "You're their sister, though?"

She laughed, and it wasn't a happy sound. "Trust me, the old school bastards who run our companies, don't like 'silly women' to mess with their money. Mostly we're afterthoughts that they can't quite get rid of."

We'd entered the small town, and I was surprised to see how nice everything looked. This wasn't like a lot of villages I'd seen over the years. Everything was shiny and new, no run down slummy areas, at least not in the parts we traveled.

"School is just over there," Eddy said, still driving fast through the nearly empty streets. "I'll drop you near the office, because you can't walk in heels for shit."

I groaned, dropping my head back against the smooth leather of the seat. "I should have brought flats with me. Boots at least."

"Unless you have a medical reason, you're wearing heels. Refer back to my comment about your 'availability to the dudes.'"

I waved my cast at her. "I'm broken."

"Next time aim for your leg and you might have a shot."

The worst part was she didn't even sound like she was kidding.

I shut up then because the school was suddenly in view, and I was suddenly freaking the fuck out. "I am not designed for this," I whispered, dread coiling in my chest.

It looked like those Ivy League colleges, the ones for the best of the best. Red brick buildings, immaculately designed with greenery trailing up and down intermittently, giving it an almost whimsical vibe. Buildings sprawled out as far as I could see, and I was wondering why the hell it was so huge. This town couldn't sustain a school this size.

I must have muttered something like that, because Eddy replied, "They have a waitlist of over five thousand," she said, slowing to enter the parking lot.

"What?"

"Yep." She nodded, only half focusing on me. There were a lot of kids getting out of cars, and I guessed she was trying not to kill anyone. "People from all over the world want to send their kids here. We have a boarding facility in town for those who don't live locally."

She said *we*, like the school was owned by her... or her family.

For all I knew, it was.

Eddy continued to weave in and out of the massive lot, which was legitimately filled with the sort of cars I could only dream of owning. And of course, my absolute top dream car was there, with four rich fuckers standing beside it.

"Holding court, as always," Eddy murmured lightly, but with undertones I wasn't even going to try and unravel.

"You hit any of them?" I asked, and she actually shuddered.

"God no! Discounting the fact that I grew up with all of them, they never bring chicks into their inner circle, and I wouldn't want to fall for someone when I'd always just be a screw in the back room."

No chicks? "Are they gay?"

I was trying to get their story, but it was as confusing as everything else in this town.

Eddy laughed loudly. "Holy shit. Not even remotely; they go through women like you wouldn't believe. But it's always just fucking them, you know?"

Yeah, I knew the type very well.

Eddy flipped her brother off as they passed, and I really wished she hadn't done that, because suddenly four sets of eyes were on me. Swallowing hard, I tried not to drool at how good they looked. Every tailored line of their suits were molded to their muscular frames, and somehow they looked less like students at school, and more like rich playboys, heading to work in some big business venture.

Lifting my eyes, I flinched at the darkly captivating gaze that caught me. Beck's eyes were locked on me, the icy stare sending shivers down my spine. I turned away from him with a jerk, because he was making it hard to breathe. Jasper, who was at his side, caught my stare instead. He gave me a smirk and small salute, like we were old friends now. Only I didn't trust anything about the look on his face.

There were two others there I didn't recognize, but they had to be Evan and Dylan.

"You already know Jasper," Eddy said, slowing even more. She shot me a sly grin. "Jasper Eugene Langham, since you seem to love middle names." I tried not to blush, because I couldn't quite make myself care as much about Jasper's middle name.

"Eugene," I said with a laugh.

She laughed too. "He hates it, and it's totally not worth the stress to use it. Trust me."

Advice I probably wouldn't be taking.

"The one with the facial hair is Evan," Eddy continued as she stopped near the front steps of the impressive building. "Evan Lincoln Rothwell. His family owns half of Europe, and they fund most of the big businesses in the world."

Evan was a little shorter than the other three, but still well over six foot. His hair was blond and brown, streaked together and styled messily. He looked like he hadn't shaved in a few days, rather than was trying to grow a beard, and he wore the look well. He was almost as broad as Sebastian, his thick muscles near exploding out of his white button down. Just like his friends, he was watching us closely, and I wanted to scramble out of Eddy's car to escape, but that would require me to walk in heels in front of all of them.

"The last one is Dylan. Dylan no-middle-name-because-his-parents-are-assholes Grant." Eddy said that really quickly before her voice softened. "His family is also involved in finance and banking." She shot me a wry smile. "And if I was ever going to love one of those fucking assholes, it would be him. He's not a bad guy, actually, and he has a soft spot for women. Which is a nice change."

Dylan was tall, like uber tall and beside Sebastian, he was the one which made me feel the least at ease. There was nothing in his dark stare that told me he was a lover of women, except if they were naked in his bed—all dudes loved that. His hair was as dark as Sebastian's, and his skin was darker than the other three, speaking of a mixed race background. I didn't touch on the asshole parent thing, just gonna assume he had a pair of Catherines raising him too.

"I appreciate the heads up on them," I said softly, like they could hear our conversation in the car. "I'm going to go out of my way to avoid all four."

Eddy patted my arm. "You and me both. And we'll be the only chicks in the school to do so."

As if to reiterate her point, I noticed that on both sides of them, there were groups of girls, all of them inching as close as they could in the hopes of being noticed. I narrowed my eyes on one in particular, who was doing her best to catch someone's attention. Her skirt was definitely signaling the available thing.

When she turned, I recognized that swing of flawless hair, realizing it was the one Beck had in his car that night.

"That's Brittley." Eddy sneered. "She's their pass around girl when they have nothing better to do. She's been trying to claim one of the guys for years, but they just use her like the whore she is."

Brittley. I added her to the list of people to avoid in this school. Pretty soon I was going to have to hide every second I wasn't in class.

A bell rung in the distance, and Eddy straightened. "You better head into the office," she said, her hands on the wheel again. "Text me your schedule when you get it, and if we don't have any classes together, I'll meet you at lunch."

Lunch. Shit. Would be hard to hide in a room filled with students, but at least it looked like I wouldn't be alone.

"I'll text you soon," I promised, and then taking a deep breath, opened the door and swung myself out. I made sure I was steady on the heels before I stood, bringing my bag with me. "It's the first door on the left when you step inside," Eddy said loudly as I closed the door.

I waved and then turned to face my new school. Nothing like starting second term of your senior year at a new school. I mean, what could be easier?

As I walked forward, I tried my best to ignore the stares I was getting. Eddy hadn't been kidding about the new girl thing, and if it wasn't for the fact that I'd already suffered through the worst tragedy of my life, I'd have been feeling very intimidated.

It was all about perspective. I really couldn't give a fuck what a bunch of rich kids thought of me. What did I have to lose now?

The inside of the building was as fancy as the outside, with marble floors, and the sort of decadent downlights one usually didn't see in a school. No metal detectors in sight; it was clear no one was worried that a disgruntled student was going to shoot up the place.

Following Eddy's instructions, I poked my head into the first door on the left—and almost turned around and left. It was nothing like any office I'd ever seen. But there were no other doors nearby, so this had to be the place.

I ventured in, heading toward the glass topped desk. Behind it was an immaculately dressed woman. She was typing away on a fancy computer, only glancing up when I stopped before her.

"Yes," she said, not warmly.

"I'm new here," I started slowly. "I'm supposed to get … my stuff."

She barely even looked at me. "Name?"

"Riley Jameson."

She hit a few keys on her computer, and then glanced at me before hitting a few more keys. "I don't have you in the system."

This time there was outright hostility and judging by that look, I wondered if she was planning on yanking the uniform right off me. I let out a sigh. "Try Deboise."

Debitch.

That caught her attention, and wariness washed over her features. She was suddenly very interested in her computer again. A moment later: "Yes, we do have a Riley Deboise in our system." Well, at least she hadn't changed my first name yet.

Office lady smoothly stood, and she clearly had no problem walking in her heels, hips swinging as she strolled over to a massive filing cabinet and drawer system behind her.

When she came back, she was carrying a black leather case and eight USB sticks. "Your class guides are on the drives," she said, holding them out to me. "Each is labeled. And your computer is in the case."

She dumped the leather bag into my hands, and I was surprised by how light it was. "What about textbooks?"

She shook her head. "Seniors are mostly online. The books you have will work for reference at home, but here, everything is guided electronically."

She held her hand out then, long red nails glinting in the lights. "Give me your phone?"

I stared at her hand before lifting to see her face. Hell no, lady. I wasn't giving my phone to anyone; it was my lifeline when I was at the Deboise Estate.

"I need to upload your schedule to the calendar," she said with a huff, like she was embarrassed by how backward I was.

Bitch. I thought as I reluctantly handed it to her.

She ignored me, pressing a few keys on her computer and then keying something into my phone, and with a series of beeps, I once again had my phone in my possession. "Your classes were selected by Catherine Deboise," she told me, her voice quivering on the name. "You are not allowed to change anything."

Of course I wasn't.

She dismissed me then, turning back to her screen, and I fought against the urge to plant my ass right on her desk, just to bother her a little longer. Instead, I turned, juggling the computer as I tried to shove the USB's into my satchel.

Exiting the door, I wasn't watching where I was going, and before I could think about the stupidity of that, it was too late. Two steps into the hall, my face slammed into what felt like a brick wall, and I went flying, landing hard on my ass. Thankfully I managed to keep a hold of the new laptop, but I lost my dignity completely.

Awkwardly, using my broken hand, I pushed my hair back from my face and almost groaned. Beck, flanked by the other three, stared down at me.

His expression was similar to the night he'd stared down at me after the race. Eyes that cut right through me, rigid jaw, flawless fucking beauty that hid the asshole inside.

"The last two times I've seen you, Butterfly, you were on your ass." Beck's grin was not nice.

"And while it's a fine ass," Jasper cut in. "It'd be better if you were on your knees, at least then there'd be a point to your existence."

Evan let out a low husky laugh, but Beck and Dylan remained impassive. Narrowing my eyes, I flipped Jasper off, adding a "go fuck yourself" to it. Close up, Dylan was even more intimidating than he had been across the parking lot, but Sebastian still took the scary cake. If, you know, scary cake was a thing.

He crouched down until he was on my level—seeing as I was still sprawled on the floor—and flicked that penetrating gaze over me. Slowly. Holy hell, his eyes were a gray so light they were almost silver. Intense. Scary.

Fucking hell, why are the hot ones always psychopaths?

I bit down on the inside of my cheek to squash the burn of arousal his gaze dragged from me, and glared back. One thing I had going for me, I gave a mean glare.

"You think a Ducis uniform makes you one of us, Butterfly?" he asked me in a low, quiet voice. Somehow I sensed this question was a hell of a lot more loaded than it seemed on the surface, so I tightened my jaw and said nothing in response. "You're less than nothing. You're just the child that Catherine Deboise threw away. A girl. Utterly useless in our world except for spreading her legs or sucking cock." He reached out and traced a finger over my bruised cheek, pressing hard enough that I winced. "Maybe you can't even do that right. Your gangbanger boyfriend do this to you?"

There was a menacing darkness to his voice that made me shiver with fear. Or, I was pretty sure that was fear. Yeah, let's go with fear.

Jerking my face out of his reach, I glared harder. It was all I had in my arsenal today. "Dante would never hit a woman. I suspect he has more honor and decency in his left shoe than the four of you combined." I cast my disgusted glare over the other three standing over me in what was clearly intended to be a threatening way. Of course it was. Why else would they be doing this? "Just leave me the fuck alone, *Sebastian*," I continued, snapping the words at Beck. "I don't want to be here any more than you want me here. It's only two months until my birthday and then I'm done."

Evan made a noise and when I glanced up, I caught a look passing between him and Jasper. Before I could demand to know what they were getting cagey about, Beck leaned in closer to me. His shiny leather shoes creaked and his mouth watering smell filled my nose. It was a mix of expensive aftershave and something that was all Beck. Dark and alluring.

"If only it was that simple, Butterfly," he whispered with an edge of foreboding. Giving me a long, unreadable look, he stood back up and stuffed his hands in his pockets. "Catherine Deboise is up to something, and you're her pawn. We intend to see you wiped from the board before she can make her move."

I spluttered a noise of shock and outrage. "Oh yeah?" I scoffed. "What does that make you, the king?"

This time—for the first time—his smile held real humor. But it was gone again as fast as it came, and it was Jasper who responded.

"You'd better believe it, trailer trash. Don't mess with the king." He snickered at his own oh-so-witty analogy, and I rolled my eyes.

"Clearly expensive schools don't teach chess," I remarked. "Otherwise you'd be well aware the queen is the most dangerous piece on the board."

The four of them just stared down at me before Beck shook his head. "Nice panties, Butterfly."

He smirked, then walked away as my cheeks flamed and I pinned my skirt down. Despite what Eddy had said, it was still too short to sit on my ass without flashing my black lace underwear to the world. Evan and Jasper followed him—like the brainless pawn they'd just accused me of being—but Dylan stayed where he was.

"What?" I snapped at him, as a frightened tremble set into my limbs. I was still on my backside, so he was absolutely *towering* over me.

The scary ass dude stared down at me for a really long, really awkward moment before he stuck out his hand. When I made no move to take it, he sighed. "It's not poisoned, Riley. I just wanted to help you up. You're like a baby giraffe in those shoes."

Uncertain, but not wanting to look scared—or any *more* scared than I already was—I took his hand with my un-plastered one and let him pull me back to my feet.

"Thanks," I muttered, and he just shrugged and started walking away in the direction his friends had gone.

"Hey!" I called after him, seizing the opportunity to try and salvage my safety. "I'm serious. I'm not here because I want to be. Just leave me alone and I'll be gone before you know it."

Dylan paused, turning slightly to give me a sad, pitying look. "You'll learn. It's not about what you want any more."

With that cryptic statement, he turned the corner, and I leaned heavily on the wall as all the strength drained out of me. Was this what the rest of my school year would be like? Threats and sexual innuendos? So much for the feminist movement. Clearly, old world money was exempt from things like common decency and equality.

"Hey," a guy called out from down the hall, and I startled. "Shouldn't you be in class, new girl?"

I frowned as he came closer, trying to work out where I'd seen him before but not having any luck. He was cute, in a preppy sort of way. Chocolate brown hair and a light tan, offset by mossy green eyes. The kind of guy I probably would have flirted with if Beck hadn't just stripped me of all my brain cells.

"Uh, yeah. I guess." Hunting through my bag, I found my phone and pulled it out. Flipping through my schedule, I located the class I was supposed to be in and groaned. "Economics." Fucking Catherine Debitch. A quick scan of my other classes showed more of the same. Calculus, finance, debate... The only subject I was excited about on this schedule was English Lit. It made me sad that I wouldn't have art history or photography, my favorite subjects at my old school, but office chick had made it clear that there was not a single chance of me changing this schedule.

The guy let out a low whistle, reading my schedule over my shoulder. "Guess you must be a smart one, then. Most chicks here just take the easy grades in event planning or sewing or some shit." He laughed as he said it, and I honestly couldn't work out if he was telling the truth or talking shit. "Come on, I'll show you the way to your class."

Giving him a suspicious side-eye, I shifted my bag higher onto my shoulder and followed as he strode down the marble tiled hall. He didn't speak again as I hurried along behind him, not until we stopped outside a classroom which overlooked the school parking lot.

"Hey, I should probably thank you," he said suddenly, blocking the door as I reached for the handle.

"Huh?" I tilted my head, confused. "For what?"

Just as he was about to answer, the door was yanked open from the other side and a middle aged man with a neatly trimmed beard glared at us.

"Miss Deboise?" he enquired, despite clearly already knowing who I was. "Class started almost twenty minutes ago. Next time you're late, it'll be detention."

My jaw dropped. "But it's my first day!"

"And not off to a great start, are you?" he replied with a sneer, then stepped back to indicate for me to enter the class.

"See you around, new girl," the cute guy who'd walked me there whispered as I entered the class and the door slammed closed behind me. Suddenly, every damn student in there was staring straight at me, and I awkwardly dodged eye contact with anyone until I found an empty seat near the windows. That nameless guy had been right, there were hardly any girls in the class.

Sighing to myself, I propped my face on my hand and stared out the window as the teacher continued whatever he'd been saying before I arrived. The guy from the hall was crossing the parking lot and tossed a grin in my direction—like he knew I was watching—before opening the door to a cherry red Porsche 911 and sliding behind the wheel.

Mother. Fucker.

I sucked in a sharp breath and sat up straighter. Suddenly it became clear what he was thanking me for: an easy win and eight hundred thousand dollars.

Chapter 7

The rest of my morning went pretty smoothly—as far as any first day at a new school could. I'd managed to find my way to the rest of my classes on time, and hadn't yet slipped over in my stupid heels despite the dangerous patches of ice on the outside paths between classes.

All in all, I was feeling not too bad by the time lunch rolled around. Except now, I needed to navigate whatever Ducis Academy passed off as a cafeteria and find Eddy, or I'd be eating alone.

I followed the stream of students—uniformed and not, because apparently only high schoolers wore the uniform—in the direction of the lunch room while nerves mounted in my stomach.

"Fuck it," I muttered under my breath as the entrance to the dining room came into view. "Worst case I can just eat outside."

The idea of sitting in the freezing cold to eat was unappealing to say the least, but it was better than doing something stupid like accidently sitting at Beck's table or tripping and landing face first into a bowl of soup.

Just the idea of all the ways I could humiliate myself made me groan, and I considered whether I *actually* needed to eat at all.

"Hey," Eddy called out, waving at me from just inside the dining hall, "Riley! Over here!"

Gritting my teeth, I entered the room and made my way over to the petite blonde. I still couldn't get past the transformation from the edgy, punk girl that I first met, compared to this prissy princess wearing a damn headband.

"Were you trying to stand me up?" she demanded, propping her hands on her hips in mock outrage. "I can't imagine why! This school is so welcoming." She couldn't even get through her own sarcastic statement without rolling her eyes, and I grinned.

"Come on, the food is at least good." She grabbed my unbroken hand and dragged me over to the buffet. The only way to describe the lunch at Ducis Academy: it was like the buffet at a five star luxury hotel. I was so focused on all the incredible edible options on my plate that I barely even noticed where Eddy was leading me—until I sat down.

"What's little orphan Annie doing at our table?" Brittley, sneered across the table at me. "She doesn't belong here and you know it, Eddy."

Eddy snorted a laugh even as my cheeks stained with embarrassment. "Actually, Britt, seeing as she's a Deboise she has more right than *you*. After all, didn't your granddaddy come into his money through a poker game?" Eddy clicked her tongue in a condescending way. "How very passé."

Brittley's jaw dropped open, and a small squeak of outrage exited her mouth before she scraped back her chair and stomped off in what could only be considered a temper tantrum.

"Seriously?" Jasper hissed across the table at us. "You know what she's like about her family's money."

Eddy just shrugged and ate a forkful of her pasta. "I know. That's why I said it."

Jasper let out a long suffering sigh, looking in the direction Brittley had stormed off, then turned his furious glare on both Eddy and me. "If she doesn't let me come on her tits this afternoon because she's too busy crying over what a raging bitch you are, I'm holding you responsible."

He stood smoothly before stalking off after Brittley. Eddy didn't seem fazed. She just hummed happily under her breath and ate another bite of pasta while awkward silence fell over the rest of the table. I took the opportunity to look around.

Jasper and Brittley were obviously gone now, but I was surprised to only see Evan further down the table with a pretty redhead in his lap. Dylan and Beck were nowhere to be seen. The other people at the table were all firmly avoiding eye contact with me, and Eddy seemed in no rush to introduce them.

So much for upper class manners.

"I thought your brother and his friends were in college?" I whispered, leaning forward. "Why do they have the same lunch period as us?"

Seriously, why!

Eddy wrinkled her perfect little nose. "God, I don't even know why they bother to pretend they're in college. They do what they want. Go to class when they want. And eat lunch when and where they want. There are no rules for them, Riley. Not a single one."

Her words almost sounded like a warning, and I chose not to reply because my insides were already squirming.

Conversation slowly started up again as we all ate our lunch, and Eddy started telling me all about some party that was being held on Friday night. I nodded absentmindedly as she begged me to go with her, because my attention was firmly glued to the dark and brooding asshole I'd just noticed standing right outside the dining room. He was speaking with someone on his phone, and whatever they were saying he was not liking it. His hand kept running through his hair then clenching into a fist by his side. His jaw was set in a tight scowl as he responded in what seemed to be one word answers. Tall and scary Dylan leaned on the wall opposite with his hands tucked in his pockets, looking like he had all the patience in the world. Suddenly, Beck looked over and locked eyes with me for a long, tense moment. I couldn't breathe, and I sure as shit couldn't look away. I was just... *frozen.*

"Girl, *no,*" Eddy groaned, snapping her fingers in front of my face and jolting me out of that weird trance I'd slipped into. "Did you hear nothing I said this morning? Beck would chew you up and spit you out in pieces. Trust me on this, girl. Steer well clear. I wish we didn't even have to eat lunch at this table but rules are rules." She rolled her eyes, and I shook my head, totally lost. There were rules over where we ate lunch?

"Don't worry," I muttered, embarrassed at having been so obvious in my staring. "It's just curiosity. Like looking at venomous snakes in the zoo, you know? Just because I'm curious doesn't mean I want to climb into their enclosure."

Eddy snickered at the analogy, then quickly sobered and stared up at someone behind me. "Hey, Dylan," she said. "Beck. What do you want?"

A chill ran down my spine and I turned slightly in my seat to find the two menacing creatures hovering far too close for comfort.

"Butterfly," Beck snapped. "A word."

His tone got my back up immediately, and I narrowed my eyes. "Was that a request or a statement, oh mighty king of the chess board?"

A shocked hush echoed down the lunch table, and I swallowed. I guessed when Eddy said to steer clear, she hadn't actually meant I should publicly mock them?

"A statement," Beck's voice got low, and that was when I really started to get scared. "Now."

As tempted as I was to dig my heels in and tell him to go to hell, I was actually curious. Was this something to do with whoever was on the phone? If so, what the shit did it have to do with me?

"You too." Beck snapped his fingers at Evan, who unceremoniously dumped the redhead into a vacant chair and came to join his friends. "Where's Jasper?"

Evan grinned, scratching at the attractive stubble on his chin. He wore the scruffy, just rolled out of bed look well. "Gone to comfort Britt after Eddy said some shit."

Beck's jaw tightened for a second, then he glared down at me. "Why are you still sitting, Butterfly? Move."

Blame it on morbid curiosity, because contrary to what I'd told Eddy, I wanted to see inside the snake enclosure. Casually, so I didn't look too eager, I pushed back my chair and slung my bag over my shoulder.

"Well?" I prompted, popping a hip and giving what I hoped was a seriously sassy glare. "What do you want, Sebastian?" Didn't matter that I referred to him as Beck in my head. As long as I pissed him off out loud.

Beck's gaze trailed over me for a moment, lingering on the bare expanse of skin between my skirt and the tops of my socks.

"After you, Butterfly," he replied, giving me a smug smile and indicating I should walk ahead of him out of the dining hall. It was a stupid power game, and not one I gave a shit to enter into with him so I just shrugged and strutted my stuff out to the hall.

I was still female, and I could feel more than one set of eyes on my ass as I moved, so I made sure to throw just a little extra swagger into my step. Just 'cause. Luck was on my side, because I didn't stumble once in the stupid heels.

"Well?" I repeated once we were in the empty hallway. "What is so important that you deigned to speak with a mere *useless female* like me?"

Beck glared at me, Evan looked intrigued, and Dylan... I couldn't tell if that was a smirk or a sneer.

"You're to attend a meeting on Friday after school," Beck announced, folding his thick, muscled arms across his chest. His shirt sleeves were rolled up to the elbows, and I needed to bite my cheek not to check him out.

"Huh?" I blurted when his words sunk into my brain. "What sort of meeting? Where? About what?"

Beck narrowed his eyes, but the corner of his mouth twitched in what *could* have been a smile. Hell could have also frozen over.

"Don't ask questions, spare," Evan commented in a bored voice. "If Beck says you're to attend, then you attend. Simple as that."

Outraged, I glared at the disinterested playboy. "What did you just call me?"

Evan rolled his eyes. "I called you spare. Because you're the Deboise's *spare* successor. You're Catherine's dirty little secret that she tried very hard to keep secret, but of course everyone knew she'd gotten herself knocked up a second time." He pressed closer to me. "Only, you're supposed to be dead … so how are you here, mere months after Oscar's death? Seems convenient."

I bristled at his thinly veiled accusations. Did these assholes seriously think I was some sort of gold-digger? A fake? That I had deliberately sought out the Deboise family and demanded my inheritance? I guessed that meant I was somehow responsible for my parent's deaths too?

Bile rose in my throat, and I pressed the back of my hand to my mouth.

After sucking in a few breaths and making sure I wasn't about to cry or vomit, I leveled a death stare at the three of them. Mostly Beck, because he was their *king*. "You can take your demands and your summons and shove them up your ass, Sebastian Roman Beckett. If anything else will fit in there alongside your fat head. I'm no one's pawn. Not Catherine's, and *certainly* not yours." I spun on my heel, intending to storm off down the hall but a huge hand clamped down on my plastered arm and yanked me off balance.

I stumbled two steps, then caught my balance against Beck's rock hard chest. That intoxicating scent of his invaded my senses and made my head spin, but he held me so close I couldn't look up at his face even if I tried.

"You'll be there, Butterfly, or Eddy will pay for your disobedience." His words were low and delivered right into my ear. How fucked up was I, that a shiver of arousal ran through me while he was literally threatening my new friend?

Gritting my teeth, I pulled back just enough to glare up at him. "Let. Go. Of. Me." I demanded, biting each word off in anger.

For a long moment, we remained locked within each other's hard stare, but it was Beck who broke first, releasing my cracked plaster wrist—made worse by his tight grip.

"Go and see the nurse, Butterfly. That cast looks like it was done at a free clinic."

"Bite me," I snapped back. Probably not the most creative insult I'd ever come up with but he set my nerves on edge like no one I'd ever met before. This time when I spun around and stalked away, he didn't stop me. He also didn't let me have the last word.

"Make smart choices, Butterfly. Eddy is awfully attached to that mustang."

My step faltered, but I didn't give him the satisfaction of arguing further. I just kept walking, and feeling those eyes burning into my backside.

Chapter 8

The next few days passed surprisingly uneventfully. I had gone to see the school nurse; not because Sebastian had told me to, but because the cracked plaster only got worse, and I knew I was only hindering my own recovery by refusing to fix it. As it turned out, she'd been able to give me a black sort of exoskeleton thing that secured with Velcro straps. It instantly eased the pain, and although I hated to admit it, it *looked* a shit load better than my old plaster cast.

On Wednesday Dante went back to Jersey to take care of some "business." He told me I appeared to be "handling my shit okay," and he promised he'd be back soon. He wasn't wrong either, I was dealing better than I expected. Eddy drove me to and from school every day, and I'd managed to avoid any *major* arguments or run ins with Beck and his crew. Best of all, I hadn't seen Debitch at all.

By the time Friday rocked around, I was actually in an okay mood.

Eddy had been bubbling with excitement all day about the party she was dragging me to and had made me promise to sneak out if I had to. Not that it should really be an issue when Catherine was nowhere to be seen.

My last class of the day was Economics... a subject that I had been shocked to find I actually enjoyed. I was catching up fast, a fact that was evident by my results in the Friday afternoon pop quiz, so I was in high spirits as class let out and I headed out to the parking lot to find Eddy.

When I reached her, my good mood dropped like a ton of bricks.

"What's wrong?" I exclaimed, noticing the mascara streaks down her face and her puffy red eyes. "Eddy, what happened?"

She sniffed hard, but wouldn't meet my eyes as she fumbled for her driver's side door and slid into the seat. "I'm sorry, Riles," she whispered as she revved her ignition and slammed her door shut. "I tried to tell you, they're in charge." Not pausing to explain any further, she reversed out of the parking lot and left me standing there in confusion. Until I saw who was parked in the next place over.

"Get in the car, Butterfly," Beck ordered, smug as fuck. Furious, I stared in the direction Eddy had gone, silently begging her to come back. But she wouldn't. Beck had delivered his threats directly to her—no doubt he knew I wasn't going to break so easily.

"I can always make things worse, if I need to break you," he commented, somehow sensing my inner thoughts. "In fact, I think I'd quite enjoy that. Just try me, Riley." His eyes were hard. Totally devoid of emotion.

I shuddered, but this time it was in fear. Every fiber of my being knew he was serious and I badly didn't want to know what he would do next. He already had my number. He'd figured out that I didn't give two shits what happened to *me* but my friends... I'd do anything for my friends, even if I had only known them a week.

"Last chance. Get in the car." His tone was so casual, so devoid of caring that it set my danger radar off in a big way. He *wanted* me to refuse. This was some sort of sick game to him!

Dropping my bag from my shoulder to my hand, I fished out the little bottle of hand sanitizer and packet of tissues that was tucked in the front zip. "Sure thing," I replied in a sickly sweet voice. "Let me just sanitize my seat real quickly. The last thing I need is to catch a disease from whatever tramps have been sitting there with no panties on."

Beck muttered something under his breath then snatched the sanitizer *and* my bag from my hands before holding the passenger door to his Bugatti open. "Get in the car," he repeated for the third time, and seeing as I'd run out of sassy comebacks, I did as I was told.

"Where are your boyfriends?" I asked when he slid into the driver's seat and pulled his door shut. This was the first time all week I'd seen him without Jasper, Evan and Dylan shadowing his every move. When he didn't reply, I decided to run with it.

"How does that all work anyway?"

This seemed to pique his interest and he arched a brow at me as he revved the engine of my beautiful unicorn car. "How does what work?"

My breath caught, and I needed to bite the inside of my cheek to stifle a moan. This *car*...

"Your four-way gay relationship," I pressed on with my snark and desperately prayed my face wasn't flushing.

A small smile twitched at his lips. "You're asking who is top and bottom, Butterfly? Does that sort of thing turn you on?"

The rumble of the engine seemed to purr through the seats, and I tightened my thighs as Beck smoothly pulled out into the street and gunned the accelerator. "Fuck me," I breathed out before biting my lip as the speed pressed me into my seat like a firm hand. Had Beck just heard that? Why, why, *why* had I gotten into this sexy, wet dream of a car? With *him*? I wasn't strong enough for this type of torture.

Licking my lips and twisting my plaid skirt in my fingers, I risked a quick glance at Beck and found an arrogant smirk on his face that equally made me want to throat punch him and rip his clothes off. It was in that moment that I first considered therapy.

"Where are we going?" I asked, desperately changing the subject from what turned me on. The last thing I needed to do was lose my tenuous hold over my tongue and blurt out that fast cars and asshole guys with god complexes were what made me wet.

Beck turned his attention from the road long enough to give me a pitying look. Long enough for the danger of his inattention at high speeds to spike my adrenaline and quicken my breathing. Thank the gods of school uniforms, my heavy woolen sweater was thick enough to hide how hard my nipples were in that moment.

"We have a company meeting to attend. I told you on Monday and you chose to ignore me, remember?" His tongue trailed across his lower lip in what *had* to be a deliberate move. The bastard was too damn aware of his own looks for that to have been accidental.

Using my nails, I pinched the side of my thigh to remind myself who I was messing with. This was Sebastian Roman Beckett. Self-confessed *king* of Ducis Academy. Gorgeous or not, I'd still rather punch him in the face than kiss him.

I think.

"I remember," I gritted out. "I meant, *where* is this meeting being held?"

His cocky smirk said he was totally aware of his effect on me, but he *thankfully* let it go as he navigated the winding roads back toward the compound where I was currently residing. There was no way in hell I'd ever call it home.

"My house," he announced with a sarcastic lilt. "Congratulations, Butterfly. You get to step inside the snake pit."

Anger and dread settled in my stomach, and I realized that Eddy must have repeated what I'd said earlier in the week. I was fast coming to learn that she really couldn't keep her mouth shut when it came to these guys. She really believed that they ruled her world.

For the first time, I was starting to think she might have been right.

#

The Beckett mansion was technically next door to the Deboise estate. If you considered the three acres of manicured gardens between each property "next door." I wasn't sure how I felt about Beck living so close, but there was no time to ponder on this as I was ushered through his front door. If one could call that fifteen-foot-high, six-foot-wide beast a door. On the inside, I was not at all surprised to see long expanses of white inlaid with gold marble floors. This place was cold like the Deboise mansion, filled with expensive artwork and minimalistic furniture. Rich people hated clutter, this was a truth I was coming to realize.

"Stay here," he ordered, leaving me in the front entrance.

I glared at his retreating back, but he didn't notice because he was already out of the room. Wandering closer to the large fireplace that was the centerpiece of the room, I briefly thought about just running out the door and hightailing it back to my place. Surely Beck couldn't forcibly remove me from my own house.

The moment I had that thought I actually laughed out loud. That bastard was capable of anything. He'd been king of this place for far too long, and I was pretty sure part of him actually thought he was royalty.

"Well, if it isn't the spare."

I spun to find Evan and Jasper in the doorway, their eyes skating across me. Evan, who had clearly decided "the spare" was my nickname, strolled forward before circling around me.

Crossing my arms, I refused to move and give him the satisfaction of knowing he made me uncomfortable.

"How about, fuck off," I suggested lightly. "I was kidnapped and forcibly dragged here. If you don't want me, I'm more than happy to stroll my ass out that door."

Jasper moved then, until he was right in my personal space. Which at least made Evan stop circling me like a vulture. "Are you nervous, pretty girl?" Jasper said softly, reaching out to touch my hair. I resisted the urge to jerk my head from his hold. His platinum hair glowed under the lighting, and his piercing blue eyes were locked intensely on me. I could see why he always had ten chicks hanging off him, why all of them did. Stupid chicks—these dudes were the sort that crushed everything around them, and I had to get out before I became the next casualty.

"You disgust me," I said plainly. "Nerves have nothing to do with it, I just hate being in your presence."

He grinned, and the hold he had on my hair tightened, pulling painfully against my scalp. "Is that righ—"

He was cut off by Beck. "They're ready for us."

Jasper released me immediately, turning to join his friend. Evan did the same, and I sucked in a deep breath before I swung myself around and marched over to where they waited for me. "You don't look like you're enjoying the game," Beck said, his expression unreadable.

My heart was beating so fast, and for once, I couldn't seem to bring my usual snark to the table. They were wearing me down, and Jasper had been right before, I was nervous.

"I don't even know what game we're playing," I said honestly. "I don't even want to play a game."

"There you go again, thinking you have a choice." Dylan strolled in, seeming more pissed off than normal. It took him from scary to fucking terrifying

Beck and Dylan were neck in neck for the scariest guys I'd ever met. Evan and Jasper weren't far behind. It all made sense how they'd managed to form the brotherhood they had. Sociopaths were clearly drawn to each other.

"Let's do this," Beck said, and I was surprised to see all four faces change. Smoothing out like they'd pulled a mask across their features. There was no way to tell what they were feeling now, no way at all. If I faced any of them in poker, it'd all be over.

But it hadn't been like that a moment ago, even if it had only been their semi-cruel mocking expressions. What was this meeting that it had them all on edge this way?

I must have hesitated too long, because Beck shot me a look. For a flash there was something burning in his eyes, and then it was gone just as quickly. "Move your ass," he said without inflection.

My body obeyed, even when my mind was terrified. Speed walking, I caught up to them, trailing just behind as they moved through the main entrance and down a long hall. We passed many closed doors, and I still couldn't figure out why anyone needed this many rooms. I was so busy paying attention to this, that I almost walked right into Evan when he stopped outside a closed door at the end of the hall. I tried to peer through the four, hoping for a glimpse of something when the door opened. Of course, this didn't work, because they were too fucking tall and well-built, blocking out any chance of seeing a thing. "Patience, spare," Evan said, shooting me a look over his shoulder. "You'll see it all soon enough."

"My name is Riley," I said through gritted teeth. "The next time you call me spare, I'm going to throat punch you."

I would do no such thing, he was a scary bastard, but I liked to make the threat anyway.

Evan's brown eyes went even darker as he reached out to caress my cheek. "We're going to enjoy breaking you, princess," he whispered. "All that pretty skin. Those bright blue eyes. When we're done with you, there won't be a piece of you untouched."

Swallowing hard, I tried to control my breathing. "You're a fucking psycho, you know that, right?"

He grinned before shoving my face away. "I'm well aware."

He turned then and followed the others into the room, and I stumbled after them on shaky legs. My gasp was audible when I realized that Catherine Deboise was in the room, seated behind a long desk. She wasn't alone either, there was a man on either side of her. All of them dressed in ten thousand dollar power suits. As I stepped closer, I noticed a phone on the desk which was lit up.

"The meeting of Militant Delta Finances is now in session," my birth mother said coldly. I startled at the name, because I'd heard it many times before. We'd even studied them in Economics earlier this week. They controlled a lot of the world. Banks, oil, mining, and so much more. You named it, there was probably a Delta label on it.

Were they actually telling me ... Deboise banking was part of Delta? *Holy fuck.* All of the guys were part of this company. Everything was starting to make sense to me now.

The door closed behind us then, and I had no idea who had timed it that way, but it was eerie, and I suddenly felt trapped.

"Delta successors, take your position," the man on her right said. He had dark, menacing eyes, which reminded me a lot of Dylan. His skin was a lot paler though. All of the oldies before us had that rich, white, old money thing going on, reiterating what Eddy had told me earlier, and it had me looking at Dylan with new eyes.

The guys moved, each of them standing in front of the table, Dylan right across from the man with the eyes like his, but he stood back a little. Like he wasn't fit to be in the same line as the rest of us. For a moment, I fought against the urge to reach out and pull him closer.

Evan snarled at the man across from him, who, upon closer inspection, had the same gold streaks in his dark hair and the same brown eyes.

Beck stood at Dylan's side, the chair in front of him empty. Jasper pulled me along and deposited me right before Catherine, and it was suddenly all making sense to me now.

Successors. This was exactly why Catherine had dragged me back into this world. It was as I'd somewhat guessed: she needed an heir. We were the heirs to these rich bastards—banking and finance billionaires who controlled the world.

"Why am I here?" I demanded, not wanting any part in this bullshit.

Catherine's cold eyes met mine. "You will not speak unless a direct question is asked of you. Remember how easily I can remove your privileges."

Memories of being trapped in my room came back full force, and I shut my mouth, even though it was more than a little difficult to do so.

"Langham and Beckett are here via phone from the New York offices," Evan's dad said. "We shall proceed."

The boys remained silent, their masks remaining firmly in place, and I understood then that the game playing had started long before my four tormentors. Their parents were the original psychos.

"We have a job for you five," Catherine said, leaning forward in her seat. "As you're all well aware, there is trouble from our *competitor.* They're still trying to muscle into our market share of oil and weapons, and we need to stop this now before it grows any larger. All this *new* money, and they don't understand the rules. It's time they understood."

Weapons? That sounded scarier than it probably should have. Then again, the last movie I watched with people smuggling weapons to the Middle East hadn't exactly worked out with a happy ending for the smugglers. I wouldn't even be surprised if this was the shit Delta was up to. After all, Catherine was one of them, and she was Satan's daughter. "Sebastian," a deep voice came through the phone in front of Catherine. "I expect you to deal with this. I don't care what you have to do, make it happen."

Beck's jaw tightened, just minutely. I doubted anyone else would have noticed, but I was watching him closely. Almost obsessively.

Because apparently I was fucked up that way.

"When do we leave?" Jasper asked.

Evan's father answered, his European accent deep and thick. "Private plane will depart at fourteen hundred hours tomorrow. Be on it."

The four nodded, I just blinked, my expression no doubt a combination of horror and what the fuck?

Remembering Catherine's threat, I raised my hand in the air. She let out a suffering sound before nodding at me. "What?"

"Uh, why am I here? I'm not part of your company, I don't have a fucking clue why you would bring me to this meeting." Okay, I sort of had a clue with the whole successor and stand before your parent thing, but I really didn't want to be here. "Is this a mistake?"

Please let it be a mistake.

Catherine stood then, her shoulders broad in the black suit jacket. The evil twist to her lips had my stomach clenching tightly. "Did you think I brought you back into my life for love?" She looked her nose down on me. "I told you I needed you. Delta is a five part company, formed by your great-great-grandparents. We have a lot of control in America ... we have a lot of control in the world. But you need an heir to remain on the board and vote. I'm not giving up my vote." She smiled with saccharine sweetness. "Blood is thicker than water, daughter."

My gaze flicked to Evan, and I could almost see him thinking *spare heir* in this head.

A thought occurred to me. "So how do you have a vote at all, Catherine? You're not blood. You don't have a dick. What gives?"

My bio-mother's face tightened into a deep scowl, but it was one of the other men—Evan's Dad, maybe—who answered me.

"*Catherine* doesn't have a vote. Deboise does. She is simply Richard's proxy while he grieves the loss of his only—er, oldest—child."

"You should have just taken the cut, Catherine," Beck said coldly, drawing everyone's attention from me. "You still receive your shares, you just don't get to make the final decisions any longer on Delta business. It was not a bad fate for Deboise."

Catherine flushed, anger marking red splotches across her cheeks. "You might be the oldest successor, Sebastian, but don't forget your elders. We still have power, and I can make your life hell."

He smirked. "You don't stand a fucking chance against me. If you push, you might find your second heir is no longer a viable option."

I spluttered before blinking at him. Had he just threatened to kill me to get rid of Catherine from their group?

The threat hit its mark though, and she shrank down into her chair. Beck turned then, and his friends fell in at his side. The four of them moving almost as one entity, so used to each other, they were that in sync. "Be on that plane," one of the men called after us. "All further instructions will be onboard."

No one said anything or acknowledged those words, and I was just wondering what the fuck I was supposed to do, when Beck swung toward me, his strong hands wrapping around my biceps as he all but picked me up and hauled me out of the room. My skin tingled and burned where he was touching me, and I sucked in as much air as I could, because his close presence was … intense.

The door closed behind us, leaving the five of us standing in the hall.

"Those bastards," Evan said, his voice low. "Always making us do their fucking dirty work. How many this time, Beck?"

He shrugged, his face awash in secrets. "Family business, we have no choice."

"There's always a choice," I said softly, and suddenly four sets of eyes were on me, as they moved to surround me.

"You have no idea what you're talking about, Riley," Dylan said, speaking for the first time since he entered the room. I wondered if that was a *thing*, just like him standing back. Was he allowed to speak to them? "You've only just stepped foot into our world, and already it's trying to break you. Imagine living this life since birth."

"What happened to Oscar?" I whispered, because true fear was driving me now. It didn't sit right with me, my brother's death, and even though I had more information coming at me, it wasn't enough. So much still didn't make sense, and unless I unraveled the secrets soon, I had this sick sense that I might meet the same fate.

In one swift move, Beck wrapped his hand around the base of my throat, pushing me back against the wall. His hold was tight enough that I could feel it, but not so tight that my breath was cut off. His hard lines were pressed everywhere, and I had to clench my thighs together because a hot, desperate need was clawing at my center. "Don't fucking mention Oscar to us again," he growled, lowing his head so close toward my face, that I could almost taste him on my lips. "Our brother was a casualty of this war, and if you don't watch yourself, you'll be next."

His fingers twitched, and despite my deepening desire for this sick bastard, I still had to say something. "Stop threatening me," I whispered, our gazes locked together so I could see the storminess in his gray depths. "I've already lost everything, death is not my worst fear."

Those last words were choked as I thought of my parents, of the simple but perfect life I'd lost. Beck stilled, and I could tell I'd confused him. It felt like a minute fraction of hostility bled out of him, and his eyes dropped to my lips then, and I sucked in a shocked breath.

He was going to kiss me?

I wasn't sure if I would combust or freak out, but I never got to find out, because he pulled back and said softly. "I knew the first time I caught sight of you, Butterfly, that you were going to be trouble." He released me from his hold. Before turning and striding along the hall, a grinning Evan and Jasper trailing after him.

I remained slumped against the wall, my heart frantically pounding against my chest. Dylan was doing his scary silent thing nearby, but he never left me there, not moving until I pulled myself together and followed the others along the hall.

"I'll give you a lift home," he said, when we neared the empty front entrance.

Shaking my head, I shot him a wan smile. "No, it's okay, I could use the walk."

My head was racing. My heart pounding. If I didn't get behind the wheel of a car soon, I would probably lose my mind. I needed some speed.

Before I made it outside, I swung back toward him. "Actually, what car do you have? Can I drive it?"

Beck's dark mocking laughter reached me before he did. Then he stepped inside, having been out on the front step. "The last car you drove you totaled. Why the fuck would we lend you a car?"

Trying to forget how good his body felt pressed into mine in the hall, I narrowed my eyes on him. "I didn't ask you, I asked Dylan. And ... those were extenuating circumstances. I don't normally drive that badly."

"I'll take her," Beck said, his eyes on me even though he was talking to his friend.

Dylan just let out a low amused sound, which for him was almost as much as a full on belly laugh. "Whatever you say, Beck. You two try not to kill each other."

He then strolled out the door and a moment later a powerful engine thrummed to life before taking off.

"Are you letting me drive the Bugatti?" I asked. The thought of that was turning me on almost as much as his little move earlier.

He laughed darkly. "Not a fucking chance, Butterfly. Now get your ass in the car."

I grumbled at him but didn't argue. Suddenly I was exhausted and the mile and a half back to my house felt like three hundred. When I was in, Beck didn't wait, spinning us out of his driveway, and taking off down the long straight path of the entrance to his estate. The Bugatti engine really opened up as he pushed her harder, and some of that tension in my chest relaxed.

He side-eyed me. "You need the speed."

I didn't want to give him any more ammunition to use against me, and it felt like anything about my personality was a weapon he'd use, but it was no doubt clearly written on my face.

"I need it," I confirmed before closing my eyes so I could feel the thrum of the powerful turbocharged engine. The silence between us should have been awkward, especially since he continued to threaten to break me, but it almost felt ... comfortable. Like in this moment, we got each other, in a way that no one else would. We got the fucked up darkness riding us both.

That moment was over though, when his car slid to a stop and he reached over and flung my door open. "Get out of my car," he said shortly, and I wondered what had put that new tension in his jaw, causing his knuckles to whiten as he gripped the wheel.

Not wanting to argue with him when he was in this sort of mood, I scrambled out and hurried to the cart I'd left at the front entrance. It was only as I neared the Deboise house, that I suddenly remembered everything that had happened during the "meeting." How in the hell could I have forgotten that I was supposed to be on a plane tomorrow at fourteen hundred hours. *What time was that anyway?*

Assuming this was not going to be a fun vacation, I still really needed to know how long we were going for. And ... did I need to pack clothes? Most importantly, would anyone miss me when I was brutally murdered by the four sadistic assholes that I was stuck with?

Dante! I really needed to tell Dante before he raised hell thinking I'd disappeared again. He was my only real friend in the world, Eddy was slowly making that list too, but knowing those guys owned her made it hard to completely trust her.

Her tears had been very real though when she took off today, and as I dumped the cart, I reached into my pocket for my phone. I had a few missed calls from Dante and ten messages from Eddy. Each with varying degrees of remorse and apology.

Hitting her number, I lifted the phone to my ear.

"Do you hate me?" she said.

I laughed, stepping inside when Stewart opened the door for me. "Of course not. I know how those assholes can be. We're all cool."

A relieved breath gushed from her. "And we're still on for the party tonight, right?"

I hesitated. Was it a good idea to go to a party when I had to be on a plane tomorrow, going fuck knew where? Anger at my situation bubbled up inside of me and before I could think about it, I was saying: "Hell yes, we're goin' to this party. I need to release some tension."

The sweet as fuck Bugatti ride had helped, but it wasn't enough. I needed to be the one who snapped her up through the gears, who drove her to top speed. The world slowed when I was driving, like all I could feel was the engine, and all I could think about was freedom.

Nothing else mattered. It all faded away.

"I'll be over in twenty to help you get ready," Eddy squealed, and I realized I'd tuned some of what she'd said out. My mind stuck on that car and its driver.

"Okay, great—" I started to say, but she'd already hung up.

Deciding I would call Dante later, I rushed up the stairs and into my room. After a quick shower I was standing there in just a towel when Stewart let Eddy into my room.

She rushed over to me, and like the first time I'd met her, she was back to her punk rock chick perfection in a tight black mini, torn up white shirt that showcased her flat stomach, and enough jewelry to sink a ship. "You look gorgeous," I exclaimed, hugging her tightly. "Now can you work your magic on me?"

She snorted. "Right, like that would be hard. You're standing there in a towel with wet hair and I want to bang you. And I'm not even into chicks."

Flipping her off, I hurried back into the bathroom and pulled out the hair dryer. It took us twenty minutes to tame my hair, leaving it in long silky strands that fell halfway down my back. Eddy insisted on doing my makeup, and I wondered if she'd ever had this sort of girl time before. It was rare in my world, and it kind of felt like it was in hers too.

"They don't really let me have friends," she said softly, and I blinked, wondering how she had read my mind. "Or … it's not so much that they don't let me, more that I don't see the point in getting close to anyone when I can't really share my world with them. I can never have anyone over to our house. My family is scary as hell, and my brother is tied up in Delta business all the time. He's owned by our parents, all the duties and company rules."

"I can't believe Militant Delta is you guys. I mean, legit the most well-known name in business." Dante used to talk about them all the time. No wonder he'd had Catherine's number, he was half a fanboy over their rise to power.

Eddy grabbed an eyeliner, talking again as she lined my bottom lid. "Yeah, that's us. Company Delta. Team Delta. Control the fucking world and turn all humans into mindless drones."

"So, it's just the five families? All of the ones that live in this compound?"

She nodded. "Oh yeah, it's old school around here. They started this together, and there are all these rules to follow so that it remains a family business."

And they had been secretly controlling the world ever since.

I couldn't see her face now, because I had my eyes shut for her to finish lining them, but I sensed her irritation. "You'll never take over any part of the business?"

She snorted. "No way. I'm here to look pretty and probably make an alliance marriage with another company they deal with."

"If girls are such shit in this Delta group, then how is Catherine one of the five?"

A light touch on my eyes, and then she moved to the next. "She's not really. Your dad—" I coughed, and she paused. "I mean, Richard, took Oscar's death really hard. I haven't even seen him since then. Think he's been in New York, at the main offices there. Catherine steps in for him."

I could understand that. The pain of my own family's death was still too raw for me to really face, but I would have loved the luxury of hiding myself away to deal with my grief. Catherine had taken that away from me.

"What was he like?" I asked Eddy, obeying her murmured instructions to open or close my eyes while she worked.

"Oscar?" she replied, and I nodded. "He was different from the rest of them." Her voice was soft as she spoke of the brother I'd never met. "Oscar was kind. That's why they were always so hard on him. Why he was always getting singled out." She shuddered. "Let's just say when he turned up dead, I was devastated—but not surprised."

"Who? Beck and his crew? You think they hurt Oscar?" I sat up sharply, pulling away from the strip of fake lashes Eddy was about to position on my lash line.

"Not them." She shook her head. "The successors are all in the same shit filled boat, and are beyond loyal to each other. Brothers ... more than brothers. No, I mean the elders."

My brows shot up. "You mean their *parents*? What exactly are we talking about here? Beatings?" My mind flashed back to the smack Catherine had delivered on my first day. She was definitely not above beating her children.

Eddy let out a low, sad laugh and grabbed my chin between her fingers to hold me still while she finished my makeup. For the longest time, she just worked in silence, then stepped back and surveyed her work.

"Perfect," she commented. "You look so much like Oscar it's crazy. Except, you know, less dick and way more tits and vag." Illustrating her point, she squeezed one of my above average sized breasts and I slapped her hand away with a laugh. Her expression sobered then. "Beatings were the least of it, Riles. When I say you need to be careful, I *mean* it. I have no idea what goes on behind the closed doors of Delta, but they are big on control. I'm a girl, and second born, so have never been in the inner circle—but I'm all too familiar with the haunted look in my brother's eyes when he comes back from meetings. Not to mention the toll it took on Oscar..." She trailed off with a shiver and quickly turned her back on me. Not quick enough to hide the water welling up in her eyes though.

"So, what are you wearing?" She changed the subject with a bright voice, and I let her. She was grieving just as badly as I was, and I could hardly believe it'd taken me this long to recognize it.

"Uh, I have no idea," I murmured, following Eddy through to my massive walk-in wardrobe.

Eddy seemed suitably impressed as she ran her hand over the hanging garments, even letting out a low whistle when she spotted the wall of red soled shoes.

"Damn, girl," she breathed, turning to face me with bright eyes. "*Louboutins.* Catherine may be a psychotic bitch, but she has *taste.* Where do we even begin?"

Grinning at her enthusiasm, I pulled open one of the drawers and took out a pair of black jeans. "Uh, I'm not really a dress sort of girl so..." I waggled the jeans at her and snorted a laugh at her horrified expression.

"Thank God I'm here to help," she whispered, shaking her head slowly and creeping closer to the hanging dresses. "You'll wear what I choose and you'll rock it so hard that Beck will be cleaning up a puddle of drool when you walk in."

I coughed a laugh and tried to ignore the fact that my cheeks were heating. Damn fair skin made blushing impossible to hide. "I thought you said Beck was off limits?"

"He is. But that doesn't mean you can't knock him down a few pegs." She winked at me then produced a tight, black bandage dress. "Valentino. Perfect."

Rolling my eyes, I took the hanger from her. I wasn't even going to pretend I didn't like the idea of seeing Sebastian Beckett drooling.

It took a bit of wiggling and a lot of sucking in, but when I was finally outfitted in the little black dress and had sky high metal studded stilettos to complete the look, I had to admit Eddy knew what she was doing. I looked sexy and dangerous all at the same time, and somehow my black wrist brace wasn't even out of place. It almost looked like a fashionable accessory, especially after Eddy decked it out with a ton of thick gold bracelets.

"I'm going to freeze in this," I said, even though I was definitely not taking it off.

Eddy laughed. "No way, alcohol is a warm friend."

She wasn't wrong about that. I studied my reflection again. "My first Ducis Academy party," I murmured. "This ought to be fun."

Chapter 9

The party was hosted by none other than Jimmy—ball cap wearing, race organizer Jimmy. When he saw me walk through the door to his impressive home, he let out a low whistle and shook his head.

"Damn, new girl." He grinned a greasy grin at me. "You clean up *well*."

"Back off, Jimmy," Eddy snapped, shoving him in the chest. "She's a Delta successor now."

Our host visibly paled under the brim of his ball cap and swallowed a couple of times before just nodding and walking away. Eddy snatched my hand and dragged me through the rabbit warren mansion until we reached the back of the house, where the main party was set up. We stopped in front of a full bar that was decked out with what looked like every type of alcohol in the world. Plus a bartender.

Rich kids really knew how to throw a party, I could admit it.

"What are you drinking?" my friend asked, yelling a bit to be heard over the loud music. When I took too long to reply, she ordered for me, shouting the name of a drink I'd never heard to the bartender.

The man understood her though, and after throwing around a few liquor bottles and occasionally pouring some liquids in a cocktail shaker, we were presented with two iridescent blue drinks.

"Dare I ask?" I arched a brow at Eddy, and she snickered as she took a sip of her own drink.

Shaking her head, she shoved my drink into my hand. "Nope, don't ask. Just drink. You look like you could do with letting your hair down." She flapped a hand at my silken locks lying loose over my shoulders. "Metaphorically speaking. Come on, let's see who's all here."

Back home I'd never really been into the party scene. Dante as my closest, and only real friend, was not a fan of dressing up and shaking his ass, so we tended to avoid them. I realized then that I'd forgotten to phone him back, and I decided to try to remember before the night was over. It was too loud to chat on the phone right now.

Eddy knew a lot of people here, stopping for hugs and fake air kisses. But it was all superficial, clearly none of these people gave a fuck about her. It was like, kiss her ass, ask about the guys, and then brush her aside.

Fuckers.

My drink disappeared far too quickly, and I lifted the empty glass to Eddy, and she nodded, leading us back the way we'd just come. Before we reached the bar though, there was a commotion near the entrance, and I spun around to find a familiar face pushing his way toward me.

"Dante!" I screamed, the alcohol already heating my blood. I rushed for my friend, not quite registering how odd it was that he was even here. I mean, not only was he supposed to be back in Jersey, but how the hell did he even know about this party.

Still, in that moment, all I cared about was getting a hug.

I slammed into him, and he hauled me up into his arm, the scent of that rich, spicy aftershave he loved so much washing over me. That smell took me back to a million memories. Fun nights. Family dinners. Everything that was now tainted in pain, because my parents, who had been part of both of our lives, were gone.

That was what I needed the alcohol for. To forget. To not hurt for one night.

"What are you doing here?" I yelled when he dropped me down.

Dante leveled a look on me, it was almost exasperated. "You never phoned me back. I was checking on you." His lips twitched. "Are you drunk already, Riles?"

Shaking my head, I swung my hips in time to the beat. "Not yet, but if this night goes to plan, it won't be long."

Concern knit his brow together. "What have I told you about losing control around strangers? We don't know these people, and from the little I've learned, they're definitely not the sort you should trust."

"Don't play stupid with me, Dante. You and I both know it's Delta. Seriously, you don't have to tell me twice that they're bad news. All rich people are."

Something dark flickered across Dante's eyes, but it was gone before I could really discern the reason. "Just watch your back," he pushed. "Delta did not become a global leader by playing by the rules. They're big business, and there is always corruption in big business."

"Is there something else about this situation I should know?" I pushed him. "I mean, you had Catherine's phone number, so clearly you have been doing a lot of *research* on them."

Dante shook his head. "That was pretty much all I could get. One lousy contact. I'm getting a lot of run around in my normal circles. No one wants to incriminate themselves and rat out Delta, seeing as it's a massive, corrupt, rich as fuck corporation, and they can destroy anyone. But I'll keep digging. Stay vigilant. No trust."

"I don't trust any of them except Eddy. She's my friend," I said stubbornly. Speaking of…

I spun to find her standing almost awkwardly behind me. Reaching out, I hauled her in closer. "Dante, you remember Eddy, right?"

Dante's green eyes were dark as they leisurely rested on Eddy. "No way I could forget someone as beautiful as Eddy," he said softly, with a rumble in his words.

Eddy smiled at him. "I remember you too, big man. Hard to forget all of that ink…"

She drawled the last few words, making them sound almost naughty.

Dante's return smile was predatory, and I knew that I was not going to be able to stop these two from screwing each other very soon. There was an attraction between them. It was fucking clear as anything.

All I cared was that neither of them dumped me when they inevitably got sick of each other.

Eddy reached out and grabbed my hand and Dante's before she started pulling us toward the bar. "I wanna dance," she said with a pout. "And I need more of the delicious alcohol now."

"You like to drink, girl?" Dante asked, watching her closely.

She shrugged. "If you were in my position, you'd like to drink too. Trust me."

We were almost at the bar, when a familiar voice had Eddy skidding to a halt. "What have I told you about dragging in the trash, sis?"

Jasper was not alone, as he leaned on a nearby pillar right beside the bar, dressed in designer jeans and a black shirt that molded to his muscles. Beck, Evan, and Dylan were all there as well, and none of them looked happy. Beck had his serial killer eyes locked on me, or … maybe on Dante's hand which was wrapped around my arm.

Eddy shot Jasper a glare. "Fuck off, Jay. I told you last night, I won't interfere in your fucked up shit, as long as you stay out of my life. You don't own me. I'm not Delta. So back the fuck up!"

Beck surged forward then, moving so fast and smooth I almost missed it completely. He edged himself between Dante and me. The pair sized each other up as they faced off. They were virtually the same height—stupid giants towering over everyone else.

"You might not be a true part of Delta," Beck said, talking to Eddy even though his gaze remained locked on Dante. "But Butterfly is. She belongs to us."

Those words did something fucked up to my insides, sending them squirming while heating me to the point where I felt like I was going to pass out or something. "You don't own her," Dante snapped. "*Riley…*" He snarled my name, clearly not a fan of the nickname. "…is her own person. I will kill anyone that takes that away from her."

Beck grinned. A scary, fucked up, evil grin. "I know all about your life, gangbanger. You're playing outside your league now. I'd be very careful who you threaten."

In that moment, I feared for Dante. I'd never had to worry about him before, because he was tough, and he did have solid friends in his gang, ones who'd had his back before, but I trusted what Beck was saying. Dante was out of his league here, and this was a scary game where probably no one was going to come out alive.

Something I would no doubt learn more of tomorrow, when I ventured out on my first official Delta business. Before Beck could do or say anything more—or kill my best friend—I swung on my heels and sashayed my way across to the bar. Hoping like hell that if I left, it would diffuse the tension which was holding us hostage. Eddy was right with me, both of us practically diving across the bar to get the bartender's attention. "We need drinks," Eddy demanded, and the dark haired dude started to nod quickly, his eyes locked on my cleavage which was spilling out over the front of my tight dress.

Before I could get mad about it, and why should I bother, my tits were practically hanging out in this stupid dress, he disappeared and was back in a flash with two more cocktails. Heat pressed along my spine, and I took a huge gulp of this new drink, something orange and fruity, before turning to face the inevitable.

If billionaire bastard was a style of dress, Beck would have nailed that look. Dark jeans that hugged his muscled legs and ass in all the right places, clearly expensive and custom fitted. He wore black boots, which topped his height out at 6 and a half foot, and his white long sleeved Henley—pushed up to showcase his bronze skin and muscular forearms—was molded to his broad chest. It was like rich met prep met fucked up darkness—which was mostly all in his eyes. Beck wore the uniform that people expected, but his face was where the real truth lay.

"What do you want, Beck?" Eddy said, almost tiredly.

He didn't bother to look at her. Instead, he snatched my delicious, fruity drink from my hand and dumped the contents onto the floor, the sticky liquid splashing my designer shoes.

"You shouldn't be drinking," he told me. His gray eyes flashed with danger, and I burned with the need to push him further. Holding his gaze, I reached out and took Eddy's drink from her hand—which she willingly handed over—then brought it to my lips, tipped it up and chugged the whole thing.

When the last drop was gone, I licked my lips and slammed the glass down on the bar.

"Kiss my ass, Sebastian," I suggested.

Almost immediately I regretted those words. Challenging him, even if it had been an insult, was not my smartest move. His chest rumbled as he reached for me.

From about ten feet away I saw Dante react, expression fierce as he strode forward, but Eddy got there first, jumping in between us before she wrapped her arms around me and dragged me away. "We're going to dance," she shouted over her shoulder.

I couldn't help myself, I had to look back. He was like a bad addiction, capturing my attention even when I really didn't want to think about him. His eyes were dark as he watched us leave, and thankfully he didn't follow.

Eddy hadn't lied, dragging me right out into the middle of the sweaty bodies. Most of the eyes of those around us were glazed, expressions vacant as they moved with the beat. There was definitely more than alcohol flowing at this party, which was pretty standard. A couple near us were devouring each other, his hand up her skirt as they moved together.

Eddy swung her hips into me, and I closed my eyes as I danced, the drinks I'd had keeping my body warm and pliant. A hard body pressed into my back at one point, and normally I would have pushed them away with a well-placed knee in the balls, but this body I recognized.

Dante's hands pressed to my sides, and I leaned back against him. Part of my brain, a tiny non-drunk sliver, realized it was a bad idea to dance with my very platonic best friend this way, but the much larger drunk part didn't give a fuck. Especially when I opened my eyes and found a set of steely gray ones locked on me. Beck stood with his friends, the four of them watching us closely, and I had to say, the looks on their faces were not at all reassuring. There was a warning there, a warning I didn't quite understand, but I knew enough to fear for Dante. And myself.

"What's wrong?" Dante asked. I'd stopped dancing, my heart pounding hard in my chest.

"I have to go with them tomorrow for a company meeting … or something," I said slowly, and at this point Eddy had stopped moving too, her eyes wide as she watched me closely. "I have no idea where we're going," I continued breathlessly. "I have no idea what we're supposed to do when we get there. All I know is I've been dragged into a fucked up family business, and another person from my family just died because of it."

Dante's face went dark and menacing, as a scowl tightened his lips. It was a look I'd seen from him plenty of times over the years but not usually directed at me. "You can't go, Riles. I mean it."

Throwing my hands in the air, I let out a long sigh. "A week ago you were telling me there was nothing I could do but play their games, and now you're telling me to bail. How? They're too fucking powerful."

I had no choice. Even if I ran, I'd never stay off their radar. I was trapped.

Dante clenched and unclenched his hands; his frustration had nowhere to go and I knew he would be in some sort of fight before the night was through. He fought the way I drove, because he needed the release.

Eddy, who was clearly used to powerful, dangerous, damaged men, didn't seem worried or scared, she just reached out and took one of Dante's hands, stopping his obsessive movement.

"Dance with me," she whispered, and I smiled at the look on his face.

Maybe fighting wasn't the right F word for his release tonight. *Thank you*, I mouthed at her, and Eddy mimed a hip thrust at me. That, teamed with the look on her face, told me this was no hardship for her. She was feeling my best friend hard.

Deciding I was in need of another drink, I pushed my way through the tightly packed dance floor.

Rough hands grabbed at me as I passed, spinning me around so my front was pressed into his. Throwing my head back to see who had me, I stared into an unfamiliar face. Blandly handsome with blond hair and blue bloodshot eyes. "What the fuck do you think you're doing?"

Nothing I hated more than handsy dudes who couldn't take no for an answer.

"You might be the hottest bitch I've ever seen," he said with a smirk.

Placing both of my hands on his chest, I pushed as hard as I could. He barely budged at all. Annoyance spiked through me, and I balled my fists, ready to do exactly what Dante had taught me in these situations. As I swung, I braced myself for the pain. This wasn't the first guy I'd clocked, and last time I hadn't been able to move my hand for a week. It was always worth it though. When my hand connected, there was a crunch and his head snapped back. They never expected a chick would punch them like that, and it took them by surprise every time. He let me go, and I was already rushing away, not wanting to deal with his retaliation. "Bitch!" he shouted and there was a new commotion.

I knew I shouldn't have looked back, but human nature and all that … I had to see.

I skidded to a halt when I found no one was following me, instead everyone was crowding close to Jasper and Evan, who stood over the top of the dude I'd just punched. My gaze sought out Beck, knowing he'd be there somewhere as well, but there was no sign of him or Dylan. Pushing my way back, I cradled my aching hand.

"Did you really think you could touch one of us and get away with it?" Jasper said, staring down at the blond, who had a blossoming red mark on his cheek, and another around his throat. "You've been warned, Todd. Consider this your one and only."

Todd held both of his hands up, pure terror on his face. "Dude, fuck, seriously. I didn't know she was yours."

"I'm not," I spat at the same time Evan said, "We own her. Body and soul."

My eyes widened at that. "No fuckin—"

Jasper turned violent eyes on me. "Shut up. You're just lucky Beck was called away on some business outside, otherwise you'd be cleaning lover boy's blood off the ground."

"Lover boy," I spluttered. "Did you miss the part where I punched him?"

His words were like acid as he replied. "Go home, Riley. You're just causing trouble here."

I seethed in anger, stepping closer to the blond boy with bloody knuckles. Todd, my would be 'lover boy' scrambled away like an overgrown crab. Clearly he recognized the danger in the room and was wisely getting the fuck out of the way.

"News flash, Jasper," I hissed, jabbing him in the chest with my finger. "No one *owns* me. One pissy little meeting with a few old misogynistic fucks doesn't change that. Now leave me the fuck alone. That goes for *all of you*." This time my glare encompassed Evan and Dylan, who had just stepped into the room. "I didn't ask for this shit, and the second I get the chance, I'm gone."

With more sass than I really thought I was capable of, I tossed my silken hair over my shoulder and stalked out of the room in search of ... I didn't really know what. I was just focused on making a dramatic exit.

"Going somewhere?" A dark, husky voice seemed to come straight out of the shadows and I jumped in fright, stumbling in my spike heels and falling headfirst into the rock hard chest of the dickhead himself—Beck.

"Yeah," I muttered, instinctively grabbing his biceps to regain my balance. "To the bar." As I said this, I flipped my hair out of my face and met his gaze by tipping my head way back. Damn tall bastard.

His eyes narrowed, and his nostrils flared a little in anger. The fact that I could recognize this sent a spike of smug pleasure through me. A few days ago, I'd have said his face was as unreadable as ever, but now I was picking up on those tiny mood cues.

What did that say about how closely I'd been watching Beck?

"You've had—"

I cut him off by clapping a hand over his mouth. "If you try to tell me I've 'had enough' then I will deliberately march back out there and slam six tequila shots in quick succession." I didn't remove my hand, but his eyes were mocking. Taunting. "Oh, you don't think I will? Try me."

Slowly, deliberately, he peeled my hand from his crazy soft lips and smirked. "You've had enough, Riley."

I had to admit, I didn't think he was actually going to call my bluff. That said, I wasn't one to make empty threats, so I shrugged and took a step back in the direction of the bar. I didn't make it far, though, before Beck's huge hand wrapped around my wrist and held me firm.

"Don't be childish, Butterfly," he told me in the sort of condescending voice that made me *rage* inside. "You're part of a respected, old-money company now. We have standards, and they don't include getting white girl wasted at some new-money party."

Gritting my teeth in anger, I tried to wrench my wrist out of his grip, but his hand only tightened and pulled me closer. When my balance finally faltered, I found myself pinned to the wall with his other hand pressed across my chest, holding me in place.

"Do not defy me, Butterfly," he breathed in my ear, his voice dripping danger and sheer *power*. His fingers tightened across my collarbone, slipping up to the base of my throat, where he pressed just hard enough to spike fear and arousal in equal measures. Damn I was fucked up.

"Sebastian?" I whispered, meeting his dark eyes from just inches away and hating the fact that my own eyes probably conveyed how turned on his little show of dominance was making me. "Go fuck yourself."

Not giving myself another second to sink into whatever this messed up attraction between us was, I brought my knee up. Hard. Nailing him right in the nuts, just the way my mom had taught me to do if I was ever attacked in the dangerous streets around home.

Instantly, his grip on me relaxed enough that I could slip out of his hold and race back down the hall in the direction I'd come after the altercation with Todd.

Where the hell were Dante and Eddy?

Halfway across the room I hesitated. Maybe I should just find Eddy and ask her to take me home? My head was already spinning, and a nasty hangover was looming even without those six tequilas I'd threatened Beck with. Chewing my lip, I glanced over my shoulder and spotted the furious, gorgeous, infuriating object of my frustration storming toward me.

"Fuck it," I muttered, hurrying across to the bar and ordering from my favorite person of the night—the bartender. On edge, I drummed my fingertips on the bar while he poured the little glasses.

Someone was smiling down on me, though, because Beck was waylaid by a gaggle of fawning drunk girls. One of them must have been someone important, because instead of brushing her aside, he was giving a tight, forced smile to whatever she was saying while his eyes remained glued to me.

I was all kinds of mixed emotions. Angry, that was a no-brainer; these rich pricks kept saying that they *owned* me. Frustrated, because it seemed like I was wading through a sea of secrets which no one was inclined to share. Jealous, because Beck just laid an all too gentle hand on that girl's waist to move her out of his way. But more than anything, I was sad. I was sad and lonely, because that small act of kneeing Beck in the balls reminded me of my mom, and she was gone. She was dead and never coming back. I was all alone in this world now, and my bio-family were the worst kind of people. They would never be my real family, not like mom and dad had been. So I was alone.

Holding Beck's furious gaze as he crossed the room, I grabbed a shot in each hand and gulped them back. Quick like lightning, I exchanged the empty glass for a full one the second I could so when Beck reached me, I was wiping my mouth with the back of my hand and feeling the whole world spin.

"You stupid, stubborn shit," he said with an angry growl as he grabbed my arm in that bruising grip that I was coming to love just as much as I hated it. "Come on."

He started dragging me away from the bar, but I wasn't anywhere *near* drunk enough to just let him manhandle me like that. Everyone knew it took a solid twenty minutes for alcohol to really kick in, so if he thought I'd be compliant he was severely mistaken.

"Take your hands *off* me!" I yelled, deliberately trying to make a scene as I wrenched my arm out of his grip. My raised voice brought far too many eyes down on us, but the moment they saw it was Beck, everyone scattered.

Beck's jaw clenched, and I imagined I could hear his teeth grinding as he let me step away. Over his shoulder I could see Evan waving him down, and I jerked my head in that direction. "Your friend needs you, Sebastian," I said, my words sounding a little slurred already.

He took his focus off me for a split second, and it was enough time for me to turn and not that gracefully slip away.

I made it out near the pool. "Hey!" I shouted, spotting my missing friends beside the Jacuzzi. They were both holding drinks and dancing close. Really close. "What the hell, you guys? You just disappeared on me!"

"Riles! There you are!" Eddy beamed and threw her arms around me in a drunken hug. "We were looking for you everywhere. This house has a really shitty layout, but I guess that's what you get with these new-money builds."

Her breath held so much alcohol I suspected it was a fire hazard, but then mine probably wasn't much better.

"Uh huh, really looks like you were looking for me," I replied with light sarcasm, glaring at Dante. The look he gave me back was... confusing. Way too complex for my tequila fuzzed brain to figure out, so I shrugged it off and let Eddy coax me into a swaying dance with her.

Soon, Dante joined us and the three of us danced together while the pounding beat of the music reverberated through us. Hands seemed to be everywhere, but it wasn't until Dante's lips brushed the back of my neck in a light kiss that I became uncomfortable. Was that a platonic friend-kiss? Or something more?

"Um, I think I need to pee," I told them, and started weaving my way over to the pool house where I imagined there would be a bathroom. It was just on the opposite side of the pool, so I waved away their half-hearted offers to accompany me. It was pretty obvious Eddy was into Dante, so maybe they needed a bit of alone time.

Who knew, maybe there was something sparking there? I hoped so. Dante deserved to be happy.

Chapter 10

After I'd taken my sweet ass time peeing in the pool house bathroom, then spent twice as long struggling to resituate my lace G-string and skin tight dress, I was exhausted. Instead of heading back around the pool to join my friends again, I sat down on a sun lounger to people watch for a few minutes.

At least, that had been my intention. I could only assume I passed out, though, because I awoke to huge, strong hands picking me up and cradling me into a broad, muscular chest.

"Sebastian?" I mumbled, trying to squint up at the person carrying me. My tongue was slow and fuzzy. Damn tequila. "Where are you taking me?"

When he didn't reply, I started struggling to get out of his grip. It was about as effective as an insect thrashing for freedom after being pinned to a board. Or a butterfly, perhaps...

"Stop it," he ordered me. "I'm taking you home."

Desperately trying to work some saliva into my dry mouth, I looked around us. Dante and Eddy were nowhere to be seen, but the party was still raging.

"I don't need your help, Sebastian. I can handle myself. Just put me down." I wiggled a bit more, but he didn't seem bothered. His steps didn't even falter as he carried me farther from the party and out to the drive where expensive cars were parked all the way back to the front gates. Of course his sexy as sin Bugatti was right by the front door. God forbid Sebastian Roman Beckett be expected to walk any great distance. Lazy prick.

"Stop muttering curses at me under your breath, Butterfly," he said. "It's annoying."

I squinted up at him, but the fucker had somehow perfected the art of standing directly in front of the moon, so his face was in shadows. Just as I opened my mouth to reply, the distinctive sound of his car unlocking beeped, and he slung me over his shoulder while he opened the passenger door. I'd barely managed to squeak a protest before he manhandled me into his car and clicked the seatbelt into place.

"That was brave," I slurred when he took his seat and slammed the door shut. "I could have happily vomited down your back right then." Even as I said it, my stomach roiled and lurched. I'd been joking, but come to think of it...

Beck leveled a serious glare at me as he started the ignition. It gave a throaty purr and I relaxed back into my seat with a sigh, totally ignoring Beck's glare. What was he looking at me like that for anyway?

Whatever it was all about, he kept his trap shut and rolled the sexy beast of a car down the driveway then hit the accelerator when we turned into the street.

"Fucking shit," I moaned as quietly as I could handle in my inebriated state. It was all just becoming way too much for me. Between the booze, the car, the speed... *Beck*... I was quickly losing my tenuous hold on dignity and resolve.

Almost like he could read my mind, Beck pushed the car faster. He threw us around corners so fast the scenery was a blur outside my window. His shirtsleeves were rolled up to the elbow, and somehow my eyes became glued to the muscles in his forearm flexing and moving as he handled the powerful car with ease and confidence.

As much as I hated to admit it, suddenly the roiling in my stomach was no longer arousal. It was something else. Something significantly less sexy.

"Shit," I said, swallowing frantically. "Beck, you need to stop."

He flashed a look at me, confused, but didn't even so much as slow. "What? Why?"

"Beck, seriously. You need to stop *right now*." One of my hands gripped the arm rest for dear life while the other held the seatbelt away from my body, like that could stop what was about to happen.

He must have seen something in my face—possibly sheer terror and total lack of blood—that made him click that I was being serious and not fucking around.

Shifting down gears as quick as he could without hurting his car, he slowed from the insane speed we'd been traveling. I pressed a hand to my mouth. He wasn't stopping fast enough. Oh god. Shit. Fuck. Please don't let this happen.

The car came to a stop on the side of the road and I frantically opened my door and threw myself out—except I hadn't undone my seatbelt. The black fabric strap did exactly as it was designed to do, locking up and throwing me back into my seat.

Horror rolled through me, and my stomach rebelled.

#

My head pounded like a bass drum, and I rolled over in my plush bed with a groan.

Why?

It was the pained, desperate mental cry of all hungover girls, wasn't it? Why did I drink so much? Why didn't I use better judgement? *Why?*

The sour tang of vomit reached my nostrils, and I gagged. Oh my god. Not again.

Scrambling as fast as my stiff, sleepy limbs would carry me, I ran into the attached bathroom and cradled the toilet bowl as I dry heaved. Apparently there was nothing left inside me to come out. What the *hell* had happened?

Peeling myself off the marble floor, I used the wash basin to pull myself up and peer at my bedraggled appearance in the mirror.

Holy. Fucking. Shit.

My makeup was smeared halfway down my face and my hair looked like something seen on the wife of Sasquatch, with a crusty patch of vomit dried into the ends.

Worse. I was practically naked. All I had on was the little black lace thong from the night before. Where was my bra? My dress? Wait, I hadn't been wearing a bra under that dress. Rubbing my face with my hands, I frantically tried to remember the night before. After the tequila and the dancing and the drive home...

Oh *shit.*

Beck's car. I threw up in Beck's Bugatti!

Groaning, I sunk back to the marble floor in a puddle of shame. I vomited in Beck's goddamn million dollar car. *He's going to murder me and rightfully so.*

But then what happened? My memory was totally blank, and that made me feel even more ill. Had I passed out on the side of the road in a pool of my own vomit?

"Jesus fucking Christ, Riley," I muttered, dragging myself back to my feet again. I still needed to use the basin for balance because the room was dipping and swirling something awful.

Cold water would help. I turned the faucet on and splashed my face a few times before giving up and staggering over to the shower. My hair desperately needed washing anyway.

"Ugh, gross." I cringed at my image reflected back at me from the full length mirror directly outside the shower. It was not a pretty sight, and I could only hope the steam would obliterate my own image soon.

Just as I squirted a handful of shampoo into my palm, something caught my eye in that narcissistic shower sex mirror.

"What the fuck..." I mumbled, peering down at my body to find the unfamiliar mark. My hair was everywhere so I pushed it over my shoulders to get a better look at my chest.

Sure enough, there was a small, blue pen ink drawing on the side of my left breast.

"Mother *fucker!*" I screamed when I saw what it was. A fucking *butterfly* drawn mere inches away from my nipple. If there had been any question about who took my dress off, Beck had made sure I damn well knew it was him.

Dripping water everywhere, I stomped back into my bedroom in search of my phone. That fucker was about to catch a piece of my mind for this invasion of privacy. It didn't faze me that I didn't have his number. A man that arrogant would have put it in my phone, I had no doubt. He probably installed a tracking device too.

Finding it on the bedside table, plugged into the charger, I snatched it up and paled. It seemed Beck had also taken the liberty of changing my clock to twenty-four hour time because the numbers thirteen thirty flashed at me.

Thirteen thirty. That meant I had thirty minutes until this jet was scheduled to leave on some mysterious Delta mission which I was supposed to be partaking in.

Well, fuck it. I didn't want to go anyway.

But something wasn't sitting right... I stared at my phone a bit longer. Beck had changed the clock to twenty-four hour time *and* turned my phone on silent. Why?

Suspicion burned in my belly. That fucker turned my phone on silent so I would sleep all day, then made sure I would see the time and know I'd missed the flight when I woke up. Which meant he didn't *want* me to go.

"Sebastian fucking Beckett. When are you going to learn?" I shook my head, tossing my phone on the bed and hurrying back to the shower. I had a flight to catch in thirty minutes.

Chapter 11

My borrowed car came to a screeching halt beside the shiny white Cessna at fourteen hundred hours exactly.

"Suck it, bitches." I snickered to myself as I climbed out of the white Mercedes and left the keys in the ignition. I had no doubts someone would see it safely back to the Deboise McMansion.

Grabbing the railing, I skipped up the steps and ducked into the jet with a supremely smug grin on my face. I wasn't sure what reaction I expected, but it wasn't the casual indifference they greeted me with.

"Oh great, the spare made it," Evan muttered as he sipped on an amber liquor in a crystal rocks glass. "Thought you said she'd still be asleep, Beck."

Beck didn't reply to Evan's bored sounding enquiry, instead flicking a glance over me from head to toe, then turning back to his laptop open on the table in front of him. The bastard looked incredible, which was only made worse by how utterly dog shit I was feeling.

I'd managed to drag myself through the shower, washing my hair and cleaning my teeth, but then I'd had little time to do anything more. I'd thrown on my comfort clothes—jeans, converse sneakers and a wonder woman tank top—but my hair was still wet and my face totally devoid of makeup.

"Yikes, you look like crap, trailer trash," Jasper sneered, grinning at me from behind the girl who was seated in his lap. One of his hands was buried up her skirt and from the speed of her breathing and the flush to her cheeks, it wasn't hard to guess what was going on. "Didn't you get the memo, this is a business meeting? Right now you barely look old enough to handle a fucking Chuck E. Cheese party." He tilted his head back to watch the chick again. She let out another moan. "Celia here can help you sort out your appearance before we get there, can't you doll face?" He pressed a possessive kiss to her neck, and she just moaned.

"Where *are* we going?" I demanded, folding my arms and desperately trying to ignore the writhing woman in Jasper's lap. "In case you forgot, no one has filled me in on *anything*, least of all where the fuck we're going today. I don't know shit about your business, so it's pretty stupid to drag me into any sort of meeting."

"You don't need to know, Butterfly," Beck answered, not taking his eyes from his computer for even a second. "You're only here as a show of power. To prove that the Delta is not weakened by Oscar's death. We are still five successors strong. Five votes."

I wanted to argue, but the pilot stepped through the little cockpit door and cleared his throat. "Uh, Celia? We need to take off." He gave the woman who was clearly mid-orgasm, writhing all over Jasper's lap—and hand—a pointed look and indicated toward the open door. For a moment I thought he was telling her to get off the plane, but when she huffed and stood up, tugging her skirt back in place, it suddenly clicked. This was our flight attendant.

"Sit down, Butterfly," Beck ordered me casually, nodding at the plush, cream leather recliner facing his. "We have a decent flight ahead of us and I'd rather not find out if you get air sick." He arched a brow at me and my cheeks flushed hot. Goddamn tequila.

I wanted so badly to cut him down with my words, but my head still pounded and my stomach hurt from the earlier vomiting. So instead of whipping out my sassy pants, I slid into the waiting armchair and buckled my seatbelt.

When I said nothing, Beck cleared his throat, his gaze turning to the small drinks table near the window. A bottle of water and packet of painkillers sat there, waiting for me, like freaking magic.

"If you knew I'd be here, why mute my phone?" I asked, taking the pills out of the packet and washing two down with a gulp of water.

Beck sighed and closed his laptop, sliding it into a pocket beside his seat. "When you noticed I'd muted your phone, what was your first thought?" The way he looked at me, I knew I'd walked into a trap, but my poor hungover brain couldn't figure out how or why.

"That you didn't want me to make this flight," I replied, then took another long sip of water. Holy crap I needed that water.

Beck raised one of those dark brows at me, his gray eyes full of dark amusement. "So what did you do?"

Realizing I'd done exactly what he wanted me to do, I sighed heavily and put my water down. I needed a damn minute to get a hold of my temper because I was too fucking tired to start stabbing people. Also, I had no sharp objects on hand.

"You're a prick, Sebastian," I murmured. Tipping my head back, I closed my eyes and tried to block his presence out.

Sometime later, the plane gently rocked as it began moving, and I tried to breathe deeply. I'd never been airsick before, but I'd also never vomited in a Bugatti so never say never.

For as long as I could, I kept my eyes shut and prayed for sleep. I had no idea where we were going, or how long it'd take to get there, or even what the fuck we were going *for*. But I was sick of asking and getting no answers, so I kept my mouth shut. Only seven weeks until I was eighteen and legally free of Catherine Debitch. No matter what she thought, she couldn't make me run her company. I just had to bide my time.

Eventually, I gave up on sleep. When I opened my eyes again, I was totally unsurprised to find Beck staring straight at me. He didn't even have the grace to look away when I caught him, he just continued staring.

"Take a picture, it'll last longer," I grumbled, shifting in my seat and reaching for my water again.

His lips curved up in an evil sort of smile. "I took plenty last night, thanks. Nice tits, by the way."

The water I'd just sipped shot down the wrong pipe and I choked a bit. "You'd better be fucking joking," I snarled, glaring daggers at the flawless asshole opposite me.

He just shrugged and grinned. Fucking psychopath.

Looking around the plane, I hunted for a change of subject. "Whose plane?" I asked. "Yours?"

Beck shook his head. "Delta's."

I rolled my eyes. "Of course. Militant Delta Finances. Care to tell me any more about your world dominating company? What do you do anyway besides deal in illegal arms? Hang out and make threats?"

He just stared at me with that blank gaze, and I knew he wasn't going to suddenly start spewing out answers so I sucked another deep breath and released it with a long sigh.

"What sorts of speeds do these planes get up to?" Why I was trying to make small talk, I had no idea. The fact that he'd just so casually alluded to having seen me practically naked left me on edge, and it was nerves that made me chatter.

Beck leveled another blank stare at me, and I huffed, folding my arms.

"Why don't you go annoy Darren with your questions?" he suggested, already turning his attention to his phone. Clearly, I'd been dismissed.

He'd been sarcastic, but chatting with Darren—the pilot I assumed—sounded considerably better than dealing with Beck's surly attitude. Unclipping my seat belt, I decided I'd go and learn a bit about jets.

Beck raised a brow at me, but I ignored him and made my way through the cabin toward the cockpit. Celia, our lovely flight attendant, was back in Jasper's lap so no one stopped me when I tapped on the little white door. A sound came in response, which I assumed to be something along the lines of "come in," so I let myself in.

"Hey, Darren?" I greeted him, latching the door and then admiring the vast array of buttons and levers, not to mention the *view*. "Wow, this is incredible," I breathed, in total awe of the fluffy white clouds ahead and the tiny glimpses of land below.

128

Turning to the pilot, who was yet to speak, I gasped. In his lap, clutched in his shaking, white knuckled hand was a sleek black handgun.

"Uh, Darren?" I prompted, "Why..." My words faded out and I needed to lick my lips a few times before trying again. "Why do you have a gun?"

My words seemed to jerk him out of the trance he'd been in, and his bloodshot eyes snapped up to my face. "I'm sorry," he whispered. Sweat ran down his forehead in beads, and tears leaked from his eyes. Every vein in his face stood out with the sheer tension thrumming through him. "I'm sorry, I'm so sorry," he started to sob as he apologized and panic seized me. I froze, totally unsure what the hell to do. Was he going to shoot me? Why?

"Darren," I started, holding my hands up, palms out. I had no idea why, it just felt like a calming sort of gesture. Or maybe I'd been watching too much TV. "Darren why don't you put the gun down?" I was aiming for soothing, like I was talking to a wild animal.

He shook his head slowly, tears still running from his red, puffy eyes. "I'm so sorry; they made me do it. I had to keep my kids safe."

I'd been so focused on the gun, I hadn't noticed the device in his other hand until it was too late. Not that I could have done anything, anyway. Without any further hesitation, he pressed a button on the little remote, and an explosion rocked the aircraft from the left side, followed by one on the right. Still holding my horrified, stunned gaze, Darren raised the gun to his face and pulled the trigger.

Blood splattered the walls, the controls, the windows, me. It was everywhere. Frantic screams ripped from me as Dylan and Beck came bursting into the cockpit, and found the mess which was once their pilot. But that was the least of our problems. The plane shifted and Darren's lifeless body fell forward, leaning heavily on a large lever and sending us hurtling toward the ground.

"Move!" Dylan barked, shoving me aside. I was still frozen in shock, whimpers ripping from my throat, and I didn't even flinch when Beck grabbed me around the waist from behind and held me firm within his strong arms. As I watched, Dylan heaved the dead pilot from his seat and sat down. He hesitated only a moment before taking the important looking lever thing in his strong grip and slowly, *painfully slowly*, pulling it back in an attempt to control our descent. Or, that's what I had to assume he was doing.

The plane was shaking and jolting like we were in a giant blender and it was only by Beck's impressive strength that I hadn't been thrown clear across the cabin.

"Sit down," Dylan yelled at us. "Strap in, we're going to crash."

I couldn't have moved if I'd tried. My whole body was locked up in sheer terror, and my gaze was fixed on the smears of crimson decorating my arms. Somehow, Beck manhandled me into the co-pilot's seat and buckled my seatbelt with cold efficiency. He yelled short, sharp commands back into the cabin—for Evan and Jasper—then strapped himself into the jump seat.

"Can you land us?" he demanded of Dylan, whose pale, tense face was firmly fixed on the controls and displays in front of him.

It was only a brief hesitation before Dylan replied, but it seemed like a *lifetime* while we continued hurtling toward the ground. Fast. Too damn fast. "No," he said, and my stomach dropped through the floor. We were going to die. Holy shit.

"He blew the left engine, and seriously damaged the right," Dylan elaborated, coldly calm in the face of our impending doom. "The best I can do is try and control our crash. But we will crash."

I looked to Beck in panic, but he just nodded. "Do your best."

"Do your best?" I repeated in a shriek. "That's it? We're about to die in three seconds!"

"Not that quick," Dylan replied, still totally devoid of emotions. "Cessna 172s travel at a maximum altitude of twelve to fifteen thousand feet. On average, we would drop at approximately five hundred feet per minute. We're currently at nine thousand feet, give or take a bit. That means we have a full eighteen minutes until impact, but I'll round it to ten minutes to account for the fact that our engines are on fire and we're in a nose dive."

"Right, ten minutes," I repeated, my voice high pitched with terror.

My life would be over in ten minutes. There was so much I hadn't had a chance to do. So many experiences I had missed out on.

"Looks like I'll see my parents sooner rather than later," I said stupidly, and for a moment, that was a comfort. I didn't want to die, but if they were there on the other side, it wouldn't all be bad.

Beck was looking at me, I could feel his steely gaze, but I was focused on Dylan. Watching as he wrestled the Cessna, doing whatever it was he was doing to slow our deaths.

"You're not going to see your parents," Beck bit out, finally dragging my attention to him. "This isn't our first plane crash, and it won't be our last. Someone is always trying to take out Delta's successors. To weaken us. But those fuckers always underestimate Dylan's skills and my determination to live so I can put a bullet in each of their skulls."

My stomach lurched as the plane rattled again. It was so rough now that I almost felt like my insides were going to be shaken out. No doubt I'd have bruises where the seat belts were cutting into me.

"How in all fuck is this not your first crash? Like … what the fuck?"

His eyes were merciless. "We're important people. The inheritors of a fortune that out masses the rest of the world's combined. We control so much more than you can even imagine … and we have enemies."

"Oscar?" I whispered, realizing that this was a decent explanation for my brother's death.

Beck shook his head, a scowl tipping his gorgeous face into something darker. Sinister. For a moment I almost believed he was as invincible as he implied.

"Oscar's death was not by their hand."

Before he could elaborate, Dylan swore again, and for the first time some of the cool detachment from his face disappeared. "Get into brace position," he barked.

I looked around frantically, finally noticing that the ground was a hell of a lot closer than it had been before. Below us was what looked like a world of trees, and I wondered if we were still in America. Was I about to die in another country? Would anyone find us or would we be a bunch of burned corpses?

"Are you fucking deaf, Riley," Beck snapped. "Brace yourself!"

I'd never been on a commercial flight, but I had seen movies before, so I leaned forward best I could with the harness belt. It was doing a really good job at holding me in place, and I hoped that harness trumped brace position.

Dylan never took his hands off the plane, fighting to save us until the very end. Panic almost had me passing out when we first clipped the top of the trees, and everything after that was a blur of screaming and pain and fear. We crashed for what felt like forever, thrown around like clothes in a washing machine on the fastest cycle.

Eventually I stopped screaming because my breath was completely knocked out of me, and everything went fuzzy when my head slammed hard against my chair.

Chapter 12

Darkness must have stolen me for some time, until I eventually woke to frantic hands running over me. With a groan, I tried to wave them away, only to have shooting pains in my arms, tearing more cries from my mouth. They were weaker this time, and for a moment, I forgot what had happened.

Until… "Butterfly, don't make me strip you down again and check for injuries. You need to open those gorgeous blue eyes and tell me where you're hurt."

Whether it was the unexpected of Beck giving me a compliment or whether it was the sudden realization that I'd just been in a plane crash, I gasped and forced my eyes open.

Beck was crouched before me, holding me up from where he'd clearly undone my seatbelt.

"We're alive?" I whispered, almost unable to believe it.

Beck shrugged. "Most of us."

I gasped again. "Dylan? Jasper and Evan?"

"Dylan is fine, that bastard is too tough to die."

Apparently so was Beck. Outside of what looked like a small cut on his temple, I couldn't see another injury on him.

"Jasper's hurt," he said, voice tight. "We don't know how badly right now; Dylan is patching him up."

"And Evan," I whispered. He'd said most of us were alive, which meant someone had to be dead.

"He's good," Beck replied, and my heart slowed down.

That only left one other than the pilot though. Looked like the flight attendant hadn't made it, and that had my stomach lurching as I tried to pull myself up. Beck stayed with me, his strong hands lifting me with ease.

My stomach screamed at me when I straightened, as did my broken arm, and the side of my head. "I think I'm okay," I whispered, testing out my limbs. "Just bruised."

Beck touched a finger to the side of my face, pulling it away to show me the fresh red of my blood. "Dylan will have to patch you up as well," he said abruptly. His face cold again. "Come on."

He turned and started to push his way through the door of the cockpit. I followed slowly, still working out my aching body. On the other side it was a mess: chairs had been ripped out on impact as the cabin was torn up, and there was shit everywhere. I understood why Jasper had been injured; his chair was basically ripped in half, that side having taken most of the impact.

Beck was standing over his friends … his brothers.

"How bad is it?" I heard him ask Dylan.

He got a grim stare. "He has broken ribs, a large gash on his thigh, and any number of internal injuries I can't assess with the equipment I have."

Jasper let out a weak laugh, and I choked in some air at the relief he was at least conscious. "I'm fine, assholes. You know nothing gets me down. Besides, Dylan has stitched my thigh, taped my ribs, and acted like a pretentious dick. He's practically a doctor."

He coughed, and it sounded raspier than I would have liked.

Hobbling forward, I peered around Beck, and met Jasper's stare. "Spare, you made it," he said, sounding almost cheerful. "I was afraid you'd die on us. Then what would Deboise do … they'd be fresh out of heirs."

I wanted to kick him in the balls, but the dude already looked like he's been kicked by a bull, so I settled for smiling sweetly. "Maybe it'll be Eddy joining me in the old-white-man club instead, you know, if you don't make it."

Dylan's lips twitched, and he looked up from where he was fussing with Jasper's leg. Our gazes met, and some of my ire died off at the worry I saw there. Shivering, I rubbed at my arms, wondering why it was so freezing in here. Evan popped his head in from somewhere near the back of the plane then, snow coating his hair. Where the hell had we landed?

Evan hurried along to us, his walk an uneven gate like he'd been hurt in the crash as well, but was managing. "The forest is huge," he said, talking to his friends. "I went pretty far and didn't see any signs of civilized life. Anyone work out where we are?"

"Canada," Dylan and Beck said at the same time.

"It's the only trajectory that makes sense," Dylan continued. "The pilot deliberately took us off course. This crash … and location was planned."

Beck swore, and when he spun around and I saw his face for the first time,

I shrank back. Holy scary motherfucker. I waited for him to bowl me over as he set off in my direction again, but he didn't. His hands were firm as he lifted me out of the way before he strode past and disappeared back into the cockpit. He emerged a few minutes later with two guns clutched in his hands.

I gulped. "Uh, what do you need those for?"

"This was a setup, and they're going to make sure they finish the job."

"Who? Who is going to make sure they finish the job? What job?"

I looked frantically between the four of them, trying to calm my breathing, but with each of their expressions growing grimmer, my panic only increased. "Riley," Dylan barked, clearly seeing hysterical when it was about to happen. "You need to pull yourself together. We're not the spoiled rich boys they seem to be expecting. We're not going to let you get hurt, and we will kill every single person who comes after us."

"That's a promise," Beck added, checking both guns and sliding them into the waistband of his jeans.

For some reason, their calm confidence helped me calm down as well, and I decided that I wouldn't be a liability to them. Well, not too much of one. Starting at the front of the cabin, I searched through each of the drawers and overhead compartments I could find, gathering together anything I thought was important. I ended up with three fluffy blankets, two medical kits, a few snacks and bottles of water, and a shit-ton of cash. The cash was probably useless, but maybe we could bribe someone in the forest to help us.

There were two duffle bags which held guys' clothing. Dumping the contents, I found a couple of thick jackets, and a few more snacks, and even more cash. "Riley, we're moving out now," Dylan said from where they were still crouched around Jasper. "We can't stay here … they'll be coming for us, and we're not in a good spot to defend ourselves."

With a nod, I slung both bags over my shoulder and hurried back to them.

"I gathered some supplies," I said softly, my gaze going straight to a very pale Jasper. He didn't look good.

"Any painkillers?" he half joked.

Holding a finger up, I dropped one of the bags and riffled through it. "You're in luck," I said, pulling out a small bottle, plus the packet Beck had given me earlier.

Dylan smiled at me, and I was pretty sure that was the first time I'd seen a true smile from him. "Thanks, Riley," he said softly, taking the bottle from me.

He gave Jasper three of the small white pills and some water.

"Put the jacket on," Evan said, noticing a thick black hood sticking out of the bag. "That's mine. I'll be fine."

He was wearing a thick long sleeved shirt, unlike me, so I decided to take him up on that offer. "Thanks," I said, slipping my arms in the sleeves before hauling the bags up again.

Beck leaned down then and helped Dylan lift Jasper to his feet. Gone was his cocky arrogance, and in its place was a pale, sweaty guy. "I think you should leave me here," he bit out. "I'm a fucking liability to you like this."

"No!" Beck snapped the word with force. "No man left behind. We'll be fine."

Jasper shook his head at his friend but didn't argue. These four were close, and I was starting to really see it, especially in moments where their guard was down. Like right now. There was a true bond there, one which told me they would have each other's backs no matter what.

"Did you try and call for help?" I had no idea where my phone was, but surely someone had theirs on them.

"No service," Dylan said. "We'll have to move toward a more populated area."

"Is there anything around here like that?"

I had no idea about Canada except that they had a lot of uninhabited land.

"Guess we're about to find out," Jasper joked and then groaned as he leaned on Evan. They moved toward the back of the damaged plane. Beck gestured for me to go ahead of him, and I stepped in behind Dylan. On the way, both of them found two more fancy leather bags, and pulled out more warm clothing and other essentials. Apparently I was the only dickhead on this flight without clothes or a coat.

The heavy weight of the duffle bags was lifted from me, and I turned to find Beck with them both over his shoulder. "If you fall behind, you get left behind," he warned me. "Keep up."

I bristled, but I was too fucking tired and scared to fight with him, so I just turned around and moved closer to Dylan. I cursed myself for choosing last night of all nights to get wasted. Had I known today I would be in a plane crash followed by a trek through a snowy forest, I'd probably have rethought the alcohol.

The plane had landed in a densely packed part of the forest, and it was clear where we'd smashed through the trees and undergrowth. I almost couldn't believe how much damage there was in the foliage around us, and it made me shudder all over again thinking about the fact that all of us could be dead right now. If Dylan didn't know how to fly a plane—and how the fuck did he know that?—then we'd no doubt have landed nose first. Dead. Like my parents.

The pain was more of a dull slash this time, probably because I had some other things to worry about. Nothing like a fight for survival to take your mind off your dead parents.

No one spoke as we moved, and despite Beck's warning, the pace wasn't that fast. Jasper was just too injured to move quickly. Dylan stepped up at one point, and slipped Jasper's other arm over his shoulders. It didn't work that well because he was so tall, but they sort of figured out a rhythm.

We moved faster then, and I tried to ignore the pains in my body that pushed me to stop and rest. I was taking Beck's warning seriously, fall behind and get left behind. And since they'd basically said we were being hunted by whomever had orchestrated the crash, I really didn't want to find myself out here alone.

After what felt like days of walking, but was probably only three hours, Dylan held up a hand. "Jasper has to rest," he said.

Evan and Dylan slowly lowered their friend to the ground. He groaned and dropped his head back against the tree he was leaning on. "More painkillers," he said, sounding a little breathless.

Beck found them quickly, along with the water I'd packed, and handed them to Jasper. "Anyone else?" he asked.

I was half tempted, because my body was starting to hurt like a bitch, but Jasper needed them more. Touching my fingers to my temple, I remembered that Dylan was supposed to patch me up. "Let me look at that," Beck said, catching me by surprise. I hadn't even seen him move back my way, dude was stealthy. "I don't have Dylan's training, but I do okay."

Dylan snorted from nearby, and I realized he had been sweeping the ground and setting up a makeshift shelter. "Don't listen to Beck. He has as much, if not more survival skills than me. Our parents raised us to survive."

"What do you mean?" I asked, looking between them while Beck lifted a white medical kit out, opening it and using something from inside to dab at my face.

I flinched when something cold and stingy hit my cut before gritting my teeth and staying still to let him finish. "Delta started out with five friends who were survivalists. They had a vision for a better life, and they worked together to make it happen. Ever since then, it's been part of the successors' training. Survival skills, martial arts, weapons training. We aren't just rich, we're ruthless and deadly," Beck said slowly, tracing his fingers across my face, and sending a shock of energy through my body as I clenched my thighs to ease the ache he seemed to create in me with nothing more than a touch. "Dylan and I have been dropped in the middle of nowhere before, with nothing more than a knife and a bottle of water."

"How old were you?" I asked, trying to wrap my head around what he was saying. I mean, these were the kids of billionaires. Not Bear fucking Grylls. How the hell did they survive?

"The first time we were eight," Dylan said, still building his shelter. "The last time … fourteen."

Beck released my face then, and I managed to start breathing normally again. His touch was lethal.

"Eight?" I couldn't really wrap my mind around what they were saying. Their world was so foreign to the one I grew up in.

Beck froze then, and for a moment, I wondered if I'd said something to piss him off again, but when his head snapped to the side of the forest where we were, I knew it was nothing to do with me.

"Incoming," he said softly.

"Incoming?" I repeated, feeling like the dumbest person in the forest.

"What's incoming?"

"Shhh." Evan appeared beside me and covered my mouth with his hand. His attention wasn't on me, though. It was glued to Beck, who had his head cocked slightly to the side like a wolf listening for hunters... or prey.

Beck's sharp gaze jerked to his friends and he gave them a few short hand gestures before they all burst into action. Dylan hoisted Jasper over his shoulder and quickly deposited the injured boy into the makeshift shelter while Evan disappeared into the trees like a fucking shadow. In less than a second, he was just *gone*. Beck hesitated only a moment longer, staring at me with a totally unreadable expression. When he turned to leave, someone burst out of the trees and without a second thought, Beck raised one of his guns and shot the newcomer clean in the head. The gunshot cracked through the still night air, echoing and reverberating off the hills like some sort of fucked up foreshadowing.

I gasped, then clapped a hand over my own mouth as Beck fired another shot into the person's body. He didn't even glance back as he made like Evan and faded into the shadows.

Survivalists. I was starting to get a much clearer picture now. They literally would do anything to survive, and they had the training to back it up.

Sweet baby Jesus.

"Get in the shelter," Dylan whispered in my ear, and I flinched at his nearness. *How did he just move so silently?* "Jasper is defenseless; I need you to stay with him."

Something told me that was a pretty way of Dylan telling me to get the fuck out of the way, but I wasn't arguing. Not by a long shot. Doing as I was told, I scurried into the shelter and watched with wide eyes as Dylan covered the whole thing with fallen leaves and tree branches. Just before he blocked our entrance, he crouched down and pulled a deadly looking knife from his boot.

"Here, take this," he said softly, handing me the weapon. "From now on, you're never to be unarmed. Understood?"

Stunned, and clutching the heavy knife in shaking hands, I just nodded.

"Stay silent, no matter what." Dylan gave me a long, serious look, then shot a pointed one at Jasper. My injured companion gave a small, pain filled salute, but Dylan was already covering our opening and disappearing into the shadows.

For a long, tense moment, Jasper and I sat there. Neither of us spoke, and I barely breathed. The knife was still clutched between the cold and trembling fingers on my unbroken hand, and Jasper had sweat beading on his forehead.

"Jasper," I started to whisper, placing my knife down in the frosted dirt, but he gave me a sharp head shake. It was clear he was telling me to shut up, but there was a pool of blood growing on the snow dusted ground beneath him. "Jasper," I tried again, this time placing my lips against his ear and just barely breathing the words. "You're bleeding. Lie down."

I pulled back just enough to catch his brow rise in surprise. He did what I said, which worried me even more. It took longer than I'd have liked, but eventually he shifted until he was flat on his back—and all without making noise. It was fucking impressive.

The extent of my medical knowledge came from watching *Grey's Anatomy* a million years ago, but I wasn't going to tell him that. Instead, I carefully peeled his sweater up and found a deep puncture wound just above his hip. Like something had stabbed him and then been pulled free.

The blood was...

I faltered, swallowing past a lump in my throat and taking a few deep breaths. Jasper tried to pull his top back down—silently telling me not to worry—but I was determined. Dylan had asked me to take care of Jasper, and what had Beck said? No man left behind?

Gritting my teeth against the cold, I whipped my coat off, then pulled my tank top over my head. Jasper's lips parted in confused shock, but I ignored him as I put my jacket back on and zipped it up over my bra. The bulky outer garment would have been no use as a compress—any idiot could have known that—but my soft cotton tank would work. Folding it up into a pad, I gently placed it over Jasper's wound.

I hesitated—again—but then pressed down firmly. He needed pressure on the wound or he'd bleed to death out here in the middle of butt-fuck-nowhere. Jasper grimaced, but gave me a small nod and placed his hand over mine. Encouraging me.

A sound nearby made me jump, and I whipped my head around to see what it was. Dylan had left small cracks of visibility between tree branches, and I used my free hand to reach up with the intention of widening one gap.

Jasper's hand tightened on mine, and he shook his head. Clearly, he meant, don't be an idiot, there's someone out there and we're supposed to be hiding. But I knew how to be careful.

Ignoring him, I slowly wiggled my finger into a gap and slid the leaves and twigs aside. Just the tiniest bit. Just enough that I could peer out and see what was happening.

Nothing. The clearing we'd been in was totally empty.

Or was it? Another few muffled sounds came from the tree line and a black clad body dropped into the clearing. Whoever it was, they were too small to be one of my guys—uh, *the* guys—and his head was at a sickening angle. I was assuming it was a man. Somehow it helped me disassociate from the memory of my mother dying of a broken neck.

I held my breath to keep from gasping as Dylan stepped into my line of sight, engaged in a fist fight with another black clad individual. Except, this was no high school brawl of flying hands and wild swings. This was like an art-form. Poetry in motion. I'd never realized how beautiful martial arts could be until I saw Dylan calmly and efficiently dispatch of his attacker. It was horrifying, fearsome, and a little bit awe-inspiring. When they'd said they were trained, they hadn't exaggerated.

With his opponent dead at his feet, dumped on top of the other body, Dylan flicked a quick glance over at where Jasper and I hid. Could he see me? Did he know I'd just watched that? That I'd just seen him *kill* two people with his bare hands?

Before my panic could grip its claws into me any deeper, Dylan disappeared back into the forest once more.

In his absence, I let out the breath I'd been holding in one, long, shaking exhale.

Jasper's fingers tightened on my wrist again, and I knew he was asking if I was okay. Don't ask me how I knew, but somehow I was learning to read these crazy, broken boys.

"I'm fine," I breathed, so quiet I could barely hear myself. Chewing my lip, I turned my attention back to Jasper's wound and made sure I hadn't released pressure while I'd been distracted.

We stayed like that for ages. Neither one of us spoke, we barely even moved. My leg fell asleep under me, but I was too damn scared to move. What if I made some noise and one of those scary dudes in black was out there?

Jasper kept his hand on my wrist the whole time, but his grip got noticeably weaker, until it seemed like he was about to pass out. It was only that, that made me move.

"Jasper," I whispered, patting him gently on the cheek. His eyes were slits, barely open, and all I could see was the whites. "Jasper, come on," I urged him. "Don't pass out. Everyone knows you need to stay awake in crap like this." I patted him harder, just short of a slap, and it seemed to rouse him slightly.

"Why though?" he murmured back, his voice thick and sleepy. "Why can't I rest? Sleep is restorative." His eyelids fluttered again, and his head rolled away from my hand.

Panic gripped me, and I smacked him a bit harder.

"Hey," I snapped in a harsh whisper. "Do *not* go to sleep, Jasper Eugene. That's an order."

I had no idea if that would work, but Eddy seemed to think he would respond to the use of his middle name, and I was all out of tricks.

If it did or not, I didn't get a chance to find out.

Someone burst through the flimsy covering of our shelter and grabbed me in a tight hold. I screamed, kicking and thrashing as my attacker pulled me out of the shelter and into the clearing.

"A girl?" The black clad man grunted. "No one mentioned a girl. Whatever, job's a job." He hauled me off my feet then threw me down on the ground and kicked me in the ribs. I howled in pain, curling over the injured site. This dude wasn't fucking around, though. He dropped down on top of me, his gloved hands curling around my throat.

"Sorry kid," my would-be-murderer muttered. "Lost my gun back in the woods there."

The absurdity of how damn *casual* he sounded blew my freaking mind. All while his grip tightened and cut off my air supply. My fingers clawed at his hands, and my whole body thrashed, but I was no match for this dude. He was a professional fucking killer, and I was a damn *high school student*.

My vision darkened at the edges, my lungs screamed, and a high pitched noise began ringing in my ears. This was it. I'd survived a car crash, and a plane crash, but my number was up.

I started to give up, my head dropping to the side as the fight left my limbs. But something caught my eye.

Jasper had dragged himself half way out of the shelter and waved Dylan's knife at me, getting my attention before he slid it across the frost covered grass. His aim was true, and it skidded right into my side, beside my attacker's knee. Thankfully near my hand that wasn't broken.

The black clad dude didn't even notice it, he was so invested in strangling me. Scrabbling around with my hand, I snatched it up and stabbed it into the closest part of him I could reach—his side.

He let out a hoarse shout, but his hands loosened on my neck and I sucked in greedy gasps of air, filling my burning lungs and coughing as I choked on saliva and air.

"You little bitch!" my attempted murderer screamed, like *I* was in the wrong here?

My limbs were weak and heavy, but my desire to live was strong. I yanked the knife out again with considerable effort—having maintained my grip on the handle—then used it to slash at the man. He stumbled backward, dodging my wild swings, and I used the distance to scramble to my feet. Now

JAYMIN EVE + TATE JAMES

we were some feet from each other, with nothing between us except a bloody hunting knife clenched in my trembling fist.

"S-stay b-back," I stuttered, my throat aching as I waved the blade in what I hoped was a menacing way. Cold and shock and pain, combined with oxygen deprivation, had made my whole face numb, and the words were hard to force out. Not to mention he'd been trying his best to crush my throat.

The man must have noticed my severe lack of experience with my weapon, because his guarded posture relaxed. Noticeably so. Fear for my life gripped me, and I stepped forward and slashed my blade at him again. Maybe I didn't know how to use it, but how hard was it to stab someone? Besides, sometimes the unpredictable was harder to fight. Right?

My attacker must have agreed with my mental ramble, because he took a couple of quick steps backward, avoiding my blade and holding his hands up.

"Now, that's not necessary, little girl," he mocked me. "Put the knife down and I promise I'll make it a quick death, yeah?"

I slashed at him again, forcing him back another two steps. "How does *get fucked* sound?" I spat back at him. I didn't need to follow through with anything more threatening. He'd done exactly what I'd been aiming for.

His retreat away from my blade had carried him directly in front of Jasper's hiding place.

As quick as a striking cobra, Jasper slashed the man's Achilles, then dragged a second blade across my attacker's throat as he dropped to the earth.

The whole thing was over in less than three seconds.

For at least double that, I just stood there frozen in horror as blood spread in a rapid pool around the black clad man's body. It was so... thick. So dark. So fucking *final*.

Bile burned a path up my throat, and I dropped to my knees, coughing up the meager contents of my stomach into a bush.

We weren't safe yet, though, so as soon as I was sure I had nothing left to throw up I wiped my mouth on the back of my hand and dragged my shock shaken ass back to Jasper.

"What now?" I asked him in a stricken hoarse whisper. I couldn't seem to peel my eyes from the dead man. Not even when Jasper tried to get to his feet and collapsed again with a hiss of pain.

"Riles, I need you to pull it together," he muttered, grimacing as he clutched a hand to his side. My tank top was still acting as a compress, but it looked heavy and wet with blood. "We need to get out of here. Hide until we're clear."

I nodded, but barely felt the motion. My head was so numb it was like I'd become a bobble head. "Hide. Right. Where? How?"

Having a task, a purpose, it helped me get a grip. Jasper was hurt and he was relying on me for help. We were sitting ducks, and he was dead right that we needed to move.

"Just help me up," he suggested. "Probably help me walk too. We don't need to go far, we just need to not be *here*."

My head bobbled again, and I crawled over to him. He draped his free arm over my shoulder and leaned heavily into me as we stood.

Fuck me, he was in a seriously bad way.

Without wasting breath on pointless words, I let him direct me. All that mattered, was making it out of these woods alive. I wasn't qualified to make that happen on my own, so I needed to place my faith fully in my companions—rich, pretentious assholes or not.

Chapter 13

To my intense relief, we didn't need to wait long before the others found us again. We'd been in our new hiding place—a fallen, hollowed out tree trunk—for only a short time before Evan's grinning face appeared in the opening, scaring the living shit out of me.

"Sorry, Spare," he teased. "Didn't mean to frighten you." The way he said it implied that I was only scared because I was a pathetic little girl, and my blood boiled with fury.

"Don't be a dick, Evan," Jasper replied for me then coughed a wet sound. "Get me out of here, I need stitches."

Shoving Evan aside, I scrambled out of the tree trunk to make room for Jasper to get out. A hand appeared in front of my face, and I took it before even noticing who it was attached to.

"Thanks," I murmured to Beck after he pulled me to my feet. He didn't immediately release my hand, and I frowned. "What?"

My voice was still hoarse, my throat and side ached, and I was in no position to deal with Beck right now. He scowled down at me, doing his infuriating well-placed-shadow thing that only seemed to deepen his frown. "Are you okay, Butterfly?" His eyes trailed all over me—checking for injuries? I'd zipped my borrowed coat right up to the chin and pulled the hood up, so he wouldn't be able to see the bruising that was sure to be showing on my throat. Neither could he see the horrible stabbing pain in my ribs, so I just gave him a tight smile and nod.

"Yep, totally fine," I lied, wishing I could talk without rasping. Tugging my hand out of his grip, I took a couple of steps away and wrapped my arms around myself, watching as Dylan peeled my soaked tank top from Jasper's wound and inspected the bloody hole.

"Riley," Beck snapped, jerking my attention back to him. He stared at me with an intensity that made me shiver and tighten my arms around myself.

"I'm fine," I repeated, dodging his stare and taking another step away from him.

He continued staring, but it was Evan—of all people—who nailed why I acted so cagey.

"She's in shock, Beck. Leave her be."

The gorgeous, scary bastard nodded slowly. How had it *not* occurred to him I might be in shock? We'd just been in a plane crash, he'd *shot* someone, Dylan had killed two men with his bare hands, I'd almost died, I'd stabbed someone, then Jasper had—

My stomach roiled again and I hurried a few yards away to retch into the bushes again. I don't think I would ever forget the sound of Jasper's knife cutting through my attacker's throat. That wet, gurgling, tearing sound...

Gentle hands gathered my hair up and held it back from my face while I heaved what seemed to be pure stomach acid. I didn't even remember where my hair-tie had gone, but I was grateful nonetheless.

"You throw up a lot," Beck murmured when I was done. He was sitting in the dirt beside me, his hand rubbing soothing circles on my back while I shivered and sobbed. Vomiting always made me cry. Or maybe that was a result of all the killing I'd just seen?

"Shut up," I whispered back. It was half demand, half plea. I knew he was teasing, but it just wasn't the time.

"What happened to your throat, Riley?"

I shook my head, not wanting to relive my almost-death. Beck, for once, took my feelings into consideration and didn't push me. We didn't speak for a while. I just sat there with my head on my knees, and Beck continued rubbing my back. I was sick and twisted, the worst kind of broken, but fuck if I never wanted him to stop.

Finally Dylan announced he was done. Where he had found a needle and thread to sew up Jasper's wound, I had no idea. But Jasper was looking vaguely better, probably thanks to the painkillers Evan had given him.

"Come on," Beck said softly, standing up and holding out his hand to me again. "We need to get away from this area."

I took his hand, letting him pull me to my feet, and didn't protest when he started walking without releasing me. "Do you think there are more of them?" I asked, eyeing every shadow with fear and suspicion. "What will happen to all the bodies?"

I didn't want the guys to end up in jail for defending us, but they had killed a lot of people here today.

"No, we got them all," he replied with total confidence. "And either they'll be cleaned up by the ones who sent them, or the wolves will get them..."

My step faltered, and it was only Beck's grip on my hand that kept me from falling. "Wolves?" I squeaked. As if everything wasn't bad enough, now we had *wolves* to deal with?

"It's not as bad as it seems," Dylan offered, falling into step beside me. "They're much more likely to take an easy meal than one that fights back." To Beck, he nodded ahead of us. "There's no town within sight, but if we continue uphill we can probably get enough cell reception to raise an S.O.S. signal."

I shook my head in confusion, even though he wasn't speaking to me. "How do you know that? Maybe there's a town right over that hill." I pointed at the steep incline ahead of us and grasped at hope.

"Nope," Dylan disagreed. "I just climbed a tree to check."

I blinked at him. "You climbed a tree. Of course you did." I dropped the subject and rubbed my eyes with my free hand. My whole body hurt, the burning in my throat felt like it was getting worse, my head was pounding and I was so cold my skin hurt. If Dylan said there was no town nearby, I was just going to believe him.

"Guys," Evan called out. "We need to make camp soon. Jasper can't go much farther."

He'd been helping Jasper walk but now seemed to be pretty much carrying his friend's unconscious form. Dylan and Beck exchanged a long look, then Beck nodded.

"We'll make camp here. Dylan can continue on until he gets service for a distress call." Beck's orders were final, and no one questioned him. Not even me, for once.

Extracting my hand from his tight grip, I went to help Evan with Jasper. I wasn't as strong as the boys, but I wasn't useless. So many near death experiences in quick succession were reinforcing my desire to live, and I knew that meant I needed to be *useful*. These boys had no room in their world for dead weight.

"I'm fine, Riley," Jasper mumbled in a sleepy, pain-addled voice as I propped my shoulder under his other arm and took some weight from Evan. "Don't worry about me, you've been through enough."

"What does he mean by that?" Evan asked, keeping his voice pitched low and quiet while I helped him prop Jasper against a tree. Beck was some distance away, looking like he was building a fire, but I still glanced nervously over at him before replying.

"Doesn't matter," I whispered, deciding to evade rather than outright lie. "We're all still alive, right?" I met Evan's gaze over Jasper's head.

"For now," Evan muttered. "If you're hurt, you need to tell Beck. We don't keep secrets from each other. Not when it concerns our well-being."

I gave a bitter, raspy laugh. "All Catherine has done since the day I arrived here is keep secrets."

Evan shook his head, like I was misunderstanding him. "Not Delta, Riley. Us. The heirs."

It was the first time he'd called me anything other than "spare" and it was enough to shut me up. The four of them had an intense bond, but it was only in that moment that I recognized it as something totally independent of Militant Delta Finances.

A soul deep shudder chased through me as I glanced over at Beck. His broad back was to us as he crouched over his pile of tinder, and I wondered for the thousandth time what the fuck I'd gotten myself into. These four were closer than blood, but they were killers. Brutal, cold blooded killers. The world they ran in was dark, so dark that this wasn't even their first plane crash. So, when faced with the prospect of being *one of them*, why wasn't I running for the hills? Why did a thrill of excitement chase through me and warm my ice cold veins?

Jasper groaned in pain then, breaking the weird trance that I'd fallen into.

"I'm fine," I insisted again, trying my best to talk clearly through the pain in my throat. Whilst evading Evan's knowing stare. Dylan reappeared from wherever he'd gone and tossed a bag each to Evan and me. I hadn't even noticed that they'd collected up the supplies from our previous camp, until now. In my defense, there was a lot going on in my head.

"Hop up, Riley," Dylan told me, nudging my knee with his hand. "Evan, let's put Jasper beside the fire, he needs warmth."

I stood aside, feeling a bit like a spare wheel while they got Jasper situated and comfortable near the fire Beck had managed to get going.

"Butterfly," Beck said softly, holding out a hand to me. Again. Was this some sort of weird symbolism? "Come here." He held a warm coat in his hand, and when I moved closer to him, he gently unzipped the one I was wearing. "You have blood all over this one," he explained as he pushed it open then paused. Numbness was overtaking my brain, and it took me way too long to understand his sharp intake of breath, rumbling chest, and intense perusal.

"Oh." I looked down at my black bra. "I used my shirt for Jasper's... cut thing." I waved a hand, failing to find the right word for his injury. I was done pretending to be a doctor for one lifetime. But it wasn't my bra—or the breasts within it—that held Beck's stare. His thumb trailed over the rapidly darkening patch on my ribs where I'd caught a boot from my attacker.

"What the fuck is this?" Beck demanded in a low, deadly voice. His fingers then trailed up over my skin, sending a fiery path along my body before he brushed across my neck. "And this?"

I just shrugged, pulling my blood stained coat the rest of the way off and exchanging it for the clean one Beck held. "One of those... people... found me and Jasper," I murmured, keeping my gaze down to avoid Beck's. My fingers fumbled with the thick buttons of the coat, too cold to function properly. I just knew I needed to cover those injuries, because Beck didn't appear to be doing anything except silently losing his shit.

"Dylan," he said, that word a snap of sound.

In a flash, the deadly second to Beck was at our side. "Check her ribs," Beck bit out, his eyes a gray so dark it was almost black. "And her throat. Some fucker tried to choke her."

Dylan shot me softer eyes than I'd seen from him before. "Jasper told me you saved him," he said as he pushed my coat open and gently stroked his fingers across my side.

I snorted before tiredly dropping my head back, clanking it against the tree trunk behind me. "Jasper saved me. That … assassin or whatever was strangling me, and he dragged himself out to shoot your blade my way."

Soft fingers brushed across my throat then, and since Dylan was still prodding my side, I knew it was Beck. Touching the marks blooming on my fair skin. I didn't open my eyes, somehow content in this moment to have two of the deadliest guys I'd ever met in my life, touching me. Protecting me.

"I think your ribs are just bruised," Dylan said, breaking me from my stupor.

"Let me know though if the pain gets worse, or if you have any trouble breathing."

He moved on to my neck then, and this time I flinched as he pressed near the center.

"Your throat is bruised as well. But since you're still managing to talk, somewhat, I think you'll be fine."

I nodded, finally opening my eyes. Beck allowed me to zip the new jacket up, and after that I moved closer to the fire. Dylan took off, heading to put out our distress call, and Beck went out to scout the area and make sure we were definitely alone. Creeping closer, I grabbed one of the blankets and draped it over Jasper. I pressed my hand to his head, worried by the slightly flushed look of his skin. "His vitals are steady," Evan said from his perch nearby. "As long as Dylan can get the call out, we'll be out of here by morning, and Jasper will have the best medical care in the country."

I snorted. "Which country, Canada or America?"

It truly hit me then that this was my first time out of America. Shit, I didn't even have a passport.

Evan and I remained close to Jasper, both of us checking on him. I forced some water into him at one point, and he didn't even curse at me. Beck reappeared, scaring the ever living fuck out of me, because he made like zero noise. Despite the fact he was tall and built like a high level athlete.

Whatever those survival skills were, they'd definitely excelled.

For four dudes who had done nothing but torment and scare me in the short time I'd known them, I felt awfully safe right now, especially as Beck settled in on the other side of me, his heat seeping into the colder parts of my body.

"Still clear?" Evan asked, and Beck nodded.

"Nothing is trailing us, we took out the entire team."

Swallowing roughly, wishing my throat wasn't burning like a bitch, I had to ask. "Who tried to kill us?"

Beck met my gaze, and for a moment I thought he was going to tell me it wasn't my business.

"Huntley Incorporated."

I blinked, wondering why that name sounded vaguely familiar.

"They started in oil," Evan supplied from the other side of Jasper. "Not that long ago, which is why they're 'new money.' Those fuckers are quick to throw their green and power around, but they lack the foresight to think long term. They've decided now they want to own it all, control the world, and they're not taking it well that we still manage to come out on top."

What was this fucking world? They were supposed to be civilized people, and they sabotaged planes and sent out teams of hired killers?

"They tried to kill us?" I all but screeched. Or I would have screeched had I been capable of that sound right now. "A little step up from buying shares out from under you to take over your companies."

Beck shook his head, drawing my attention to him. "You don't understand, we've all moved past the point of shares and hostile takeovers ... now it's about control. Control of the world. Of wars. Of resources. At the moment Delta has more, and Huntley wants it. They also know we have a strong set of rules which govern us. Company shares can only be passed to heirs ... the inheritors. If there are no heirs ... you have a weakness that can be manipulated."

"Not to mention we're the first inheritors, since our great-great-grandfathers, to have a bond stronger than simply being part of Delta," Evan added. "We're loyal. We're even more highly trained than our fathers, and we can't be bought or manipulated. They're afraid when we rise up and take control of our companies, we will decimate them."

Beck's chest rumbled, and I shivered as he pressed closer to me. "We need to figure out what our retaliation is going to be."

"How can you be sure it was them, though?" I asked, wondering if they might be overlooking another enemy. "I know this Huntley is the competition, but surely you have other enemies to worry about?"

Beck and Evan exchanged a glance, and I reached out to check Jasper's pulse and temperature again, adjusting the blanket that had fallen down.

"No one else has the resources to get to our people," Beck finally said, answering my question. "That pilot, he'd been with us for a long time."

My hands trembled as I recalled his drawn face, the tears in his eyes as he lifted the gun. "He said he had to protect his family," I whispered, my own eyes burning as those dark memories tried to edge further into my head.

A thought hit me then. "Why don't you guys have bodyguards? I mean, Huntley sent hired killers after us, and clearly after the pilot, so why are you always…"

Alone. They handled everything themselves, and considering they were rich and powerful, clearly had dangerous enemies—I already knew of more than one attempt on their lives—but there was never any sign of bodyguards.

Jasper chuckled then, and I was relieved to see him open his eyes a touch. "Our parents tried to keep a team around us," he rasped. "But we ditched them so often, they eventually gave up."

"We don't need any others," Beck said without emotion. "We have no weaknesses in our group, the four of us are a team. We trust no one else. We have each other's back, and no team of bodyguards could do what we can."

That was for sure, I'd never seen anybody move the way they did when those hired killers showed up. That was cool, capable, kill-without-remorse sort of shit that I expected from hardened soldiers. Not dudes only a year or two older than me.

"What about my brother?" I asked, reaching for the water again, and making Jasper drink a few more sips. My throat seized then and I took a few drinks myself before continuing, "Was he ... part of your inner circle?"

A somber air fell across them, and I got the sense that they didn't like to talk about Oscar. "He was," Beck said simply, and that was the most I got out of them on that subject.

Evan, who was eyeing me with more interest and warmth than I'd ever seen from him, leaned forward. "What's your story, Riley? How did Catherine pull you back into this world?"

Darkness pressed on the edge of my mind then, because my story was filled with enough pain to drag me into a place I wasn't sure I could go. Not yet.

Only, it felt like we were on a precipice right now, the five of us. A shared pain existed between us, and it was bonding us. It felt like maybe they had stopped thinking of me as a spare heir, at least for the moment. Maybe if I shared my past, they would accept I wasn't just a pawn for Catherine, sent here to sabotage them, just like Huntley was trying to do.

"My parents died," I whispered those words, letting them fly into the world. Wishing the pain, that was so much worse than any bruised throat and ribs, would fly with them too.

Before I could say another word, Beck jumped to his feet, gun in his hand as his eyes did that predator thing again. I tensed, half pulling myself into a crouch position in preparation for an attack. A sigh left me a moment later when Beck relaxed, somehow knowing it was Dylan, even though the other boy didn't appear in the clearing for three more minutes.

Jasper's hand on my wrist had me shooting him a worried glance. "Are you okay?" I whispered, my eyes running across his wane features.

He shot me a grin, and it looked genuine. Not like those smiles he gave all the chicks he fucked—those were fake, designed to make them feel comfortable, to think that he liked them as much as they liked him. Not many saw the real Jasper, but I felt like in this moment, I might be.

"You positioned yourself in front of me," he said, amusement in his weak voice. "I knew you wanted me."

I snorted, gently shaking his hand off. "In your fucking dreams. I just don't feel like dealing with your friends if you die. All that crying..."

I sensed it wasn't in my best interest to let them know about my newfound softer emotions regarding the four of them. To let them know that I was starting to ... like them. That *I* would cry if Jasper died.

And Beck ... I refused to even think about him not being in the world.

Dylan settled in near Beck. "Did you get a call out?" Beck asked him.

Dylan nodded. "Yep. Reinforcements are on the way. They tracked our location." He checked that fancy watch with a thick black dial that he always wore. "They'll be here at 0300 hours. Which gives us six more hours to camp out and wait."

I shivered because night had well and truly fallen now, only the light of the fire illuminating the area, and the moment that sun disappeared, the temperature had dropped. Could we survive another six hours in this sort of environment?

JAYMIN EVE + TATE JAMES

Beck reached out and draped an arm around me, pulling me closer into his side. We were both padded up in thick jackets, but somehow I could still feel his warmth right along the parts of my body he pressed. As he tightened his hold, I flinched at the sharp pain in my ribs, but I didn't complain. I was finally warm.

"Body heat is essential to survival," Dylan said softly, his eyes glittering in the half light as he watched Beck and me. "I'm going to make another shelter, and then the five of us … we're going to get very well acquainted."

A blush stole across my cheeks at the mental images of his words. All four of the Delta heirs were hot as fuck, and deadly in a confident way that definitely did it for me. But I was a one dude sort of girl, unfortunately, because that might have been fun.

We did have six hours to kill.

Dylan and Beck managed to pull the shelter together in about thirty minutes. It was close to the fire, but not so close that we had to worry about burning to death in our sleep. One of the blankets was laid down over the half-frozen ground.

"I'll take first shift," Evan said, as he helped his friends lift Jasper inside. "Keep an eye on things."

He situated himself on a log just near the opening of the shelter, and I handed him one of the remaining two blankets.

"I'll take over in two hours," Beck said. "Dylan will be the final shift."

Once that was agreed, we all ate a quick snack—some soft cheese, because it was all my throat could handle, and a quarter of a bottle of water for me. Then I crawled in next to Jasper. The first thing I did was feel for his temperature and pulse. His skin was clammy again, and his pulse felt fast, but he was still alive, so I just brushed a hand over his head to wipe the moisture from his skin before settling in next to him. My head was cushioned on my arm, and I immediately had to change positions then because my bruised ribs screamed at me, but on the other side, my broken arm screamed at me, and I was left flopping around like a fish.

Beck let out a rough sound before he reached out and pulled me into his chest. It almost felt like all my breath was knocked out of me, as I sprawled across his firm body, everything inside of me relaxing. "Do you want some painkillers?" he asked, his voice rough.

Knowing that would probably require him to leave, and I was far too comfortable for that to happen, I shook my head. "I'm okay … but can you sleep while I'm sprawled across you like this?" I asked, my eyes already starting to close.

I might have been more comfortable, but Beck needed sleep too.

His chest shook as he laughed in a low, sexy way. "I think I can manage."

Dylan crawled in then, I felt him slide in on the other side of Beck, the four of us—mainly due to their stupid, sexy ass muscles—were a pretty tight fit. But it was warm, and cozy, and for a moment I forgot the traumatic events of the day.

For a moment, I just drifted in a sea of comfort.

"You didn't finish telling us about your parents," Jasper said, startling me out of my half asleep state.

His voice sounded pained, and I worried immediately that he was getting worse. It felt like he wanted me to talk him to sleep—or distract him—and even though I really didn't want to speak around my aching throat any longer, I would talk for the rest of the night if it kept Jasper alive.

"It was a car accident," I said softly, knowing even Evan in the doorway could hear. "We skidded on black ice, which I know is a common occurrence, but my dad ... he grew up driving those roads. He'd never had an accident before. I still don't understand how it could have happened."

For some reason, in this moment, my deepest pain was spilling from me, and considering my company, I should have been more careful with the weapons I was giving them, but I just couldn't bring myself to care. "My mom died on impact, broken neck..." A memory teased me then ... a random thought that there was important information about that night that I had forgotten. "My dad died at the scene from massive internal injuries."

"But you survived, somehow?" Dylan asked, propping himself up so I could see him on the other side of Beck.

I shrugged tiredly. "I was the only one with a seatbelt on, both of theirs malfunctioned the day before from the cold. Our car was a piece of shit."

The silence after that was heavy, and I realized that it sounded stupid, said out loud, to think that my parents' seat belts would malfunction when mine didn't. I mean, we'd all assumed that at the time, but ... could it really have happened? Like a terrible twist of fate on the very night that we would roll from slipping on black ice. When my dad had never slipped on black ice before.

"Could it have been Huntley?" I whispered, because I knew they were all thinking the same thing as me. "Trying to take me out before I had the protection of Delta?"

Beck's arms tightened around me, and I buried my head in the padding of his jacket, trying to calm myself. "When was the accident?" he asked slowly.

I blinked. "Just over three weeks ago."

Three weeks. Was it possible that it had only been twenty-one days since

I lost everything in my world. A hot burning in my eyes and throat sent tears cascading from me before I could stop them. A sob escaped, and even though I sucked it back, there was no way any of them could have missed it.

"It'll get easier," Beck said, his hand on the back of my neck, tangling in my mess of hair. "The pain won't ever go away, but you'll breathe easier one day."

Another sob rocked through me, and I wondered who Beck had lost.

They let me have my moment, and no one asked anymore questions about my parents, no doubt worried I'd cry all over them again. Eventually I drifted to sleep, an uneasy sleep filled with shadows and death, the color red coating everything in sight.

A sliver of clarity returned when Beck shifted out from under me, placing me directly on Dylan's chest. "Keep your hands on her back, and only her back," I heard him rumble, and then he was gone.

Dylan had a nice chest, but it wasn't as comfortable, and I barely slept for the two hours that Beck kept watch.

When he crawled back into the shelter, bringing with him an icy cold, I settled into my new favorite place in the world. Beck's chest. His arms wrapped me up, and he pulled me higher—gently enough that it didn't hurt my ribs too much. I ended up with my head cradled in the crook of his neck while his hand rubbed gently up and down my back.

"All clear out there?" I whispered sleepily.

"Go to sleep, Butterfly," he murmured back, and in seconds his breathing evened out and he was asleep.

Evan, who had moved over to make room for the changeover of guard, shot me a knowing look before he dropped back down. "Beck definitely likes to keep things interesting," he said, turning his back on us.

"What do you mean?" I whispered, my words brushing across the skin on Beck's throat, because I was basically pressing my lips to it.

"Never seen Beck sleep with a girl … fuck them, yes, but the day he trusted a chick to stay longer than that…"

He trailed off, and I tried not to let any sort of hope blossom inside of me. These were not normal circumstances, and sure, Beck could have left me on the hard ground, my ribs screaming in pain—he had that option, but still … not normal. I couldn't count anything that happened here as what would be back in the real world.

That would only lead to him ripping my heart from my chest and destroying whatever crumbs remained.

Chapter 14

Beck was gone when I woke, my head and side now cradled in one of the extra blankets. It was still dark, but the light of the fire remained strong. Rolling over, I realized it was just Jasper in the shelter with me. With practiced hands, I reached out and felt his pulse, letting the rhythmic thrum calm the panic I experienced at waking and not knowing if he'd still be alive.

"Thank fuck," I whispered before shivering in the freezing early morning air. Dylan had not been kidding about body heat, it had made a world of difference. Especially since they'd made sure I was always in the center, protected.

A girl could get used to that.

Evan poked his head in then, and I reached up to try and smooth the absolute mess I knew my curls were in. "Lost cause, Spare," he said, his eyes laughing as he watched my failed attempts at getting my hair flat. "You're going to need four tons of conditioner and some pruning shears."

I flipped him off before wrinkling my nose. I wanted to be angry that he'd called me spare again, but this time when he said it, it was almost like … a pet name.

"You're probably right," I said with a sigh. "Where are the others?"

He shifted positions so he could get his hands under Jasper. "On their way back with the medical team. Our ride is here."

Helping best I could, we got Jasper out and waited just near the fire. Someone had kept it going through the night, which was good because it was still dark and freezing, and I felt like a damned zombie. My ribs hurt. My face hurt. My throat hurt when I breathed. My arm hurt, and my broken arm really fucking hurt.

But we had made it. I was alive, and help had arrived…

"Are we going to have to fly again?" I whispered, and Evan flashed me a perfect white-toothed smile.

"Don't stress, Riley. What are the odds of two plane crashes in the same twenty-four hour period?"

Apparently pretty high when you were the target of rich bastards who were trying to take you down.

Before I could let the fear consume me, because it seemed I was now going to have PTSD when it came to flying, there was a scuffling sound through the trees ahead, and then there were people everywhere. Medics rushed straight for Jasper, relieving Evan of the weight, gently strapping him onto a gurney style device, with handles on all four corners so they could carry him out. Before they moved him though, blood and something in a clear bag was hooked up, and I could have cried as they rushed off, taking Jasper away from us.

"Come on," Evan said. He quickly used dirt to smother the fire then took my hand in his. "They're waiting for us."

There was a short climb up a hill to reach a small clearing where two helicopters were waiting. Jasper and his medic board was being slid into one, and I wasn't at all surprised to see Dylan head in after him. They'd never leave their friend alone while he was unconscious and vulnerable.

"I'm going with them," Evan said. "Beck has you."

I noticed Beck then, standing in the shadows of the second metal beast. He was having a serious looking conversation with a man dressed in a black suit. Beck's gaze was on me though, and I tried not to think about last night … sleeping on him … trusting him.

No doubt he'd go back to king of the assholes today, so I had to get my game face on.

I moved closer and surprisingly he met me halfway. "Ready to go home?" he asked, expression unreadable.

I nodded. "Yeah, so ready. Oh wait … I don't have a fucking home."

The thought of a hot shower and proper food was definitely enticing, but knowing it would come at the cost of spending one more night under Catherine Deboise's roof. Fuck that.

Beck's eyes narrowed. "Keep playing the game, Butterfly. Oscar is the result when you try and get out."

"Who killed him?" I asked, sick of not having answers.

Beck grew tenser, more shadows lining his eyes. "I don't know, but I'm going to find out."

No idea why, but I believed him, and it was a relief to know he hadn't killed my brother.

When we settled back into the second helicopter, a medic approached me, kneeling down. He looked to be in his late twenties, with dark hair that curled almost to the collar of his white uniform. "I'm here to assess your injuries, Ms. Deboise," he said, reaching for me.

Beck, who was on my right side, made a low rumbling sound and the medic froze, his eyes darting between me and the scary dude. "I-I," he stuttered, fear apparent in the way he pulled back and swallowed hard. "Does she have any injuries?" and just like that, I'd been relegated to nothing more than property.

"Sitting right here," I said with a snarl. "And yes, she does have injuries."

Beck's smile was slow and not particularly nice. "She'll be fine. We have doctors at home that I trust."

The medic scurried away then like his ass was on fire, and I glared at Beck. "What the hell was that about? You don't want me to get medical help? Why work so hard to keep me alive if you're ready to let me die now?"

He smirked at me. "Butterfly, anyone who can bitch me out with this sort of aggression, is far from death." He paused, and something darker washed his face into that shadowy place he lived in at times. "I don't know this team of medics. If I don't know them, I don't trust them."

"But Jasper…" I started.

"I have no choice … he's in a bad way. Which is why Dylan and Evan are there. Both of them will watch out for him."

Shaking my head, I settled back into my seat, fatigue and pain rendering me silent. I was confused. It almost sounded like Beck cared enough about me to want to make sure that none of these medics were under Huntley control. Was this just because I was one of the successors to a seat in Delta's company?

I mean, after a trusted pilot shot himself and tried to kill them, it was pretty obvious why they had trust issues. Maybe I should do the same…

"Can I trust Eddy?" I whispered, scared that the only real friend I'd made in years, outside of Dante, might be fake.

Beck didn't turn to me, he just continued staring out into the main body of the helicopter, keeping an eye on those around us. "Trust her with limits," he said. "She's not one of us, but she's as close as you'll get to a friend in this fucked up world. It's smart to always remember, Butterfly … money corrupts everything."

I cleared my throat, my pulse skyrocketing as the helicopter blades picked up speed, and the giant metal beast started to move. Without thought, I reached out, gripping Beck's hand.

"Nervous flyer," the female medic on the other side of me said, her voice muffled by the noise of the helicopter.

Swinging my head around, I leveled her with my "what the fuck" face. I'd just survived a plane crash...

She must have realized what a stupid statement that had been, giving me an apologetic look, but it was too loud in here now for conversation. Beck freed my hand from where it was wrapped around his, and I almost got my feelings hurt, until he slipped some headphones on me. The sort with a tiny speaker.

By this time we were in the air, my fear had eased, so I simply clasped my hands together, jumping when Beck's voice echoed in my headphones.

"These are programmed so no one else can hear us," he said, his voice a rasp of darkness and danger. A rasp my body responded to with almost embarrassing intensity.

"So … Delta … are you guys into bad stuff as well as the legit business practices?"

I had no idea why I asked that, but ever since the plane crash, I'd felt like I was missing something big about my *family company*.

Beck's gaze finally met mine. "Delta controls sixty-five percent of the money in the world. We see all. We control all. We are all. I'll let you figure out if that could all be legit on your own."

They were egomaniacs. *We see all … we control all…* Come on.

Maybe that was the part all of them struggled with the most; there was only so much they truly could control. I wondered if that was what had happened to Oscar … Beck had implied it was because he wanted to get out. Maybe my brother hadn't quite been able to stomach this life. One of cruelty and sabotage. Of trusting no one and always looking over your shoulder. Why then, was I not wanting to run screaming from them? Why did I fit when my brother, who had been born and raised into this life, could not handle the world of being a Delta successor?

What the fuck was wrong with me?

The helicopter ride smoothed out after the takeoff, and except for my initial panic, it did not cause me undue stress. Beck and I talked on and off for the rest of the flight. I learned he owned ten cars, six of which were dream cars of mine, and four others that I wouldn't turn my nose up at. He had no siblings, but there had been a catch in his voice when he said that … which made me wonder if he was telling me everything.

"So your favorite food is steak and lobster?" I said, laughing a little. How typical of a rich boy.

He shot me a smirk. "Too predictable for you? Sounds better than grilled cheese and tomato soup."

I swung my elbow into him, gently because it would have hurt me more than him. "My mom made it for me whenever I was sick, or sad, or tired," I explained. "It was her way of cheering me up, and it … it's more than just sandwich and soup." I stopped talking because I was too choked up to say more. To know I'd never see her carrying a special tray with my favorites was beyond devastating.

Beck was quiet, and some of that restless energy he always carried with him seemed to ease. "I'm sorry about your parents, Butterfly."

My hands clenched, and I squeezed my eyes shut, willing myself not to break down. "I'm sorry too," I managed to say. "It's just so fucking hard. Some days I'm not sure I can keep living with the pain of losing them."

He turned to me then, and it was such a sudden movement I almost fell off my seat. Until then, we'd remained side by side, his long body pressed along mine, but we hadn't looked at each other. Instead staring across the helicopter.

Now, locked in the intensity of his gaze, I almost couldn't breathe.

"You will keep living," he told me seriously, bite in his words. "Because they would want you to. Because the pain will get easier. And because we … Dylan, Evan, Jasper, and me … we fucking need you to keep living. We're five again."

I blinked at him, my eyes no doubt wide and glassy from the tears I was trying desperately not to shed. "I promise," I whispered. "I won't ever give up. If that dude trying to kill me in the forest taught me anything, it's that I'm not ready to die."

Beck relaxed back in his seat, and we resumed our previous positions. We did not talk for the rest of the flight, but his long body remained pressed to my side, and I couldn't stop the deep seated ache in my center to reach out and touch more of him. He'd let his guard down with me today, and it showed me the sort of man Beck could be. And I wanted to see more of it.

When we landed, I was helped out by a medic, and then I just kind of hovered around awkwardly while more doctors and security personnel crowded us. No one touched Beck, and he strode away toward Jasper when the second chopper landed.

"Ms. Deboise, we're going to need you to come with us," a female medic said. She wore a different uniform to the ones who had rescued us from the mountain. It was a dark olive green, with a red cross stitched over the front pocket.

"Uh," I hesitated, unsure if this was one we trusted or not. I mean they … they trusted.

She must have thought I was confused or something, because a firm hand landed on my shoulder, and she started trying to direct me toward a nearby ambulance. My feet dragged as I wondered if I should be fighting her or not.

I mean, Beck had just taken off without a backward glance at me, so most probably he was over giving a shit, and was back to being an asshole. I might as well get checked and get some of the good pain killers.

When she got me to a nearby ambulance, another medic helped me inside, and forced me to lie back on one of the long beds. "A doctor will be right by," the medic said, her expression cool. "Just relax. We'll get you patched up and good as new."

She didn't like me, that much was obvious, and I wondered why that was—I'd never seen her before in my life. There wasn't time to figure it out before she spun and disappeared out the double doors of the large white vehicle.

Before I could panic about being alone and vulnerable in the back of an ambulance, a familiar face entered my line of sight. Jasper, looking a lot worse for wear, was gently helped into the other bed next to me.

"Still alive, I see," I joked, so happy to see him.

He shot me a slow grin, and it would have looked normal if not for the macabre splash of blood across his platinum blond hair, face and neck. I'd probably not noticed in the forest, because we were in some hectic situations, but Jasper was a mess. Lifting my hands, I squinted at the blood staining them as well.

We were all messes.

Unfamiliar faces followed Jasper's, and then the ambulance started up. Just before the doors were about to close, a hand slipped between them, pulling them open again.

"We're full..." a doctor began until she saw Dylan's face. Her words trailed off, and she got out of the way to allow him to sit right at the head of our beds.

Whatever nerves had been assaulting me died off then, and I felt safe. Which was ironic considering Dylan could kill everyone in this vehicle with his bare hands without breaking a sweat.

"You okay, Riles?"

They'd taken to calling me Riles like Dante, and it made my heart ache a little.

"Just ready for some decent pain killers," I said seriously.

"Fuck yes," Jasper said weakly. "Give me all the shit. I want to be seeing fairies or someone is getting fired."

I chuckled then. "I don't think they work for you, Jasper. Their bosses might have something to say about you randomly firing their staff."

Jasper's laugh was weak and raspy. "So much to learn, new girl."

Dylan was watching me with an odd expression, and I lifted an eyebrow. "What?"

"Your innocence is refreshing," he said simply. "The dynamics are changing … you're changing them."

I still didn't really understand what he meant by that, but I could tell he meant it as a good thing, so I smiled in return.

Our conversation was interrupted by a doctor reaching over to hook Jasper up to another IV. His first one was pretty much sucked dry up on the pole above his head. The woman turned to me then. "I'm going to start you on some fluids," she said quickly. "All of you are dehydrated, and it will help us assess your injuries better."

I nodded, not in any sort of mood to argue. Even though I really hated needles. Dylan helped me into a half sitting position, lifting me just enough that I could get the thick jacket off. Underneath was the bra and nothing else still, but I didn't care. Caring required energy I just didn't have.

Dylan's gentle fingers pressed against my ribs again. I flinched, but the pain was dull, only really kicking in when I breathed too deeply.

"You're going to be fine," he told me, his dark eyes softer than I was sure I'd ever seen them. Everything about Dylan was dark, including his gorgeous skin, but his ultra-scary vibe, the one that had sent spikes of panic through my blood the first time I saw him, was no longer there. Not for me. Something had shifted for us in the forest; I trusted them now, which was possibly the stupidest thing I'd ever done in my life, but it didn't make it any less true.

"I'd like to assess her before making that call, Mr. Grant," the medic tentatively interrupted. Clearly she wasn't over the whole fear thing he inspired.

Dylan leveled her with a steady, calculating stare, and she swallowed hard, her eyes wide and pupils dilated. I could almost smell her fear. When he finally nodded, she swallowed again, her breathing audible even over the sound of the engine. Stepping closer, she quickly ran a hand along my side, pressing and probing, asking me what hurt. While she was evaluating me, another person hooked up my drip, and when that needle came into view, I focused on it.

"It'll only hurt for a moment," the second medic said. "I'm very good at my job."

Somehow I fucking doubted it. No one was good at needles, they always hurt far more than they should. Before I could refuse, a swab was wiped across my skin, and then the needle was coming for me. I flinched just before it made contact and the medic pulled back. "If you move, it'll be much worse."

I glared. "Right now I've got a woman feeling me up and another medic about to stab me. Let's just say I've been in more comfortable positions in my life."

"Always so difficult," Jasper rasped. "You're definitely the Deboise heir."

If I could have moved, I would have flipped him off.

Dylan reached out and took my hand, holding it in his firm grip. "I won't let anyone hurt you," he promised, and I let out a sigh before closing my eyes.

"Okay, just do it," I grit out.

Another brush of cool alcohol wipe across my skin, and then a short pause while the medic waved her hand to dry the alcohol before inserting a needle with the smallest prick of pain. I squeezed Dylan's hand so tightly I worried I might be cutting off circulation, but he never complained or tried to get free. Deciding it was easier to just keep my eyes closed until we got to the hospital, I tried not to think about Beck. From the moment Dylan climbed in with us, I knew Beck was going back to icing me out of his life. He'd sent his friend to keep an eye on us rather than doing it himself.

I'd be a liar if I didn't admit it cut me up inside to have Asshole Beck back.

But it was also good. I needed this lesson. To learn to protect myself, because if there was one thing I knew about the heirs of Delta, they now had the power to really hurt me. I couldn't let that happen. I had such little left in my life, if I lost one more thing...

I wasn't sure I'd survive.

Chapter 15

The doctors wanted to keep me in overnight, but I refused. Desperation to put some distance between the boys and myself pushed me to run, and to run fast. I had to get my emotions back under control. I also needed to have a conversation with Debitch, because there were things I needed to ask her. Important things. If she wanted to use me as her heir, then she would need to bring more to the party. For too long I'd let her hold all the cards, have all the power, but that shit was over today.

When I was dropped in front of the Deboise estate, the gates slid open, and I found a cart waiting for me. My ribs were aching again after all of the prodding and poking, so I gently eased myself onto the seat and hoped that the painkillers would kick in soon.

The trip back to the giant mansion was fast, and when I got off, Stewart was waiting in the front hall, his face creased in concern.

"Ms. Deboise ... Riley. I was so worried about you," he said as I limped inside. Reaching out I patted him on the arm.

"I'm fine, Stew, don't even worry about it. Riley Jameson is one tough cookie."

"It's Deboise." Her cold voice had Stewart jerking back from me, a mask falling over his face.

I smirked at Catherine as she slinked into the room, dressed like she was off to fucking fashion week—or an upscale funeral. Knee-length, perfectly tailored black dress, dark hair piled up on top of her head, makeup flawless and dark.

Bitch.

Meanwhile, I was over here looking like I'd just been in a plane crash and trekked through a forest filled with lunatic murderers.

"Black for mourning, *Mother?*" I said with as much sneer as I could manage. In this moment I wanted to rip her fucking head off and kick her lifeless body off a cliff.

She waved an elegant, red-nailed tipped hand at me. "Always so dramatic. You survived. You needed to toughen up, it's not easy being a Deboise, and this was a good introduction for you."

There was this ticking in my brain, like the anger was so huge now, that my head felt like it was about to explode.

"Why the fuck did you bring me into this world?" I seethed, taking a step closer to her. I had nothing on me but a borrowed shirt, ratty jeans, a new brace on my broken arm, and one small pill bottle of pain relief.

But Catherine still flinched back slightly, as if I was coming at her with a weapon.

She recovered quickly though. "I brought you into this world because

Deboise needs an heir to keep our vote in Delta. It's our most important rule. Blood is thicker than water. And thanks to you, I cannot have any more children, so you are it for us."

You're welcome, bitch.

"What if I don't want to be part of your billionaire club? What if I don't want to be one of the inheritors of a corrupt, evil, archaic company?"

Catherine laughed, an evil Disney villain kind of chuckle. "Dear child. Whatever made you think that you ever had a choice in this matter? You have no rights here. No choices. You belong to me."

I crossed my arms over my chest. "I won't do it. You can't make me."

Whatever sliver of unease she had shown before was gone now as she closed in, standing right before me. In her heels she was taller than me, but I was too angry to feel intimidated. "You have weaknesses, Riley," she whispered. "Do you want to lose Dante the way you lost your parents? Or … how about Eddy? I've heard you two are great friends now. Would be a shame if anything happened to either of them."

That. Fucking. Bitch.

She had me exactly where she wanted me.

A thought hit me so hard and fast that I actually gasped. "Did you kill my parents?"

Until I talked with the guys last night, I'd never thought the accident was anything other than an accident, but now…

Catherine chuckled again. "No, I can't claim credit for that. The storm timed itself perfectly, and I was able to maintain my seat at the table."

If she was lying, she was the best liar I'd ever seen. My limbs actually shook in that moment as I considered the possibility that my parent's death had been orchestrated by someone. Either Delta's goons, or Huntley's. Either a possibility.

"I don't believe you, bitch." I decided to shake her up.

Catherine turned and before I could react, smacked me hard across the face. Stewart, who must have been hiding in the wings, rushed out then and caught me. My injured side and arm screamed at me, because they'd both been jerked as I fell.

"Mistress, she was just in an airplane crash," he said softly. "You could really hurt her."

Not wanting her to turn her ire on the poor guy, I shook my head and straightened. Then I swung my broken arm, the one with the hard shell, and smashed it into the side of her head. I hadn't given myself a second to think about it, so it took both of us by surprise.

Catherine let out a low shriek, teetering on her heels for a moment before landing heavily against a nearby table with a large vase on it. The vase, which was tall and expensive looking, with dozens of colors woven through the glass, smashed to the ground. The sound echoed around the cavernous front entrance.

When Catherine finally regained her feet, her eyes were molten pools of blue fury, and she came at me with both arms extended. I prepared myself for her violence, but just before she reached me, a tall man rushed out from a side door and intercepted her.

It took me a minute to realize he was dressed as nicely as she was. Charcoal suit, custom fitted to his tall, well-built frame. Thick black hair with just a few touches of gray at the temples, and eyes that were a deep chocolate brown. I stumbled back as our gazes met, his over a struggling Catherine's shoulder, from where he'd spun her around to try and calm her down.

"Who are you?" I asked, breathing rapidly.

He didn't say anything at first, instead taking a moment to stare at me in what might have been an awkward way, but there was nothing sexual in that gaze. It was almost … sad.

Catherine had finally stopped fighting him, but I could see the way her back heaved as she breathed deeply, trying to get herself under control.

"You look just like him," the man said, his voice hoarse. "Like my son."

My breath caught in my chest, and I felt a sting of pain at those words. This was my birth-father, the elusive Richard. He'd stopped Catherine from attacking me.

After another few minutes, he released her, and she spun around to face me. A hand on her shoulder kept her from striding forward. "You're lucky I need you alive," she spat at me, her face awash in hatred.

I smiled sweetly. "That's right, bitch. You need me. And if you'd like me to continue to do your bidding like a good little heir, there's a few things I will require."

Richard waved a hand tiredly at me. "Whatever you want, you've got it. Just ask Stewart. I give him permission to purchase anything."

"No cars," Catherine spat out. "You can have anything but a car. Don't want to make it too easy for you to run."

More than likely she was aware of my love for racing, knew that it was the only way I could ease that painful tension which twisted my gut up and sent my pulse racing at times. We all knew I could steal a car if that was the only thing stopping me from running. Catherine just wanted to exercise whatever power she could.

My *parents* left soon after that and I stumbled up to my room, and into the longest hottest shower I'd ever taken. It felt like years later I pulled myself out, took the painkillers and, dressed only in a shirt and underwear bottoms, crawled into my bed. It was barely past midday, but the sheets and mattress had never felt so soft, and I figured I'd be out cold in seconds. Yet the moment I closed my eyes, all I could see was the plane falling from the sky. Feel the terror that gripped me when the pilot shot himself. Mental images from the past twenty-four hours filtered across my mind, one after another. Death. Blood. Fear. Pain. It intermingled until I felt like I was going to scream.

A knock at the door pulled me from my panic, and I called out "yes?"

Stewart walked in slowly, a tray of food in his hands. "I just wanted to check on you," he said softly. The tray went down on my bedside, and I tried to find my appetite. He pulled a phone from his pocket then and handed it to me. "Also, I figured you might need a new phone. I wasn't sure if yours was damaged in the flight."

I actually had no idea where the phone Dante had given me was. It could have ended up anywhere, but was probably still in the wreckage. "Mr. Deboise had me program his number in there for you." Stewart's eyes were glittering with something unspoken. "If any more … problems occur, he wants you to call immediately."

Ah hah. If Catherine Debitch lost her shit and tried to hit me again, more correctly. Thankfully this time she hadn't used her rings, so it'd just be one more bruise to add to my collection.

Couldn't say the same for her, because I'd hit her hard enough to break skin. I wasn't sure if I did or not, but part of me hoped she got more than just a bruise. Stewart left me, and as the door closed, the phone in my hand rang.

Glancing down, a familiar number flashed up on the screen. *How in the…* "Dante, how the hell did you get my number already?" I asked as a greeting.

"You're in so much fucking trouble Riley. Open your damn door so I can yell at you in person."

The line went dead then.

Pulling the phone from my ear, I blinked at it before pulling myself out of bed. Crossing to the bedroom door, I slowly opened it up, not at all expecting Dante to be waiting on the other side.

Only he was, his face dark with anger as he pushed his way in the room.

"Eddy," I squeaked, seeing her there as well. She must have been hidden behind Dante.

I didn't ask how they had gotten into the house; when Dante wanted something, nothing stopped him. I was just glad that the parental assholes had left already so we could have this fight in peace.

Turning, I let out a long breath. "I'm sorry I worried you," I started, clearing my throat to try and ease the raspiness. Thankfully the painkillers had kicked in. "I promise, I didn't mean to be on a plane that was sabotaged and crashed into Canada. Like … that was not how I thought yesterday would go."

Dante appeared to be too furious to speak; his hands were clenching and unclenching into fists. His shoulders looked extra broad in the leather jacket he wore, ripped up jeans and a Metallica shirt the only other clothes. Outside of his favorite boots.

A warm feeling settled into my chest as I stared at him. My best friend.

I got to see him again.

When he finally took a step forward, I held my breath, prepared for his explosion. I'd only been on the receiving end of Dante's temper a few times in my life, and while he was never physically violent with me, he certainly didn't hold back in the verbal ass-kicking.

When his arms wrapped around me and he hauled me into his body, I let out a low huff and groan. The hug was painful, but I would gladly take it to have this moment with Dante. For a second, when the plane was hurtling toward the ground, Dante's face had crossed my mind. Knowing I'd never see him again, it had hurt almost as badly as the crash did.

This was a precious moment.

When Dante finally let me go, he seemed marginally calmer. "Tell us everything," he said softly, holding my hand. He left an opening for Eddy to hurry forward and wrap her shaking arms around me. "I just came from seeing Jasper," she said in a choked voice. "He went in for surgery, but he's doing okay."

Surgery didn't sound good, but I was relieved that she seemed to think he was okay. He'd been rushed away at the hospital, and I hadn't seen him again.

The three of us sat on my bed, and I told them as much as I felt safe in saying. I didn't mention all of the murder that the boys did, because that was … that was something I would take to my grave. I would not be the reason they all ended up in prison while they'd been keeping us safe.

"The world of Delta is dangerous," Eddy whispered, her eyes darting around the room. "But there's no way out now, Riley."

Dante and I just stared at her. "Very comforting," I said with a laugh, because what the hell else could I do?

At least I wasn't in it alone. Beck might have disappeared the moment we returned, but Jasper and Dylan had acted the same. Like I was one of them.

That would have to be enough.

Shuffling across my huge bed a bit, I wrapped Eddy in a hug as tight as my damaged ribs would allow. "I'm sorry about Jasper, babe. He'll be okay though. He's a stubborn fucker."

Eddy gave me a watery smile, but I could see the fear in her eyes. "He told me you saved his life. I think he's a bit in love now."

I scoffed a laugh and bumped her with my shoulder. "Yeah right, pretty sure Jasper falls in love at least twice a week."

She grinned and waggled her eyebrows at me but didn't push the subject. Thank fuck. The idea of Jasper liking me as anything more than a good friend made me all kinds of tense and uncomfortable. Not that he wasn't gorgeous. He *was*. But Beck...

I let out a heavy sigh and flopped back on my pillow mountain. "So what do you want to do? I don't have a TV in here or anything."

Eddy laughed and shook her head. "Oh my god, you're so working class right now, Riles." She said it with a teasing grin, reaching over to the bedside table and pressing a button that I hadn't even *seen*, let alone associated with a TV.

From the bench at the foot of my massive bed, a huge flat-screen TV rose up like fucking magic.

"Get out," I muttered in awe. "To think I actually read my school books when I couldn't find that sucker last weekend."

Dante laughed at this and I whacked him in the stomach with the back of my hand. Then immediately regretted it, because it pulled my side and I cringed with pain.

For the rest of the afternoon, the three of us stayed snuggled up in my

JAYMIN EVE + TATE JAMES

bed, watching Disney movies and eating the popcorn that Stew delivered to us. Eventually, though, Stew came to tell us that it was my "curfew" and that Dante and Eddy needed to leave.

I wanted to argue, but exhaustion had been creeping over me like a black cloud, and I was already half asleep when my friends hugged me goodbye.

"Can I bring you some dinner, Miss Riley?" Stewart asked after my friends were gone.

I yawned heavily and tried to rub my eyes with the backs of my hands— only to scratch my face with that damn hard shelled wrist brace.

"Fuck," I groaned. "No, I think I just need to go to sleep. Thanks, Stew."

The old man gave me a small frown, but nodded and exited my room. "Call if you need anything, Miss. Oh, and I placed the codes to the house alarm, and the front gate on a note for you." He waved the yellow post-it note. "As per Mr. Deboise's orders."

That made me chuckle, because Richard Deboise was definitely doing everything he could to piss off Debitch, which made me like him. Just a little.

Shutting the door after Stew and turning the lights off, I dragged my feet back to the bed and fell in face first. My whole body hurt, but I wasn't due for another dose of painkillers for another two hours. I groaned into the plush bedding, then wrestled my way under the blankets as best I could without hurting myself further.

I'd been so sleepy while Dante and Eddy were here. My eyelids were like lead and my brain like a ball of cotton wool. Yet the second I actively tried to sleep ... I was wide awake.

"Come on, Riley," I whispered into the darkness of my room. "You need sleep. Just ... sleep."

Yanking a pillow over my face, I tried to block out the world. But within seconds, the overwhelming feeling of suffocating washed through me, and I sat bolt upright, throwing the pillow across the room.

My heart thundered and my breath came in harsh gasps.

Great. Amazing. Lingering psychological effects from being nearly killed. Just what I needed.

"Fuck," I groaned, pulling my knees up and dropping my head to my folded arms. I closed my eyes again—only for a second—but instantly I was hit by a barrage of images that I badly didn't want to relive. The black-masked man on top of me, his hands around my throat as he squeezed the life from my body. The blood spraying from his throat as Jasper dragged his blade across it. The view from the cockpit of the plane as we hurtled toward the ground.

"Shit, shit, shit." I was shaking now, my breath coming so fast I was sure I'd pass out soon. I needed to get out, get fresh air or space or *something*. I just…

Stumbling from my bed, I pulled on a fluffy bathrobe and a pair of black Uggs. It was the middle of the night, and I doubted anyone would see me or give a fuck what I was wearing, but I was amused to think a Deboise was heading out in her pajamas. Catherine would lose her mind.

Grabbing the yellow note with the codes, I made my way through the dark house. I disabled the alarm on the front door before I hobbled out to stand on the small front porch. Lifting my head I breathed in and out, enjoying a moment of silence and fresh air. My feet started to move while my hands reached for keys I didn't actually have on me. I was desperate to drive. To feel that power under my hands. To forget everything else in a rush of speed and horsepower.

Noticing the golf cart there, I decided that would have to do, and slowly pulled my broken body into the seat, starting her up and taking off. When I reached the front gate, I programmed in the code to leave, relieved that I finally had some freedom. My foot was flat to the floor, and I must have looked like a deranged lunatic as I flew along a small road that led between the five estates that all coexisted here. I wasn't sure why I headed in the direction of Beck's estate, but I found myself slowing down and letting the cart just coast when I reached the impressive gates that barred his even more impressive house from the world. Coming to a stop, I just sat there, staring up at the full moon. It was a cold night, my breath visible in the air as I breathed in and out deeply, trying to calm the fractured state of my mind.

"What are you doing here, Butterfly?"

His low voice wrapped around me, and since a part of me had been waiting for him, I didn't even jump. "How long until I can close my eyes and not see death?" I asked, not turning away from the moon.

He didn't answer for a long time, but he braced his hands against the roof of my cart and stared down at me. His shadowed form blocked out the moon, and I shifted my attention to his frown.

"I'll let you know when I manage it," he finally said, his voice soft. "In the meantime, you just grow ... accustomed to it. Numb."

"That sounds awful," I whispered, shuddering.

Beck frowned at me a moment longer, then nudged my shoulder. "Shift over."

"What? Why?" My fingers gripped the flimsy steering wheel tighter. "I'm not letting you drive my sweet ride."

Beck glared, and when he seemed to accept that I wasn't joking, let out a low grumble and stalked his sexy ass around to the passenger seat. A little clicker in his hand opened the obnoxious front gates and he indicated for me to drive in.

"Too lazy to walk?" I teased, turning my cart through his gates and beginning the *long* drive up to the house.

He gave me a long side eye. "More like I don't trust you cruising around the Delta compound in this thing." He tapped the plastic frame holding my roof up. "Knowing you, I'd find you crashed into a lake or something."

The dark look on his face reminded me that my brother had been found dead in a lake, but I ignored the shiver of fear and huffed at the implication I was a bad driver. You lose one race and your reputation was in the shit.

"Come on," Beck said when I pulled up outside his front doors. He didn't even wait to check if I was following, just strode up those steps like he was Zeus and this was his Mount Olympus.

Damn him for making me predictable, but curiosity had me in its tight grip, and I reluctantly followed him inside.

"Through here," he called out when I hesitated in the foyer, peering up at the massive crystal chandelier. Following his voice, I wandered through a fancy sitting room until I found him in a lounge area with an impressively stocked bar.

He was pouring two glasses of a deep amber liquor and as I stood there—awkward as fuck—he dropped a couple of ice cubes in each one then picked them up.

"Here." He held one out to me. "It'll help with the sleep thing."

Gingerly, I reached for the glass. I probably wasn't supposed to drink alcohol while on the painkillers from the hospital, but I was desperate.

Our fingers brushed as he handed it to me, and a deep shiver of desire shot through me. Something told me, I'd live to regret taking this drink with Beck. But at least I'd live. Not asking questions, I blocked my nose and took a huge swallow of the liquor.

At first, it just tasted sweet and smoky, and then it burned all the way down my throat and pooled like lava in my belly. Coughing, I blinked moisture from my eyes and peered into the glass. "Wow, uh, what is this?"

The corners of Beck's mouth picked up in a small smile, and he *sipped* his own. "Port Ellen, forty years old." He paused when I blinked stupidly at him. "Scotch," he explained in plain English. "Really rare, expensive scotch. Which is totally wasted on your unrefined taste buds, apparently." This last was muttered in a dry tone as he turned away from me. He took another sip of his fancy scotch as he messed with the sound system, flicking through tracks until he settled on one he liked. All the while, I scowled and simmered.

"Are you really so arrogant, Sebastian?" I demanded, my anger at his jab finally boiling over. "Is it really so revolting to you that I was raised in a two bedroom unit on a dodgy street in Jersey? That my best friend is in a gang, and I met my last boyfriend on community service?" Beck had tensed, I could see it in the lines of his back. He was wearing a black, short sleeve t-shirt like the cold held no power over him. He was in charge of his core temperature, not the weather.

"You should never have grown up like that," he bit back, and I got even more riled up.

"Why the fuck not? We might have been poor, but I've at least never been in *multiple* airplane crashes. Your fucking life is a joke."

I really pissed him off then, his eyes darkened as his full lips narrowed.

"Make no fucking mistake, Riley, you are one of us. This … life, is something that you're part of, and should always have been part of. Don't fool yourself into thinking that your trailer trash life was superior."

"There's something seriously wrong with you," I shouted back before coughing at the pain in my throat. Bruised vocal cords did not like shouting. Taking another sip of the watery remains in my glass, I finished. "Oscar is the one who was a Delta successor. A true heir. I'm Riley Jameson, not Deboise, and don't you ever forget it."

Beck dropped his empty glass. "Maybe you'd like to just be a Beckett fuck toy then? Since you don't seem to want to be part of Delta?"

The heavy crystal tumbler flew from my hand, hitting the wall beside Beck's head and exploding in a dramatic spray of glass.

"Fuck you, Sebastian Beckett," I hissed at him. "I wouldn't touch you with a ten foot pole. No pretty exterior is worth the rotten interior. Call me crazy, but I have standards."

I whirled on my heel, my dressing gown swirling like a cape, but Beck grabbed my upper arm in an iron grip before I made it even two steps out of the room. With a strong tug, he turned me back around to face him.

"You really think so, Butterfly?" he taunted. His hand still gripped my arm, holding me close enough that I needed to tip my head right back to glare at him. "You want to tell me you don't feel this magnetic pull between us? That sexual tension that just keeps fucking building every time we're near? That's all in my head, is it?"

My chest was heaving, my emotions in a messy, ugly tangle that I didn't have the energy or will to address. "M-must be," I retorted, my voice shaking with anger, pain and arousal. "Guess you secretly love slumming it with us poor girls."

He laughed then, a cold, dangerous sound. His eyes held me prisoner, burning with determination and I knew if I didn't get out of here soon ... he'd win. "You're right," he murmured, his gaze taking a cruel edge. "Even if you weren't one of us ... Delta, I wouldn't fuck you. Poor little orphan girls are too needy."

Rage burned in me, and my free hand cracked him clean across the face. It was a better slap than the clumsy hit I'd delivered to Catherine earlier. This one was crisp, snapping across his face with a satisfying sound but instantly, I regretted it.

What the *fuck* was I thinking? This was a man I'd literally seen *kill people* a mere twenty-four hours ago. He'd shot them as casually as turning on the TV, and here I was ... slapping him. Had I damaged my fucking brain in the plane crash?

"Beck..." Panic gripped me, and I froze, waiting to see what he'd do. My hand was tingling from the slap, and a red mark was coming up on his cheek already, but he just stared at the wall. His jaw was so tight as his cheek ticked, and his hand still gripped my upper arm like a manacle.

Licking my lips, fucking terrified, I tried again. "Beck, I—"

Whatever I was going to say, I cut off with a squeak of fright as his furious glare swung from the wall back to me. His other hand came up to the back of my head, his fingers tangling in my long hair and I braced myself for his retaliation. Beck seemed like the tit for tat sort of guy.

My whole body tensed, but the blow never came. Or rather, it did ... just not in the way I was expecting.

Tightening his grip on my hair, Beck tipped my head back and crushed his lips to mine in a bruising kiss. For a long moment, shock held me totally immobile and I did nothing to push him away. Instead, I just stood there and let him kiss me while my brain ran around and around in circles screaming *what the fuck is happening?*

When my body finally caught up with my brain, I braced my hands on his hard, muscled chest and shoved him back from me, glaring up at him in fury.

"What the *fuck* do you think you're doing?" I shouted, feeling a bit like a banshee.

Beck shook his head slowly, breathing deeply as his gaze remained glued to my lips. "I have no idea," he admitted. "This is insanity."

But sanity was overrated. Right?

Impulse overtook my better sense, and my fingers curled in his black t-shirt, dragging him back to me and returning his kiss with one of my own, just as rough, violent and demanding as his had been. Our lips parted and our teeth clashed. It wasn't pretty, but it was primal and needy and as hot as all fuck.

Beck's huge hands grabbed me by the ass while my arms wound around his neck, desperate to get closer to him. Apparently he was on the same page, hoisting me up and letting my legs wrap around his waist as he walked us out of the room. Where he was taking me, I didn't care. So long as he *took me*.

Ugh, that scotch was fuzzing my brain and making me cheesy even inside my head. Whatever, who wouldn't short circuit from kissing Sebastian Roman Beckett.

That thought sent my mind down a dark path, and I peeled my lips from his with conflicted reluctance.

"Nope," I announced, shaking my head. "Nope, I'm not doing this. Put me down."

Beck just chuckled, a shadowed noise that wasn't humor so much as disbelief. "Not a chance in hell, Butterfly."

"Sebastian," I snapped, struggling in his grip and getting nowhere. His hands still held me tight against him, and his steps didn't falter once as he carried me up the stairs and into the first bedroom on the right. "Put. Me. Down."

"Or what?" he taunted, kicking the door shut.

Glaring at him, my hands braced against his chest, and I desperately tried not to caress all those hard muscles. "Or I'll scream."

This seemed to bring a genuine—if not mocking—smile to his face. "Maybe I'd like to hear you scream." He said it in a way that left no room to mistake his meaning. He'd like to hear me scream ... *his name in ecstasy as I came all over his cock.* Yeah, I could fill in the gaps.

Even so, he did what I asked. Sort of.

He took a couple of long strides across the room, then released me rather abruptly, dropping me onto a ridiculously soft bed before standing over me.

"Do you really want to leave, Riley?" he asked in a more serious tone of voice. His eyes were dark, guarded, and his expression unreadable. "You can walk out of my house right now and we can pretend this never happened. Just go back to how things were. Is that what you want?"

Fuck no! My conscience was screaming, *howling* denials, but I just bit my lip.

Was that really what I wanted? To pretend this never happened and potentially miss my opportunity at ever exploring this fucked up chemistry between Beck and me?

"No." The word fell from my lips like a fucking prayer, reverent and loaded with conviction.

196

It was all he needed. His weight dropped down on me, his lips on mine and his hands on my body. My mind was made up, I was all in. Fuck it, even if things *did* go back to normal tomorrow, at least I wouldn't be wondering anymore.

Beck's hands shoved my robe off my arms, then stripped my t-shirt over my head in one quick move—barely even breaking our kiss for a moment. Damn he was good. Must have been all the practice...

Ugh, stop it. So he's a man-whore. Who gives a shit? It's not like you want to date him!

The thought of anyone—let alone me—actually dating Beck, being in a monogamous relationship with him ... it was hilarious, and I couldn't prevent the small laugh bubbling out of my throat.

"What?" he asked, pausing with his hand over my breast. My legs had somehow parted and he rested between them.

"Hmm?" I replied, blinking up through a haze of desire. My own hands had made it up under his black t-shirt, and I could see the edges of some ink designs. The possibility of exploring them further had me practically salivating.

He pulled back a bit further. "You just laughed. Why did you laugh?"

I frowned, then a slow smile spread over my face. I hadn't even been fully aware that I'd laughed aloud, and I surely couldn't explain my thoughts ... *ah fuck it.*

"I was just laughing at the idea of you with a girlfriend," I explained, then froze. "Not that I want to be her," I back peddled. "Oh my god, that sounded so creepy clinger. I was just laughing at the idea of you staying faithful to *any* girl." I shook my head, regretting ever opening my mouth. "Forget it, it was funnier in my head. Are we doing this or what?"

Not really waiting for him to change his mind, I tugged his shirt up and over his head to expose ... a body I definitely wasn't ready for. Holy. Fucking. Shit. Was it even *legal* to be that ripped and sexy *and* have such perfectly placed ink?

"I think I just came," I muttered, sweeping my eyes—and my hands—all over his body.

A sly grin crept over Beck's lips, and I knew my foot in mouth comments were forgotten ... for now. "Not yet, but you will," he promised, dipping his head back to my neck and kissing his way down to my chest. Deft fingers stripped me of the crop top I'd been sleeping in—big boob problems— tossing it aside and palming my breasts. Beck groaned, his breath warm against my exposed nipple. "You really do have great tits, Butterfly."

His compliment reminded me of his little calling card, after I'd vomited in his Bugatti then passed out, but this time I grinned at the memory instead of being mad.

"Thanks," I replied, hooking my legs around his waist and rolling us over—giving myself the dominant position. It wasn't even subtle, this was a clear battle for supremacy even if it was a fun one. "You're no slouch yourself. These tattoos are..." I trailed off with a noise of appreciation. My fingers traced the black ink designs before I gave over to my more primal instincts and ran my tongue across the geometric wolf on his chest. He indulged me for about half a minute, his hands busy with my naked breasts, before he turned the tables and flipped us again.

"I'm going to need you more naked than this," he muttered, dragging his fingers into the waistband of my soft pj bottoms. He took his time peeling them down my legs, torturing me with anticipation before tossing them across the room. A curse slipped from his sexy mouth as he ran his rough hands back up my body. "You have no idea how often the sight of you like this has crossed my mind since Friday night," he admitted, his voice gruff and needy. "You've been torturing me and you never even knew it."

His fingertips brushed a little too hard across the purple-black splotches on my ribs, and I hissed. My whole body tensed, but he just stroked the injured patch before doing the same to the hand prints around my throat.

"Beck," I breathed out on a frustrated sigh. "Are we fucking or what?"

His gentle hands stilled. He peered up at me, his eyes dark and glittering like the gateway to Hell or something. Instantly, I suspected that was the worst thing I could have said. Or was it the best? It was all a matter of perspective.

Either way, my question tore through his soft, gentle side like claws through tissue paper. His tongue ran across his lower lip, then without any warning his thumbs looped in the sides of my lace underwear and tore it clean off my body.

A shocked squeak escaped me as I gaped at him in equal parts fear and admiration. I'd read books where that happened but they were always some form of paranormal romance where the hero had extra powers. I had *no clue* it was possible in real life.

Beck took advantage of my open mouth, grabbing me by the back of the neck and claiming my lips in a rough, possessive kiss which left me panting and gagging for more.

The bruises around my throat ached where he held me, but it was just adding to the whole fucked up situation. Once again, the idea I needed therapy crossed my mind because *fuck me* if the pain of his hands on my bruises wasn't turning me on even harder.

"Beck..." I started to say, but my brain short circuited as his lips made their way down my body. He kissed lightly over my bruised throat and ribs, sucked at my nipples until I cried out, then dragged his tongue down my belly. His strong hands gripped my thighs, forcing them apart and I gave up even trying to reclaim dominance.

I was done. Done lying to myself that his alpha male bullshit didn't push all my buttons in the best possible way. If he wanted to go down on me as a sign he was in charge, who the fuck was I to complain?

Dropping back onto the bed, I twisted my fingers in the thick sheets as Beck's hot breath teased at my lady bits. He shifted his weight, freeing up one hand to use. He stroked his fingers across my flesh, playing with me before he followed with his tongue.

Hot spikes of sheer pleasure zapped through me as his mouth met my throbbing clit, and I moaned my encouragement. He knew what he was fucking doing, but there was no space in my brain for jealousy over his past lovers. It was just us now. Somehow, deep down, I knew this was different from his casual fucks. *We* were different.

"Fuck, Beck," I panted, my hands coming to his head and gripping on tight while he slid two fingers inside me. It was the perfect complement to what his tongue was doing to my clit and nerve endings all through me started exploding with sensation. My hips bucked. I couldn't work out if I was begging for more or begging him to stop, but who the fuck was I kidding? It didn't matter when Beck was in charge.

"Jesus fucking Christ," I breathed in a lusty whisper, my back arching as his fingers fucked me in time with his mouth. "Beck, you asshole, I'm going to come way too fast like this."

He didn't stop for a second—fucker—but I could feel his smug grin against my pussy as he ramped up the intensity until I was crying out in climax. My thighs tightened around his face, and I needed to force myself to release him as my body shuddered and spasmed through that first, explosive orgasm.

In my defense, it had been too damn long since I'd come with anything other than my rabbit.

"Who says you're only coming once tonight?" Beck seemed to fucking *purr* as he kissed my inner thigh then shifted off the bed. For a moment, he just stood there and stared down at me, and I had a fair idea of what he was seeing.

Long hair spread around me like I'd been in a hurricane, flushed cheeks, swollen lips, heavy lidded eyes. My chest was heaving, drawing attention to what Beck had dubbed "great tits." My legs were still spread apart, and I thanked all sorts of Gods that I didn't believe in, that I'd maintained my laser hair removal appointments in recent months. It had so been worth bussing tables at that shitty diner for a year to get the funds.

While he stared at me, I looked my fill of him. Without his shirt, and wearing only a pair of jeans, he looked like he'd walked straight off a Calvin Klein photoshoot. If Calvin was into the dark, dangerous, bad boy look. Actually, who fucking cared if Calvin liked it. Riley sure as shit did.

My tongue dragged across my lower lip as I watched his hands fall to his waistband, his fingers working his fly undone, and then the denim dropped to the ground. He still wore black boxer-briefs but they weren't leaving much to the imagination.

The awe must have been as plain as day on my face, because that asshole smirked and grasped his *impressive* length through the fabric.

"Birth control?" he asked me in such a casual tone I could have sworn he just asked if I preferred hard or soft cheese.

"Excuse me?" I spluttered.

His smirk spread wider. "Are you on birth control, Butterfly? Although given that response I think I can guess the answer."

Half pissed off at his cocky attitude and half shocked that he'd even thought to ask, I just shook my head. "No." I cleared my throat. "I broke up with my ex months ago and with everything since my parents..." I took a deep breath, swallowing past the painful words then just shook my head again. "Taking the pill just hasn't been on my radar."

Beck just nodded, like it really didn't bother him either way. He stepped over to his dresser and opened the top drawer, pulling out a handful of foil wrapped packets and tossing all but one of them onto the bedside table.

"Uh..." I eyed the extras with interest, then raised a brow at him. I was propped up on my elbows now, but still seriously in a bad position for sass. "Expecting company?" I asked with a small laugh. I'd been joking, but something triggered a dark, dirty part of my brain which I quickly stifled.

Beck took his time before answering. He held my gaze as he stripped off his boxer-briefs and rolled on the condom—almost like he was daring me to break eye contact and ogle his junk.

I mean, obviously the second he glanced away I took a long, *hard* look. It's what any female would do in my position.

The mattress dipped as he knelt on it, nudging my legs wider so that he could take the space between them. Space I was all too damn willing to relinquish to him—and his ogle-worthy erection.

Instead of just pouncing on me and jabbing around with his dick until he found the right hole—thanks Nathan for that experience—Beck took his damn time, kissing me like I was his queen, tangling his tongue with mine and imprinting the memory of his lips into my brain as sure as carving it in stone.

Right when I feared I'd come just from his damn kissing—I was starting to think his tongue was scary talented—his fingers ventured south of the border. Not that I needed any further prepping thanks to the mind-blowing orgasm he'd already delivered, but he still stroked his fingers in and out of me a few times before replacing them with the broad tip of his cock.

"Fuck yes," I groaned in encouragement, tilting my hips up and silently begging for more. He was teasing me, and he damn well knew it.

"I think I'd like to hear you beg, Butterfly," he murmured in that husky, seductive voice that should have been illegal. "I think I'd enjoy hearing you tell me what you want." Only his tip was inside me, which showed a level of self-restraint that was so typically Beck.

"Sebastian," I growled, turned right the fuck on and also stubborn as hell. "I'm not playing your bullshit games. I'm not going to lie here and beg you to fuck me. I won't ask you to sink the rest of that gorgeous cock inside me, to fuck me hard, fast and deep until I'm hoarse from screaming your name. I certainly won't ask you to flip me over and fuck me from behind while you pull my hair and whisper in my ear with that orgasmic voice of yours. I simply, *won't* do it." I grinned as I said this, watching his pupils dilate with a need equal only to my own. My words pushed him over the edge of control, and I knew we were done playing games.

Slowly, deliberately, he sank deeper inside me as he held my gaze prisoner with his hooded eyes. One hand cupped my cheek, and for a moment, I felt like I was seeing the real version of him. The one with hopes and dreams, with softness and light inside him. The one who desperately wanted—needed—

to be loved. But as soon as I saw it, it was gone.

He broke our intense stare down as he became fully sheathed within me and I groaned with satisfaction. Satisfaction and pure need.

"You know what to do," I teased, whispering in his ear as he paused with his forehead against my neck.

His head raised back up, and that vulnerable version of him was gone like it had never existed. Sebastian Roman Beckett, king of Ducis Academy, lead heir to a global corporation, and all round playboy asshole was back. And more than ready to deliver on what I'd *not* begged for.

By the time I screamed my way into my second orgasm, I was already questioning my own sanity. Not for the obvious—why the fuck I was screwing this dickhead who was making my life into an invisible prison—but for the fact that I was never going to get over this. How in the fuck was I going to be able to date "regular" guys after experiencing all that Beck had to offer?

Ugh. I was so screwed. Literally and figuratively.

Beck didn't even wait for me to finish riding out the aftershocks this time. Instead his strong hands grabbed me by the waist and flipped me over. His grip dragged my ass straight up in the air while I scrambled for balance, and he thrust straight back into my tight, spasming pussy.

"Fucking shit, Butterfly," he groaned, pausing for just a second and allowing me to find a comfortable way to balance without hurting my broken arm. "Every now and then," he murmured, so quietly I wondered if he was talking to himself, "I think Catherine brought you here to test me."

His hands gripped my hips so hard I knew I'd have even more bruises in the morning. I fucking loved it. I still rode the lingering shocks of my last orgasm, and he was already fucking me hard and fast, his skin slapping against me with a delicious smacking sound that I never wanted to forget while his breathing grew ragged.

Beck released one of my hips, reaching forward and gathering my long hair in his fist before yanking my head back to an angle that danced the line between pleasure and pain. *Exactly* where I loved it and exactly where my vanilla ex, Nathan, had been too scared to go.

"If you really are a test," Beck growled, his pace increasing in speed and force. "It's one I'll happily fail."

My center was already throbbing and clenching, warning me of a third impending climax—a serious record in my book and not something to scoff at—even as Beck released my hair and slipped his hand under me to toy with my clit.

This time when I came, my screams harmonized with Beck's panting groans as he joined me in sheer ecstasy.

My body must have been in shock or something, because as we both collapsed onto the bed in a boneless heap, I blacked out for a few seconds. Or maybe that was my brain short circuiting from the insanely good sex. Either way, I was fucking *wrecked*.

For an indefinite amount of time, we just lay there. Our naked, sweaty limbs entwined and our bodies heaving as we panted together. Eventually, though, I needed to wriggle out and run to the attached bathroom to pee. It was a girl thing, I was *so* sure.

As I returned to the bed, I eyed the pile of metallic wrapped packets on the bedside table, then noticed the sly, wolf-like grin on Beck's stupidly handsome face.

Fuck sleep. It was way overrated anyway.

Chapter 16

Sunlight warmed my face, rousing me from what had been a deep, dreamless sleep. For a split second, that moment before reality and dreamscape clash, I forgot the nightmare that was my life. I forgot that I'd lost my parents, and had found myself in a scary world that would probably be the death of me. For that moment, everything was okay, and I was a normal chick ready to take on the world.

Then reality smashed that moment to pieces.

Opening my eyes, I blinked up at the unfamiliar ceiling above me. Fuck. I was still at Beck's.

Barely daring to breathe, I slowly rolled to my side, and when I saw the bed was empty, I let out a low gasp of relief. What the hell was I thinking?

I just lost my mind whenever he was close by, and no matter how much of an asshole he was … how much he scared a part of me … a larger part was addicted to the rush in my blood when he was near.

And I had slept. For the first time since the crash, I'd closed my eyes and there hadn't been death.

It couldn't happen again though. Pulling myself from the bed, I glanced down at my nakedness before looking around to find my clothes. It took me ten minutes to track them down, and my panties were completely torn, so I just tucked them in the pocket of my robe.

Once I was dressed, I poked my head out the room and was relieved to find that there was no one in sight. I barely remembered the path we'd taken last night to reach that room—I was going to assume it was not Beck's actual bedroom because I remembered Evan saying he never let chicks sleep in his room.

I made it undetected to the front door, and was thankful that it was unlocked and had no alarm as I strode out and hurried to my golf cart. Firing it up, I tried not to think of myself as a coward, but as I took off I was almost certain I'd never slammed my foot quite so hard to the floor.

I'd fucked Sebastian Beckett. Like … I could number the amount of guys I'd slept with on one hand. Dante was an intimidating best friend, and I had standards. So this was not a normal thing for me.

This was a big fucking deal.

The gate to his compound was open as well, and I had a sneaking suspicion he'd left the pathway clear to make it obvious he wanted me out of his house. Damn him. I didn't care what he did at school today, I was not going to give him the satisfaction of knowing that last night meant anything to me at all.

It was just sex.

Fucking amazing, mind blowing, multiple orgasm sex.

Who needed that in their life?

My thighs clenched at the memories, and I mentally told them to stop it, because that was it. That was their only Beck experience.

When the Deboise estate came into view, I opened the gate and drove to the house. A few of the staff stared wide eyed when I rushed inside, hurrying as quick as my injured body would let me. Today there were less sharp pains in my side, but the dull ache felt like it might have settled in permanently.

In my room, I ditched my clothes and went straight for the shower. Stepping inside, the hot water sliced across my body, and I groaned at how good it felt. There were some new pains and a few bruises from last night. Running my hands across my hips, I could see marks from Beck's fingers gripping me. He had a way of holding just tight enough to hurt, but it was hurt in a good way. A way that made my body ache with need.

Stop it, Riley!

I had to stop thinking about him.

Focusing on not being late for school, I quickly washed my hair and then jumped out. The hair dryer took most of the moisture out of my long waves, and I ran some product through it to stop the frizz. Makeup next, and that took longer because my face was still a mass of bruises, along with some wicked dark rings under my eyes. I didn't actually get that much sleep last night, and the days before that had taken its toll.

By the time I was done though, I looked like my normal self, and I could have kissed my makeup for giving me that shield against the world.

I needed it today.

When my uniform was on, I noticed the phone Stewart had given me last night was flashing on the bed. I'd forgotten to take it with me, and no doubt Dante was pissed that once again, I hadn't answered his calls.

I was a shitty best friend these days, and thank fuck he was less so. He continued to commute between Jersey and here, always around when I needed him.

Swiping the screen I had five messages. Two were from Dante, checking in with me, and I quickly shot back a reply. One was from Eddy, checking if I needed a ride to school today. After confirming that with her, I focused on the other two.

Neither was a number I knew, but it was immediately obvious who the first one was from...

Unknown: Hey, Spare Heir. I won't be in school today, almost dying is a real bitch. But the boys will keep an eye on you. Don't fuck anyone I wouldn't.

Jasper.

With a laugh, I texted back. *Me: Dude, is there anyone you wouldn't fuck? You've given me free run of the school.*

After sending that I turned my attention to the other unknown text. *I'm going to put a butterfly permanently on your skin. Right on those dimples just above your ass.*

My body heated, like set me the fuck on fire and call it a day.

Beck.

Jesus.

He had spent a lot of time with his hands on my ass...

My phone vibrated, and I focused on the new text. *Jasper: Well, no guys or my sister, but the rest ... think of it as a free for all buffet. Just make sure you wait so I can watch.*

Me: You're sick, dude. Now fuck off and get better.

I ignored Beck's text, because I really didn't know what to say. Saving his number in my phone felt like a big deal. I could contact him now, whenever I wanted.

With that in mind, I changed his name to *drunk booty call*, and laughed as I turned around to finish getting ready. Ten minutes later I was dressed in my uniform, uncomfortable heels on, and bag slung gingerly over my shoulder. The golf cart took me to the front gate, and Eddy zoomed up a minute later.

She examined me closely as I slid inside, and the smile she shot my way was genuine.

"Girl, you look hot. I wouldn't even know you almost died two days ago."

I snorted out a laugh. "I still feel like I almost died two days ago."

Groaning, I leaned down to yank off the ridiculous heels and stuff my feet into the converse sneakers I'd smuggled out of the house with me. Given all I'd been through, anyone who wanted to reprimand my breech of dress code could kiss my ass.

Eddy waved a hand at me before she spun the wheel and took off. "How you look is all that matters." She paused for a brief moment, and I felt like I knew her well enough now, to know that something pretty big was on her mind.

"What is it?" I said with a sigh. "Spill it."

She shot me a look before a grin that was mostly grimace lifted her cheeks. "Word got out." Her voice was soft and I sensed some sympathy in there. "About you and the guys being in the crash together. Uh, there are a lot of rumors."

Shaking my head, I stared out at the scenery flying by. "Let me guess, I'm now the company whore, and each of the guys fucked me before passing me to the next one?"

I turned to find her staring at me, her expression stunned. "How did you know? Did Dante tell you?"

Sitting straighter, I narrowed my eyes on her. "Dante knows? I texted him this morning, and he never said anything."

Eddy shrugged. "He was ultra pissed when he found out. He's really protective of you, girl."

Needing a subject change, I shot her a slow smile. "Care to tell me what's going on with you two? I mean, I'm not blind. I see all the touches and lingering looks. And you came to my house together…"

Eddy's hands flexed on the wheel like she was uncomfortable, and I wondered where my confident friend had gone. Dante had her all tied up in knots.

"We've messed around a bit," she said in a rush. "And he is … amazing. Sexiest fucking guy I've ever had my hands on…"

"But…" I said, pushing her.

"But…" She sighed. "He reminds me of my brother."

I coughed and she burst out laughing. "No … no, not like that. I mean, he has that same dangerous and dark vibe. I'm not sure I want to fall for someone whose world is dark. I've been trying my entire life to get away from it. I've seen what it has cost Jasper. What it will continue to cost him for the rest of his life."

We were in the school parking lot now, and when she pulled into a spot near the front, she turned the car off and faced me fully. "Do you know what Dante actually does for the gang?"

I shook my head. "He never really talks about that part of his life. He says he doesn't want me involved, and the less I know, the safer for me."

Eddy didn't looked surprised by this. "Yeah, he brushed me off when I tried to ask, but Riles, I'll be honest, I think Dante is a pretty important part of it. I know authority. I know a leader when I see one, and he has head honcho written all over him."

This gave me a moment's pause as I considered what she was saying. Dante was so young, only a few years older than me, that I never expected he could be anything more than one of the outer members of whichever gang he was part of. He'd never told me their name either, but I knew there were only two major players in our area. The Grims and the Slayers. I'd seen his tatts, and he was definitely a Grim—the reaper kind of gave it away.

Eddy opened her door, and the sounds of nearby chattering students filled the car. "So yeah, I'm not sure I can risk my heart on someone like Dante, but if we can keep the casual cool thing going, then I'm not going to complain."

I nodded, opening my own door and hopping out. Before I could get more than a step away, some bitch I'd never seen before knocked into the frame of my door, pushing me back into the car. My ribs screamed in protest, and as I straightened, I leveled her with the darkest fucking glare I could manage.

"Why don't you watch where you're going," I snarled, adjusting my bag.

She flashed me a falsely sweet smile, her face heavy with makeup, her blond hair so peroxide it was as white as her shirt. "I figured you'd spent most of the weekend on your back. I was just helping you get back there."

And so it began.

Returning her smile with a false one of my own, I tilted my head. "Well, actually, I spent most of the time on my hands and knees, because it's hard to fuck four dudes when you're on your back."

Her smile faltered for a beat, because she'd clearly been hoping I would run crying from the school. Riley Jameson was made of tougher shit than that.

Eddy joined me then, her eyes narrowed on the bitch. "Fuck off, Kate. No one gives two shits what you say."

A deep voice joined us then, and I realized we were drawing a bit of a crowd. "Last time I saw you, Kate," Evan said, slipping in next to me and putting an arm over my shoulders to draw me closer. "You had Jimmy's dick in your mouth. He said you suck like a fucking fish, gulping all over his dick, but the rest of us were grateful that it at least shut you the fuck up."

She opened and closed her mouth, like she was demonstrating Evan's words for him. Some girls nearby were laughing, and when Kate looked around and saw no allies in the vicinity, she took off across the parking lot and into the school.

Tilting my head up to him, I was surprised by how happy I was to see Evan. His smirk was almost comforting as he winked. "Always getting into trouble, Spare. Looks like we're not going to be able to leave you alone."

Over his shoulder I could see Beck and Dylan talking, and the conversation was tense. I couldn't help but let my gaze linger on Beck's broad shoulders and trim hips. I recalled every naked detail of his perfection. Those tatts which I'd traced with my hands ... and mouth.

His eyes snapped to me, and I gulped at being caught checking him out. The air practically sizzled between us, despite the distance. I'd just made up my mind to walk toward him, when he turned away and started talking to someone I couldn't quite see.

Or rather, I couldn't see her until Evan, his arm still around my shoulders like he was staking his claim on me, started to maneuver me toward the school.

Her shiny chestnut hair was the first thing I saw, draped across Beck's arm as she hung from his side. My teeth slammed together as rage clouded my mind for a beat. Fuck. Brittley. That fucking skank was hanging off Beck like he was the last dude in school.

He didn't push her away either, if anything, this was the most animated I'd ever seen him as he stared down, talking to her. Dylan stood by, watching his friend with an odd expression on his face.

With a low growl, I forced myself to stop staring at that spectacle, and instead focused on Eddy.

"We have calc or history today?" I asked her, desperate to think about anything other than the raging jealousy coursing through me. Those were the two classes we shared, and having Eddy with me, made them almost bearable.

Beck was not mine. We'd fucked, end of story, and he'd shown me exactly how he felt about that this morning.

Fucked and forgotten.

Eddy pulled up her schedule, and I remembered that mine was on my old phone. I hadn't memorized it yet, and apparently neither had Eddy.

I was just wondering if I was going to have to head back to that snobby bitch in the office for a new schedule, when a reminder popped up on my phone to tell me I had English in ten minutes. Must have synced across somehow.

"Calculus and history are both after lunch today," Eddy said, scanning her phone. "Damn. Guess I'll see you at lunch."

"Ugh, okay, girl. See you then."

I set off to homeroom alone. Or at least I thought I was alone until Evan slipped in after me. He stopped at the table next to where I'd just dropped my bag, and stared at the guy sitting there. He wasted no time scrambling out of his chair and leaving the seat free for Evan.

"What are you doing?" I hissed, my eyes darting around the room as I realized how much attention we were drawing.

He grinned before stretching back in his chair. He didn't have a book, or computer, or fucking pencil in sight. "I'm on Riley duty today."

I must have looked like a stunned idiot as I blinked at him, but I couldn't quite figure out what he meant. "Riley duty? Why?"

Reaching out, he ruffled my hair, that smirk he did so well firmly in place. "Because you belong to us now."

The teacher walked in before I could refute that claim.

Facing the front of the room, there was this odd feeling in my chest. It was warmth, and for the first time since my parents died, a little piece of me felt … okay. When Evan said *us* I knew he wasn't referring to Delta in that situation. He meant them. I was one of them now, and … I *fucked* Beck.

Damn. I had no idea how that was going to go, but hopefully we would both just pretend it didn't happen.

My phone buzzed in my pocket, and I pulled it out before checking on the teacher. She wasn't paying us any attention, so I quickly read the text.

Dante: I'm out front. I need to head back to Jersey for a few days, but I wanted to say goodbye first. It's been too long since I got a Riley hug.

The bell rang then, and even though I knew I'd be late for my first class, I rushed out the door and headed toward the parking lot. Despite the light hearted nature of that text, I was worried. When Dante took off abruptly, it usually meant something was going down with his gang. Since Eddy's words about him being a leader, I was now even more stressed about what his absence meant. The dangers he would face.

Evan caught me just before I made it down the stairs, sliding in front of me and blocking my path. "You need to get back in school, it's not safe out here for you." For the first time he was serious, the smile gone, and his eyes much darker than usual.

"Dante is waiting for me," I said shortly. The Delta heirs might have been scary as fuck, but I wasn't letting them walk all over me. Not today. Not. Ever.

Evan shook his head. "I don't give a fuck, girl. It could be God himself waiting for you, and I'd still be here stopping your ass from walking out into danger."

"You've got to be shitting me," I said, getting irate. Maybe it had been a bad idea to befriend these controlling fucks. "I'll be five minutes."

Shaking him off, I tried to step around him, but he was much larger and moved a lot quicker than my injured ass. Before I could start screaming, and I was pretty damn close to that, a shadow washed over us, and Evan swung around, his body moving into a defensive position. He placed himself in front of me, and I wondered if maybe I'd underestimated how dangerous it was here in school. I mean, I hadn't forgotten that someone had forced our pilot to blow up the plane, but I'd thought I'd be okay in public.

Evan was acting like we could be taken out at any moment, and a trill of fear raced along my skin.

This time though, it was only Dante, dressed all in black and wearing a fucked off expression. "What the hell do you think you're doing?" he demanded, getting right in Evan's face. "If you step in front of Riley one more time, I'm going to end you. I don't even care who your family is."

Evan was a few inches shorter than Dante, but he didn't look remotely intimidated. The memory of the boys stealth missioning it the forest was strong in my mind, and I feared for my best friend. He had no idea how dangerous Delta was.

Edging around, I tried to slip in between Dante and Evan, but before I could, strong hands wrapped around my biceps and lifted me full bodily out of there. Beck's face was awash in fury as he maneuvered me behind him.

"What the hell?" I shouted, slamming my hands on his back, and getting … stinging palms in return. I legitimately wanted to hurt Beck, but he didn't even turn his head.

"What are you doing here, gangbanger?" he said, his voice low.

I'd heard this sort of lethal tone from him one other time, and it turned my blood to ice, because I knew Beck was pissed. I glared and edged toward Dante. "Leave him alone, he did nothing to you."

Dante was smirking at them, taunting them, because that was his style. But he had no idea how dangerous they were. Especially Beck.

Dylan, who I hadn't even noticed until now, stepped forward. "I think it's time you left town. Permanently," he advised Dante. "We'd hate to have to send you back … in pieces."

The look in his eyes was making me nervous. Sucking up as much courage as I had, I met each of their dark stares. "If you touch one hair on Dante's head, I will hunt you assholes down and cut your balls off. Right the fuck off!"

I waved my hands to emphasize my point.

For the briefest moment, it almost looked like the corner of Beck's lips twitched, but I knew I was wrong when he turned those dark as sin eyes on me, because I could see nothing but pissed.

"Did Evan tell you not to leave the building?"

I blinked. "Well, yes. He said there was danger."

Beck stepped into me, and I fought against an urge to back up. "And you decided not to listen?"

Crossing my arms, I scoffed to hide my nerves. "You don't own me. I'm my own person. I take my own risks."

Beck just shook his head, one hand wrapping around the back of my neck as he pulled me into him. "That's where you're wrong, Butterfly. You're in the circle now, and once you're in, there's no way out."

"We have rules, Riley," Dylan added, backing up his best friend.

Dante made a rumbling sound from where he'd been edged out. "What the fuck do you mean she's in and can't get out? You bastards are involved in some dangerous shit! Why the hell would you drag Riley into that?"

My head was starting to ache, and my body was starting to ache, because Beck still held me captive. And all I could think about was him … the strength in his hands and body as he fucked me.

Beck didn't turn from me when he replied. "Riley was dragged in long before she met us. Her birth dictated the rest of her life. Now she has to fall into line."

Sucking in a deep breath, I jerked my head out of Beck's hand, and he let me go. Two steps to the left, and I was standing with Dante. "What if I just take off now?" I said, sounding desperate and devastated all in the same tone. "Can I run?"

Evan snorted. "Maybe if you run to Mars. Otherwise Delta's reach is too far."

Dante's huge hand cupped my shoulder, and he pulled me closer to him. My side ached as he did, and I tried not to flinch. Beck's eyes followed that movement, and I shivered at his dark stare.

Dante saw the same thing, and that only made him hold me even tighter. "You're hurting me," I bit out quietly, hoping the others didn't hear.

His grip loosened a little, and it must have been the opening Beck was waiting for, because he moved then. Faster than I'd ever seen a person move. I was in his hands and then passed off to Evan before I could blink. Beck went at Dante, and my tough as nails, highly trained, badass best friend, was knocked to the ground in about a tenth of a second.

Dante got back up quickly, and even managed to get two swings in. Both of which Beck dodged before he stepped in and punched Dante so hard I heard bone crack.

"No," I screamed, struggling against Evan, my pulse racing as I frantically ran my eyes across Dante. "Leave him alone. Please."

Beck swung around, and I shrank back. "Make him leave. Now. Before I lose my fucking mind."

He turned and strode away, and I was shaking as Evan lowered me back to the ground. "Say your goodbyes," he said, giving me a little nudge forward.

I stumbled to Dante, wrapping my arms around him. "I love you," I said softly, "But it's too dangerous here for you. You have to go."

He groaned before hugging me back. "If you need me, Riles, I'll be here so fast their heads will roll. And I mean that literally. I can have a lot of very bad people here..."

It'd be war if that happened, and I was so scared that I might lose one of the guys I cared about. Which unfortunately also included the stubborn assholes in Delta.

"I'll be okay," I promised, letting his familiar arms hold me for a minute more.

Dylan cleared his throat, and I shot him the meanest glare I could muster. But I did step back, my eyes hot and irritated as I tried not to cry.

"I'll text you," I told Dante. His jaw had a dark red splotch on it, and I wondered if Beck had broken anything. "Please be safe."

"I love you, Riles." He was so serious. "I'll be watching."

That appeared to be directed at both me and the two guys behind me. Then Dante turned and left. I watched him until he got into the unfamiliar car and then disappeared.

A part of me broke then, and I couldn't stop the tears that trailed down my cheeks.

Evan and Dylan moved so they were framing me on either side, and while neither of them said anything, they did reach out and take my hands. Holding me while I fell apart. I wanted to hate them, because they were insane and damaged and violent. They'd forced my best friend out of my life, the controlling fucks, but ... maybe it was for the best. If my life was as dangerous as they were implying, then Dante could only be in danger being around me.

It was the five of us against the world.

"Let's go to class," I said, freeing my hands to wipe at my tears. Dylan's fingers gently wiped away the ones I missed.

"You're not alone, Riles," he said softly. "It's better this way."

I shrugged because I somewhat agreed with him, but they needed to work on their delivery.

All the violence was exhausting.

Chapter 17

We'd missed the first class, but my teacher didn't even bat an eyelid when I slipped into my second class with Evan's arm wrapped around me possessively. I was too emotionally drained to argue with him about this "Riley Duty" bullshit, and his closeness was bringing me a weird level of comfort. Especially in the wake of Beck's macho bullshit with Dante.

Evan guided me to the back of the room where two younger boys—younger as in my year group—hurried to grab their shit and abandon the desks they'd been sitting in, so we could have them.

"That was rude," I murmured, sitting down so we weren't causing any *more* of a fuss. "We could have just found empty seats."

Evan shrugged. "I wanted these. Now stop chatting and learn things."

The rest of my morning classes were strangely enjoyable, thanks to the little paper airplane notes which kept landing on my desk. Apparently I needed to learn, but Evan was bored as shit.

"How do you know that?" I whispered to him as we left my last class before lunch.

He grinned and waggled his brows at me. "How'd I know that Mr. Bundaing likes to dress in women's clothes and occasionally wears the underwear to school?" He snorted a laugh. "For one, our company holds leverage over *every* employee—teachers included—and for two, I saw the lace thong one day when he bent over to pick something up."

"Wait, Delta owns the school?" I frowned. Did I already know this? "Is there anything Delta *doesn't* run?"

Evan shrugged. "Huntley."

The mention of the rogue group who tried to have us all killed was like a bucket of ice water over my mood, and by the time we reached our usual lunch table, I was firmly under a dark cloud.

"Hey, girl," Eddy greeted me with a bright smile. "Saved your seat!"

"You save it every day," I replied, my smile much weaker. Still, I placed my food tray down and sat with a heavy sigh. Evan had finally peeled himself off my hip and gone to sit with the other boys—minus Jasper. Thinking of Eddy's brother sent my gaze wandering over his usual spot, which so happened to be beside Beck's.

That's when my mood soured even further.

Brittley was sitting in his lap. Like … right in his fucking lap, and he wasn't shoving her to the floor where she belonged.

Worse. Beck made eye contact with me over Brittley's shiny chestnut head, and when she reached over and pressed her lips to his neck, he didn't shove her trashy ass away. Blood rushed to my face and bile curdled in my belly. Obviously, I'd known last night was a one off but what the fuck was this all about? Did he seriously think that I was so pathetic that I'd fall in love after one—admittedly mind blowing—fuck? Was that what this was? Proving he was a player?

Fuck. Him.

Just as I was about to snap a witty, sarcastic remark, Brittley lifted her face and shot me a look of pure triumph. For a moment, a rage so potent hit me that I was half out of my chair, ready to rip her right off him, until I remembered that Beck didn't belong to me.

That was what this little display was all about, after all.

Gritting my teeth, I sank down again and grabbed at the sandwich on my plate. Two bites and it tasted like shit, so I threw it down, and concentrated on breathing in and out and not looking in his direction.

"You okay?" Eddy asked, shooting me a concerned stare.

"Can we get out of here?" I asked. "I could use some decent food and something about this is turning my stomach." By "this" I meant the company, not the sandwiches.

Discounting that this place served food that was like a Michelin starred restaurant compared to my last school, it was really about getting away from Beck and his whore.

Eddy's gaze shifted to their table then, and when she came back to me, her face held understanding and sympathy. Then, like the best fucking friend ever, she threw her sandwich down as well and declared that she needed a burger. We were up, moving through the cafeteria, and I didn't turn my head once to see if the guys noticed. "They're going to follow us," I said urgently the moment we were out of the door.

Eddy nodded, and before I could say another word, she grabbed my wrist and we were sprinting. With bruised ribs.

"Come on, girl," she said in a breathless laugh. "Pick up the pace."

I groaned, almost stumbling over a slightly uneven surface. "I'm injured!" Thank fuck I'd swapped the heels out for sneakers though.

Somehow we didn't die, making it to the parking lot before anyone ran us down. Eddy's car beeped before we even reached it, and we slid inside. I held my side, feeling the tenderness of my ribs, but I was pretty sure I hadn't done too much damage. Eddy peeled out in a screech of tires on pavement, and then we were zooming away from the school and heading into the main part of the town. Since I'd arrived here, I'd never gone any further than the school, so I was actually interested in taking it all in.

"It's small, but the elders of Delta like it that way," Eddy explained as we stopped at a red light. "They control everyone in the town, and no one gets up in their business."

They were going to be so pissed that I'd taken off without one of them. Tension pressed on my chest at the thought of what would happen when they caught up with me. "Maybe we shouldn't be doing this?" I said in a breathless whisper.

Eddy eyed me with a strange look on her face. "Too late to chicken out now."

Reaching out to grab the "oh shit" handle, I sighed. "It's dangerous to be around me. I shouldn't be risking your life like this, even if I'm cool with risking my own."

"Everyone knows I'm a Langham," Eddy said, sounding completely unconcerned. "Danger follows our family around. I'm not in any more just because we're together."

I wasn't sure I believed that, but I felt somewhat better.

Eddy pulled into what looked like a miniature mall.

"Center Court," she said, shifting into park and opening her door. "It's small, but it has some wicked designer stores. Half this town is rich thanks to Delta."

When we got inside, I realized that small did not equal lame. It was fancy, like marble floor with gold inlaid patterns-similar to the Delta mansions—chandeliers, leather couches, and security on all entrances. "Wow," I said softly, trying to take it all in. "Kinda wish I had a credit card now."

Eddy threw her head back and laughed. "You're literally the daughter of one of the richest people in the world, and you don't have a credit card."

I shrugged. "Catherine doesn't want me having any freedoms. Money is a freedom I might use to escape her."

She didn't say anything, but I knew Eddy was thinking the same thing as me. There was no escape.

Passing the fancy stores, we ended up in the food area, and I wasn't even surprised to see tablecloths on the tables, with cutlery and wine glasses. In the middle of a friggin mall food court.

"Pick your poison," Eddy said, waving a hand around.

There were multiple choices, and we settled on Italian. Deciding to split a pizza and salad between us.

"You want wine?" Eddy asked.

I blinked. "We're not even eighteen, let alone twenty-one."

She shrugged. "Age is just a number, and here no one asks for numbers."

"Sure," I said, deciding I might as well. I'd pretty much decided I was too scared to venture back to school today and face the wrath of the guys, so getting wasted seemed like a decent alternative.

Eddy squealed before she jumped up and returned a moment later with a bottle of Moscato in an ice bucket. "Figured we'd start on the light stuff and see how we go."

I already had my glass in hand, because I was ready to let loose. Eddy filled both of our glasses almost to the top, and just when I was about to take my first sip, a flash caught my eye. It was a brief illumination, but I thought the guy sitting at a table across from us had just taken a photo of us. I couldn't see any camera though, and he was focused on a menu in front of him. A dark suspicion took root in my stomach as I watched him for a moment longer.

"Do you know that guy, Eddy?" I asked, inclining my head in his direction.

I couldn't really see much about him outside of the dark jacket and blond hair, but he was creeping me out.

Eddy stared for a few moments before shaking her head. "Never seen him before; don't think he's local."

My uneasy feeling increased.

"Fuck," Eddy said, distracting me from the dude.

"What?" I looked around and almost died when I saw them.

Beck was in the center, Dylan and Evan were on either side, and their pissed off faces were very obvious for all to see. The three of them were heading right for our table, and even Eddy looked pale as they closed in.

"Should we run?" I whispered.

She shook her head. "No, that will only make it worse."

I believed her. Reaching out, I wrapped my hand around the knife there, even though I knew there was no way I could use it on any of them. For some reason, it made me feel better though.

When they reached us, there was a charged silence, and I could finally see the tumultuous gray of Beck's eyes.

"You ran from us," he rumbled in a voice so dark and dangerous it sent a shiver down my spine. Or maybe that was arousal… the lines were becoming blurred.

I shook my head. "Nope," I lied.

It was only partly a lie, actually, because I had only run from him … well, him and his skank.

"Figured you were too busy to notice me leaving anyway," I said with a shrug. "You had your hands full."

Beck tilted his head to the side and ran his gaze across my face. He'd done the exact same thing last night, just before he slid inside of me. Like he was seeing through my bravado to the pain in my soul. Leaning over, he caged me in, a hand on either side of my chair.

"You jealous, Butterfly?" he asked in a voice like velvet.

I snorted a nervous laugh that not even I believed. "In your dreams, Sebastian. What the hell would I have to be jealous about?"

He considered my bullshit for a long moment, then his lips twitched in a fractional smile.

"Don't ever run from us again," he told me in that same dark, dangerous voice. "This is your last warning."

Swallowing hard, I could have cried when the server brought our pizza and salad to the table. It was the distraction we needed though, as Evan let out a whoop and pulled a chair out to sit down. "I'm fuckin' starving," he said. "Someone interrupted our lunch." He winked at me though, and it was clear

JAYMIN EVE + TATE JAMES

that he wasn't angry with me anymore.

Dylan sat as well, and Beck, who was still leaning over me, reached down and yanked me up out of my chair. Before I could protest, he sank down, pulling me onto his lap. I struggled for a moment because all I could think about was his skank, but a firm hand on my stomach halted my movements. "This is apparently the only way I can keep an eye on you," he said into my ear. "It's this, or I take you over my knee and spank your fucking ass. And I really, *really* want to spank that creamy white ass." This last part was delivered in a husky whisper that made my lady bits heat.

I had to get a grip on my raging hormones before I could even think about an answer to that. I took too long, though, and Beck growled in my ear, this low rumbly sound which basically set my panties on fire.

Turning slightly, I groaned at how sexy Beck was. So much for keeping a clear head.

It should have been uncomfortable for me, being in his lap like this. Especially after he'd all but ignored me since last night and then basically flouted his fuck buddy at school, but I felt mostly relaxed. Relaxed and turned on, because his body was hot and hard as he cradled my softness. His hand still splayed across my stomach as he held me in place, and I couldn't stop from wiggling as I remembered the strong grip of his hands on my hips last night.

I didn't fool myself though. This was Beck showing me who was in control. That if I defied him, he would come after me and put me right back in place. This was dominance plain and simple, and I was way too into it.

The pizza disappeared, even though Beck didn't touch a slice. Evan made up for it though, eating over half on his own. When it was done, I reached out and grabbed my wine, gulping it down because I needed … wine. I really needed wine.

My eyes drifted across the tables, noticing most were empty around us now. *Shit.* I'd been distracted by the arrival of the guys, and I'd forgotten about the creepy dude. Eddy noticed me looking at that same table. "Girl, obsessed much. What's up with that?"

"He just … I thought he took our photo before."

I felt tension press across the guys then. "Who?" Dylan snapped, his eyes already taking in the tables around us.

"Butterfly…" Beck said, warning in his tone.

"I don't know," I told them. "Eddy didn't recognize him, and he's gone now. He was at that table over there."

I pointed out the now empty table, wondering if maybe he'd taken off the moment the guys arrived. Or if that was just a coincidence. "Time to go," Beck snapped. He stood, lifting me off his lap as he did so, before setting me gently on my feet. His hand wrapped around mine, and he started dragging me out of the food court so fast I needed to power walk to keep from falling flat on my face.

"Sebastian, what the hell?" I demanded, trying to yank my hand free of his iron grip.

Looking around I found Eddy and Evan hurrying alongside us, but Dylan was nowhere to be seen.

"Guys, what the fuck is going on?" I barely got my question out before Beck popped open the door to a cherry red McLaren P1 then shoved me inside.

He slammed the door shut, barely missing my foot, then came around and slid behind the steering wheel. "Maybe nothing. Dylan will find out."

Confused, I shook my head. "Okay, so what the fuck are we doing if it may be nothing?"

Beck gunned the engine, reversing out of his space and speeding when he hit the main road. "Because it may be *something*."

This shut me up. What was he thinking? Huntley? Oh shit, was that one of our attempted killers?

My blood ran cold, and I wrapped my arms around my body. We didn't speak for a long time, and I stared out the window wondering how close I'd possibly just come to death again. Finally when the morbid thoughts became too much I decided to change the subject.

"Where's the Bugatti? Not that I'm complaining." I about died when he told me he had a McLaren in his ten car collection. I ran my hand over the soft leather trim and listened to the sexy purr of the engine. His Bugatti Veyron was my unicorn car, but this baby came a damn close second.

Beck gave me a long side eye. "My Bugatti needed detailing," he remarked in a dry tone. "Some drunk bitch threw up in it."

My cheeks heated, and I bit my lip with embarrassment. Whoops.

"Sorry," I murmured, turning my attention back out the window again. Try as I might, though, it was impossible to ignore the sexy growl of the McLaren engine or the way Beck hugged each corner tight.

My fingers twisted in my plaid skirt, and I clenched my legs tightly together. If I had thought driving with Beck was an erotic experience before sleeping with him... this was something else entirely.

Thankfully, we came to a stop outside the Deboise mansion gates before I could embarrass myself.

"Get out," Beck ordered me in a voice like ice. His hands gripped the steering wheel in a white knuckled grip while his gray eyes remained locked dead ahead through the windscreen.

He was angry—furious, even—but at fucking *what?*

"What the hell is your problem, Sebastian?" I demanded. "You mood swing harder than a girl with her period. One minute you can't keep your hands off me and the next you can't stand the sight of me. Make up your fucking mind because you're giving me whiplash."

Beck said nothing. Did nothing. I may as well have been speaking another language for all the reaction I got out of him. Shaking my head in disgust, I unclicked my belt and popped the door open. "Maybe just leave Evan or Dylan on Riley Duty the rest of the week. I'm sick of navigating your bullshit."

I stepped out and slammed the car door behind me before stomping toward the Deboise gates. My entire body hurt, and I wasn't looking forward to running into Catherine in the middle of the day, but Beck and his moods could kiss my ass. A car door slammed behind me, and before I could even turn to look, a pair of strong hands grabbed me. Beck whirled me around and crushed his lips to mine in a wild, possessive kiss that made my whole resolve melt into a puddle of mushy goo at my feet. Blame it on a head injury, but I kissed him back like he was my damn soulmate.

With a growl, Beck pushed me away, and we both stared, our breaths coming out in harsh huffs. "What are you doing?" I pleaded, imploring him with my eyes to fucking make a choice.

He shook his head, hands reaching up to run through all that glorious dark hair. "I don't fucking know! You're just everywhere. In my fucking head. I can't … I need to stop. This is not a world that works with…"

He waved a hand between us.

"Then stay away from me, Beck."

I was tired. This shit was tiring.

He shook his head, and I was drowning in his eyes. How the hell did they change color the way they did? From the lightest gray to a dark stormy night, which was where he was right now.

"That's the thing, I've tried…"

I barely heard those words and then he spun on his heel and was back in his car. I resisted the urge to both scream and cry, because I was desperate to release all of my angsty emotions to the world, but I wouldn't give Beck the satisfaction.

When I got inside, my phone started to ring, and for some reason I expected it to be Beck, but it wasn't.

An unknown number flashed at me, and even though I wouldn't normally answer it, something compelled me to.

"Hello," I said.

"Are you home?"

The male voice was familiar, and I relaxed. A part of me had been worried it was going to be a scary call from one of those Huntley fuckers.

"I'm great, Dylan. Thanks for asking," I replied sweetly.

A beat of silence. "Are you home?"

"Yes," I said as bluntly. And then I remembered that he had been investigating the creepy guy. "Did you find anything in the mall?"

His reply was instant. "Can't really talk on the phone, it's not secure, but … security footage was erased."

Shit. That had to mean something, because why erase footage if nothing suspect was going on.

"I'll be there in ten minutes," Dylan said, and I heard the roar of an engine before the line went dead.

Needing to change before he got here, I dragged myself upstairs and kicked off my shoes. The uniform followed, and I pulled on jeans and a white shirt, tying my long hair back into a loose braid.

When I got downstairs Stewart was opening the door, and it was almost as if our huge front entrance shrunk around the giant badass that was Dylan. When he looked up and saw me at the foot of the stairs, he inclined his head asking me to follow him outside. I nodded, figuring that whatever he wanted to tell me was Delta business.

We walked across the soft grassed area away from the house, and when he stopped, he ran his gaze over me. "I was worried about you," he said in that quiet, confident way of his. Dylan from the start might have looked like the scariest, but he was the most caring. I'd seen it enough times now to know he was the one that held the others together. Beck was their leader, their fury, their fear. But Dylan was their heart. Loyal. Lethal. And … lonely.

"You think Beck could hurt me?" I asked, because what else could he have worried about.

The smallest of smiles tilted up his lips. "There are many different ways to hurt someone. And some are harder to recover from."

There was pain in his voice, hidden deep under the neutral tone he used.

Unable to stop, I reached out and took his hand. "Who hurt you?" I demanded, surprised by the venom in my words. It pissed me right off to think of his pain.

All of their pain.

It was becoming my pain too.

Dylan glanced at our hands before lifting his flawless face back to meet my gaze. "You're never afraid to touch me," he said, his fingers tightening around mine.

I tilted my head to the side as I stared, trying to figure out what he was talking about.

"Why would I be…?"

Cynicism washed away every other expression. "My mother would never touch me because I was the result of an affair with the nanny. My father was fucking ashamed of me because he likes to whitewash his world, but of course, he couldn't keep his dick out of the not-at-all-white hired help and here I am."

I'd wondered how an ancient as fuck, bunch of old assholes had accepted someone like Dylan into their inner circle. I personally, loved the creamy darkness of his skin, the slightly exotic tilt to his cheekbones, and the scary glint in his eyes. But that wasn't Militant Delta Finances. They were about being rich, white bastards.

"Your real mom?" I whispered.

He shook his head. "Disappeared. Probably dead."

My hand clenched around his, and he shrugged. "Can't miss what you've never had, and since my father's wife couldn't have any children of her own, I was raised as a legitimate child. But only in public. Behind closed doors…"

Jesus Christ. I couldn't even imagine what had gone on. "Is that why they made you do all that survival stuff?"

Dylan shook his head. "Nope. I think they would have preferred I didn't learn how to defend myself, but it's tradition. And they're all about tradition."

Another broken boy. Desperate for love and acceptance. This was why he cared so much, why he'd gone the opposite way to Beck.

His beautiful face was still, staring down at me with depthless eyes. For a moment I wondered why it couldn't have been Dylan. Why the fuck was Beck the one who ripped my heart out of my chest every single time he was around me?

"I'm always here for you," I said to Dylan, because he was important to me now. "If things get hard at home, come and find me."

He shook his head, and like watching someone wipe a slate clean, he pulled all of the sorrow away and was back to being cool and collected. Gently untangling our hands, he crossed his arms over that impressive chest. "I actually stopped by for another reason," he said all business. "It's clear someone tampered with the security footage at the mall. Something was going on, and since the guy you saw was close to you, I'm going to hazard a guess that Huntley has figured out that you're a weakness in our ranks now. The rest of us, we can take care of ourselves. We're trained and dangerous. You…" his eyes ran down me slowly. "Are a lot of things, but you're not dangerous."

I snorted. "You've clearly never seen me during shark week."

He flashed me a lopsided grin. "Hormones aside, I think you need to do some training. At least learn basic defense and to shoot a gun. It won't be enough, but it's better than nothing."

I closed my eyes and let out an exaggerated gust of air. "You're probably right, and I'm actually pretty good at anything athletic, so hopefully I pick it up quickly."

Dylan nodded. "We're good trainers."

"We're…" I said with a groan. "All of you will be training me?"

His lips tilted up. "There's no one better with a weapon than Beck."

I should have guessed that. Dylan was the martial arts expert, and Beck was the "shoot them in the fucking head" expert.

"Okay, but can we start tomorrow. I'm pretty beat already." I paused. "And beat *up*. Let's not go too hard on me, yeah?"

It felt like today had been going for a million years.

Dylan nodded. "Yep. I'll pick you up in the morning. Around ten."

"Uh, school?" I said.

"Not tomorrow, this is more important."

That was fine by me. I'd always been an average student, and while I used to be interested in decent grades to get into college, now I was apparently inheriting a seat on a billion dollar company without even having to pass senior year.

More importantly, if I didn't figure out how to keep myself alive, it wouldn't matter about school or grades or anything.

Dylan left after that, and I made my way back to the monstrosity of a house that I now called home. Stewart greeted me. "Are the birth parents in?" I asked, needing to know if I was about to be ambushed.

He shook his head. "No, miss. They're at the New York office."

Looked like the day was finally turning around. "I'll be in my room," I said.

"I'll bring you some food," he called as I started to walk.

I flashed him a smile before traipsing up the stairs, and crawling into bed. Now that I had my new nifty television, I was going to enjoy some relaxing time watching trashy movies and eating whatever I could get my hands on.

The first thing I did was text Dante though. *Me: Are you okay?*

It was a few minutes before he replied. *Dante: I'm good, Riles. Just dealing with some business. Are you okay?*

I had to think about that answer for a moment before deciding that I was as good as could be expected. Under the circumstances.

Me: I'm okay. The guys are being crazy protective, and I can't decide if I'd rather be kidnapped or not just to get away from them.

It was in my nature to joke about the more serious shit ... made it easier to deal with.

Dante: Lay low. Please. For me. I'm gathering as much information as I can; we'll make it safe for you. I promise.

Me: Love you, Dante. Stay safe.

Dante: Love you too, Riles.

I plugged my phone into the charger and turned my attention to the television, scrolling through the million and one choices before I settled on *The Fast and the Furious*. I'd seen these movies so many times that by now they were comfort food for me.

Stewart arrived some time later, and he had a tray filled with more junk food than was possible for any one person to eat. Along with a delicious boscaiola pasta.

"You spoil me," I gushed at him, wondering if maybe I should just set my sights on a man that brought me food. If only Stewart wasn't forty years older than me, he'd be almost perfect.

I made it through three and a half movies before sleep pressed in on me. I dragged myself into the shower, changed into the softest cotton pajamas with roses on them, and snuggled under the covers.

Then I closed my eyes, and ... the pilot's face flashed right across my mind.

Chapter 18

Tears actually sprang to my eyes as they flew open. This could not be happening. I needed to sleep, it was one of my favorite things to do, and having dead people appear every single time I closed my eyes, was really going to impact my life.

There was only one other time I remembered having insomnia. When I was ten my childhood best friend, Jessie Mcglee, moved away. Outside of Dante—and now Eddy—she was the only true friend I'd ever had, and I'd missed her so much. My mom had to sleep in my room with me for three weeks before I could finally relax my brain to sleep alone. This time though, I had no mom…

My chest got tight and I tried not to break, despite the pressure in my throat and behind my eyes. Scrambling out of bed, I was sucking air in and out, trying to get myself under control.

Without thought, I was pulling on my dressing gown and Uggs again, stumbling downstairs, and throwing myself into the golf cart. The codes were memorized now and I barely even stopped at the gate before I was flying down the road between my house and Becks.

Don't think. Don't think. Don't think.

I needed to do anything except think about my dead parents. The dead pilot. The dead assassins. Or even the alive assassins who were still trying to kill me.

What if he's not alone?

My foot lifted from the gas, and I let the cart slowly idle forward. I wasn't quite at the front of his house, and I slammed my hands on the wheel, hating myself for this fucking weakness.

Dropping my head forward, I let the tears finally fall, dripping down my cheeks in hot torrents of pain. Tonight I wished that I wasn't so alone.

He appeared soundlessly, which was always his way, and wrapped me up in his arms. I didn't fight him, letting him lift me from the cart before he jumped in to drive. He never let me go the entire drive back to his place.

I expected him to take me straight to that generic bedroom again and fuck me, use my body because that's all it was good for. I would have even welcomed it, in my current state of mind. But when I finally lifted my head from his hard chest, I realized that we were in a completely different section of the house.

Beck dropped me gently into a large chair, one with a reclining footrest. We were in a cinema room. One which had like twenty luxury seats and the biggest screen I'd ever seen.

"What ... why?" I asked, my voice husky.

"I'll be right back," he said, brushing a thumb across my cheek, collecting stray tears. "Pick a movie."

He dropped a complicated looking remote in my hand, and then strode toward a bar at the back of the room. It took me a few failed attempts but I finally figured out how to get the files open, and then I scrolled straight to *Fast and Furious* 4. Might as well pick up where I left off.

When Beck returned, he had two heavy glasses, filled with ice and an amber liquid.

He handed me one before settling in at my side, his muscled thigh and arm pressing right down my body.

Everywhere he was touching was on fire, and I gulped down a mouthful of the alcohol, recognizing the flavor from the last time I was there. The fancy old scotch that I'd been too unrefined to appreciate. "Nice choice," he said, and I had no idea what he was talking about, until his eyes shifted to the screen.

I laughed. "Yeah, I was half way through a marathon tonight. They're classics."

He didn't ask me why I was crying. Why I was sitting in a cart in front of his house again. He didn't ask me one thing as we sat together, watching the screen, sipping on our alcohol.

"Where are your parents?"

The question slipped out, and I expected him to do his usual evasive half-answer bullshit. The silence felt heavy, but surprisingly he answered. "My mother is in France, living with her lover. The secret everyone knows. I haven't talked to her in five years. My father's in New York. He basically lives in the office there, doing ... business."

"Are they divorced?" I asked, trying to understand.

Beck snorted. "Delta doesn't do divorce. We keep it all in the family and the 'til death do you part is literal."

Knowing everything I did about them, I wasn't surprised. "How long has it been since you've lived under the same roof as them?"

Beck took a drink, finishing it in one long swallow. "I've been on my own, off and on, since I was ten."

Ten? What the actual fuck. What sort of monsters would leave a child alone? Oh, right, Delta sort of monsters.

He must have read my expression in the flashing lights of the movies, because his lips tilted into a cynical smirk. "It was for the best. They're a fucking mess, and whenever I was in the middle of their fights, I had to watch my father beat the shit out of my mother. Lucky they took off before I was old enough to fight back, because I probably would have killed Dad."

Fuck. Fucking fuck.

"I'm sorry." I couldn't think of what else to say.

He didn't reply, and at that moment, his jaw was like cut glass. Rigid and sharp. I fought against the urge to trace my fingers along those perfect, dark planes of his face. He'd shut off from me again, so I focused on the movie. Enjoying the thrum of cars as they raced at stupid speed, doing impossible things, and yet somehow still making it work.

Neither of us spoke again, but the silence between us wasn't uncomfortable. This Beck ... the one who found me crying outside his house in the middle of the night and offered me comfort ... this wasn't the infuriating king shit of Ducis Academy. He wasn't whiplashing my emotions, pushing and pulling me until I felt like an old piece of elastic.

That Beck was sexy, dangerous, enticing and terrifying. But this one?

This was the kind of guy I could easily fall in love with—and that scared the shit out of me.

Clearing my throat, I awkwardly shifted away from him in a lame attempt to distance us. But it wasn't our physical closeness that was making my skin crawl with fear and anxiety. It was our emotional closeness and that wasn't something I could easily run from.

"What are you doing, Butterfly?" he rumbled, not taking his eyes from the movie screen. His fingers curled a little tighter around my hip and tugged me back into the gap I'd created.

Licking my lips, I desperately resisted the magnetic pull of *him*. "I should, uh, I should go home."

This made him shift slightly, turning his attention from the screen to peer at me with those intense gray eyes. "Why?"

Bullshit excuses flitted across my mind, but none made it past my lips. Eventually, I let out a frustrated sigh and opted for the truth. "Because I *just* accused you of sending crazy mixed messages and yet here I am in your house in the middle of the night. Again." I shook my head, breaking eye contact with him and fidgeting with my robe.

There was a long pause before Beck replied. Long enough that I was bracing myself, ready to run from the thick tension between us. "I like you being here," he finally admitted in a soft whisper. His hand picked mine up from where I was twisting my robe and tangled our fingers together. "I keep pushing you away, hoping you'd hate me. That you'd stay away, because being near me is a death sentence." He paused, and I was too much of a coward to look up at him, even though the heat of his gaze was setting me on fire. "But you're a part of this, whether we like it or not. So, maybe instead of pushing you away, I should hold you tighter."

The air all rushed out of me from a breath I hadn't noticed I was holding. "What are you saying, Beck?" I asked, my voice holding an edge of pleading. "This shit between us is exhausting."

He shook his head, looking down at our linked hands. "I don't know, Riley. But I don't want you to go."

Slowly, I nodded. I didn't want to move from this spot. "So where does that leave us?"

Finally I found the courage to look up, meeting his conflicted gaze as he, too, raised his face. "I don't know," he repeated, soft and confused. "I just know..." He trailed off with a frustrated sigh, then leaned forward and touched his lips to mine. For a hot second, we both froze.

Giving over to the moment, I brought my hand up to his cheek and returned the gentle kiss, slowly, carefully moving my lips against his.

Beck let out a small sound, a pained groan as our lips parted and our tongues met. It was such a stark contrast from the rough, demanding, possessive way he'd kissed me until now. Still, he didn't push it any further. My whole body was flushed with heat, greedy for more, but he pulled back and swiped his thumb across my lower lip.

His gaze was drenched in lust, need and ... something more confusing. It scared me, and I wasn't emotionally prepared to explore it further. Not yet.

"Just watch the movie, Butterfly," Beck ordered me in a husky voice, settling back onto the cozy chair and wrapping his arm around me.

I hesitated only a moment longer before sinking into his embrace and losing myself in those deliciously fast cars on the screen.

Chapter 19

I must have fallen asleep sometime during the sixth Fast and Furious, and when I woke up I was curled up in the cinema chair at Beck's house. He was nowhere to be seen, but there was a pillow under my head and a cashmere blanket was tucked over me.

"Dammit," I groaned, sitting up and rubbing my eyes. "I need to stop doing this."

Stifling a yawn with the back of my hand, I peeled myself off the chair and stretched the kinks out of my back. Part of me wondered why he hadn't woken me up to send me home, but a bigger part suspected he *knew* I couldn't sleep alone right now.

Pressing a button on the remote, I checked the time and gasped.

"Fuck!" I exclaimed. School started in less than thirty minutes, and I was still at Beck's ... in my jammies. Tossing the soft blue blanket onto the chair,

I rushed out of the cinema in search of the way out. Why was Beck's house *so fucking huge?* Last time it had been a clear shot down the stairs and out the door, but I hadn't paid any attention to how we'd gotten to the cinema last night.

Frantic, I rushed through the marble tiled halls and rooms, then came to a skidding halt in the enormous kitchen.

"Oh," I blurted, finding Beck sitting on a stool at the kitchen counter. He was dressed in fitted workout clothes—I tried really hard not to drool over all the muscles on display—while casually sipping a cup of coffee and reading something on a tablet. Beside him, another place had been set with fresh, steaming coffee and a plate of waffles. "I didn't ... uh..." I awkwardly shifted from foot to foot as he watched me like a predator. "I need to get home, did you see the time?"

A smile teased at the corners of his mouth, but he shook his head and indicated to the seat beside him. "Sit down and eat something. Your clothes are in the guest bathroom."

There was no room for negotiation in that statement, and I was still too sleepy to even try and argue—despite the fact that my clothes had no reason to be in Beck's guest bathroom. Mute, I slid onto the stool beside him and took a long gulp of my coffee. It was exactly how I liked it—pitch black.

I was starving, so I didn't put up a fuss about eating the waffles in front of him. They looked like they'd been prepared by a chef, topped with sliced bananas, fluffy mascarpone, and drizzled with maple syrup. Mouth-watering heaven.

"Jesus Christ," Beck muttered on a laugh, looking at me from the side of his eye. "If I'd known, I would have fed you waffles sooner."

"Hmm?" I frowned at him, my mouth full, then blushed hot when I realized I'd been moaning my appreciation of the food. How. Embarrassing. I swallowed, then cleared my throat and took another sip of coffee to cover the awkwardness. The bitterness of my black coffee contrasted perfectly with the sticky sweetness of the waffles, and I needed to bite my lip to keep from making anymore borderline sexual noises over my breakfast.

Beck just snorted a laugh and powered off his tablet. "I'm going to take a shower," he declared, then eyed me meaningfully. "A cold one. Take your time with that, we're not expecting Dylan until later but I think I'll get you started on basics before he gets here."

"Huh?" I squinted at him in confusion. Maybe I needed more coffee.

Beck shook his head at me. "You forgot? We're teaching you how to shoot today, Butterfly. It's time you became a bigger badass than you already are." With a flirtatious wink that was *so* not Beck, he departed the kitchen in search of that cold shower he mentioned.

I had totally forgotten Dylan was going to teach me defense and shooting today, and now that Beck had reminded me I was strangely giddy with excitement. Just more evidence that I was a bit fucked in the head, I guessed.

Quick as I could—without wasting it—I finished off my breakfast and stacked the dishes in the sink. I couldn't see a dishwasher anywhere and wasn't comfortable enough to go poking around in cupboards looking for one. Besides, I had no doubt the Becketts had staff lurking around waiting for me to leave so they could clean up.

Thankfully, the guest bathroom wasn't *too* hard to find. It was back in the direction of the cinema where we'd spent the night.

There was a neat, folded pile of clothes on the vanity and I didn't pause to look at them until after I'd showered and dried off.

"Huh," I muttered, picking up the spandex items and inspecting them. At first, my reaction was along the lines of, "where is the rest of it?" and then quickly my mood shifted to more of an evil chuckle. Silly Beck. He'd clearly picked out my outfit—high waisted leggings and a black strappy crop top—thinking he was pissing me off. Instead, I was just going to make his day *long* and *hard*. All puns intended.

Once I'd dressed, I tied on the black sneakers that were parked in front of the vanity then admired my reflection. He'd gotten my sizes spot on, but that didn't even surprise me. Beck had that next level possessive thing going on, and despite the fact that I still had *no idea* where we stood with each other, his knowledge of my sizes was no shock.

For lack of any idea where else to go, I headed back through to the kitchen while weaving my long, unruly hair into two French braids. Thankfully, I had some spare hair ties around my wrist, so I could secure the ends.

"Hey," I said, coming up behind Beck who was pouring another mug of coffee.

He turned, and his gaze darkened, dragging over me from head to toe before he handed me the beverage. "Come on, trouble," he growled. "We're heading to the range."

The fact that he already knew I needed more than one coffee to function in the morning showed a level of understanding I wasn't ready to acknowledge. So I just sipped my drink and followed him through the rabbit warren house, wondering what in the hell the *range* was.

"Oh," I blurted as Beck led me into a literal gun range. In the basement of his house. What the fuck...? "Right, this makes total sense."

He flicked a quick look at me, then gestured for me to come closer. From a small table he picked up a highly polished wooden box and held it out to me.

"What's this?" I asked, curious and excited. My parents had done their best, but money was seriously tight in our household. I barely even got gifts on my birthday, let alone for no good reason.

Beck gave a half shrug. "Just figured you needed something more girly than the guns we use." He said it casually. Too casually.

Suspicious, I opened the box. Inside was a delicate handgun, its handle a pearly cream enamel with a blue butterfly painted on it. The engraved plate in the box said it was a Smith & Wesson M&P9 Compact 2.0. I knew nothing about guns, maybe less than nothing, but this one was prettier than most I'd seen.

"Sebastian," I breathed out. "It's beautiful."

"It's just a weapon," he muttered, turning to a locked door and scrolling the combination to open it. Inside was a collection of guns that would put a private security company to shame. It wasn't just a cupboard, like I'd thought. It was a full walk-in supply room with every variety of gun imaginable mounted on the walls. Or ... that was what it looked like to me, anyway.

"Holy shit," I whispered, staring at the collection with a slack jaw.

Beck threw a cocky grin over his shoulder at me, but selected a normal looking handgun and several boxes of ammo. I kept peering into the storage room, and he coughed a short laugh.

"You can play with the big guns after you learn some basics," he told me. With his hand on my lower back, he guided me away from the arsenal and over to the little cubicles set up in front of a long room. Running down the ceiling, tracks were set up to mechanically place targets and return them with a click of a button. Only the best when you're that stupid rich, I supposed. For the next while, Beck taught me "the basics" as he called them. It was difficult with my fractured arm to hold the gun completely steady, but if I used that hand just as a guide, I managed to figure out a way.

After our discussion in the cinema last night, the training session was strangely ... enjoyable. No trace of the prickish asshole surfaced. He was calm, patient and understanding to the point that I started watching him from the corner of my eye with fears he'd been body snatched.

Dylan arrived early—around the same time Beck actually let me fire real bullets from my very own gun. The look on his face as he entered the gun range in the Beckett basement was one of pure confusion. No doubt he'd expected to find us tearing shreds from each other, blood splashed all over the walls and curses being screamed. Instead, what he walked in on was me jumping up and down with excitement as my target returned to show I'd actually hit the paper. Turning to Beck, almost on instinct, I high fived his waiting palm—awkwardly with my casted hand seeing as I still held a gun in the other one—then beamed at Dylan.

"Hey!" I greeted him. "Did you see? I hit the paper!"

I proudly waved my hand at the target which hung in front of my station. Admittedly, the little hole from my bullet was still a *long* way off the colored rings, it was barely even on the page. But fuck it, that still counted in my book!

Dylan gave Beck a cryptic glare over my head, then turned back to me with a smile. "You sure did, Riles. Good work."

"Keep practicing, Butterfly," Beck instructed me, brushing his hand across my bare back and sending an instinctual shiver of arousal racing through me. "Dylan and I need to discuss you."

"Excuse me?" I demanded, whipping around to scowl at him.

"Your *training*," he clarified, cocking one brow at me. "What did you think I meant?"

My face heated, and I turned back to my target to hide the embarrassment. "Uh, nothing."

"Mm hmm," Beck murmured with a small chuckle. He and Dylan stepped outside

Fighting the urge to follow and listen in, I instead examined my beautiful gun. Trying to decipher the hidden message there. Why did Beck buy me something so ... personal?

Okay, yeah, I was clearly fucked up enough that this was akin to jewelry for me. My very own, pretty gun. It had to mean something. He'd said as much last night, but there had been so little good in my life lately that a very large part of me was screaming not to trust Beck. To not trust his words, which were so perfect. Too perfect.

But I was so fucking invested at this point, I couldn't walk away, even if I wanted to.

Even if they would let me.

The guys returned a moment later, and there was no tension between them. If anything, Dylan looked amused while Beck was mostly expressionless.

"Come on, killer," Dylan said, indicating I should put my gun down. "It's time to learn how to defend yourself."

Checking the safety on my gun, because that was the first thing Beck drilled into me, I placed it gently on the bench and followed the guys from the room. Dylan was first while Beck slid in behind me. The two of them towered over me and it was like I had my own personal bodyguards as we moved into the room beside the range.

"Whoa," I said when we entered the gym. And by gym, I meant a fucking state of the art area with every piece of equipment or weights one could ever need to become Mr. Olympia. There was also a ring, where I assumed Beck beat the shit out of people he didn't like, and a padded area which was where Dylan led us. Beck stayed back and let his friend take the lead. Dylan's expression was serious as he stood across from me. "It would take me years to make you sufficient in martial arts, there's no fast tracking true skills. So today I'm going to focus on Krav Maga."

I blinked at him, not having heard that before. "I don't know what that is. All I know is Jackie Chan and Jet Li."

Dylan chuckled, and his eyes flicked to Beck. I followed that line of sight, and was surprised to see that Beck also looked amused. "Let's save the Wushu training for another time, Butterfly."

I shrugged, again having no idea what the hell Wushu was.

"Krav Maga basically translates to unarmed combat. It's about getting out of there alive and using natural instincts to do so. You already have a lot of fight in you, so it shouldn't be too difficult for me to hone that into quick, more instinctive reactions."

I nodded. "Yep, I like it. Sounds down and dirty, which is how I fight."

Beck's laughter rumbled out, and I flashed him a grin before giving Dylan my attention again.

The big guy stepped into me, and maybe it was the simple fact that we were fight training, but suddenly he seemed really huge and menacing. He wore workout clothes too, his tank cut off at the sleeves, showcasing his massive arms. Between him and Beck, I was on ripped body overload.

It was almost too much for one chick to handle. Thank fuck for my rabbit.

Swallowing hard, I shuffled back a little. "I mean, you could kill me with one punch. Are you sure I could get away from you?"

His smile was slow. "I'm not going to punch you," Dylan said, spreading his arms to the side like he was proving his innocence. "I'm going to teach you how to punch me."

Now that sounded more like it. I stopped moving, and he got really close. There was a sudden tension in the room, and it wasn't coming from Dylan or me. "First thing you'll learn is the open hand strike," Dylan said, and he was suddenly all business. "You can cause a lot of pain if you hit them in the right spot."

I cocked an eyebrow at him. "Need I remind you of my currently broken state?" I waved my braced wrist, then indicated to all my various bruises.

"You're not broken, Butterfly," Beck commented in a dark voice, "Not yet, anyway."

Dylan just shook his head and scrubbed a hand over his face. "I'll be careful, but you need to learn this. The idea of you being defenseless…" He trailed off with a grimace, and I could have sworn Beck *growled* like a pissed off bear.

"I'll be careful," Dylan repeated, reassuring me.

He demonstrated how I should use the heel of my hand to strike over and over, aiming for the throat, back and front, the nose, and the thinner bones on the bottom of the face. Since I only had one working hand at the moment, I just mimed the action with my broken one.

"Pivot your hips a little," Beck said from the sidelines, and I met his gaze. Dylan's hands landing on my hips had me gasping as I turned back, and I could have sworn Beck made another low growling noise, but I was too distracted to confirm it.

"What are you doing?" I asked Dylan, feeling his strong fingers pressing into my hips.

"Showing you," he said seriously. "You'll get way more power if you move your body into those strikes. And always aim for the vulnerable spots like I showed you."

It took me a few seconds, but my natural athleticism kicked in and I was able to start striking harder. "Good," Dylan said, stepping back. "I want you to do this over and over, until it becomes like second nature. Practice it every single day."

I nodded, my arms tingling from the adrenalin. I had no fucking idea why this was so awesome, but I was wondering if maybe I was born to fight. Like my blood and body had known all along I was part of this billionaire company, even if my brain did not. Or maybe I was just sick to fucking death of being a victim, and it was nice to have some control for once.

"The next thing we'll focus on is the kick to the groin," Dylan said, stepping back slightly. "For this one, I'm definitely using the pads."

I snorted as he walked to a shelf and pulled down a medium sized black pad. "A groin kick can take down almost anyone," he told me when he returned. "And there are ways to do it much more effectively."

I snorted. "Hello, not a novice at the dick kick, my friend. Guys have trouble with the word no. It's in every girl's arsenal."

Dylan grew serious, and I was just wondering what I'd said, when I felt heat at my back. Beck pressed right into me, and I almost groaned at the feeling of him behind me.

"Who?" he said softly, and I really had no idea what he was talking about.

Dylan moved forward, not touching me, but I could feel his heat as well.

"Who couldn't take no for an answer?" he breathed.

Oh. That's what this was about.

Furious, dangerous men surrounded me, and instead of scaring me, it turned me right the fuck on. "No one you need to worry about," I said a little breathlessly. "I got in a good dick kick, and then Dante dragged him away, and I never saw him again."

I'd never asked Dante what had happened to Peter Topher, probably because I had a sneaking suspicion he was floating in a river somewhere. Some things were better not to know.

"We deal with things like that from now on," Beck warned me. "Dante has been relieved of Riley Duty."

I spun, glaring at him. "If you don't want me to test my new skills on you, you better back up on the Dante thing. He's my best friend. I won't give him up. You're just going to have to learn to play nice with him."

The funniest thing was, Dante could have been in part of Delta. Hell, he'd wanted to be part of it before they'd dragged me into this life. I mean, he fit all the requirements of their inner circle, tough, tall, tatted, had a dick. But I knew they trusted no one else, so I had to ease the suggestion into a later conversation.

"Can we get back to kicking ass please?"

Beck grumbled but backed up, and Dylan resumed with instruction of how to perfect a groin kick. He showed me how to put the most speed and power into it, and I slammed my leg into the padded bag he held.

"You've got strong legs, Riley," he said when we were done. "And with one of your arms weak at the moment, it's the perfect weapon for you to use if you don't have your gun."

I nodded while pushing back a few strands of hair that got loose. Dylan moved closer to me in a single smooth stride, and suddenly his arms were around me, and he was holding me tight, but not too tight to hurt my ribs. "Next we'll deal with an attacker that grabs you."

I gasped at the long firm lines of his body, forgetting for a moment this was supposed to be an attack. "Dylan," Beck said, that one word held so much warning, that my stomach clenched. There was the scary Beck.

Dylan wasn't worried though, and I thought I felt his body shake a little as amusement creased his face. "Just self-defense, brother."

I edged out from Dylan's hold and met Beck's gaze. Fuck. Dark storm clouds filled his eyes, and his jaw was locked in place, arms rigid at his sides. Dylan leaned down, his voice brushing over my bare skin near my throat. "This is interesting," he murmured. "Beck and I have never thrown down over a chick. Wanna push him a little?"

I shook my head quickly. "No," I spluttered, louder than he'd been. "Definitely not. He'll kill us."

Dylan was for sure laughing now. "Come on, babe. I finally found Beck's weakness. Might as well take advantage."

"No," I said more firmly, and he winked.

"Whatever you say, Riles."

I tried to pull away, but he held me tightly, and suddenly this wasn't fun anymore. "An attacker is not just going to let you go," he said, his voice low and rumbly. "You're going to have to make them let go."

"How?" I asked, unable to move an inch in his firm grasp.

Dylan started to pull me across the workout space. "What would you do if someone started dragging you away like this?"

JAYMIN EVE + TATE JAMES

I blinked. "Uh, that hand punch thing?"

He nodded. "I want you to use everything I showed you, and when I pull you, don't try and go the other way. Come at me with force. Knee kicks, swing your arm, push back at me in the direction I'm trying to take you."

His words from before about firing Beck up appeared to be forgotten as we focused on this new maneuver, and it was some time before Dylan was satisfied with my counter attack.

Then he took me to the ground, and I hit with a thump, all air leaving my lungs as his heavy form landed on me. He instantly absorbed some of his weight onto his forearms that were braced either side of my head, but it had still hurt like a bitch. "Ground attacks are another thing completely," he whispered, his eyes twinkling at me.

That lasted a fraction of a second, though, before he was hauled right off me, and a pissed off Beck was looming over both of us. "Enough," he said. "You're only teaching her basic moves. I can fucking do that."

Dylan, looking slightly pissed himself, jumped to his feet. "You were the one who wanted me to do it because you're more interested in fucking Riley than in teaching her."

Beck growled, like his freakin' chest rumbled, and he swung at Dylan before I could blink. The pair clashed, and I scrambled back out of the space they were occupying.

"What the hell are you doing?" I screamed, on my feet and trying to figure out how to get between them. Only there was no fucking way. I hadn't been kidding when I said one punch from Dylan would kill me. One punch from either of them.

"Beck!" I demanded, getting closer than I should have.

He ignored me. Both of them ignored me, and I had a sneaking suspicion they were enjoying beating the shit out of each other.

Fuck this. I spun around and started marching from the room. I didn't have my phone on me, but I'd memorized Eddy's number in case of emergencies. Something Dante had always drilled into me. I found a landline at Beck's, and I called Eddy.

"Uh, hello?" she said, sounding unsure.

"Hey, girl, it's me," I said quickly. Can you get me from the front of Beck's place?"

I heard shuffling as she moved, and then: "Yep, be there in five."

"Riley!" Beck shouted. Knowing he was coming for me, and that he was pissed, I sprinted for the front door, grabbing a heavy woolen coat from the stand near the door and made it outside in a flash. My cart was sitting there and I jumped on it, gunning it out of there. Despite my stolen coat, I was fucking freezing, but not enough to send me back into that pissing match.

Beck needed to learn I wasn't going to sit there and watch him beat the shit out of his friend for touching me. I mean, I liked he felt possessive, but we were a team. That's what they always said. I wouldn't come between them; that was the last thing I wanted.

When I reached his front gate, it was open, no doubt from Dylan entering before, which made it that much easier for me to get out and ditch the cart. Eddy pulled up a second later, and I practically dove into the passenger side.

"Go," I said, waving my arms at her.

She laughed as she spun the wheel and hit the gas. "Girl, what's going on with you?"

I shook my head before sinking back into the soft seats. "Fucking Beck and

Dylan. Seriously. Those assholes think they can solve everything with violence."

Eddy must have noticed my workout gear then. "Defense training?" she guessed.

I nodded. "Yeah. Beck lost his shit when Dylan touched me, and I left the two of them smashing each other in the face."

Eddy shrugged. "Violence is in their blood. You're gonna have to get used to that if you're hanging around."

"Do I have a choice? Not to hang around?"

She shot me a side-eye. "No. Like ... not a fucking chance. You're in and there is no getting out."

I dropped my head into my hands. "I don't know what I'm doing? Beck ... the guys. It's a lot. I have already gone through so much pain with my parents, I don't know if I can live this sort of life where I'm constantly afraid to lose one of them."

Eddy swung her car around a bend, and we exited the compound which held the five Delta estates.

"Beck will never let you go," she said seriously. "I know I warned you about staying away from them, but things are different now. I've never seen or heard of him throwing down over a chick, and he would especially never do that with the other guys. They're a strong unit. A brotherhood. You might be the first thing that's ever come into their midst that they want to fight over."

I couldn't wrap my head around it. Something about me being one of them, an inheritor of this Delta legacy, had them all screwed up. "Where are we going?" I asked when it finally clicked that Eddy hadn't taken me home.

"Jasper told me you were ditching today for training, so I decided to ditch too and visit him for a few hours. Figured you might want to go?"

The thought of seeing Jasper filled me with excitement. "Absolutely. I've been worried about him."

He'd texted me a few times, and I knew he was supposed to get out in a day or two. He'd had to have minor surgery on his spleen, but his recovery was going really well now. I'd been dying to pop in and see with my own eyes that he was okay. The hospital we pulled up in was the same one where I'd been checked over after the crash. "This is our hospital," she said softly. "With Delta approved doctors. You'll be coming here from now on, if you're ever injured."

"Your hospital?"

She laughed. "I mean, they treat other patients too, but we have priority, and we do all the hiring and firing. Everyone is vetted through the company. It's safe here."

Yeah, like the pilot vetted through Delta. Nowhere was safe, and Eddy was naive to think otherwise. When we got inside, no one stopped us at the desk. Eddy just walked through like she owned the place, which apparently she kind of did. Jasper's room was really nice, with a huge bed, fancy flat screen television, and a scantily clad nurse in his lap.

"Ew, Jasp, seriously." Eddy covered her eyes before snapping at the chick. "Get the fuck out of here, skank."

The nurse glared before she slid off his hand—Jasper's signature move—and straightened her clothes. "I'll see you later," she said to Jasper, shooting Eddy a sly grin as she passed.

Eddy shook her head before turning to her brother, who had thankfully tucked any body parts away, and was once again sprawled back with just a pair of gray sweats on.

"You're looking much better," she said, hurrying forward.

He shrugged. "Genetics. Mine are perfect."

I snorted before I crossed to sit on the other side of him. He reached out with an arm and hauled me closer. "Better get my hug in before Beck shows up here and puts me back into surgery," he said against my shoulder.

With a laugh, I gently pushed him away. "What?"

"Dylan called me. Seems our boy has a little problem with a pair of blue eyes and perky tits."

Despite his injuries, I couldn't help but slap him on the arm. "Seriously, dude. You need help."

Eddy made a small sound from nearby, and Jasper turned to her. "What, sis?"

She shrugged. "Nothing, just never seen you treat a girl nicely before. It's … weird."

Jasper was suddenly serious, and I preferred this side of him to the joking sleaze. That one was his facade for the world. I like the glimpses of the real Jasper I'd gotten in the forest. Strong and loyal, badass and brave.

"Riley is not just any girl. She's ours. One of us. And despite the tension, I've been thinking about how the dynamics have changed. She's good for us … she makes us better."

He was talking about me like I wasn't in the room, but when his face turned in my direction, there was so much emotion in his eyes, that my body tensed. It wasn't romantic, per se, but it was something.

"Can you do me a favor?" Jasper asked, taking me by surprise.

"Uh, sure, what do you need?"

He grinned, and then reached across to a small side table to grab a set of keys. He dropped them into my hand, wrapping his fingers around mine for a moment. "There's a race on Friday. It's my race. I've won every year since I started. I need you to take my place and keep the legacy alive."

I blinked, looking down at the fancy keyring with the Lamborghini symbol. "Are you serious?"

I mean, he'd seen me race once and I crashed the fucking car. I still wasn't sure I wouldn't have another freak out and do the same thing if I raced again.

Jasper chuckled. "Firstly, it's just a car."

Wrong, it was an effing Lambo, but sure.

"Secondly, I watched some race videos of you. Pretty sure my baby couldn't be in better hands."

No one called their "just a car" baby. He loved that yellow flashy number, and he was placing her in my hands.

"I'm going to win for you," I said, determination lacing my words. "Those fuckers will wish they never underestimated me because I'm a chick."

Jasper laughed. "Might be best if you don't tell Beck until it's too late for you to back out." He turned to Eddy. "Can you make sure she has the cash for buy-in, we want this to look legit as possible."

Eddy grinned a wicked smile. "You got it big bro! Oh, this is going to be fun."

Chapter 20

We ended up spending the rest of the afternoon hanging out with Jasper in his hospital room, and it was the most fun I'd had in a long time. Actually, the whole day had been—with the exception of Beck and Dylan's little pissing contest.

When Eddy dropped me back off at the Deboise estate, though, my heart began to sink. If luck was on my side, Catherine and Richard would still be in the New York office, but that meant I was all alone in this massive mausoleum.

My golf cart was still at the Beckett house, so I took my time walking across the perfectly manicured grass to get up to the house.

"Miss, you're home late," Stewart commented as I let myself in and wandered through to the kitchen. "Good day at school?" He gave my obvious *not*-school uniform a pointed look, and I blushed.

"Uh, something like that. Are the DNA donors still in the city?"

The elderly servant smothered a smile and nodded. "Yes, I believe they are due to return tomorrow or the next day."

"Cool," I murmured, looking around and feeling a bit lost. "Uh, do you think I could order pizza for dinner or something?"

"Absolutely, Miss," Stewart replied with a warm smile. From a drawer, he pulled out a stack of paper menus and presented them to me. "Master Oscar was particularly fond of Romano's, but I'll let you choose. Just call down when you decide and I'll get it ordered on the house account for you."

Smiling back at him gratefully, I took the menus and headed up to my room. Nightmares or not, I was determined not to go fleeing into Beck's embrace again tonight. Sooner or later, I needed to learn to face my demons alone.

After my pizza and a long shower, I decided to tackle some school work in the hope that it would send me to sleep. After about an hour of staring at quadratic equations, my eyelids were drooping like they were coated in lead.

Satisfied that I was tired enough to actually sleep, I flicked off the lights and crawled into the middle of my huge bed. It took a couple of tosses and turns, but eventually I found a comfy position and closed my eyes.

Gloved fingers bit into the soft skin of my neck, squeezing tighter and tighter, cutting off my air supply until—

"Fuck!" I yelled, sitting bolt upright and gasping greedy lungfuls of air. "Fuck, fuck, shit, fuck." Tears streamed from my eyes, and I began to shake as residual terror washed over me in waves. "This can't keep happening," I sobbed into my arms as I hugged my knees.

Dimly, I heard my phone vibrate softly—again—but I ignored it. Beck had been messaging all afternoon, and I'd been clearing the notifications without reading them. He needed to learn that I wasn't a leg of mutton that he and his friends could fight over like hungry wolves. Checking his messages would have only made my resolve crumble, especially after how sweet he'd been last night in the cinema. The way we had kissed... I groaned, but happily let the confusing, fuzzy emotions push aside the fear that had been dominating me.

Something made a sound outside my windows, and I startled. Sitting there, frozen, I waited. What had it been? It sounded like...

There it was again! It sounded like someone had just pried the intruder mesh off my windows. Holy shit, someone was breaking into my room!

Frantic, I scrambled out of bed and hunted for a weapon. Stupid me, I'd left my beautiful new gun at Beck's house so the next best thing was a heavy, carved wooden lamp.

I yanked the shade off it, tossing it aside, then brandishing the base like a bat as I waited for my intruder to enter the room.

Seconds later, the window clicked open, and a huge, dark shape slipped through and pushed the gauze curtains aside.

I didn't hesitate for a second. With a wild battle cry, I swung my lamp and smashed it into the intruder's head. Or, I tried to. He was taller than I'd expected, and I mostly hit shoulder.

Good thing I did too.

"What the fuck, Butterfly?" Beck roared, clutching his shoulder and stumbling back a few steps. "What the hell did you just hit me with? Is that a *lamp?*"

Gaping in horror, I dropped my weapon and clapped my hands over my mouth. "Oh my god, Sebastian." Laughter started to bubble up and I did my best to swallow it down. "I'm so sorry, I thought you were coming to murder me! Wait, what the fuck are you doing climbing through my damn window like a creeper? I'm on the second floor! How did you even get up here? Why didn't you use the damn door, you psychopath?"

Beck just scowled at me and stalked across the room to flick my *other* lamp on and inspect his injuries. "I think you cut me," he muttered, pulling his shirt off to get a better look at his upper arm. Dear God. Drool.

"Beck!" I snapped, desperately trying to keep my hungry eyes off his tatted up muscles. "Answer me!"

He huffed and actually rolled his eyes. He broke into my room like a fucking cat burglar but he was *rolling his eyes* at me? "If you had checked your phone, you would have known I was coming," he informed me with a sarcastic lilt. "Besides the fact that we just spent all damn day teaching you to defend yourself and you still decided to attack with a *lamp?*"

I sighed and rubbed my eyes as I flopped back down on my bed and cuddled a pillow. "Why are you here, Sebastian?" I asked *again*. "I think I made it pretty clear I didn't want to see you tonight."

"Yeah, well I wanted to see you." He shrugged, sitting on the side of my bed and peering at me with way too much insight and understanding. "How were you sleeping, Butterfly?" he challenged me, propping his leg up and leaning over me as I lay back down to cuddle my pillow defensively. "No bad dreams?"

I scowled at him. "You know full well I wasn't sleeping," I whispered in a hoarse voice. Fear and desperation threatened to overwhelm me again, and I clenched my jaw to force them away.

Beck just gave me a knowing look, then stood up and stripped his jeans and boots off.

"Uh," I stuttered, not even trying to stop from staring. "What are you doing?"

He kicked his clothes aside, then climbed over me and wriggled under the blankets. "What? I'm not sleeping in jeans, Butterfly. Now shut up, you actually have to attend school tomorrow." His strong arms gathered me up, and I released my pillow as he tucked me into his warm embrace.

Yeah, I was still pissed at him and annoyed as fuck that he turned up uninvited ... but I was so glad he was here. My whole body seemed to sigh as the tension dropped away and the steady beat of Beck's heart lulled me to sleep.

If I was more interested in psychology, I'd have been questioning why such a dangerous, secretive, violent person could make me feel so utterly *safe*. But I wasn't second guessing shit.

#

Sunlight streaming into my room woke me, and I scrubbed the back of my hand over my eyes. Why were my fucking curtains open?

Warm hands tightened around me, hugging me tighter against a hot, hard body and I grinned. That's right. My late night intruder must have left them open.

I yawned and snuggled back into his embrace. It was the first time I'd woken up after a night with Beck, and he was actually still there.

He mumbled a sleepy noise, his hands shifting on my belly and his lips pressing to the back of my neck in a way that caused a delicious wave of half-asleep arousal to roll through me.

"Good morning, Butterfly," he murmured in a rough, thick voice. His hands shifted further until one large palm cupped my breast. The thin fabric of my tank top may as well have not been there at all, because my nipple hardened under his fingers as though I were naked. His lips moved lazily across the back of my neck, and I moaned a little.

"Sebastian," I breathed in warning. Warning of what? I had no idea. All my sensible thoughts had flown out the window. Or maybe part of my brain was still asleep.

He breathed a sigh into the back of my hair, his hardness pressing into my ass as he pulled me closer. "I fucking love when you use my name," he confessed in a dark whisper.

I snickered. "I do it to piss you off."

He kissed the spot behind my ear, and I could *feel* him grinning. "I know. It's such a turn on, Butterfly."

I smiled like a damn fool, arching my neck and groaning encouragement as his hand not on my breast ventured south, slipping inside the small shorts of my pajamas and under the soft cotton of my panties.

For a long, indulgent moment, I let him work me over with his hand until I was panting and writhing against him. As much as I was loving how talented his fingers were, I was craving something more.

His teeth nipped at the bend of my neck, and I gasped. "Sebastian..." I trailed off with a groan. "I don't have any..."

Beck's lips paused against my neck, and his fingers stilled for a moment. "Shit," he cursed. "I didn't bring any either."

A strangled, frustrated noise escaped my throat. "You didn't?" I was shocked. He seemed like the type who had condoms permanently stuffed in his pockets.

"I wasn't coming over here to fuck you, Butterfly," he informed me, his forehead dropping to rest on my shoulder. That statement clicked something inside me, and I lost a little piece of my heart to him. He hadn't climbed through my window for a booty call. He'd come because he was worried and wanted to help me sleep…

I might have to change his name in my phone after all.

Wriggling around until I was facing him, I clasped his face in my hands and kissed him long and hard. "I don't suppose you've had a health check recently?" I suggested when our kiss ended and both of us were breathless.

Beck's dark brows shot up, and his lips moved soundlessly for a moment. "Um, yeah," he finally said. "Last week, actually. It's sort of a Delta requirement to get regular checkups. I'm clean…" He shifted back a little to peer at me with lust-filled curiosity. "You?"

I knew my cheeks were flaming red, but my pussy was demanding a more satisfying ending to this wake up. "Yeah, I got the full medical after the accident." I bit my lip. "So … I mean…" I gave a little shrug and hoped he could grasp my meaning without having to spell it out.

A slow grin spread over Beck's face, and his hands slid my shorts and panties down together. When he got as far as he could reach, I wriggled the rest of the way out of them and kicked them off my feet while he did the same with his own boxers.

Our lips returned to each other like magnets, and Beck hitched my leg up and over his hip. It put us in the perfect position, so it barely took any effort for him to slide his steely cock inside me.

"Shit," I hissed, tipping my head back as he filled me and hit all those needy nerve endings in just the right way. There was nothing between us, and I refused to read too much into it. This was just sex, right? Just really, *really* great sex. I wasn't deluding myself into thinking Beck wanted to date me or anything crazy like that.

"Fuck, Riley," he murmured, burying his face in the side of my neck as we rocked together. It was such a stark contrast to the wild, angry way we had fucked just a couple of nights ago. This was lazy and relaxed ... almost— cringe—like we were *making love.*

That L word crossing my brain scared me, so I pushed Beck's shoulder until he was flat on his back with me straddling him. We didn't lose our connection for even a second, but the new position allowed him much deeper into my pussy, and I gasped, bracing my hands on his chest as I adjusted to the new sensation.

Beck's eyes widened as I began to move, riding him slowly. For one, I was loving the sleepy, languid early morning sex. For two, my thighs still burned from my work out with Dylan, and I probably couldn't have picked up the pace if I'd tried.

Reveling in my position of power, I shifted my weight back a bit. Just enough that I could take my hands off his chest and strip off my pajama tank top.

"Butterfly." Beck groaned as my naked breasts jiggled while I fucked him. "This is unfair." He reached up and palmed them both, rolling my nipples between his fingers while I chased down the orgasm that was slowly building. I leaned back a fraction farther, then gasped as the tip of Beck's cock found my g-spot.

"Oh my fucking God." I whimpered, ignoring my tired leg muscles as I set the exact speed and depth I needed until my climax crept up and crashed over me. My pussy clenched tight, spasming as I cried out and Beck's hands tightened on my waist.

He waited until I slowed, then flipped us over and reclaimed *his* place. The dominant one. Controlling fucker.

Beck's hands pressed down on my thighs, spreading me wide and pinning me down as he re-entered my tight, post-orgasm core. Hissed curses fell from his sexy lips as he thrust into me, and I arched my back. It made it an even tighter fit for him, seeing as he still held my thighs pinned wide apart, but it also meant that as he fucked me, his hard dick rubbed my clit.

Selfish? Fuck yes, but if I could milk a double orgasm before school, I damn well would.

We fucked harder now. Within moments I scored that second climax and screamed my satisfaction while my good hand tangled in the sheets at my side. Apparently that was the last straw on Beck's will-power and seconds later he hurriedly pulled out of me and spilled his hot load all over my stomach.

Thank fuck he'd understood what I meant. Accidental pregnancy was *not* on my to-do list, and I already had plans of sorting out some birth control asap.

We stared at each other for a long moment, both panting and sweaty, then Beck leaned down in a stupidly sexy push up to kiss me.

"Good morning, Butterfly," he whispered, then hopped off the bed and disappeared into the bathroom. I figured when I heard the water running that he was taking a shower, so color me surprised when he returned with a warm cloth for me to clean up with.

"Thanks," I mumbled, taking it from him. Beck just gave me this weird sort of half smile, then sauntered his tight, naked ass back into my bathroom.

I wiped up and tossed the cloth into my washing basket, then sat on the edge of my bed and scrubbed my face with my hands. What the fuck had that all been about? Was he going to ice me at school again today? I had to be honest with myself, if he let that Brittley slut hang all over him again, I'd probably bitch slap her. Then throat punch him. And thanks to Dylan, I could now hit damn hard.

"Butterfly!" Beck called from the bathroom, and my blood ran cold. Was this the part where he told me to keep this our dirty little secret and not tell anyone? "Get that gorgeous ass in here."

I froze. What? Did he just ... hesitantly, I wandered over to the open bathroom door and peered inside. Beck met my curious gaze through the steamy shower door and raised his brows.

"Well?" he prompted me. "Are you joining me?"

It was probably a terrible decision, but a huge part of me wanted this. I ignored all the warning bells in my head, telling me I was heading straight for a broken heart. My heart could only be broken if I fell in love with him, and that was insanity. Beck was just ... *Beck*. So I threw caution and common sense to the wind and stepped into the shower with him.

Chapter 21

The surprises continued after our shower, with Beck declaring that he was driving me to school, and that he'd already told Eddy not to stop by.

"Possessive much?" I muttered, pulling up my knee high socks and arching a brow at him. "You know people are going to *talk* if I turn up to school in your car?"

His gaze heated, running over the length of my leg that I had propped up on a chair. "Good," he growled. "It's time they know you belong to me." I spluttered a noise, and his eyes darted away from me. "*Us.* Delta, I mean. Anyway, go have some coffee and breakfast, I'll be back in fifteen to pick you up."

I assumed he needed to go and get his car, or a change of clothes, seeing as he had literally climbed through my window the night before. Whatever, the double-O before breakfast had me in too good of a mood to argue with him.

A stupid grin seemed glued to my face as I headed into the kitchen after

Beck left. I couldn't seem to wipe it off, but no one else was around to see me looking like a fool, so who cared?

"Oh, uh, good morning," Richard said as I walked into the kitchen, and my smile slipped off my face. He and Catherine were seated at the elaborately laid breakfast table and Catherine was glaring at me like I was dog shit stuck to her Jimmy Choos.

"Hi..." I dragged the word out, awkwardly assessing how I could get the fuck out of there without being too obvious?

Richard gave me a tight smile and indicated to a third place set at the table. "Please, join us. Breakfast is such an important meal for a growing teenager." His face was drawn, his words underscored with sadness and my heart went out to him a bit. Catherine was evil to the core, there was no doubt about that, but Richard just seemed like a grieving father.

I hesitated, rocking on my stupid heels for a moment, but my mind was made up by the subtle headshake Catherine gave me.

Oh, what's that? Don't want me to join you? Suck my dick, Debitch.

Smiling sweetly at my birth mother, I politely accepted Richard's offer and sat down for breakfast.

She scowled at me like she was plotting my death, and it only made me want to piss her off even more. If I'd been a more callous person, I'd have asked about Oscar. But I sensed that Catherine didn't care much for her son as anything more than the Deboise legacy. A title I now held. No, bringing up my dead brother would only hurt Richard and so far I didn't see how he deserved that from me.

"Riley," Catherine started, clearing her throat and folding her hands in front of her. "I don't know what sort of loose morals your adoptive parents raised you with, but you're part of a very respected company now. That comes with certain expectations of *behavior*." She said this last word like it was distasteful, and I suspected she was talking about my less than subtle fuck session with Beck this morning.

Ordinarily, I'd have been mortified. Or, I would have been if my *real* parents had heard me getting my freak on. I shuddered even thinking about it. But Catherine's insinuation that my parents were irresponsible or just generally shitty parents, made me see red.

"Insult my parents one more time, Catherine," I spat at her. "I fucking dare you."

My cursing made her jaw clench, and I watched her fists tighten on the table. She wanted to hit me so badly, but was holding back for some reason. Because of Richard? Or because I'd fought back last time?

"Regardless," she hissed. "No heir of mine will be gaining a reputation as the town bicycle, nor will she be giving birth to some illegitimate bastard before graduating high school." Her words were laced with venom, and I wondered what she'd say if she knew it had been Beck who was riding *this* bicycle.

"Not to worry, mommy-dearest," I replied with sickly sweet sarcasm. "If that happened, I could just dump the baby and pretend it never happened. You know all about that, don't you?"

Her face turned a splotchy red, and her lips parted in fury. Before she could respond, though, Richard cleared his throat.

"Don't you have a meeting with Langham this morning, dear?" he reminded her, taking an innocent sip of his coffee.

Catherine glared daggers at me for another beat then sucked a sharp breath and turned back to her husband. "I think you mean *we* have a meeting with Langham, Richard. They expect to see both of us."

Richard just shook his head. "I'm not ready. You go on without me and give me the abridged version later."

It was a clear dismissal, if I'd ever heard one. Catherine huffed, but threw down her linen napkin and stormed out of the kitchen with a sharp clicking of her heels.

"I apologize about her," my biological father said softly when she was gone. "I'd like to say this is a result of Oscar's..." His voice broke over the missing word—death—but he cleared his throat to continue. "But in truth she's always been a cold bitch." He dabbed at his mouth with a napkin then pushed back his chair. "I don't mean to cut your breakfast short, but I wondered if I might show you something? I'm so rarely here and time ... time is just not on our side." His words dripped in melancholy, and my heart broke for him.

"Of course," I agreed. I hadn't even touched the food, but whatever he wanted to show me must have been important. This was the longest he'd ever spoken to me, which I knew was because of my resemblance to Oscar. The son he'd loved, and the one he'd lost.

Richard led me through the house to a room which was quite obviously his office. It was all leather bound encyclopedias and heavy furniture. So old-fashioned-rich-man. He gestured for me to sit on the chesterfield and wandered over to the huge oil painting behind his desk. It was of a severe looking old man and based on the clothing it was from a generation long past.

Richard flipped the painting forward on hidden hinges, and spun the combination dial of the safe behind it. He took out a manila folder from inside, and left the safe open while he returned to me.

JAYMIN EVE + TATE JAMES

"Riley," he started, then cleared his throat and perched on the other end of the couch. He placed the folder on the leather between us and laid his hand over it. "I wanted you to know..." He trailed off with a sigh, and I sensed that this was causing him pain. "Catherine ... when she was pregnant with you, we had a falling out. I left her, moving into my apartment in New York City. I regret it more than I can say, but I wasn't there when you were born."

He fell silent, his gaze fixed firmly on the packet between us.

I took a wild guess at what he was trying to tell me. "She got rid of me before you arrived?"

Richard nodded, and my opinion of Catherine dropped even further.

"She told me you were stillborn. That it almost killed her as well. She had a body..." he broke off, clearing his throat before he continued. "I'm telling you this now, because I have been trying to distance myself from Delta ever since. I might have been born into this legacy, but it was always something Catherine wanted. More than me."

Catherine was a right old gold digging bitch.

"Why did you marry someone as toxic as her?"

Richard closed his eyes for a beat, like a bad memory had taken him by surprise. "In the very beginning, she was different," he said when he recovered. "We actually met at a board meeting with Huntley, and I thought she was charming and funny and beautiful."

I gasped at his casual use of our enemy's name. He met my stare with a hard one of his own. "The drama between our companies didn't used to be so drastic and deadly. We've actually done a lot of business together. Catherine is the daughter of one of Huntley's CEOs."

I gasped again, and it almost sounded comical. "Have you stopped to think that maybe she's just here to sabotage Delta?" I asked bluntly.

Richard let out a sad laugh. "She's proven her loyalty to us time and again. She rejected her family when all of the underhanded bullshit started."

Yeah, right. I knew women like Catherine. She was playing both sides, there was almost no doubt of it. "I wish that she'd never come back into my life," I told him bluntly. "Not only did I lose my parents, but I'm now stuck with a legacy I never wanted."

"Just like me," he said with a nod.

He nudged forward the folder that had remained between us, and I hesitated to pick it up. Part of me was scared to see what was inside. Like, it might be information that would destroy the tenuous happiness I'd found in the last few days.

Unable to control my curiosity any longer, though, I reached out and gripped the edge, pulling it toward me. My hands were shaking as I flipped it open, and I blinked when the contents came into view.

"What is this for?" I asked, flicking through each piece.

"Riley…" The pain in that word drew my attention. His eyes were filled with a sadness that almost drowned me. "I can't lose another child," he whispered. "You need to run. Now. Run and never look back. Leave the country; everything you need is inside."

The tremble in my fingers increased as I opened the passport, finding my photo but none of my correct details inside. There was also a license, birth certificate, bank cards, cash, and a few other pieces of paper, all with the same fake name: Chelsea Smith.

"It's top of the line," Richard said. "If you keep your head down, no one will find you."

A week ago I would have been all over this, even with the shitty reality that I'd have to run and hide my entire life, but now…

I would be leaving my guys. I would be leaving Beck.

Like Richard had heard that thought, or at least read the resistance on my face, he leaned forward. "You can't trust him, Riley. You can't trust any of them."

I blanched, sucking in a deep breath. "What … why?"

"Delta, the company, it controls them, and whatever is happening with you and the successors right now, that's all part of the plan."

A denial sprang to my lips, because there was no way those guys were faking emotions with me. Except … I knew they were highly trained and intelligent. If they needed to pretend, to gain my trust for some reason, then I had no doubt they could do it. But could Beck really fake that shit when he was buried inside of me?

Was I being played in the greatest con that had ever crossed my path?

"I don't believe you," I whispered, pushing the folder back toward him. "I appreciate you looking out for me, I really do. I haven't had many people in my corner since my parents. But I know these guys. We're a team."

He looked at me like I was either stupid or naive, but he didn't push it again. "I'll keep this in the drawer here," he said, showing me exactly where it would be. "You can take it and run at any time. If you need to get out."

I felt queasy now, whatever good mood I'd had from Beck last night and this morning gone. Richard had instilled the smallest sliver of distrust inside me, and while I was nowhere near close to believing him, I did start to wonder if I'd been a little too quick to trust the guys.

Standing, I took a few steps back. "You can't fake the bond," I whispered, smoothing down my skirt. "They're a lot of things, dangerous and violent, but they don't lie. They made their dislike obvious at the start, but things changed between us. When we were fighting for our lives … it shifted the dynamics."

Richard didn't argue, he just nodded, lips flattening. "I hope you're right, Riley. I've seen what happens when Delta puts its power to use, demands the successors fall into line. Bond or no bond, I'm not sure they could deny the order."

"For me they would," I whispered, hoping I wasn't as fucking naive as he clearly thought I was.

Spinning on my heel, I rushed from the room, and hurried back through the house.

I wasn't watching where I was going, still upset from the conversation with Richard, and I missed the fact that Beck was waiting for me right in the middle of the foyer. I let out a huff of air as I crashed into him, and his arms went around me to steady us both.

"You okay, baby?" he said, in his low rumble of a voice.

My head shot up, and I drank in the perfect dark planes of his face, and those eyes which were lighter and more silvery today. My heart did that lurching thing that always happened around him, and my stomach went all swirly. "Uh, yeah, just a weird conversation."

Concern tilted his eyes down, and he examined me closely. My breathing got a little faster, and then he stilled before slowly lifting his gaze from my face. Turning, I saw Richard. Beck and he exchanged a long look, and it wasn't one filled with any warm or fuzzy emotions. Richard actually backed up, and I was surprised to see what looked like fear crease his face as Beck stared him down.

"Come on, Butterfly," Beck finally said, wrapping an arm around me, and half lifting me toward the door. "We're going to be late for school."

A dark energy radiated off him as he opened the door and buckled me into the Bugatti. Secretly I was glad this gorgeous ride was back in action, and I was going to make a conscious effort not to vomit in it again.

"What did Richard say?"

Beck's words were low and thrumming with anger. I hadn't quite realized, until this moment, but he was majorly pissed.

"Just … I don't even really know. He was warning me about Delta. The amount of power and control they have."

For some reason I didn't tell Beck about the new identity waiting for me in that folder. Because there was now a small part of me unsure in this new life, in the bond and relationship. A part of me wanted to keep an out, just in case.

"He needs to be careful," Beck said. "Don't bite the hand that feeds you."

Not so veiled threat there. "Can you really blame him?" I said angrily, feeling somewhat protective of my birth father. "He doesn't want to be part of this world any longer, but he can't get out. I mean, it cost him a son."

Beck's hands flexed on the wheel, and he must have called ahead for the gate out of the compound, because it was open and waiting for us to just fly through without pause.

"There is no point fighting against things you can't change."

That almost sounded resigned, even though the anger was still underlying each word.

"Delta is and always will be. It's different for their generation of inheritors. They're … not family like we are. Not bonded. They have no loyalty."

He made that sound like the worst kind of crime. "I told him I wasn't interested," I said softly. "I'm choosing to remain loyal. Not to Delta, I don't give a fuck about that misogynistic old as fuck, white-washed corporation. But I do care about you guys. I have your back."

And I did. That much I had no doubts about. Maybe that part of me that remained unsure was the same part of me that always wondered how I could have been thrown away as a baby. When my parents had told me I was adopted, it had hurt, despite me loving them more than anything. It was still ... rejection. It damaged a fundamental part of me, making me question why I wasn't enough. Illogical, but it was what it was.

"We're a team now, Riley. Forget what Richard said, he's just grieving for Oscar."

I decided he was right, and to lighten the mood, I flashed him with a bright smile. "You called me baby. Getting soft in your old age, Sebastian?"

His returning smile was slow. "Don't push me, Butterfly. I might be tempering the darkness for you, but any time you need me to ... break you a little, I'm more than capable."

He accelerated hard when he said that, and I bit back my moan, tightening my hands into fists as I resisted the urge to climb over into his lap.

I compromised by reaching across and taking his hand. He met my gaze, and I gave him a genuine smile. "I liked it."

He untangled our hands before brushing a thumb across my cheek, and then focusing again on the road. The drive was over in less than a minute, mostly because Beck's car was a fucking masterpiece of design and engineering. His spot was free, as it always was, and when he pulled in, two other cars parked on either side of him. I hadn't realized that the guys were following us. Dylan, in his black on black G wagon, and Evan in a lime green

JAYMIN EVE + TATE JAMES

… whoa, I hadn't actually seen the Lamborghini wagon before, but I knew they were fast and badass. These guys had the best fucking cars. I'd have been jealous, except I wasn't sure I wanted the strings which came attached to them.

My door was opened, and I startled before looking up to see Dylan and Evan grinning at me. "Come on, Spare," Evan said, holding out a hand.

Beck edged his friends out of the way, getting to me first. "I'm on Riley Duty today," he said shortly. "Let me know if you hear anything."

Both of them reached out and fist bumped Beck, as if they were all sealing a pact. I resisted the urge to roll my eyes before crossing my arms and settling back against the side of the Bugatti. I knew these guys hung out in the parking lot until the first bell, establishing their rule over the school and world in general.

Hangers-on gathered closer, and I wasn't surprised to see that I was getting confused- intrigued looks from the guys, and confused-angry looks from the chicks. Beck and Dylan fell in on either side of me, their arms brushing against my shoulders as they chatted casually about a party on Friday night. "You're gonna be there, right?" Evan asked, nudging me.

I snorted. "Uh, I'm not sure. I guess I'll see if Eddy wants to go."

My last party experience hadn't ended so well, but hopefully this time Beck wouldn't give me a reason to down half a bottle of tequila … yeah, okay, I needed to own my actions, so I'd admit it was only partly Beck's fault. He hadn't poured the alcohol down my throat.

"Wait, did you say Friday?"

I was supposed to be driving for Jasper on Friday.

Beck nodded. "Yep, but we won't be there until after the race."

He said it so casually, and I tried not to react. "Oh, awesome."

Oh, fuck. I was going to have to pull a fast one if I was going to race without Beck trying to stop me. I wondered if I should just tell him what Jasper wanted and then put my foot down if he refused. Beck always got his own way though, and I needed this. I needed to race. The stress and trouble sleeping, some of it could be alleviated with a fast car under my hands.

Beck would understand once it was all over and he saw I was actually really fucking decent at driving.

The bell rang then, and I straightened, noticing, that Eddy had just arrived and was waving at me from beside her car. "See you guys at lunch," I said with a wave before I hurried to my friend.

Beck gave me the slightest illusion of freedom, remaining with the others for a moment longer before he followed me across the parking lot.

Students watched us like we were the latest drama on television. Eyes wide, mouths open, well, all those that weren't talking about us in hushed whispers. "Beck's right behind you," Eddy muttered when I reached her side. She looped our arms together and dragged me into the school, hundreds of students joining us.

"He's on Riley Duty today," I said, leaning closer to her. "Until the Huntley threat is dealt with, they're basically on my ass."

She shook her head. "Don't kid yourself, girl. Huntley is never over, the level of threat just changes with whatever is going on in the world."

"So why are they…?"

She shrugged. "I'm guessing that they're feeling a little possessive and protective of you for some reason." She looked over her shoulder at Beck before turning back to me. "I wonder why that might be…"

I had to look at him then, it was a pull that I couldn't resist. He stood a head above most of the students around us, and even though he was a few feet away from us, his eyes were focused on me with intensity. Fuck, when he gave me all of his attention like that, my knees did the cliché weak thing, and I almost couldn't stay upright.

Eddy squeezed my arm when she left me at my homeroom before she disappeared into the crowds. I slipped inside and took my usual chair. I heard gasps when Beck entered the room, and I had to shoot him a grin and eye roll. The way he was treated in this school was ridiculous. He wasn't a god.

He slid into the table beside me before he extended his giant arm out and wrapped it around the back of my chair. More gasps. Eyes watched us closely before turning away like they were afraid to get caught.

"You're drawing attention," I drawled, shaking my head at him.

He shrugged. "Can't help that."

I kind of thought he could, but all of the Delta heirs—the male ones anyway—got off on the power and attention. Beck and Dylan were scary, Beck more so because Dylan was nurturing by nature. Evan and Jasper went for the sex on tap thing, using their power and popularity to get the chicks. It didn't hurt that they were hot with rockin bods either, but it was mainly the power and popularity thing which brought the skanks in.

"Hey, Riley," a low voice said from my other side.

Turning in my seat, I met a set of light blue eyes. "Hey Jake." I returned his smile.

He'd talked to me a few times before; he was shy, with a serious face and dark rimmed glasses. He mustn't have noticed that Beck was with me today, which didn't surprise me because he usually had his head in a book wherever he went.

"How are you?" he continued, pushing his glasses up on his nose.

I shrugged. "Can't complain."

Had two screaming orgasms this morning.

Beck leaned forward slightly in his chair, and shot Jake an unamused look. Jake's pale features went as white as the wall behind him, and he swung around to face the front.

I narrowed my eyes on Beck. "Was that really necessary?" I snapped.

He shrugged again, his broad shoulder brushing against me, and sending shivers across my skin. "Didn't say anything," he said, a smirk playing around his lips.

Beck didn't need to say anything to get his point across. Fucker.

The teacher didn't blink an eye at Beck being in the wrong room, and wrong grade since he was technically in college at Ducis, and shouldn't be in any classes with me. When the bell rang, I waited in my seat, wanting all the staring students to leave before I did. Beck remained in his relaxed position, hot ass leg spread going on in front of him as he leaned back in the chair.

I caught the edge of his ink creeping out the side of his black shirt, and tried to resist my strong urge to touch him.

"Are we sitting here all day, Butterfly?" he asked, amused. He'd caught me checking him out, and I didn't even care.

Rising, I straightened my shoulders, trying to act like I didn't care about all the new attention coming my way. It was worth it to spend time with Beck. To be part of the inner circle. I finally felt like I was part of a family again, and I wasn't giving that up.

Richard's words washed through my mind, but I dismissed them. I wasn't being stupid and naive. He didn't know Beck, Dylan, Jasper, and Evan like I did. He didn't understand. He hadn't gone through blood and fear like we had. Beck had confirmed that this morning: the previous generation of inheritors didn't have this bond.

When we reached the hall, lots of students watched us. Beck remained close to my back, his heat washing down my spine, and for some reason, I threw extra sass into each step. Swinging my hips.

Beck's hands wrapped around my sides, pulling me to a halt. "Keep that up, Butterfly, and you're not going to make classes again."

A moan choked off in my throat. This was not the place, but, shit.

I wanted him.

Needing to get myself together, I spotted the bathroom and darted toward it.

"I'll be right back," I called over my shoulder, ignoring the huff from Beck.

I half expected him to follow me in, but he didn't.

Deciding I might as well pee while I was in here, I entered one of the free cubicles. The other two were occupied, and I heard toilets flush a moment before I finished and flushed as well. Stepping out, I stopped when I saw Brittley and one of her friends at the sinks, washing their hands. Trying my best to ignore them, I moved to the remaining sink, and placed my hands under the automatic soap dispenser first, followed by the water.

"It'll never last," Brittley said brusquely. "You're just the new flavor of the week, but they'd never actually care about trailer trash like you."

Her friend laughed, crossing her arms across a very ample chest.

Exhaling loudly, so she knew she was pissing me off, I dried my hands and faced the pair. "And I give a fuck what you think because?"

It was her turn to laugh. "Because Beck and me are soulmates. He knows that. He always comes back to me."

I tried not to let jealousy rear its head, but the thought of this skinny bitch wrapped around Beck made me feel sick. "You don't mean shit to him," I countered, knowing this for a fact. "But since you seem so sure about it, we should ask Beck to choose. Let's go out right now and do that."

I waved a hand at the door, and for a moment, fear flashed in her eyes before her natural confidence reasserted itself.

"Would probably be the fastest way to get rid of the trash," her friend chimed in, boosting Brittley's confidence further.

She nodded. "You're right, Jade. Beck and I were together last week, I'm sure he wants more of what I brought his way."

My hands clawed, ready to rip her head off, but I refrained for the moment. *Last fucking week.* I was going to kill him. My fury was bubbling over as I slammed the bathroom door open, startling a few students lingering in the hall. Beck was leaning back on the lockers across from the door, seeming relaxed, but he had been waiting for me, because he straightened immediately. I stormed across to him, and before he could say a word, I slammed both of my hands into his chest and shoved him as hard as I could.

I'd been hoping he would hit the locker, but he didn't move at all.

"What's up, Riles," he asked, looking amused.

I jerked my head toward Barbie one and two behind me. "Britters here seems to think you two were fucking last week. You know. When you were…"

"In a plane crash with you," he cut in, that amusement going nowhere.

Brittley shifted uncomfortably, and it almost looked like she was about to take off, so I reached out and snagged her arm dragging her closer. "When was the last time you fucked her?" I asked Beck.

He shook his head. "Never. I don't touch chicks like this."

"I—" I opened and closed my mouth, words dying on my tongue.

Brittley let out an aggrieved sound, fighting against my hold now. When she jerked herself free, I just stared at her. "What sort of overconfident cumbucket pretends she's important to someone, when he's never even touched her?"

She sniffled, crossing her arms in a protective manner. "He's touched me plenty, and it was only a matter of time before he realized how good we would be together. That we're meant to be together."

Jesus. She was delusional.

Beck had dismissed Brittley completely at this point, his gaze scorching me with its intensity. "You hit me, Riley Jameson," he growled slowly. "You didn't trust me, believing the word of a fucking lying skank. Right now, I'm about ready to take a hand to your ass."

I swallowed hard, trying to keep my expression neutral, even though my insides were doing a happy sexy dance at the thought of Beck losing control with me. "Promises, promises," I purred. It got me hot pushing him, because angry Beck might be scary, but he was also sexy as hell.

"What is wrong with you?" Brittley screamed then, her hands fisting in her hair. "She's trailer trash. Poor and pathetic. She's not good enough for you."

Beck's attention went to her for the first time since she'd stepped into the hall, and I almost felt sorry for her, because the look on his face was not one I would want directed at me.

"Riley is worth a hundred of you," he said soft and menacing. "If you value your life, and the life of your family, you'll stay the fuck away from her.

Don't talk to her. Don't look at her. Don't breathe in her direction."

Brittley looked like she was going to pee herself right there in the hall, and it took Jade three attempts to finally get her friend moving away from us. I still felt somewhat sorry for her, because I'd been reasonably sure of how this situation would go down.

"Come on, heartbreaker," I said with a smile. "We're late for class."

This was becoming the story of my life.

Chapter 22

That night, Beck didn't even give me a choice. He just drove me straight to his house after school, and I didn't complain. As badly as I hated to admit it, I was falling for him. He made me feel safe, and in a world where people were literally trying to kill me, that was a big deal.

Once again, I slept in his arms and didn't have a single nightmare. He kept my darkness at bay. Thursday was much of the same, and I kept waiting for something to burst this perfect little bubble my world was currently in.

Friday at school I spent the day giddy with excitement and anxious Beck would catch me out on my lie of omission. Eddy had already declared that I'd be getting ready at her house, and we would meet the boys at the race. I didn't believe for a second that Beck would actually just leave me alone with Eddy, but at least it was Evan on Riley Duty again, and we were pretty sure he'd be curious enough to let it all play out.

"Fuck me, you look dangerously sexy," Eddy muttered as she admired her handiwork a full half hour before the race was due to begin. Once again, she'd chosen my outfit, and done my hair and makeup for me. She was right, though. I looked all kinds of dangerous in charcoal jeans, black crop top and leather over-the-knee boots with killer heels. "You're going to kick their asses," she breathed, grinning from ear to ear. "Are you okay driving in those heels though? I thought you needed like... flats or some shit?"

"Yeah, if you're an amateur," I snickered. Not that I had a huge amount of experience driving in heels but I had total faith in my abilities, heels or not. Laughing nervously, I tossed my dark curls over my shoulder. Eddy had put some sort of magical serum in it that made it look like I'd just stepped out of a shampoo commercial. "Let's just hope I don't choke and end up totaling Jasper's baby."

Eddy cringed. "Don't joke, babe. Jasper would murder you ... and that's only if there was anything left after Beck was done. Come on, we have a race to get to." She grabbed her phone and started tapping out a message while we headed through to the garage where Jasper's canary yellow Lamborghini waited for us. "Just telling Evan to keep his trap shut," she told me, waving her phone in the air. "He'll see Jasper's car and assume it's me driving, but the last thing we need is for him to mention it to Beck. A suspicious Beck is a scary Beck."

I grimaced at the idea of Beck catching me out before the race. His temper ran hot most of the time but something like this, I could imagine him finally making good on that promise to turn me over his knee and smack my ass right there in the street in front of his friends.

Ugh, why did that idea turn me on so hard?

JAYMIN EVE + TATE JAMES

I clicked the key fob and the gull wing doors lifted to allow Eddy and me into the car. From the glove compartment, she pulled out a wad of cash and handed it to me.

"Keep that in your lap," she suggested, "I don't want anyone seeing me give you money when we get there. Jimmy gets really worked up about people paying their own entry to race."

"Got it," I said, glancing at the wad and estimating it was a similar amount to the last buy-in. Two hundred thousand at least. So much money it made me ill, but then again I was driving a car worth more than double that.

"Let's do this." I grinned at Eddy and gunned the engine as the automatic doors opened. Evan was lurking near the gates in his own car—a Porsche 918 Spyder this time—and he smoothly pulled out into the road behind us. The Lambo had such darkly tinted windows that I knew Eddy was right, Evan would assume it was her driving, so I kept my speed checked and didn't show off. Not yet, anyway.

Eddy directed me to the race start point, and instructed me on the course as we drove. It all sounded pretty straight forward, and we'd driven over it casually during our lunch break, so I wasn't too worried. Nope, the deranged butterflies that were flapping around madly inside of me were all for Beck.

We pulled up directly beside Jimmy, and I rolled down my window.

"New girl," he said, tilting his ball cap up in surprise. "Driving Jasper's car. What ... uh ... what am I to make of this?"

Smiling, I took the cash from my lap and held it out to him. "Jasper's still in the hospital, I'm his proxy."

Jimmy hesitated, glancing around him. Probably looking for Beck.

"Hey," I said, bringing his attention back to me, "You're in charge, right?"

Jimmy nodded slowly. "So what's the issue? No one even needs to know they're racing a girl if that's what you're worried about."

The race coordinator rubbed the back of his neck, then sighed and took my wad of cash. "Fine, you're in. But if you total this car, I want *nothing* to do with the fall out. Understood?"

Beaming, I nodded. "I absolve you of all responsibility."

Jimmy grumbled something under his breath but tucked the money in his pocket and walked away while I hit the button to wind the window back up.

Eddy waited with me, right up to the point that the racers—just four of us this time—needed to line up. Then she popped her gull wing door and stepped out.

"Kill them all, babe," she encouraged me with a sassy wink. "I've got money on you for the win."

As her door closed and she walked away, I spotted Evan's horrified face in the crowd.

Shit. Beck was about to find out in about five … four … three … two…

Sebastian Roman Beckett's furious glare was the last thing I saw before the flag fell and my foot slammed down on the gas pedal. He could curse me out later because right now, I had a race to win and a reputation to repair.

\#

Jasper's yellow Lambo didn't let me down. We flew across the finish line several car lengths ahead of the next driver, and I gently eased down my speed until I could safely loop around and return to Eddy. She was standing beside Jimmy, jumping up and down and screaming like a lunatic. I could hear her even through the closed windows of Jasper's car.

Crazy bitch.

It was the three scowling, scary as fuck dudes waiting behind her that made me hesitate on exiting my vehicle though.

Crap. They looked *really* pissed off. So much for Jasper's idea that Beck would be fine if it's "all in good fun." Little bastard set me up!

Grabbing my phone out, I shot him a quick text.

I won your race, but I think Beck's about to murder me. Say nice things at my funeral.

His reply came almost immediately.

Hah! Murder you with his dick, more like.

Classy. I replied with a deadpan emoji face. Fucking Jasper.

A knock on my window saw me fumbling my phone before I peered up at Eddy's beaming face.

"Come on," she shouted through the glass. "Stop being a pussy!"

I sucked in a huge breath and released it in a heavy sigh. Time for those metaphorical big girl panties. With shaking fingers, I popped open my door and waited for it to raise before I got out. People were whooping and cheering for me, and it reminded me of old times. If only Dante was here to see me...

My gut panged with guilt, remembering that I still owed him a car to replace my butterfly.

"Hey! I know you!" Some random dude called out, pointing at me. He was clearly wasted, but he squinted at me and nodded. "Yeah, you're that chick."

Eddy snorted. "She's clearly a chick, that much is obvious."

I smirked at her, and she laughed.

"Nah, nah, nah." Drunk guy waved his hand in the air. "You're *that* chick.

The one who used to race the butterfly car down in Jersey. Didn't you get in a crash and like ... kill your parents or something?"

Shock ripped through me and my jaw dropped. "Excuse me?" I breathed in outrage.

"Yeah," drunk guy carried on, slurring his words badly. "You were like some kind of racing urban legend and then you just *poof!* Disappeared."

My lips moved, but no sounds came out. This dude had clearly combined the crash that killed my parents with the crash that destroyed butterfly. But the accusation that I was responsible for my parents' death left me utterly speechless.

I needn't have worried for long, though. Seconds later, Beck's fist met drunk dude's face and sent him sprawling—unconscious—on the ground.

Shock saw me gasping, covering my mouth with both hands as I frantically looked around. Was anyone going to intervene? Beck could *kill* that guy! He was more than capable, given all his training.

But everyone was just staring like this was some sort of half time entertainment. Eager, fascinated, but not in the slightest bit concerned. Only one person wasn't watching Beck as he stalked over to where drunk dude was sprawled.

"Hey," I grabbed Eddy's arm, "isn't that..." My words trailed off as I searched the crowd again and came up blank.

"Isn't that who?" My friend asked, peering in the direction I was looking.

I shook my head. "Nothing. I thought I saw that creepy guy from the mall filming us again, but maybe I imagined it."

Jeering yells came from the crowd that had closed around drunk guy and Beck. They pushed me into action, and I shoved my way through the spectators until I saw Beck holding drunk guy by the neck of his bloody shirt, whispering something to him.

"Beck!" I snapped with as much authority as I could muster. He cast a look over his shoulder at me, then dropped bleeding drunk guy back to the ground and straightened up. He dismissed his victim without a second glance and grabbed me by the upper arm.

"What the fuck, let me go!" I shrieked as his fingers bit into me. When he ignored me and kept dragging me toward his Bugatti, I decided to take matters into my own hands.

Using a series of basic maneuvers that Dylan had taught me, I broke Beck's hold on my arm and backed away from him cautiously. "You were hurting me," I explained in a shaking voice as he glared death at me.

"Get in the car, Butterfly," he ordered me in a low, dangerous growl. From the corner of my eye I could see Dylan and Evan hovering nearby looking ... concerned.

"No," I replied, backing away from him a few more steps. "I came here in Jasper's Lambo, and I'm leaving in it."

Beck took another menacing step toward me, and I backed up three more.

"Riley," he snapped. "Get in the fucking car." His jaw was so rigid that his cheek was ticking, and his whole frame was strung as tight as a piano string.

"You don't own me, Sebastian," I said with a stronger resolve. "A couple of fucks does not give you the right to manhandle me and order me around."

We had a huge crowd, everyone from the race was hanging off our every word like a reality TV show, and it was turning my stomach. These rich kids were fucked in the head.

"That's where you're wrong," Beck bit back. "I own *everyone* in this town, and in eight months that'll extend to a significant portion of the world. Don't embarrass yourself by pretending you have free will."

He started to step toward me, probably to put me in his car by force, but Dylan and Evan intercepted him, forming a human shield between us.

"What do you think you're doing?" Beck demanded, his fists clenching at his sides.

Evan responded quietly, probably hoping that our audience wouldn't hear. "Saving you from making a stupid mistake, bro. This is Riley, not some cheap skank. Think about what you're destroying here."

Beck stared down his friend for a long, tense moment then shifted his gaze to Dylan.

The big, scary dude just folded his arms over his chest and glared right back. "You need to calm the hell down, brother. Walk away now, or I'll make you walk away."

My eyes widened, but I wasn't stupid enough to say anything. Beck stared at his best friend for a long time before glaring past him at me. "We'll be discussing this later, Butterfly," he promised me, and I shivered with fear. Or arousal. Yep, I needed therapy.

He stormed back to his car then, and gunned the engine. The Bugatti purred in response, then escalated to a roar as Beck tore away down the road.

"What the fuck just happened?" I asked Dylan, as he wrapped his arm around my shoulders. "Would you seriously fight him to protect me?" The question came out in a shocked whisper, and I craned my neck to look up at him.

Dylan met my gaze unflinchingly. "Without hesitation."

"We all would," Evan added, stepping up to my other side and squeezing my hand. "Beck would expect us to protect you from anyone, including him." His expression brightened then, some of the dark shadows on his face disappearing. "Come on, let's get to the party. You've got a win to celebrate and maybe a few drinks will loosen up Beck's foul mood."

I snorted a laugh, because I severely doubted that much of anything was going to loosen Beck up. But I badly wanted to get away from all the prying eyes around us, so Eddy and I climbed back into the Lambo and followed Evan to the party.

Chapter 23

Despite all the tension and threats from Beck at the end of the race, he was nowhere to be seen at the party. When I finally found the ovaries to ask Evan, he told me Beck had been called in for a meeting with Delta. Apparently some of the successors before our parents were in town and wanted to chat. *Great.* Even older rich bastards. "Hey, that reminds me." I accepted the drink that Evan had just ordered for me and chewed the edge of my lip. "Beck said something about owning half the world in eight months. What's that all about?"

Evan heaved a sigh and wandered with me out to the back patio. "I don't know how much of a crash course you've had on all things *Delta*," he said, his gaze darting around us. "But basically it was set up like ... two hundred years ago. So lots of the rules are carryovers from a more antiquated time period."

I rolled my eyes, "Yeah, like the penis requirement for entry or the whole needing a blood heir to keep your seat thing?"

Evan grinned. "Well, you've already broken the penis requirement. Unless you're hiding something surprising in those pants?" He squinted at the crotch of my tight jeans then shook his head and shuddered. "Nope, no one could tuck that well. But yes, exactly like those dumb rules. This one was probably a carryover from when life expectancy was shorter, but basically the controlling seats of Delta passes to the next generation when the heirs turn twenty-one. That's in eight months for Beck."

My brows shot up, and I gaped at him. "Holy shit." I wondered then what Catherine had planned to keep me in line when I was the one in control. Was almost too scary to even think about. Come to think of it, if Oscar hadn't mysteriously died then *he* would have been the first to twenty-one. Was Catherine capable of murdering her own son?

I shivered.

"Yeah." Evan nodded, oblivious to my dark thoughts as he took a long sip of his drink. "Anyway, don't stress too much about how he was tonight. He was just crazy pissed that you'd kept secrets, and then when that dude mouthed off about your parents..." he trailed off with a shrug. "Beck has anger issues, you know?"

"I'm starting to see that," I whispered, leaning on the railing and staring out into the night. "Am I ... should I be worried?"

Evan shook his head firmly. "God no. I suspect he's taking his time at this Delta meeting because he's feeling bad about earlier."

That idea made me smile. "So this meeting ... how come none of the rest of us got dragged in?"

Evan screwed up his nose. "Ah, technically I don't know. But if I had to make an educated guess, they're grooming him to take over the Beckett chair. Basically dragging him into their meetings that we aren't privy to."

"Sounds fun," I muttered with heavy sarcasm. "But maybe that means he can start turning shit around, if he has a say in the decision?" I wasn't totally sure what I meant by that, considering I didn't totally understand what Militant Delta Finances actually *did* to maintain their hold of power. But it couldn't have been good. Not with how these boys had been raised.

Evan gave me a pitying look and shook his head. "Don't hold your breath, Spare." He raised his glass back to his lips and drained the last of it. "I'm going to grab a fresh drink. Want one?"

I glanced at the untouched cocktail in my hand and shook my head. "No, thanks. Send Eddy out to hang with me if you spot her."

"You got it," Evan said, wandering back into the house with his empty glass in hand.

The bar was only just inside from where I remained, and I didn't miss the fact that Evan kept me in his peripheral vision the whole time he was ordering his drink. When these guys were on Riley Duty, they really took it seriously.

My attention shifted when Eddy came sashaying out onto the patio with a huge grin on her face and a half empty cocktail in her hand. Not her first one, either, judging by the glazed look in her eyes.

"Hey, girl," she cooed, wrapping her arms around me in a sloppy, drunken hug. "Are you having fun?"

I laughed at her slurred words and waved away the potent alcohol fumes from her breath. "Holy shit, Eddy. You're such a lightweight."

"Am I?" she challenged, waggling her brows at me while sipping her drink. "Or do I have a Mary-Poppins-Bag stomach and this is really my twenty somethingth daiquiri? Hmm? You'll never know!" She hiccupped, then propped her ass on the railing beside me while I continued to grin at her.

"Pretty sure you're just a lightweight."

Evan rejoined us then, but instead of a fresh drink, he was scowling at his phone. "Spare, Beck called and said he needs to speak with Dylan and me urgently."

When he didn't explain further, I frowned. "Okay ... and?"

"And the reception keeps dropping out. I need to go back out to the street to hear him properly." His creased brow clued me in to his indecision, and I shook my head.

"I'm fine here, Evan. Just go and take your call, I'm perfectly safe with Eddy. Right, Edith?" I shoulder bumped my blonde friend, and she hiccupped again.

Evan scowled at her, but the look on his face when he glanced at his phone told me that whatever Beck *had* said, made him worried.

"Seriously, you'll be a couple of minutes," I continued. "Beck isn't exactly a long winded conversationalist. You can be there, make your call, and be back in half the time it'd take me to walk back to the road in these heels."

I wasn't exaggerating, either. The party was being thrown in a fancy, modern mansion on the side of a valley. The driveway to get in was a seriously steep incline, and I'd almost fallen on my ass about fifteen times when we arrived.

Evan hesitated a moment longer, but his decision was made for him when Dylan arrived and jerked his head to his phone.

"I know," Evan snapped, running a hand through his hair. "But Riley..."

Dylan shook his head firmly. "Beck specifically said no Riley."

This piqued my curiosity, but not enough that I cared to push the issue. He probably just wanted to talk about how pissed he was at me.

"For reals, guys," Eddy spoke up. "I got our girl for five minutes. I *think* I can handle that."

And outside of the plane crash, there had been zero attempts on my life since. I was pretty sure I'd be safe.

Dylan ran his gaze over me, then pulled a switchblade from his boot and slapped it into my palm. "You know what to do if anyone tries anything."

I snorted a laugh and rolled my eyes. "Yeah, like I'm going to stab some guy who gets handsy on the dance floor." When it looked like they would argue further, I slipped the knife into my back pocket. "Go. Your mighty leader will be getting anxious."

I got about twenty looks as they moved together toward the exit. It was very clear that they were not comfortable leaving me, and while I wasn't afraid for myself, I didn't like them out of sight either.

Eddy let out a low giggle, distracting me from my thoughts. "I can't believe the way you drove Jasper's car, babe. That was seriously the hottest thing I've ever seen. I wanted to bang you when you crossed the line leaving those fuckers in your dust."

I snorted, love for her swelling in my chest. I hadn't had a real girlfriend for years, and I'd forgotten how much I dug hanging out with an awesome chick. There were just some things that dudes sucked at, and girl talk was one of them.

"I almost wasn't sure I'd win," I admitted. "A flashback hit me at one point; my tires screeched the same way my dad's did when we crashed." I swallowed hard, trying to push the melancholy down again. "But I held my focus this time."

Eddy reached out and wrapped her hand around mine, holding it tightly, tears filling her eyes. She was drunk girl emotional. "I wish I could take that back for you," she half sobbed. "I hate that you've lost so much, and all for a stupid company that has more money than soul."

I blinked at her, wondering if she'd meant that the way it came out. "You think Delta orchestrated my parents' deaths?"

She stilled, some of the haziness in her eyes clearing. "You don't think it? I mean, timing alone…"

"I was in the car though," I reminded Eddy. "It's the biggest flaw I can see in the theory."

Eddy just shook her head, an angry sort of smile on her face. "You're thinking like a chick raised in the ghetto. There's a fuckload that can be done to ensure you survived and your parents didn't."

Eddy was the first person to put it so bluntly, and as the horror of her words registered, my stomach swirled with force. I lurched to my feet, ready to chuck up everything in my gut. "Be right back," I murmured, stumbling off the patio and hurrying to a nearby bushy plant.

"Riles!" Eddy yelled, almost falling down the stairs as she followed me. "You can't be out here—"

She was cut off then, and I lifted my head, my stomach heaving as I wondered what had happened to her. Stepping out from where I was partly hidden in the shadows, I saw her crumpled form on the ground. My first thought was that she'd passed out, but then a tall, broad shadow stepped out from the side of the house.

"Hello, successor of Delta," he said.

I couldn't see his face clearly, but it was not a voice I knew. My instincts told me to run, but I couldn't leave Eddy here at his mercy. Who knew what he'd do to her to get to me?

"If you come with me now," he said in a slow drawling accent, "I won't kill your friend."

Okay, that was apparently what he would do.

"Who the fuck are you?" I asked, not moving an inch.

He shook his head. "I'm no one. Just a guy doing a job."

Huntley goon. Had to be.

"Where are you taking me?" I was stalling for time because my guys would be back soon; I only had to keep Eddy and me alive until that happened.

He took a step closer, and as lights from the porch finally washed across his features, I recognized him. "You were filming us at the mall and race!" I accused.

He shrugged. "Had to make sure I had the right person. Delta hasn't had a female heir before, it's been quite the revelation."

I opened my mouth but he cut me off… "Enough fucking talking," he said irately. "You have two seconds to walk over here, or I'm going to stab your friend in the throat."

I took a hesitant step closer, wondering how long I could drag this out for. When I was within a few feet of him, he surprised me by lunging forward and wrapping a hand around my unbroken wrist. Dylan had grabbed me this way fifty times during our defense training while he was drilling a response out of me. He said that repetition was the best way to make something instinctive. Looked like he was right. Instinctively I pushed into my would-be kidnapper, breaking his hold, and then using my palms and knees, struck as hard and fast repeatedly until he was thrown completely off.

I hadn't forgotten the blade in my pocket, but right now I was focused on saving Eddy.

This guy was well trained though, and even though I'd taken him by surprise, I barely even got my hands under Eddy's body before he was dragging me away and across the rough ground. I fought and struggled, making it as difficult as possible for him, and deciding it was time, reached into my pocket to pull the switchblade out. It flipped open, and I swung my free arm, trying to reach any part of him.

I lucked out when I scraped over the hand that was clamped across my biceps. He cursed and loosened his hold enough for me to flip myself around. Holding the blade in front of me I had an immediate flash back to the plane, to the man I'd fought there with a knife. I hadn't done any training with this weapon yet, and I wished for my pretty gun. Why the fuck did I keep leaving it at Beck's?

"They're going to kill you," I warned him, backing up a little as I waved the knife in front of me. "They're already on their way back."

I'd been so busy taunting him, that I hadn't noticed just how close he was. Close enough to lunge forward and punch me right in the face. It hit with the sort of solid thud that bruised, if not fractured bone. I screamed, going down hard, black dots dancing across my vision as I fought against unconsciousness. If I passed out, I was dead. Or I'd wish I was dead when I woke up in the Huntley torture dungeon.

He loomed over me, and in my half dazed state I scrambled to find the knife that had been lost when I'd fallen. There was nothing around my hand, and I could have cried as darkness pressed in on either side of my eyes. Hands ran across me quickly, but I was so out of it, that it barely registered.

I was moving again then, my body bouncing along the hard ground, as

I weakly tried to twist from his hold. "No! Help!" I cried, but it was nothing more than a weak noise.

More darkness pressed in, blocking the light completely. I figured that this was me losing my tiny grasp on consciousness, but then the pressure around my body eased, and I heard thuds and scuffling, followed by the sort of rumbly growl that I usually associated with Beck.

Because I was free, I managed to roll myself over and started to crawl back in what I hoped was the direction of the house. My head throbbed like it was being repeatedly smacked with a hammer.

My vision was tunnel, most of it still blurry, the pain wanting to pull me under. Hands landed on my back, and I immediately started to fight, spinning to kick and punch. Dylan had said I should use my legs, and I was going to do my very best.

"Butterfly," a soft voice said, and the fight died. I slumped against him, and he lifted me into his arms. "Baby, hold on."

I had no strength to hold on, but I sort of realized he hadn't meant that in a literal sense. He was talking about not passing out on him.

"Eddy," I croaked.

He brushed a hand across my brow, pushing back all the wayward hair. "Evan has her, she's okay."

Tears leaked out of the corner of my eyes, and I finally let myself rest heavily against him, all of my fight gone.

The next however long was mostly a blur of pain. I managed not to vomit in Beck's car, and I counted that as a win.

"You managed not to get kidnapped as well," Dylan reminded me. I must have mentioned the vomiting thing out loud. Dylan was driving while Beck held me in his lap. "Proud of you, Riles."

"Thanks," I mumbled. "Need my gun."

Beck's arms tightened around me, pulling me closer into his rigid muscles. He hadn't relaxed once since I'd ended up in his arms, and the heat of his fury was burning me even through my clothes. I thought they would take me to the hospital, the Delta owned one, but we actually ended up at Beck's house. In another room I'd never seen before.

It was basically set up like a very expensive emergency room. White and sterile, with beds and as much medical equipment as I was sure most hospitals had.

"What is this room for?" I asked, wincing when I realized that was a pretty stupid question. I couldn't think straight with the pounding in my brain. What I meant to ask was why do you have a hospital in your house...

"Sometimes we get injured and we like to keep the details off public record," Beck explained, keeping his voice low and soothing. "I also have some doctors that I use and they won't step foot near a legit hospital. We've had to use this room a lot."

"Much easier to protect you from Beck's estate as well," Dylan added. He was close by even though I couldn't see him. Beck gently placed me on a reasonably comfortable hospital bed, and a warm blanket was draped over me. "Don't fall asleep on me, Riles," he said, adjusting the pillow under my head. "The doctor will be here in like two minutes."

"We could just do it." I heard Dylan argue. I'd closed my eyes at this point because the bright lights were hurting me. "Not like we haven't patched each other up a million times."

Beck disagreed. "I won't risk her. We'll just get an opinion, and then figure out what we want to do for treatment."

"Still awake over there, Riley?" Dylan asked quickly.

I lifted a hand and waved it, hoping that would be sufficient.

Beck was at my side then, and I let out a soft gasp when he reached out and took that hand, holding it tightly. My other one, the broken one, was gently held by Dylan, both of them offering comfort and support.

"We're so fucking sorry we left you alone," Dylan said, and Beck made a low angry noise. "We should have known better."

"S'okay," I whispered. "No one died."

"Not yet," Beck said softly, and the menace in his voice was enough for me to open my eyes and meet a set of steely gray ones.

"What does that mean?"

Beck's face was awash in shadows, despite the brightly lit room. He was scary right then, the ruthless Beck that didn't give a fuck who got hurt if he got his own way. "It means, that Huntley is about to be down another one of their hired help."

Oh, right. "That was the guy at the mall," I told them, not wanting any secrets between us. "He said he was confirming that I really was Delta, because you guys don't usually let chicks in."

Beck and Dylan exchanged a glance, one filled with about a million hidden messages I didn't understand. "So he'll be killed?" I asked, wanting to know for some morbid reason. He'd been creepy as fuck, he'd tried to kidnap me, and he'd punched me in the face. I couldn't find a sliver of sympathy for his situation.

But I still needed to know his fate.

Beck nodded, his eyes dragging over my face. "He's just lucky I won't be the one doing it. His death at my hands would not be merciful." He used his free hand and ran featherlight touches across the spot on my face that was throbbing. Where I'd been hit.

It surprised me Beck wouldn't be killing him, and I tilted my head to the side. "Delta upper levels are handling it," was all he said.

The doctor arrived then, his footsteps loud as he hurried across to the bed. He didn't have any medical stuff on him, but then again, he didn't need any in this room. Beck and Dylan greeted him with a head nod, and he looked wary but confident as he reached my side.

"Good evening, Ms. Deboise."

I sighed but didn't correct him.

He then spent twenty minutes checking me out, under the close and watchful eye of Beck and Dylan. When he was done, he washed his hands, and moved toward the guys.

"She's going to be just fine. I see signs of a mild concussion, but no fracture in her cheek. She needs rest and for someone to keep an eye on her for the next twenty-four hours. She can also have pain relief as required."

"Did you check on Eddy?" I asked, worried about my friend.

The doctor looked at Beck first before meeting my gaze. Every fucker thought they needed his permission to speak. "An associate of mine is checking her. The last update from him is that she's going to be fine as well."

"Yep, Evan just sent me a message," Dylan said. "She's back home resting. Jasper is home too."

Looked like the Langhams were going to need some full time medical professionals to take care of their kids for a while.

As I sank back, the doctor bailed, seeming relieved to finally be able to go. I sat up and turned to drop my legs off the side of the hospital bed. Beck was there before my feet could hit the ground. "What the fuck, Butterfly? You heard the doctor."

I raised a brow in his direction. "Yes, I heard the doctor, even though he didn't bother talking directly to me. I'm fine. Mild concussion."

Beck swept me into his arms, and I thought briefly about fighting him, but then I decided it was pretty comfortable here, and I really did feel tired and achy still. "I'm going to deal with our problem," Dylan said as we got closer.

Beck nodded, no tension at all between them, despite their earlier confrontation.

That was until Dylan leaned down and pressed his lips briefly to my forehead. Beck's chest swelled as a rumble of anger ripped from his throat. "Don't fucking push me," he said, and Dylan just winked at me before straightening and leaving the room.

"Fucker," Beck mumbled as he followed the same path out of the hospital area, taking me up the stairs again. I thought I caught a glimpse of a uniform clad man as we went past, but when I looked again there was no one. Clearly Beck liked his staff to stay out of sight.

I expected Beck to take me to the room we'd used for sex, but he continued on along that same hall until he reached the very last door. He opened it without jostling me at all, and I blinked when we stepped inside.

Unlike the generic spare room—pun intended—this one held personality. Warmth.

There was a massive king sized, or triple king sized more accurately, bed in the center of the room. It had a dark brown wood frame, and thick navy comforter. The wall to the right side of it was painted in a similar navy color, and was a feature of the room. Not just for the color, but because there was half a dozen guitars mounted to the wall on what looked like custom stands. Not in a million years would I have guessed that Beck played an instrument. He just didn't seem the type, and it immediately struck me that I really didn't know that much about Beck or any of the guys. So much of our relationship had been animosity and then fighting for our lives. I guess that was the brilliance of hoping for more years with them. It gave me time to learn everything.

Trust had to come first, and then the rest would follow.

As long as we had enough time.

Before I could examine anything else in his room, Beck placed me into the center of his bed. I lifted my butt so he could drag the cover over me. "Why did you bring me in here?" I asked sleepily, burrowing my head into cloud-like pillows. "I thought you never brought chicks to your room."

He was silent for a beat, and I opened an eye to make sure he was still there. He was. Staring down at me with an unfathomable expression.

"You're not just a chick," he told me. "You never were."

My eyes closed again, even as heat burned in my chest at those words.

For the next twenty-four hours, Beck barely left my side. Bringing me painkillers, and light meals, and waking me up all the freaking time even though the doctor hadn't told him to do that. He couldn't seem to help himself. My head improved quickly, and each time I woke it was to more clarity. I'd thought for sure I'd have a ton of nightmares, after almost being kidnapped, but I slept better than ever. Mostly because Beck was in bed with me a lot, and when I woke up I was often wrapped around him.

Early Sunday morning, when I opened my eyes to a dark, cool room, a soft strumming sound caressed my senses. It was a low, simple tune, but the beauty and darkness in each haunting note had goosebumps rising across my skin. I just knew this was Beck, and I continued to breathe in and out rhythmically so he wouldn't know I was awake and stop.

A minute later, he started to sing.

Holy fucking shit.

I'd never heard a voice like his, a low rasp of sorrow and anger and pain. I didn't know the song, but I felt every word he sang while his fingers strummed smoothly through the notes. Tears burned my eyes as I bit my lip to stop a sob from escaping. When the words stopped, the music continued, and what had seemed simple, turned more complex as the tempo changed. "I know you're awake, Butterfly," he said softly, not missing a beat on the guitar.

Wanting to see him play, I lifted myself up, happy that there was barely a twinge in my head now. I was afraid that Beck would stop playing, but he didn't. Our gazes locked, and I couldn't say a word as his song wrenched emotions from me I hadn't even realized I possessed.

He was on a chair in the corner, shirtless, his legs spread in that sexy way of his as he strummed the strings. I didn't know the sort of guitar he played, but it looked almost delicate against all the masculinity of Beck, but whatever it was, he had it mastered.

"You play and sing beautifully," I said softly, the darkness holding us in its cocoon.

His gaze stripped me of thought, and I stared like there was nothing else in the world but Beck. His hands stilled, and the guitar was slowly lowered down to rest on the wall next to him. He leaned back in his chair, that amazing, sexy-ass, inherently *Beck* pose. All of his delicious ink was on display and it pulled me from the bed like a magnet. My legs were steady as I crossed to him, clad in nothing but panties and one of his shirts which reached mid-thigh on me.

Standing before him, I held my breath as he reached out for me. His hands ran up my sides under the shirt, until he reached my breasts, cupping them and squeezing ever so slightly. My breath escaped in a hissing sigh as his thumbs caressed my nipples until they were hard aching peaks. I arched closer to him, my center aching as I desperately sought some sort of release.

"Are you feeling okay?" he rumbled, his head already lowering as he captured a taut nipple in his mouth, through the cotton shirt. I groaned, threading my fingers in his hair to hold him there. I never wanted him to stop what he was doing. When he eventually lifted his head the obvious wet spot there sent more swirls of arousal through me. "Riley?"

"Huh?" I blinked down at him, searching my sex-fuzzed brain for what he'd just asked but coming up blank.

"Your head," he elaborated with a slow, seductive smile—that bastard knew exactly what effect he was having on me. "Is your head still hurting? Because I can..." He trailed off, his brow creasing with a slight frown, and my eyes widened.

"You're not stopping!" I snapped, a little more desperately than I'd intended. "I mean, ah, apparently orgasms are the best form of natural painkiller. So technically..." I trailed off with a sneaky grin. Silently, I begged him to return to what he'd been doing a second ago, and thankfully he took the hint with a slow, smug smile of his own.

Beck's hands explored my bare skin, pushing up my borrowed shirt and allowing his mouth unhindered access to my sensitive nipples. My fingers tightened in his hair, my breathing quick as he slipped one hand down the front of my panties and stroked me in time to his tongue on my breast.

It took all of my self-control—*all* of it—not to scream in ecstasy as he played my body as skillfully as he'd played the guitar. Strong, sure fingers sent my body into a frenzy, and when I couldn't handle it any longer, I tightened my hold in his hair and pulled his head back from my breast. All so I could slide into his lap, leaving nothing but thin fabric between us as I pressed against him.

Beck hooked his thumbs into the sides of my panties and tore them clean off, leaving me spread bare as I straddled him.

A husky laugh left me. "You're hell on a girl's wardrobe, Sebastian."

He didn't comment, his expression serious and guarded as he lifted the bunched up shirt over my head, leaving me completely naked in his lap. The emotion from his music seemed to linger in the air as he kissed me with tenderness. He touched me, those huge palms of his sliding across my body, until I was nothing more than nerve endings filled with pleasure.

Beck had never been this way with me before. It felt more serious, like more than just sex. This was ... reverence. Love?

I balked as that four letter L word skittered across my mind, and pulled back from Beck's way too gentle kiss.

"What?" he asked. His bottomless gray eyes narrowed with suspicion.

"Uh," I hedged, not wanting to admit the thought that I'd just had. "Nothing, I just... remembered I forgot to call Dante earlier. He's probably freaking out if he spoke to Eddy." I shifted as if to get up, but Beck's strong hand on my waist held me still.

"Hold up," he said with an edge of incredulity. "You're naked, in my lap, my fingers literally inside you, but you're thinking about *Dante?*" His index and middle fingers moved slightly to emphasize his point, and I groaned— both in pleasure and because I instantly regretted my change of subject.

"God no," I hissed, tilting my hips forward a bit to encourage him into continuing.

Beck made a self-satisfied noise. "I figured as much. You're a terrible liar, Butterfly."

Giving up on my minor panic attack, I relaxed back into him and pressed my lips to his neck. "Are we chatting or fucking, Sebastian?"

"We're doing whatever I damn well want, Butterfly," he informed me. "Because I'm the oldest successor to this company and that means I own you." His voice was rough with desire even as he tried to maintain his King Shit demeanor. I'd never admit it to him, but the controlling Lord-of-everything bullshit was a stupid massive turn on for me, and my pussy tightened around his fingers.

An evil smile danced across my lips as I slid off his lap and onto my knees in front of him.

"Oh yeah?" I challenged, my fingers peeling back the elastic of his boxers and revealing Beck's impressive erection. "Give me five minutes and we'll reassess who owns whom."

In all honesty, I was *not* some sort of blow job goddess with superior sucking powers. I was, however, scarily in tune with Beck's subtle mood shifts, his body language, his breathing patterns. These were the things that mattered, and I put them to use as my lips closed over the silken head of his cock.

"Fuck," Beck groaned after a short time. His fingers were tangled in my wild hair, and his grip was guiding me at a pace that seemed to be driving him into madness. "Okay, fine," he growled, pulling me up before I could get him to come. His hands left my hair, and he grabbed me by the waist, lifting me up as he stood and then dropping me onto my back on his bed. "You win."

He deftly produced a condom from what seemed to be thin air and rolled it on with practiced ease. Fucking man-whore.

I watched Beck with heavy lidded eyes as he stood at the edge of the raised bed platform. He grinned, confident, then grabbed my ankles and pulled me toward him so that my butt was on the edge and my legs were free to wrap around his waist.

"Win what?" I asked, wrinkling my nose in confusion and significantly more interested in watching him position his hard, throbbing cock at my entrance.

His mouth curved in a half grin, and he gave a tiny head shake. "Nothing, never mind."

Before I could question him further, he thrust deep inside me and all coherent thoughts scattered from my brain like a cloud of startled butterflies. I cried out with pleasure, hooking my ankles together behind his back and pulling him closer. Deeper. Like I couldn't ever get enough of this man.

Sebastian Roman Fucking Beckett.

"Shit yes," I gasped as he thrust into me again, and again, and again, fucking me like he was made solely to pleasure *me*. Again, those warm, fuzzy feelings of genuine affection crept into me but this time, I let them linger. What Beck didn't know, couldn't hurt me. Right?

Regardless, I could blame it on the mild concussion, but for a little while as our bodies writhed and moved as one, I let myself wonder what it'd be like to be loved by Beck.

The fantasy didn't last long, though, because I quickly realized that to love Beck would mean only pain and heartbreak. He seemed to sense the shift in my mood, too, as he unhooked my legs from around his waist and used my ankles to flip me over.

"You better not be daydreaming of anyone but me, Butterfly," he said on a growl as he let my feet touch the ground before thrusting deep back into me. "Your first thought when you wake up, and your last when you go to sleep had better be about me, and how fucking good it feels to have my dick inside you."

His words made me gasp, but only for how accurate they already were. More than once since we'd first fucked, I'd found my mind reliving the feel of him inside me. Ugh, fucking Beck was ruining me for all other guys.

My elbows braced on the mattress as Beck's strong fingers bit into my hips, controlling me as he thrust in and out... claiming me. A deep moan escaped my throat as he pulled me back onto him, then his hands shifted from my hips to my butt cheeks.

"Tell me something truthful, Butterfly," he said, his breath short as his palms gripped my ass.

"Like what?" I replied in a breathy gasp. The tip of his cock was nudging my g-spot and I was tense all over in anticipation of my orgasm.

"Have you ever been fucked in the ass?" he asked with an edge of raw desire. His thumb brushed over that rather taboo area, and I squeaked with panic. A dark chuckle came from Beck as his thumb circled my ass once more before returning safely to my hip. "I take that as a no."

"No," I confirmed, feeling my face flaming red but also knowing my pussy was clenched tight and my whole body was flooded with an arousal I'd never experienced before.

Beck hummed a contented sound as he resumed his motions, but didn't try and push the issue any further. "Not yet, anyway," he murmured. His hand snaked around underneath me and played my clit like his damn guitar, sending me over the edge into a screaming climax that was loud enough to wake the dead.

Chapter 24

The next time I woke, the room was washed in dull light, and it was too warm. I kicked the blanket off, and pulled myself out of bed, desperate to pee. When I was done, I looked around the huge room, and a wave of loneliness tugged at my center. I already missed waking up with Beck.

Deciding that I needed a little exercise, I left his room and strolled along the hall to go downstairs.

I heard them before I saw them, laughter and the clinking of plates. When that snort-laugh of Jasper's registered, my feet picked up the pace, and I all but burst into the kitchen.

Four sets of eyes turned to me, and I didn't even care that I was only dressed in Beck's shirt, with a sports bra and panties underneath. The Henley was long enough to cover me to mid-thigh anyway. I barely caught Beck's resigned glare before Evan jumped to his feet.

"Spare!" he shouted.

He swept me into his arms, and I relaxed against him, relieved to see all of the guys together in one room. Mostly uninjured. "Been worried about you," he murmured close to my ear.

I gave him an extra squeeze, and then wiggled to get down. Jasper was next, and while he moved a little gingerly, he didn't hesitate to lift me as well, his strong arms solid around my back. "I saw your race," he said when he dropped me to the ground. "You drive like a fucking wet dream, baby girl."

I rolled my eyes at him before giving him a gentle shove.

"Your car is a wet dream, I just got to go along for the ride."

He groaned and closed his eyes. "Don't say wet dream, now all I can think about is—"

"Jasper," Beck said, sounding calm, but there was a warning underneath that one word.

Jasper just winked at me, and led me to the table. Dylan pulled a chair out for me, and dropped a kiss on my cheek when I sat. "You're looking much better," he said, relief in his voice. "You got to stop scaring us like that. I haven't slept for days."

Before I could reply to Dylan, a hand landed on my thigh, and I found Beck's warm eyes. "You okay, Butterfly?" he asked softly, and for a second I wondered if I was actually going to burst into flames.

My entire body felt warm, including my chest—which was from more than just Beck.

These four made me feel... too much. And Beck made me feel everything.

"I'm fine, just sorry that I worried you all," I said, turning to include everyone. "I honestly didn't plan on getting myself almost kidnapped and knocked out."

Expressions hardened, and some of the calm bled from the room. Now I was seeing the guys from the forest, the ones who were trained to survive, who could kill without remorse.

Didn't make me feel any different.

Wanting to change the mood, I looked at the food on their plates, and Jasper laughed. "Hungry?" he drawled.

I all but drooled at the pancakes, bacon, and toast.

"Yes! Feed me," I begged.

Beck lifted his hand from my leg, and I tried not to feel bereft. He moved to the warming plate in his impressive kitchen and started fixing me a plate. Dylan was up then too, and he placed the largest mug I'd ever seen in front of me before filling it with coffee.

"We picked that one out especially for you," he said with a wink.

Don't cry. I seriously wanted to bawl my fucking eyes out at how sweet they could be. Sweet psychos.

"A mug of my very own," I said, noticing that all of the other guys had specific coffee mugs for them.

Jasper's was yellow, like his Lambo, and it said "Pussy Magnet" on it. Evan's was smaller, because he preferred a single shot of espresso, and it said "I like it hot." Dylan had a plain black cup, and Beck had a dark blue one. His said "King can Checkmate" and I wondered if that was in reference to our chess discussion, or if he'd always thought the king ruled the board.

And now I had my own. One with no words, but a white chess piece... a queen.

"You're one of us now, Riles," Dylan told me. "You get your own mug."

Don't cry.

"Aw, you assholes are sentimental," I tried to joke, but my cracked voice gave away my emotions.

Beck placed a full plate in front of me, and then leaned over the bench, resting on his forearms so our eyeline was level.

"We have everything in the world that money can buy," he said softly. "But this…" He gestured to the four of us. "This is what money can't touch. This is the only important thing we have."

And I was crying.

Only a few tears escaped, sliding down my cheeks, and I didn't bother to brush them away. Beck returned to his seat at my side, Dylan on my other side, and then all of us ate our food and there was no tension between us.

When we were done, the five of us cleaned up.

"I gotta get back home and rest," Jasper said. "Fucking doctor's orders."

I hugged him. "Give Eddy my love," I said as I pulled back. "Tell her I'll text her whenever I get my phone back."

Jasper had filled me in over breakfast, and I was glad that Eddy was all but recovered from her ordeal. Except she now had a full time bodyguard, which I knew would piss her right off.

He nodded. "You got it, baby girl."

I wrinkled my nose at him. "You need to work on your nickname game."

He shrugged. "What? All the girls love my names for them."

"And I'll bet it helps that you don't have to remember their actual names while making them think they're special."

He dramatically grabbed his chest. "You wound me, Riley Jameson."

I laughed loudly. "There you go."

He left with Evan, who was driving him home. Dylan lingered in the doorway. "You should get some more rest too," he told me.

I was feeling somewhat fatigued again, and it frustrated me how weak I was. "Yeah, probably a good idea."

He brushed my hair back, and I wondered about the serious expression he now wore. "No matter what happens, you need to remember this day," he said to me, his voice low. "Our world … it's filled with secrets."

"And we all have to play the game," Beck finished his best friend's sentence.

It had been such a fun, lighthearted morning, but now they were back to secrets and bullshit.

"What does that mean? Is something happening that I should know about?"

Don't fucking lie to me, was how I wanted to finish that sentence.

The pair exchanged a look. It was such a fast glance that I barely even caught it, but I was immediately uneasy.

"Nothing you need to worry about, Butterfly," Beck said. "We'll keep you safe."

I snorted. "If I wasn't so out of my league in this world, I'd kick your ass for saying that. I'm not a damsel in distress, this is not the Wild, Wild West. I don't need you all to come to my rescue."

Some of the tension lifted. "Better hide her gun," Dylan joked. "She's dangerous when pissed off." He winked, and then with a salute to us both, left the house.

Beck wasted no time after that ushering me back to his room and stripping me of my clothes. Any questions I'd wanted to ask were lost in his hands and tongue and body on mine, and I figured that the next time we weren't naked, I would not let him get away with any more evasiveness. Because something was up, and I was determined to find out what it was.

I WOKE SLOWLY SQUINTING AN eye open to look across the bed, surprised by the expanse of emptiness. Where was Beck now? As I lifted myself to look over his bedroom, a scream ripped from me. Two men, dressed in black, stood at the end of the bed. Jerking the sheet up to cover my nudity, I scrambled back to put some distance between them and me. For the life of me I couldn't figure out how Huntley got into Beck's house, but I had absolutely no doubt this was who faced me.

"Riley Jameson," one of them said in a voice devoid of inflection. "You have two minutes to get dressed, and then we have to leave."

"I'm going nowhere with you," I said, my voice trembling, which pissed me off, but the fear was real. "Beck is going to kill you when he finds you in his room."

I probably needed a new threat, but he was just such an effective one, that I couldn't help but use him. Especially when I was naked, vulnerable, and once again without my goddamn gun.

"We are here on behalf of Delta," the other one said, his voice the exact same. "And you have a minute and a half now."

Pulling the sheet tighter around myself, I slipped off the side of the bed. Clothes were pooled on the floor, and without taking my eyes from them, I scrambled around to grab a shirt and pair of black sweats.

"If you're Delta, where is Beck?" I asked.

No response. Same expressionless faces. Carbon copies of each other, right down to the military-cut dark hair.

"One minute."

Fuck.

I got the pants and shirt on without flashing them, and I was relieved that no one attacked or grabbed me while I was somewhat vulnerable. If anything, they appeared to be staying as far back as they could, and for the first time I did wonder if they might actually be working for Delta.

Still, I'd be an idiot to blindly go with anyone I didn't know and trust.

Crossing my arms over my chest, I wished for a bra, but apparently this was as good as it was getting. At least I was no longer naked.

"Where are you taking me?" I demanded.

"Time's up," Asshole one said.

Fear had my blood pumping through me, and I eyed the door, wondering if I had a chance of making it. Even if I used my Krav Maga moves, there were two of them, which would lower my odds of escaping.

"Ms. Jameson," Asshole two said, holding a hand out to me. "Don't fight us. We have strict instructions not to hurt you. You'll be fine."

"I—I don't understand. Where are the guys? The Delta heirs? If this is company business, shouldn't one of them be here?"

"We're taking you to them," Asshole two told me.

Believe them or run?

I sprinted for the door, which didn't take either of them by surprise. They both moved in one smooth dive, wrapping their arms around me, and sliding me to the ground before I made it to safety. I swung out blindly, shouting abuse. They didn't care though, one wrapped a hand around my face, and the other around my shoulders, lifting me like I weighed nothing. Together they carried me from the room, even as I tried to kick and scratch them.

They were skilled. Far more skilled than I would ever be, as they anticipated and avoided my every strike. By the time we ended up outside, I was exhausted, still recovering from the numerous injuries I'd sustained in the past… I didn't even know how long. Ten days? Three weeks? A headache was back, pounding dully at the base of my skull.

I was shoved into a black Escalade SUV, and the doors were shut and locked around me. There was a metal plate that separated the back seats from the front as well, like a police vehicle. When asshole one and two got in the front, I slammed my hands against the metal.

"What the fuck are you fuckers doing? Let me go. This is kidnapping and my family is important."

Catherine Debitch had to be useful for something.

"Sit down and buckle yourself in. It's a bit of a drive."

I didn't even know which asshole said that, and it really didn't matter. The end result was the same. I was at the mercy of these two, and I would just have to wait and see where I ended up.

They turned away from civilization—and any hope of rescue—quickly. Taking me out into a back road, that led deeper and deeper into a thick forest. The darker the sky grew as the canopy thickened, the more dread settled in my stomach. I had a really bad feeling about what was going to happen next. This entire thing had a bad vibe to it. Really bad.

"Where are we going?" I asked for the tenth time. Again I got no answer.

Exhaustion pushed me into the seat, and I dropped my head back, closing my eyes as I tried to figure out what I could do to save myself from this situation. The car started to slow, and I was focused again, my gaze going to the window. The road was narrower, and just when I thought we'd reached the end of the trail, they rounded a large tree, and there was an open grassed area. It was such an odd sight after being in such densely packed trees that I blinked at it stupidly.

The car stopped, and a moment later, my door opened. I stared at asshole two. "I'm not getting out."

He held a hand out, still so polite and expressionless. "We walk from here."

"You're gonna kill me, aren't you?"

This was the perfect spot to kill someone. We were like an hour from any sort of civilization, in the middle of nowhere. If I was ever going to kill someone, this is exactly the sort of place I'd take them.

"We have orders not to harm you, Ms. Jameson."

I realized then that they'd used my real surname from the start. It hadn't registered before, but that had to mean they didn't work for Catherine. She would have insisted on Deboise.

"Who in Delta do you work for?" I pressed.

For the first time his face expressed an emotion. The exact nature of the emotion I couldn't tell, but I had a sneaking—and scary—suspicion that it was sympathy.

Which fucking terrified me.

"We work for Mr. Beckett."

Beck's dad?

Holy fuck.

Was this all a ploy to get me away from his son? Would he kill me though? I had no idea of the nature of Beck's father, but his son was certainly ruthless enough when he wanted something. I imagined that he learned that from somewhere. And Beck had said his father used to hit his mother, which spoke of a violent, controlling nature.

The door behind me opened while I was contemplating these truths, and I almost tumbled back as arms wrapped around me. Again, just like from the Beckett estate, I was dragged out of the car and carried across the grassed area.

Fighting these two was futile, I already knew that, but I still had to try. I was at least making this difficult for them. They were going to earn every cent of their blood money. The grassed area was half a mile long at least, and it was meticulously maintained. I wasn't walking myself, but it looked soft and thick, and I understood why they hadn't driven across it. Someone had gone to a lot of trouble to beautify this area.

A building came into sight, one which had been hidden back in the trees. I hadn't noticed it at first, mostly because I was too busy trying to kick asshole two in the balls, but now I couldn't unsee it. I had a terrible feeling this might be the last place I ever saw.

I was carried up to the wide front porch, and the pair held me in place, waiting for something.

"Aren't you going to knock?" I said sarcastically.

What was with the dragging out the suspense thing? They were going to give me a heart attack and miss out on the fun of killing me. *Mr. Beckett* would be so upset.

The door swung silently open then, and chills raced along my skin as my breathing increased in time to my racing pulse. There was no one in the doorway, no sign that anyone was in the house at all.

"This is a bad idea, guys," I said, wondering if maybe I was safer staying with them after all. "We should salt and burn this place before heading right back to the car."

I had no idea what signal they had been waiting for, but whatever it was they were moving again. Through the creepy ghost door. Inside looked like a billionaire's hunting lodge, and I was supremely relieved to not see any human heads mounted on the walls with all the deer and other animals. A fireplace was roaring in the center hearth, sending warmth across my skin. I hadn't even realized how cold I was until my body started to tingle from the change in temperature. We crossed through that room and another large dining area. It had two massive antler chandeliers, and I fought the urge to scream.

This place was some sort of fucked up house of horrors, I knew it.

The door to the basement was open, and of course we walked right through it and down the stairs. Because all scary shit happens in the basement, right? It was dimly lit in this room, and it took more than a minute for my eyes to adjust. Asshole one and two dropped me in the middle of the dark room, and before I could say a word, or dick punch the both of them, they spun around and were back up the stairs. The door slamming behind them.

Gulping, I tried to control the panic spiraling inside of me. What the hell was down here with me? Why had they run like that?

How was I going to die?

"Deboise Successor," an eerie whisper filled my ears. "You are called to prove your loyalty."

What. The. Fuck?

This was actually a Delta thing? A huge part of me had thought the assholes were just kidding.

One by one my guys stepped into the light, dressed completely in black. I looked at Jasper first, avoiding Beck because I couldn't handle the devastation of his betrayal yet. Jasper's eyes were filled with so much emotion when they met mine; he mouthed "sorry" to me as our gazes clashed. Tears burned my throat, because I might not know exactly *how* they betrayed me, I just knew they had. Evan, who was next to Jasper was expressionless, and I lingered on him for only a moment before going to Dylan. There was dark anger defining his features, and while I saw a glimpse of the guy who'd stood between me and his best friend, it was tempered now. He might not have wanted to be there, but he clearly had no choice.

Finally, when I couldn't ignore his darkly magnetic pull any longer, I turned to Beck. The first clue I had that this was bad, was his eyes. They were dark and cold, the look he wore on occasion that made the world think he was a sociopath. Maybe that look was the real Beck after all, because there was no sign of the guy who'd cared for me when I was injured. The one who loved my body like it was precious to him. This was straight up the Beck who shot dudes in the head.

"What the hell is going on, guys?" I asked cautiously, backing up a little. "Why am I here?"

More black-suit clad fuckers stepped out of the shadows, and the heirs were joined by their parents. I didn't recognize all of them—but it looked like even Beck's dad was there. I mean, of course he was, his goons were the ones who kidnapped me.

He looked like a slightly older, dignified, tired version of Beck. Handsome, with a strong jawline and bronze skin. Only his eyes were colder than his son's had ever been. Which was scary as hell.

Catherine addressed me. "All of Delta successors have to prove their loyalty to our company. As we've told you before, we are an old partnership, and we have rules to ensure that our five remain loyal and strong. Rules that ensure that the best interest of Delta is always upheld. You're required to do something for us, and in return, we will place your piece of history into the vault. After this you will be afforded the privilege, wealth, and responsibility of this noble company."

"Blah blah fucking blah," I said, my voice a snap of hatred. "Get to the point, bitch. I don't have time for these games any longer."

She lost her composure then, lurching toward me. If Jasper's father hadn't reached out a hand to stop her, I had no doubt we'd be on for our third bitch fight this month.

"Let's get this over with," Mr. Langham said, looking bored and resigned. "Until we have her tapes in the vault, we're running a huge security risk."

Catherine shook him off, but she didn't disagree. Waving a hand toward the heirs, she snarled, "You four get her into fucking line."

Uh oh, Deboises don't curse. Looked like I pushed her all the way this time. I was almost proud of myself.

Beck leveled Catherine with a look so dark that she slammed her mouth shut and backed up a little. "Don't ever tell us what to do again," Dylan said, sounding pissed off. "We're not the ones to push around. We don't need you. You need the heirs, otherwise the global shares end up back in circulation. And then you're all fucked."

She glared, but that was about all she had at that moment. The guys left their parents then and stepped over to stand in front of me. If I reached out a hand I could have touched them, but right then that was the last thing I wanted.

"You all knew about this?" I asked quietly, looking between the four of them.

One by one they nodded, and my heart cracked as I absorbed the truth of that. Not one of them had warned me.

"I was naked when your father's goons ambushed me in bed," I said, facing Beck.

The smallest of twitches was visible in his rigid jawline, and his eyes were as dark as ash.

A low, sickening laugh came from behind Beck, and his father said, "Might want to correct her on that one, Sebastian. I don't have goons."

My breath caught in my chest, a low sob wanting to choke out, but I held it back. *Beckett.* "Yours?" I said, realizing the truth. "You let two strange men come into the room while I was sleeping and kidnap me?"

Beck snarled. "I knew I could keep them from touching you."

It didn't matter though. That was such a betrayal of my trust. I had been asleep, vulnerable. Fuck, the only time I got any sleep lately was when Beck was with me, and now that was gone as well.

And still, as I stood here before him, my body craved his. Treacherous bastards. Both of them.

"We need you to repeat and swear your loyalty to Militant Delta Finances," Dylan cut in, looking tired. "The sooner we can do this, the sooner we can get back to destroying Huntley."

I crossed my arms over my chest, well aware I was still braless, shoeless, and wearing ill-fitting clothes. "I don't understand. I was on the plane where we were going to a company thing. Why do I have to suddenly 'prove my loyalty' now?"

Catherine was the one to laugh, and I did my very best not to look at her face, because it just made me furious. I wanted to keep a level head. She didn't care though. "That flight was taking you to a Delta meeting, within which you needed to pass a test. It's always something different, and the heir does not know about it until it's happening. This is take two on that little test, and the stakes got upped because you pissed me off."

Part of me knew my guys were victims of this bullshit, the same way I was, but they had been aware that this was coming and not one of them told me. I'd been blindsided, and the fear I'd felt for the last few hours was spreading through me. Filling me up with too much emotion.

"I refuse," I whispered, taking another step back. "You can't make me do anything."

I'd been wondering what Catherine was going to use to control me once I turned twenty-one and controlled my seat in the company. This was what it was. I knew it deep in my gut.

"Don't you even want to know what the test is?" Evan asked, tilting his head while giving me an odd stare. "I mean, you should be curious, right?"

That was his nature, the curious jokester. Always dissecting me with his stare.

Jasper reached out a hand to me. "I thought you wanted this, Riles? To be part of us."

Biting my lip, my teeth cut into the soft pad. "How can I trust you now? I thought I was being kidnapped. I prayed and said my fucking goodbyes." My voice rose at the end, and I sucked in some deep breaths to get myself under control. "I don't know what to think."

My Langham stepped forward. "You have no choice. Catherine will not release her family from Delta."

I finally met my birth mother's gaze. "You can't make me."

She grinned, and it was filled with the sort of joy that had to mean bad things for me. "You have no idea how wrong you are."

She stepped back and ripped away a black curtain. I hadn't noticed it at first because the room was so dimly lit, but on the other side a man was tied to a chair. Everyone moved out of the way so I could see him better, and I recognized him straight away.

"What the hell?" I whispered, revulsion crawling up the back of my throat. "He tried to kidnap me, why is he here?" I'd thought he would be in police custody or something by now.

Catherine moved forward and dropped a gun into my hand. On instinct, my fingers curled around the heavy piece. It wasn't my gun from Beck; this one was just a standard black, with a few shiny accent pieces.

"Kill him," Catherine ordered. "Kill him and we will record it as security against you ever betraying Delta. This ensures loyalty. If you betray us, that footage is released to the world, and you will spend the rest of your life in jail. The worst jail we can find. A much harsher punishment than simply killing you."

My fingers trembled, and for a brief moment, I wondered if I could shoot her. Catherine. The bitch who brought me into this world.

"This doesn't make any sense," I choked out. "I mean, you guys are so rich, you could destroy me if I said anything anyway. You don't need evidence."

Jasper placed a hand on my shoulder, but I shook him off. "This is how it's always been." he said sadly. "All of us have tapes. All of us had to do something which would end us if it was released. It's the bond we share, the reason we don't betray one another."

And yet in my mind, they had already betrayed me.

I looked between Dylan and Beck. "This was why I got the gun training.

Not so I could defend myself, or feel safer, but so I wouldn't miss when I had to murder a man."

Beck scoffed. "This piece of shit is not a man. If he wasn't required for your loyalty task for Delta, then I would have killed him myself."

Dylan made a sound of agreement. "Don't forget that he tried to kidnap you. You don't want to know what they do to young, gorgeous girls that fall into their hands."

"It's for the best," Evan added, also reaching out to me.

I avoided him as well. I didn't want anyone in this room touching me.

"I don't care what he did, or what he would have done had he succeeded in taking me. All I know is that I cannot shoot a person tied to a chair. Maybe if he was actively trying to hurt me, I'd give it a literal shot, but … this is wrong."

Not to mention letting these fuckers have that sort of leverage over me. Like … no way. I mean, how did the vault even work? Who got to access it? There must be an independent party who oversaw it … what if they decided one day to expose us all. This was a stupid, outdated thing which clearly came from the nineteenth century.

"You have no choice," one of the parents said. I didn't really care which one at this point.

"Not gonna happen."

Catherine made that same happy sound, and my blood turned cold. She waved her hand at Beck. "Time to bring out the incentive."

The look Beck leveled on me then was even scarier than Catherine's happy sound. "What did you do?" I whispered, already sniffling as tears burned my eyes.

I'd been insane to think I ever had a choice here.

His expression softened just for the briefest second before the mask was back in place. "You have to play the game, Butterfly," he said softly, repeating the words he'd told me long ago when speaking about Oscar. No one gets out of the game alive.

He turned and about ten seconds later, reemerged from a small side room. Another tall man was at his side, and a sob choked from me at the state Dante was in. He was barely conscious, stumbling along. His hands were bound tightly behind his back, his face a swollen mass of bruises and cuts.

"Dante," I sobbed, my fingers opening and closing over the gun as I fought the instinct to run to him. "What the fuck did you do to him?"

I directed that to no one in particular, but Beck answered. "He fights dirty. We had no choice."

Beck did this. My heart shattered then, and I crumpled forward, holding my chest as tears streaked silently along my cheeks.

Someone touched me but I violently shook them off. No one was my friend here. I'd given my trust to the heirs, and they had betrayed me. I'd given my heart to Beck, and he had smashed it into a million fucking pieces.

"Time is up, I have a meeting to get to," Mr. Langham said. "Shoot the Huntley operative, or we will shoot your friend. Easy?"

Beck pulled out a gun then from the back of his jeans, and he kicked Dante in the back of the legs, knocking him to his knees. I couldn't believe what I was seeing; the only part of Beck I recognized right then was his eyes. They were no longer dark, but a beautiful silver. Like when he'd been holding me last night.

He flicked the safety off the gun, and I cried out. "No, wait. I'll do it."

Dante managed to get one eye open enough to see me. "Riles, baby ... girl,

337

don't … do."

He shook his head, telling me that his life wasn't worth destroying mine. That's where he was so wrong. Putting on my best pissed off face, I looked around the room at my betrayers. "Promise me that if I do this, you will let Dante go. Alive. And never touch him again."

Their word wasn't worth shit, but I had to make it very clear that this was what I wanted and I would not shoot Huntley's guy without it. "I want you all to fucking promise me!" I shouted.

One by one, each of them repeated the words back, assuring me that from now on, if Dante stayed out of their business, they would not pursue him. Even Catherine, though she did so reluctantly.

With trembling hands I pushed through the guys and stood before the Huntley man, who remained tied to the chair.

I wished so hard that his eyes weren't open then, watching me closely. There was no fear on his face, but I could sense it there all the same. A desperation. Human instinct to want to save your own life.

"I'm sorry," I told him seriously. "I don't know if you have a family … friends who will miss you. I wish it didn't have to be like this, but Dante…" I inclined my head to my best friend. "He's my family. My everything. I have to save his life."

He started to struggle then, for the first time since he'd been revealed to me. I lifted the gun, and there was a whirring noise and a click, which I could only assume was a video camera kicking in so that this was recorded for "the vault."

I released the safety, my hands shaking too badly for a clean shot. I didn't want to drag it out, though, make this guy suffer, so I closed my eyes and breathed in and out. In and out. Centering myself.

The room was deathly silent, and I almost wished that someone would make some noise, because the voices in my head were screaming at me. *Don't do it.* I couldn't do this. But I knew Beck would shoot Dante. What I didn't know is if he'd be sad about doing it, but it was clear that he had no choice. He was controlled. We all were.

My eyes snapped open and without another thought, I pulled the trigger.

To be continued in...

BROKEN TRUST

Stay Connected

JAYMIN EVE

Facebook Page: www.facebook.com/jaymineve.author

Facebook Group: www.facebook.com/groups/764055430388751

Website and newsletter: www.jaymineve.com

TATE JAMES

Facebook Page: www.facebook.com/tatejamesfans

Facebook Group: www.facebook.com/groups/tatejames.thefoxhole

Website: www.tatejamesauthor.com

Newsletter: https://mailchi.mp/cd2e798d3bbf/subscribe

Also by
JAYMIN EVE

Supernatural Academy (Urban Fantasy/PNR)

Year One (May 2019)

DARK LEGACY
(DARK CONTEMPORARY HIGH SCHOOL ROMANCE)

Broken Wings

Broken Trust (2019)

SECRET KEEPERS SERIES
(COMPLETE PNR/URBAN FANTASY)

House of Darken

House of Imperial

House of Leights

House of Royale

STORM PRINCESS SAGA
(COMPLETE HIGH FANTASY)

The Princess Must Die

The Princess Must Strike

The Princess Must Reign

CURSE OF THE GODS SERIES
(COMPLETE REVERSE HAREM FANTASY)

Trickery

Persuasion

Seduction

Strength

Neutral (Novella)

Pain

NYC MECCA SERIES
(COMPLETE - UF SERIES)

Queen Heir

Queen Alpha

Queen Fae

Queen Mecca

A WALKER SAGA
(COMPLETE - YA FANTASY)

First World

Spurn

Crais

Regali

Nephilius

Dronish

Earth

SUPERNATURAL PRISON TRILOGY
(UF SERIES)

Dragon Marked

Dragon Mystics

Dragon Mated

Broken Compass

Magical Compass

Louis

HIVE TRILOGY
(COMPLETE UF/PNR SERIES)

Ash

Anarchy

Annihilate

SINCLAIR STORIES
(STANDALONE CONTEMPORARY ROMANCE)

Songbird

Also by
TATE JAMES

THE ROYAL TRIALS

Imposter

Seeker

Heir (2019)

KIT DAVENPORT

The Vixen's Lead

The Dragon's Wing

The Tiger's Ambush

The Viper's Nest

The Crow's Murder

The Alpha's Pack

The Hellhound's Legion (Novella)

Kit Davenport: The Complete Series (Box Set)

HIJINX HAREM

Elements of Mischief

Elements of Ruin

Elements of Desire

THE WILD HUNT MOTORCYCLE CLUB

Dark Glitter

FOXFIRE BURNING

The Nine

DARK LEGACY

Broken Wings

Broken Trust